Humility

Humility

BROOKLYN CROSS

HUMILITY
A Dark Aladdin Retelling

Written by: Brooklyn Cross

FIRST EDITION.

ISBN: 978-1-998015-30-6

Edited by: R. Mudawar at Just Ask Her Productions

Cover Art: DAZED DESIGNS

Created with Vellum

Also by: BROOKLYN CROSS

Fairytale Virtues

(Contemporary/Shared World Standalones/Aladdin Retelling/Dark Comedy/Mafia/RH - Dark 2-3 Spice 3-4)

Humility by Brooklyn Cross

Patience by Mia Z Staysails

Temperance by EJ Everette

Diligence by Jay Leigh Brown

Chastity by Kira Roman

Charity by Alexandra K Martin

Kindness by Sunday Mathers

The Kings of Wayward Academy

(Academy/Slow Burn/Slow Build/Why Choose/Mafia - Dark 1-3 Spice 1-4 the dark and spice will progress more as the series continues)

Disobedient Pawn

Defiant Knight

Lost Souls MC

(Motorcycle Club - Dark 3.5-4.5 Spice 3.5-4.5)

Malice

Surrender

Showbiz (Coming 2024)

Fealty (Coming 2024)

Splintered

Absolution

Handcuffed

Solace

The Righteous Series

(Vigilante/Ex Military Romance - Dark 3-4 Spice 3-4)

Dark Side of the Cloth

Ravaged by the Dark

Sleeping with the Dark

Hiding in the Dark

Redemption in the Dark

Crucified by the Dark

Dark Reunion (Coming 2024)

The Consumed Trilogy

(Suspense/Thriller/Anti-Hero Romance - Dark 4-5 Spice 3-4)

Burn for Me

Burn with Me

Burn me Down

The Buchanan Brother's Duet & Next Generation

(Serial Killer/Captive Horror Romance - Dark 4-5 Spice 3-5)

Unhinged Cain by Brooklyn Cross

Twisted Abel by T.L Hodel

Unhinged Kallie by Brooklyn Cross

The Battered Souls World

(Standalone Books Shared World Romance/Dramatic/Women's Fiction/All The Feels- Dark 2-3 Spice 2-3)

The Girl That Would Be Lost

The Boy That Learned To Swim (Coming Soon)

The Girl That Would Not Break (Coming Soon)

The Brothers of Shadow and Death Series

(Dystopian/Cult/Occult/Poly MMF Romance - Dark 3-4 Spice 3-4)

Anywhere Book 1

Anyplace Book 2

Anytime Book 3

Seven Sin Series

(Multi Author/PNR/Angel and Demons/Redemption - Dark 2-5 Spice 3-5)

Greed by Brooklyn Cross

Lust by Drethi Anis

Envy by Dylan Page

Gluttony by Marissa Honeycutt

Wrath by Billie Blue

Sloth by Talli Wyndham

Pride by T.L. Hodel

AUTHOR'S NOTE

HUMILITY IS A DARK FAIRYTALE
RETELLING AND
IS INTENDED FOR MATURE AUDIENCES
ONLY.
THIS BOOK IS FOR SALE TO ADULTS
ONLY, AS DEFINED BY
THE COUNTRY'S LAWS
IN WHICH YOU MADE YOUR PURCHASE.
HUMILITY IS A REDEMPTION STORY
WITH A MORALLY GREY BAD GUY
TURNED INTO A HERO.
HUMILITY CONTAINS SCENES AND
SITUATIONS THAT MAY BE UPSETTING
FOR SOME READERS.
INCLUDES TW AND SENSITIVE MATERIAL
THAT IS NOT SUITABLE FOR
ALL AUDIENCES.
READER DISCRETION IS ADVISED.
FOR A LIST OF TRIGGERS, YOU CAN
FIND THEM AT
WWW.BROOKLYNCROSSBOOKS.COM

PLAYLIST

GENIE IN A BOTTLE - OSHRI
IF YOU CARE - EVAN BARLOW
NEED A FAVOR - JELLY ROLL
WATERMELON MOONSHINE - LAINEY WILSON
MAKE HATE TO ME - CITIZEN SOLDIER
LAST NIGHT - MORGAN WALLEN
FLOWERS - MYLEY CYRUS
RUN - ONE REPUBLIC
A THOUSAND YEARS - CHRISTINA PERRI
FALL INTO ME - FOREST BLAKK
GRAVITY - JOHN MAYER
WHAT YOU DO - JAMES GILLESPIE
THUMBS - SABRINA CARPENTER
FORGET ME - LEWIS CAPALDI
FINGERS CROSSED - LAUREN SPENCER SMITH
YOU DON'T OWN ME - SAYGRACE
WORK SONG - HOZIER
HOME - MICHAEL BUBLE
BAD IDEA RIGHT? - OLIVIA RODRIGO
STAY - ZEDD & ALYSSIA CARA
BEFORE YOU GO - LEWIS CAPALDI
YOU WERE MEANT FOR ME - JEWEL
YOU ARE THE REASON - CALUM SCOTT
MY ANGEL - PRINCE ROYCE
A WHOLE NEW WORLD - PEABO BRYSON & ROBERTA FLACK

TO

ALL THOSE WHO
GREW UP IN LOVE
WITH A FAIRYTALE

Knight

IN SHINING ARMOR

BUT

NOW WANTS
THE KNIGHT TO

Talk Dirty,

BEND THEM
OVER A

Desk,

AND MAKE THEM

Scream.

Chapter One

ANGELO

TWO YEARS AGO

"SHIT," I growled as the alarm sounded. I looked at Enzo. "What the fuck? I thought you shut it off."

"So did I," Enzo said as we heard the guard's shouts over the screeching.

Thump. I looked at the locked door. *Thump.* It rattled again. This was not how this was supposed to happen. I quickly rolled the delicate Fabergé Egg in the protective cover and placed it in the padded lockbox. *Thump.*

"We need to move now," Dario said as he peeked out the window—our only escape. "More guards are coming up the driveway, all heavily armed.

"I'm hurrying as fast as I can here," I said as I stuffed the box in the large backpack. "This wouldn't have been a problem if Enzo had done his job.

"I did do my job. There must be a secondary alarm that wasn't on the instructions your guy gave us."

"Sure, blame the instructions." Reaching into the safe again, I grabbed a stack of folders and a velvet pouch, tossing them into the bag before zipping it up.

"You two can argue after we leave. Let's move," Dario said as the door thumped again, this time cracking.

"Okay, go," I said, running around the desk. Dario opened the window and pulled out the grappling hook. It clicked as the four claws locked into place. He tossed the black rope out the window, and I shooed Enzo out first as I struggled to get the backpack on. He was quick and disappeared.

Bang. The door gave way a little more, and suddenly, bullets burst through. Dario jumped on me and rode me to the ground as he covered my body with his own. The door splintered, and small pieces flew into the room like it was raining wood.

"Don't hurt the egg," I growled at Dario.

My best friend glared at me before yanking me to my feet when the gunfire stopped.

"That egg won't mean anything if you're dead."

Dario grabbed the hook off my pack and locked it into place.

"Fuck, are you guys alive?" Enzo called up from the bushes below.

"For now," I answered as we stepped up onto the window frame together. The door burst open, revealing a mass of guards dressed in traditional black suits and Don Falcone at the front.

"Shit."

His eyes scanned the room and landed on me just as we jumped out the window. It was dark, and the moon wasn't bright, but I hadn't pulled down my mask. Fuck. He saw me. This was not how this was supposed to go. I would take the egg and look like the hero when I found the assholes who'd stolen the Falcone family treasure. Not only would I bring honor to my family name, but I would demand a reward, and I knew exactly what I wanted.

"Leave the ropes," Dario hissed as we reached the ground, and he unclipped me. He shielded my body as we raced to Enzo just as a hail of bullets rained down on us. I had no idea how we avoided being hit as we rounded the back of the house.

A few guards running toward the alarms came straight at us across the backyard. Dario was quick and shot them both before they could get their guns raised. There was a reason he was my personal bodyguard and best friend. I'd never met another man who could kill as quickly, efficiently, and without remorse as he did. I'd also seen him take a bullet in the leg and still keep fighting like it never happened.

The Falcone alarms grew louder, and lights flashed all over the property while the barking of dogs sent a shiver up my spine.

"Shit, dogs," Enzo said, echoing the same thought in my head.

"Move faster," Dario growled as he hauled me along. I ran every day, so I was fast, but fucking Dario was a machine, and he pushed me now.

The snarling wasn't close yet, but we could hear the guards yelling to cut the dogs loose. We didn't have much further to go, but each footfall didn't feel fast enough. Blood coursed through my body as we weaved between the trees and over a fallen log. I could see the road and the glitter of streetlights ahead.

Looking back, I could just make out the shadowy outlines of dogs cresting the knoll we'd run down moments before. Shit. Their snarls were loud now, and I gave the final sprint everything I had.

The lights on our car flashed as we got near. The dogs were so close that I could almost feel their feet hitting the ground and their hot breath on the back of my neck.

"Doors open," Enzo panted into his remote. The doors silently opened, and I aimed for the backseat. "Start car." The fancy sports car fired up, and the engine was loud as it revved.

Bursting through the trees, I leaped for the back door and landed on the seat as Dario slammed the door shut. A dog rammed its head into the metal with a thud and a whimper. He jumped into the passenger seat while Enzo ran around and got inside just as three more dogs leaped at the glass. Their barks were loud, the large teeth biting at the window as their nails scraped down Enzo's paint job.

"Oh, you fuckers, I just had it detailed," he complained as he put the sports car into first and drove away from our hiding spot. The wheels squealed as he shifted quickly through the gears, pulling away from the dogs and the sound of bullets that missed the car. "I bet you're fucking thankful now that I have automatic doors."

I pulled myself upright, my chest heaving from the exertion of the run. "Yeah, I'll concede that was pretty handy." We'd all given him the gears about the car's feature when he had it installed.

"Who gives a fuck about the car. What are we going to do now? We have to run for it. Do you get that? This is our home, and now we're all dead men for a stupid egg," Dario snarled, his bark far worse than the dogs that chased us.

"We'll get something sorted out. I'm still the underboss of the Esposito family. My father will help me figure out how to spin this in our favor. You'll see Dario. Stop worrying," I said, gripping his shoulder. "We won't have to leave."

"And I think you're delusional," he said, glaring at me.

"No, I won't do it. You have embarrassed me and this family for the last time," my father, Don Mario Esposito, yelled. He pointed a finger at me, the one that held our family crest. "You will leave this house tonight. You are banned from these walls, your inheritance or claiming your name. You're dead to me and no longer my son."

"But Father...."

"No. I will not hear it. I do not care why you chose to steal a family heirloom from another Don, nor do I want to know how you managed to fuck it up if you say you had it so well planned. All I know is that my phone is ringing off the hook, and guess who is calling?" I shook my head. "Giovanni." I swallowed hard as my father said the Don of Don's was calling. He never reached out to my father personally.

"Shit."

"Shit? That's all you have to say?" My father marched behind his desk and slammed a crystal glass down before he filled it with a dark whiskey. He drank it down like it was water before pouring himself another.

"Father, I swear, I wasn't trying to damage our family name. I was only trying to solidify our position and give us more of a voice at the table. I only wanted to make you proud of me."

"What you wanted to do and what you have done are vastly different. You will leave here tonight. You are no longer an Esposito. I am ashamed of you, Angelo. This family will be lucky if we are not all found floating in the ocean by morning. Leave. Take whatever money you have and go, but you are not welcome here."

"Father...." I started as his phone rang again, and he held it up to show Giovanni's name.

As my father answered the phone, Dario grabbed my arm and pulled me from the room. What the hell just happened? I had a great plan that wouldn't hurt anyone and would make my family proud. Instead, I no longer had a home.

Anger brewed in my stomach as my eyes met Dario's. He was speaking, but I had no idea what he said.

"We need to leave. I secured us a jet out of Italy, and I've already packed your bag. Come on, we need to go before the men sent to collect us arrive."

"How?"

"I had to use the leverage we have on Giovanni to make this happen, but we have our way out and we need go before the window closes," Dario whispered.

"Are you coming with me?"

Dario glared at me as we marched down the hall. "Don't ask me stupid questions. Of course I am. Your rank was never why I chose to be your friend or agreed to be your personal guard. Where you go, I go. Until I draw my last breath."

Enzo waited in his car when we walked outside, and I stopped to turn and stare up at the mansion that had been my home for the last twenty-three years. I didn't even know where to go from here. The shock of being banished was starting to lift, leaving me chilled to the bone. I'd ruined everything. My greed, my need to improve the family and the desire to win back the love of my life had spurred me into action, and now I'd been stripped of everything I held dear. I was going to be forced to leave behind the one person that had ever held my heart. Everything I'd fought for and done had been for naught. I could already see the looks on the other Don's faces when they heard what I'd done, humiliation filling me.

"Come on, get in." Dario pointed into the car, and I slid inside, trying to picture my life without this place or my family. I was no longer Angelo Esposito, underboss, and I had no idea who I was without the title. What had I done?

Chapter Two

JASMINE

FIFTEEN YEARS EARLIER

AGE 6

"PAPA, DO I HAVE TO GO?" I sat in the large chair in my papa's office and played with the hem of my dress.

"Mia Bambolina, why do you not want to go to school?" I lifted my shoulder in a shrug. "You like the other girls, yes? Gemma, Ada, Rosa? You talk about them all the time."

"I do like them, Papa."

"Is it the schoolwork? Is it too tough?" I shook my head. "Then what is it?" His voice was soft and kind. I'd never known my papa to be angry with me, and I didn't want to make him angry now, but I didn't want to go back to class and face Angelo, Dario, and the other mean boys. They put stickers on my back, stuffed old food in my desk, dumped drinks on my head, and stuck gum in my hair. They would always laugh, but I didn't cry. Even when it took Mama hours to get the gum out, and she still had to cut a chunk of my hair off. I wore a headband so no one could see the mess and make fun of me.

I looked up as a shadow covered my feet, and Papa loomed over me. His face was happy, and after Mama was sick for so long, it was nice to see him smile.

"Tell your papa what is wrong? I don't like to see such a sad look on my pretty daughter's face."

Sighing, I just couldn't say the words. "I get scared," I said, which wasn't a whole lie. It was a baby lie. Mama told me there were different types of lies, and this one was definitely a small lie. At least, I thought so.

"Oh, mia Bambolina, there is no need to be scared." He knelt and closed his fist tight. I stared at the big shiny rings and the black artwork on his fingers. "You tell me who scares you, and your papa will take care of them," he growled, and I giggled.

Reaching out, I touched the largest of the rings on his finger. "You like that one?"

I nodded. "It's pretty."

He brought his hand closer and pointed to the letter *F* on the top and the sparkling stones that circled it.

"This stands for Falcone." He tickled my tummy, and I laughed and wiggled in the chair. "You are a Falcone."

"Stop, I can't breathe," I laughed until he stopped.

"Grab my fist," he said, and still smiling, I put both hands on his. "You feel how strong I am?" I nodded. "I will never let anyone hurt you. If someone is mean to you, you tell me, and I'll make sure they never hurt you again. I'm your papa, and it's my job to protect you."

"Okay, Papa." I cupped his checks and kissed both sides before hopping down and running for the door.

"Mia Bambolina?" I turned and looked at my papa, who was standing again. He looked so powerful in his black suit, like he could take on all the mean boys in my class for me. "Ti amo."

"I love you too, Papa."

"Leave me alone, Angelo. My papa says he will make sure you never hurt me again," I said, crossing my arms over my chest as I stuck out my chin.

"Ohhhh, did you hear that, boys? She told her papa." He made fists and wiped at his eyes. "Wah, wah, wah, look at the little crybaby."

I stomped my foot and glared at the boys. "I'm not a baby, and I didn't cry," I said.

"That's all I see, a whiny baby that had to tattle about a little teasing. What's next? Are you going to shit yourself?"

Gasping, I put my hand over my mouth and looked at the school. "You said a bad word. If the teachers hear you...."

"Who is going to hear me out here?" He opened his arms and looked around. A few other kids looked our way, but no one interfered. Not even the girls came to help. "Shit, shit, shit!" Angelo yelled at the top of his lungs, and all the boys laughed.

"Stop it. I don't want to get into trouble." I tried to march around him, but he blocked my way. "Leave me alone." I stepped to the side, and he followed me, his laugh annoying as he glared down at me.

My hands balled into fists. It wasn't polite to hit if you were a girl, but this might be one of those times that it was okay, just like lying.

"Why are you such a jerk," I asked and then covered my mouth.

His eyes grew wide, and his mouth opened. "Did you hear that? She said a really bad word."

"I heard it," Dario said and crossed his arms.

"I heard it too," another boy said.

"Me too," a third said.

Each of them nodded in agreement, and my heart fluttered with fear. Would Angelo run to the teacher and tell them what I said?

What if they called my papa, and he was upset with me? I couldn't have them do that.

"I'm going to tell on you, Tiger. You have a potty mouth," he said and turned to walk away. Panic set in. I jumped and grabbed his arm, hating that he was so much taller than me.

"No, stop! I didn't mean to say that."

Angelo stopped and glared down at me. "Get off of me, shit for brains."

"Stop calling me names." I hung onto his arm tighter.

"Ow! You clawed me." He shoved me, and I tripped over my feet, landing on the ground hard. My dress had flown up over my head, and I quickly pulled it down, but the damage was done. All the boys were staring, pointing, and laughing.

"She landed in dog shit. Look," one of the boys said, and I looked down to see he was right. There was a stinky, brown stain on my pretty dress. The laughing got louder as they doubled over and held their stomachs.

Tears filled my eyes and burned as I tried to ignore them. I wiped the poop that got on my hand on the grass, but it was no good. I couldn't block them out. Leaping to my feet, I acted without thinking and punched Angelo in the face.

Everyone went quiet as he fell on his ass. For just a second, I felt powerful, like a superhero taking on the mean people in the world. I swallowed hard as Angelo lifted his head, his face twisted in anger.

"I'm going to kill you," he growled, and I screamed as I ran for the school.

"Get her," Angelo yelled, and it felt like I was being chased by a pack of dogs.

Fear made me run faster than ever before. I looked over my shoulder and saw they were gaining on me. Tears flowed down my cheeks as I screamed again. All the other kids just stared at us, making me feel small and alone.

"I swear I'll kill you," Angelo said from right behind me.

The door to the school opened, and Mr. Nardis walked out. I skidded to a halt and heard the boys behind me do the same.

"If you snitch, you're dead," Angelo hissed.

"What is happening here?" Mr. Nardis demanded.

I didn't care about Angelo's threats and turned and pointed at him. "He pushed me into dog poop."

"She was swearing and grabbed my arm." He held out his arm and pointed to the nail marks I'd made.

"Did you do that," Mr. Nardis asked me."

"Yes, but I did it because he was being mean to me first."

"No, I wasn't. You attacked me," Angelo argued.

"Yes, you were." I stomped my foot. "Don't lie. Lying is bad."

"I'm not lying. You're the liar."

"Enough. That is quite enough from both of you. You're both going to the office, and the principal will call your parents and get this sorted."

"But Sir..."

"Now, Angelo."

The cool air of the school hit me as we walked inside, and I could smell the gross poop on me now.

"I'll get you back for this," Angelo said as we entered the office, and Mr. Nardis went to find the principal.

I stuck my tongue out at Angelo. I hated him so much.

Chapter Three

ANGELO

FIVE YEARS LATER

AGE 13

WHY DID they let girls come on these trips? I never understood it. They held us back from the stuff we wanted to do because we had to include them. To make matters worse, Jasmine Falcone was here this year.

I saw enough of that annoying girl at school, and now I had to spend an entire week with her at the yearly get together. My dad was on his phone and didn't care what I had to say about not doing this father-child event. I used to look forward to this every year. The Dons and underbosses got together, and while the men discussed business, the rest of us played games and had fun. It was the one time of year all of us guys could hang out and our fathers always set up amazing activities, but three years ago, it all changed.

One of the Dons complained that he had four daughters and no sons, and his daughters also wanted to enjoy the week. Now, here we were with girls at our guys week. Yuck.

We pulled under the grand, sweeping archway of the massive resort, and I couldn't help but feel a tiny tug of excitement in my chest. Dario and I always found cool stuff to do, and picking on Joseph was funny shit.

The driveway was long, but soon, we reached the lineup of limos and SUVs and sat, waiting. One song on my playlist later, we pulled up to the front of the sprawling villa, and I spotted Dario in the crowd.

He was dribbling a football with a bunch of guys. I jumped out of the SUV, ignoring my dad's yells to get my suitcase, and ran into the middle of the group to steal the ball. Kicking it hard away from Dario.

"Hey," Dario yelled and ran after me. We raced across the perfectly cut grass, and like God himself gave me the opportunity, there was Jasmine, walking along the path straight ahead, all alone.

Barreling down on her, I looked back once to make sure none of the adults could see, then yelled her name and kicked the ball hard. It sailed straight at her, and she looked up just in time to get hit square in the face.

She stumbled back with the impact and was crying before her ass hit the grass. I had to stop running. I was laughing so hard and couldn't catch my breath. All the guys laughed with me, except for Dario.

"Aww come on, that's funny shit," I said, but Dario shook his head and walked over to Jasmine.

She sat up, and blood ran from her nose as tears ran down her face. Okay, I didn't mean to do that, but watching her fly off her feet had me rolling around in a fit of laughter all over again.

"Leave me alone," she said, pulling her arm away from Dario. "Don't pretend you care." She marched toward me, her eyes furious. I'd gotten used to that look on her face. It was a daily occurrence between us at school.

"Hey there, Tiger. Did you know you have something on your face?" I sighed, enjoying the bright sun as I sat my hands behind me on the grass and stretched out my legs. "I hope that ball didn't make you any uglier. Your face really couldn't take it."

"I hate you," she hissed. "I hate all of you." Jasmine stomped by, and I yelled as she jumped on my hand. "Oh no, I hope it's not broken," she said, her voice sarcastic as I glared at her and held my hand to my chest. Jumping to my feet, I flexed my one good hand into a fist. "You going to hit me now, too?" Jasmine crossed her arms. "Not surprised. We all know you come from a long line of men who hurt women. Why would you be any different?"

That was a low blow. There was no proof that my father ever touched my mom, but I'd heard the whispered stories about my grandfather. The rumor was that my father killed him after he raped my mom one night while my father was at a meeting. Grandfather's disappearance was kept quiet. My mom moved out shortly after, cutting off all contact. One day I had a mom the next day I didn't.

A shrill whistle from the top of the hill got our attention. Giovanni, the Don of Dons, and his son, Lucas, stood at the top. I groaned at the sight of Lucas. Why was he here? He never came. He considered himself too good to be bothered with this retreat. He was five years older than I was and an asshole. He acted like he was better in everything, bragged about it nonstop, and always chose to make fun of me.

Giovanni waved for us to head up, and before I could spout out my comeback to Jasmine, I realized she was already way ahead, her fast strides eating up the ground. Shit, her father was here.

Dario grabbed my arm and waited until the other guys were out of earshot before saying anything.

"What is it?"

"This thing you have with Jasmine has to stop. That shit was wrong."

I narrowed my eyes at my best friend, anger burning in my gut. "Whose side are you on?"

"It's not about sides. We're older now, no longer little kids. Jasmine may be two years younger, but she is still a princess. One of these times, her father will get pissed. Do you really want your father and the Falcone family to fight?"

Dario made a good point, but I didn't want to hear it. "Screw that. I hate her, and she hates me. It's fair."

I stomped away from my best friend and caught up to the guys just as they reached the top of the hill. I looked for Jasmine and found her with her father. He looked worried as he held her shoulder and chin to inspect her face. I expected her to point her finger at me and yell out my name, but she never glanced my way. Staring at her face, I was stupidly annoyed that she acted like I didn't exist. It should have been a relief that she wasn't snitching.

Even when Don Falcone looked around, he didn't look my way and instead waved over the organizer who ushered them inside. I didn't understand why she wouldn't say anything.

A hand clamped down on my shoulder, and I knew without looking that it was Lucas.

"Looking as scrawny as ever. I thought you might've started working out or something, but you still look like a plucked chicken."

"I thought you hated these things," I said, hoping to avoid whatever insult he had cooked up next.

Lucas shrugged and pushed back his floppy white-blond hair, which made him stand out among the rest of us.

"Thought I'd slum it for a little while. I also need to pick a wife." Fear raced down my spine at the mention of the word. I couldn't say why, but I was suddenly worried he would choose Jasmine, and there was no way I would let him take that away from me, too. She was mine to torture, and make fun of.

"A wife? Yuck." I crossed my arms and looked at the large group of girls glancing over and smiling at us. "Why would you want to get married?"

"You obviously haven't had sex yet," Lucas smiled.

"He'd have to date someone first," Dario piped in, and Lucas laughed.

"Shut up. I've dated."

"Fine, who?" Dario stared down at me, and I was tempted to lay him out on his ass.

"That girl, the one that flew home. You know whatever her name was," I said.

"You mean the girl you spoke to for one afternoon at the beach? That doesn't count."

"And to think I was excited to see you," I growled.

"Hey guys, what are you talking about," Ciro asked as he wandered over from another small group.

"Angelo hasn't fucked anyone yet, and I need to find a wife," Lucas said, and my face heated with embarrassment.

Ciro smirked, and I suddenly felt outnumbered. "You're missing out."

"That's what I tried to tell him. As for choosing, I'll see who gives me the best blow job." Lucas stretched and waved at the group of girls, who waved back. This was too much. I was going to be sick watching this mating ritual. "Not that I plan on only ever fucking my wife, but you need to pick right."

"Oh yeah, and who is the right one," I asked, crossing my arms.

"One that is happy to have a ton of kids, and I can still get it on elsewhere, of course. Do you not know anything?"

Just then, Jasmine and Don Falcone stepped outside. Her face was clean, and she was wearing a new outfit.

"Fuck, she is growing into a fine piece of ass," Lucas said, and I followed his line of sight, my hands curling into fists.

"Isn't she a bit young," I asked, trying to derail him.

"There is no such thing."

That statement was creepy as fuck.

"Lucas, come over here," Giovanni called.

Lucas clapped me on the back, and I almost took the swing that was ready to go. "Well, duty calls. I wonder if Jasmine has sucked a cock yet?"

A growl ripped from my chest as he jogged away, but Dario stepped in my path.

"Get out of my way. I'm going to kill him." Dario's expression never changed, yet I knew he was mocking me. "What? You heard what he said."

"What I heard was the Don of Don's son getting ready to choose his wife, and we can't interfere. Besides, why do you care? You say you hate her."

"Hate who," Ciro asked, and I glared at him, not answering.

"You're right, I do. Whatever."

I stomped away from everyone gathered and rounded the side of the large villa. Why the hell did I care? I shouldn't care. I hated Jasmine, had from the first day I saw her and made sure she knew that every day since. The thought of Lucas or any other guy choosing her made my blood run like fire. But why? I leaned against the wall to calm down and realized my hands were shaking.

All I could picture was Lucas forcing her to marry him and what he would do to her once he got her alone. I was the only one allowed to do anything to Jasmine Falcone, and if that meant I had to go through Lucas, I would.

Chapter Four

JASMINE

I DIDN'T WANT to come to this thing. Summer break was my only escape from the war at school, and now here I was defending myself all over again. Angelo was seriously the worst, and his idea of fun was picking on me.

It was midnight, and I was trying to sleep, but no, everyone else wanted to stay up and talk about boys and do their hair. I rolled my head to the side and watched the girls. They'd moved on from hair and were now doing their nails and laughing together. This was the second reason I hadn't wanted to come.

It wasn't that I didn't like all those things. Holding up my hand, I stared at my chewed nails. It was just that I didn't seem to fit in. I felt like a round peg trying to fit into a square hole. They didn't laugh at the same jokes, and I didn't get their fascination with boys.

"What about you, Jazzy?" Shocked that someone was speaking to me, I blinked and looked at all the faces that had gone silent.

"Me what?"

"Who do you think Lucas will choose?"

"Choose for what?" Everyone laughed.

"See, she's clueless," someone said as they went back to what they were doing.

I was an alien. I was sure of it. You couldn't feel this out of touch with everyone around you and not be from another planet.

Pushing myself up, I decided to go for a walk. It wasn't like I was going to get to sleep anytime soon. No one said anything as I walked out, only adding to my loneliness.

I wandered the halls, not paying attention to where I was going but admiring the estate's beauty. It reminded me of a palace. You could easily get lost with how large it was, and there were pretty decorations and flowers all over to accent the dark, shiny wood.

Poking my head in a room, I realized it was a library and smiled. Couches and chairs that looked like they could swallow me whole were spread out, and not a single person was in sight. Perfect.

Walking over to a couch, I grabbed the throw off the back and curled up in a ball. It didn't take long for my eyes to get heavy and sleep to pull me under.

I blinked, confused where I was and what had woken me. A strange, muffled noise reached me, and I listened harder, trying to figure out what I was hearing.

"I said do it, or you're off the list. You don't want to be off the list, do you?"

Was that Lucas? He sounded different, mean even.

"No, but I've never done this before. I'm scared," a female voice said. It was so low that I barely heard it, but I could've sworn it was Gemma. What the hell was going on?

"Get on your fucking knees now, or I go and get someone else," Lucas snarled, and Gemma cried out in pain.

My heart was pounding so hard that I was sure they would hear it. Please just go away.

Then I heard the sound of a zipper.

"Please, I...."

"Just open your fucking mouth." There was a high-pitched squeal and then a muffled scream.

"Oh yeah, just like that, you little fucking slut. You're a liar, you must have sucked cock before."

No, this couldn't be happening. What I thought was going on couldn't be real. Poking my head up from my spot on the couch, I looked around and sucked in a sharp gasp. My hand covered my mouth as I spotted Gemma on her knees in front of Lucas. He had his hand wrapped in her hair, and tears streamed down her cheeks as he shoved his thing into her mouth and pulled it back out. I wanted to gag as he pushed his hips forward again, and it disappeared down her throat. I couldn't stay in here with this, but the only way out was to walk right by them.

"Please," Gemma said, coughing as he pulled out of her mouth. She screamed as Lucas yanked her head back hard. The sound of his hand connecting with her cheek was loud, and the anger that ignited in my gut was immediate.

"Hey! Let her go," I said and leaped up.

"Jasmine, I didn't know you were in here," Lucas said, smiling. "Why don't you come join us?"

I marched for the two of them and kept my eyes firmly on his face. This was so gross. He was worse than I thought he was.

"I said let her go. She doesn't want your...." I waved my hand at his crotch. "Worm down her throat."

He laughed and waved his penis at me, and I turned my head away so I didn't have to look at it. "Does that look like the size of a worm to you?" Lucas laughed. "Why don't you get over here and on your knees with your friend, and you can see for yourself."

"No, I said let her go." Stomping forward, I grabbed Gemma's arm. "Let's go, Gemma."

Lucas shoved me hard in the chest, and I slammed back into the bookshelf. "Either get on your knees or get out, but Gemma isn't going anywhere. She wants this, don't you, Gemma?"

I looked down at Gemma's large eyes and the tears staining her cheeks. She was obviously upset, and yet she nodded yes.

"Gemma, you don't have to do this. I'll go get my papa," I threatened, and her face went as white as a ghost.

"No," she yelled.

Lucas grabbed for me, but I was faster and ducked under his reach.

"Come on, Jasmine, don't be a loser. Your friend is having fun. This is what fun looks like. Don't you want to be popular with the boys? I'll teach you all you need to know. I might even pick you instead."

"Go away, Jasmine. No one wants you here, and I don't want your help." Gemma glared at me like she wanted to kill me and wrapped her hand around Lucas's worm again.

"Oh, fuck yeah. Eager thing you are now," he said, and I backed up until I was at the door.

"Gemma, please come with me," I said.

"Last offer, Jasmine. You could be the wife of the next Don of Dons. Don't you want that?"

"Not even a little. I'd rather suck on my shoe and die alone with a house full of cats."

Opening the door, I jumped out and slammed it behind me. My heart was pounding hard in my ears, and my stomach was in knots. What he was doing was wrong. I could feel it, and yet Gemma ordered me to go. What the hell would Lucas say to his father about any of this? About me? About Gemma? Was I going to get my papa in trouble?

Shit. You didn't insult—and flat-out refuse—Lucas without upsetting his father, and I'd heard many scary stories about how ruthless Don Giovanni could be.

I squealed as a hand slapped over my mouth and an arm wrapped around my waist, pulling me backward. I struggled in the person's hold as I was dragged into another room. I managed to get my teeth on one of the fingers and bit down hard.

"Ow," Angelo's voice growled in my ear.

He shoved me away, and I stumbled before turning around to see him close the door. Shit. Shit. Shit.

"You bit me," he complained and shook his hand.

"Serves you right for grabbing me like that." I crossed my arms over my pajama top, and as his eyes traveled up and down my body, I realized that I was wearing the one with small tigers all over.

"So you like the nickname?"

"No, it's just a coincidence," I said. I wasn't going to admit he was right. He'd called me tiger so much that was how I'd started to see myself. Fierce and agile. At least that was what I chose to take from it, rather than whatever reason he had.

Angelo smirked. "Sure it is."

"What do you want? Anything else you'd like to try and break my nose with? There is a vase over there. I'm sure it would do some damage."

"About that...I didn't mean to get you in the face." I cocked my hip and raised a brow. "Okay, maybe I did a little, but I wasn't trying to break your nose." He stuffed his hands into his black and silver plaid sleep pants, and it was the first time I'd seen him look anything but an arrogant asshole. He cleared his throat. "I'm sorry," he finished, and my mouth fell open.

"What did you just say?"

"Shut up, you heard me." Angelo rubbed the back of his neck.

"Is that why you dragged me in here?"

"No. What the hell were you doing in that library with Lucas?" He growled and took an angry step toward me.

"What business is it of yours what I do," I asked, not backing down.

He stopped walking and towered over me. I was always small, but he'd shot up so much in the last year that I barely came to his chin. Papa said boys did that and would grow in large spurts. I hated it. It made taking him on when we fought so much harder. My hands clenched now as I prepared for whatever he planned.

"Lucas is trouble. Stay away from him."

Again, he wasn't wrong after what I just saw, but I hated that he thought he needed to say that to me.

I narrowed my eyes. "Lucas is the future Don of Dons, and if he wants to spend time with me, so be it." I pulled my long hair over my shoulder and ran my fingers through it. "At least he doesn't lie about me, put spiders on my head, ice down my top, steal my homework, or kick balls at my head." I lifted my chin and stared Angelo in the eyes. "Considering who I'm in this room with, Lucas is an upgrade."

I expected any retaliation except for him to cup my face and drop his lips to mine in a kiss. My brain froze. What the hell was happening? My mouth had been partially open, and as his tongue touched mine, I jerked back from him, wiping at my mouth.

"What the hell was that?" I growled and stomped past him. "Yuck, it's like a dog just licked inside my mouth."

"It's called a kiss, stupid," he snarled and glared at me. "You're supposed to like it."

"I'll never like anything from you." Opening the door, I ran out and sprinted down the halls. My heart pounded as I rounded the corner to the girl's wing and stopped to lean against the wall. I poked my head around to make sure he hadn't chased me down and raised my hand to my lips.

He kissed me. What new kind of bullying was this? Why would he do it when no one could see and laugh? Why did it kind of tingle? Why had my stomach fluttered?

I shook my head, seething anger rising along with the confusion. This was what he wanted—me questioning everything. It was bad enough that I worried about what he might do at school. It was annoying that I looked behind the door of every room at home to make sure he wasn't there. Now I had to add this weirdness to my list?

No, I wouldn't do it. Angelo Esposito was not taking up any more of my mind. Boys should all be drowned at birth. Well, except for my papa.

Chapter Five

JASMINE

WE'D BEEN HERE three days, and I was ignored or excluded daily. It made me want to scream.

I wanted to go hiking, but I wasn't allowed. I wanted to ride the ATV but was told they weren't for girls. I wanted to go sailing with everyone, but there was no more room in the boats, so I stood on the dock with my life jacket in my hand and watched everyone sail away. The only one that looked bothered at all was Dario.

It had become very clear that I wasn't welcome here. No matter what I did, the other kids ignored me. Gemma had said something to the other girls about me finding her and Lucas in the library. They had all started acting strange with me after that night. I would ask to go home if I hadn't seen my papa laughing and relaxing with the other Dons. I just couldn't bring myself to ruin this moment for him.

Wandering along the path near the beach, I spotted everyone on the trail that led up to the cliffs where you could jump into the water. Running, I caught up to the group just as they reached the opening.

"Hi," I panted, reaching the girls.

I never jumped in, but I loved watching everyone else leap and do tricks. I smiled at the girls I knew from school, and just like all the other times, they acted like I didn't exist. Angry, I grabbed Gemma's arm and pulled hard enough that she had to turn around.

"What the hell? Why are you all acting like this?"

She crossed her arms and glared at me. "You know why."

"No, I don't. Does this have to do with you and Lucas the other night?" Her face went as red as my mama's tomato sauce.

"Nothing happened, and you know it. You acted like a slut, and then threatened me in the hall if I said anything."

"What?" My mouth fell open in shock. "That's not what happened, and you know it."

"Why are you making up lies about us," Rosa asked.

"I'm not. I've never said anything about any of you to anyone. Why would I?"

One of the older girls, Meesha, pushed through the group and glared at me. "Because you're trying to move your family up in the ranks by marrying Lucas. We've all seen how he looks at you, and now you are making sure that none of us has a chance with him by spreading vicious lies with your wicked tongue."

"Yeah, you said I have a foot fungus to make sure he didn't look at me," Nikki said.

"And you told him that I always smell and like girls," Ella called out.

This was crazy. I looked from one to the other, and they all glared at me like I was a troll under a bridge.

"I don't want Lucas." I looked at Gemma, and there was a glimmer of guilt in her brown eyes. "Tell them the truth. I don't want him and didn't spread rumors either."

Even though I found it awkward to hang out with them most of the time, they were the closest thing I had to girlfriends. Panic made my heart beat like wings were flapping against it. Would they tell these lies to my papa? Would he believe them?

"Don't bother trying to deny it. I asked Lucas if you were in the library with him, and he said yes. Why would he lie?" Gemma crossed her arms, and the other girls made a wall.

“Maybe because he’s a jerk face. I was in the library, but I was sleeping until Lucas and Gemma going at it woke me up, not the other way around.”

“See, I told you that was what she’d say,” Gemma said, shaking her head. Walking forward, she gave my shoulder a little shove. “Why don’t you get out of here? No one wants you around, and we didn’t invite you anyway.”

I hated crying in front of people, but I could feel the tears burning my eyes. Standing up straight, I stared Gemma down.

“I thought we were friends.”

“I guess you thought wrong. I’d never want to be friends with someone like you,” she said, and I searched her face for a remnant of the person I knew.

“I hope you get what you deserve,” I said. “Same goes for all of you.” Turning on my heel, I ran off as fast as I could along the path. Tears filled my eyes, and I couldn’t see where I was going, but I didn’t care and kept going faster and faster until I burst out of the forest onto the sand. I ran to the dock where the small sailboats and canoes were tied.

All I wanted to do was float away and never come back. Wiping my eyes with the back of my hand, I untied one of the canoes and gripped the sides as I stepped into it.

“Jasmine, stop,” I looked up and saw Ciro and Angelo running along the beach.

“Leave me alone.”

“Jazzy, you don’t know how to swim,” Ciro yelled.

“I don’t care.” I felt bad yelling at Ciro. He was my only friend, but we promised to stay away from one another here this week so that his dad didn’t get on his case about being friends with a girl and not hanging out with the guys. Ciro had a secret that only I knew about, and I would go to my grave to keep it, but right now, not even he could make me feel better.

Using the paddle, I pushed away from the dock, and the canoe rocked wildly.

“Sit down,” Angelo yelled, but it was too late. The rocking got worse as I tried to correct it, and I screamed as I flew through the air and landed in the water with a splash. The blue water swallowed me as I clawed at the disappearing surface but kept sinking.

I couldn’t breathe, and panic set in as I tried to swim up. There was a loud splash, and terror and relief consumed me as Angelo swam toward me. He’d hated me my whole life. If he wanted to make sure I drowned, this would be the perfect moment for him, but instead, he wrapped his arm around my waist and kicked. Bubbles rose around us, and the burning in my chest got worse, but we were heading up, and with a gasping breath, we emerged.

He held me against his body as he pulled me toward the shallow water where we could stand. I coughed and spit, my eyes burning from the salt water and crying.

“What the hell were you thinking,” Angelo asked as he dragged me onto the beach. I didn’t say anything as Ciro helped me to sit down. Angelo shook his body like a dog shaking off water and looked at his feet. “Great, my new sneakers are ruined. Don’t be stupid and stay out of the water,” he said, stomping away.

My bottom lip trembled as Ciro sat beside me and wrapped his arm around my shoulders.

“Are you okay?”

I shook my head no. “Why are people so mean?”

“I don’t know.”

“Did you hear what they said to me up there?”

“I pretended not to, but yeah, I overheard some of it.” Ciro rubbed my shoulder, and I shivered despite the heat of the day.

“I didn’t do any of what they are saying. I’m not like that.” I wiped at the stream of tears again.

“I know. It was Lucas. He’s been gloating about it, but we didn’t know who he was talking about until now.”

“Such an ass. I didn’t think I could hate someone more than Angelo, but Lucas found a way to make it happen.”

“Just ignore them all.”

I pushed myself to my feet and squeezed the water from my top. "Easier said than done. I'm going to get changed."

"You going to be okay? You seem like something more is going on." I stared into Ciro's concerned eyes and couldn't tell him I thought my mom was sick again. I'd heard hushed conversations about doctor appointments, and everyone was acting overly happy. But if I said it aloud, it would make it more real.

"No, I'll be fine. Thanks, Ciro."

There was no way I was staying in a room with those girls again tonight. I'd figure something out.

Once everyone had finished eating and retired to their separate wings, I snuck out and ran to the beach. There was a firepit set up and a bench to sit on. Placing my bag of clothes down, I squatted to figure out how to get the fire going.

"Need some help?" I shot to my feet and turned to see Angelo walking toward me.

"Are you following me?"

"Pfft, don't you wish. I was out for a walk on the beach."

I looked at the matches in my hand and conceded that I didn't know how to start a fire, but saying that would make me look weak.

"Oh, for fuck's sake, give me the matches. I'll get it going," Angelo said, snatching them from me.

"Why are you always such a jerk," I asked.

"I'm not."

"So only to me, then?"

"Do you want me to light this or what," he said, looking at me.

"Fine, light it." Grabbing my blanket, I sat down and wrapped it around my shoulders. It took Angelo a few tries, but he got the fire going, and I paid attention to how he did it. Leaning down low, he blew on the flame, and the tiny spark ignited.

"That should do it." He looked around and then down at my bag. "No one else joining you?"

"Go ahead, get it off your chest," I said, pulling the blanket tighter.

"Get what off my chest?"

"The teasing or rude comment about how everyone hates me. I know you're dying to do it. So say what you want and go away." I looked away from his eyes and focused on the dancing flame that was slowly growing in size.

Instead of leaving, he sat down beside me. I leaned away and stared at the side of his face.

"What are you doing?"

"Sitting, what does it look like I'm doing?"

"No way. You're not sitting with me."

"I already am, so deal with it." He glanced over, and I looked away. "Why are you out here alone?"

"I don't hang out in places I'm not welcome," I said.

"Funny, you've done that our entire lives. Why stop now?" I jumped to my feet, and he grabbed my hand. "Shit...habit. I'm sorry, I didn't mean that."

"Stop saying sorry. I know you don't mean it, and it's weirding me out," I said but sat back down.

"I do mean it," he said, letting go of my hand. We sat quietly for a long time, and it was oddly calming having him here with me.

"My mom is sick again," I blurted out. "It's why I haven't asked my dad to go home. They are trying to hide it from me, but my mom had tests this week." Tears trickled out before I could stop them, and I scrubbed at my face. "I get why they don't want to say anything, but I'm not a child anymore. I can take it."

I wasn't sure why I felt the need to share that with him after all the years of him being an ass. Maybe because there was no obligation for kind words, and I knew Ciro would try to fix my problems. I didn't want that. I just needed someone to listen.

As I suspected, Angelo didn't say anything, but he wrapped his arm around my shoulder.

"Can I sit down?" We jumped at the sound of Dario's voice, but surprisingly, Angelo didn't move away.

"Sure," he said, and Dario sat on my other side.

This felt weird.

"For the record, Lucas is a dick. Ignore him and stay as far away as possible," Dario said, holding out a package of cookies. I shook my head, no, but Angelo took some.

"Thanks for keeping me company," I said, and we lapsed into silence once more.

This trip had been strange, and I couldn't imagine two more days. I closed my eyes and listened to the rhythmical waves lapping the shore. It was true that sometimes the enemy of my enemy was my friend.

Chapter Six

DARIO

"WE CAN'T SIT out here all night. She's gonna catch a chill," I said, looking over Jasmine's head to Angelo.

"I'd be pushing my luck if I moved her."

He was right about that. Jasmine would probably wake up swinging at his face.

"Okay, I'm going to take her inside. You bring her stuff." Careful not to jostle her, I stood and slowly scooped Jasmine into my arms. Her head settled in the crook of my neck, and all the emotions I'd buried bubbled to the surface.

I was nothing, a nobody, in the grand scheme of things, and never seen as an equal. My father was one of Don Esposito's advisors, but Angelo was the only reason I got invited this week.

My hands were tied when it came to Jasmine. I was loyal to Angelo first as much as I hated to see the shit he did to her. Angelo held open the door to the villa, and the warm air felt hot against my cool, damp skin. A heavy dew had formed, and I could see the droplets in Jasmine's hair. I wasn't letting her get sick.

"Where are you taking her?"

"The small sitting room that we found in the west wing. No one is down that way," I whispered, and Angelo nodded.

The door was open, and I walked through while Angelo closed and locked it behind us. There was a couch and a chair in the room, and I picked the couch, sitting down with her still in my lap. Her hand gripped the front of my hoodie, and she was shivering. There was no way I was leaving her.

"Hey, asshole," I grumbled, and Angelo froze as he was about to sit in the chair across from me. "Take off her wet shoes and put the knit blanket on her," I ordered, surprising myself and shocked when Angelo did it without argument.

She sighed and cuddled into me as he laid the blanket on her. Angelo plopped down in the chair and stared at me. In moments like this, I saw the Don he would be. The way he held his hands and stared at me was exactly how I pictured him when it was time for him to take over for his family.

"You like her, don't you?"

This felt like an interrogation, and I squirmed under his glare. "We're just friends. If you can even call us that," I answered, and Angelo snorted and leaned forward.

"That was an answer my father would give. You're my friend. Tell me the truth."

If I told him and he ordered me never to talk to her again....

"Dude, this is me. I'm not going to be angry if you do" Angelo said.

I lifted a shoulder and let it fall. "It doesn't matter. I know my place, and it's at your back, not with a princess."

He leaned back and stared at me. I hated when he did that. Angelo had a way of telling you off without saying a word. It was so easy to feel judged. We spent every day together and half of the nights playing video games or watching movies while our fathers worked. I knew all of his looks and glares, and right now, he was telling me to stop being a dick, but it took one to know one.

"What more do you want me to say? It doesn't matter how I feel."

"What if it did?"

"What do you mean?" I narrowed my gaze and stared at my friend.

His eyes flicked to my hand, and I realized I was rubbing Jasmine's arm to help get her warm.

"I mean, what if it did matter how you felt? Would you tell me then?"

This felt like a Venus flytrap, and I'd already flown into the gaping mouth. "If it mattered, then yes, I would tell you," I finally admitted.

"Okay, then tell me, do you like her?"

I glanced down at her and couldn't believe I was going to say this out loud. "Yes, I do."

"Okay then."

"What does that mean?"

He shrugged, laid his head back on the chair, and closed his eyes. "Just means that we will figure something out, but we have years before we need to worry about it. By then, we may hate her or hate each other. So, for now, I'm going to sleep."

Jasmine shivered and drew my attention back to her. I couldn't picture hating her. Then again, I couldn't have imagined my parents hating one another, but they divorced, and now my mother was in Switzerland with her new boyfriend.

Although, that was because of my older sister's death. Trauma should have brought our family closer together. Instead, it drove a wedge between my parents. They were vicious with one another and struck out with words like a wooden stake to the heart.

My father was overprotective, and my mother wanted to let Catia grow up and have a life outside of the Mafia family lifestyle. They fought constantly about it, but in the end, my father won out, and it drove my sister to sneak out in the middle of the night to meet up with her boyfriend.

I remembered my mother's scream all too clearly. It was like her soul was ripped from her body. I raced downstairs, and the police stood inside while my mother bawled on the ground. My father looked shocked as he stared at the men who had delivered the news.

They called it an unfortunate accident, but after they left, my father called Don Esposito. Of course, I listened in on the conversation of how they found her dead from an overdose. My sister never took drugs, hated them, and was very open about it. She threatened to cut my nuts off if I ever started taking the product the other families sold, and I believed her.

They found her boyfriend trying to flee the country, and I asked to watch the execution. My father beat him until his face was unrecognizable before shooting him between the eyes.

"There are times when a man does what is necessary to protect his family. Remember that, son," my father said.

That was when the blame game started. My mother blamed my father for being too strict, and my father blamed my mother for being too lenient.

I never wanted to end up like that. I'd rather remain single forever, but if Angelo was serious...it was almost too much to hope.

Chapter Seven

ANGELO

I WAS SO TIRED. Yawning, I ran my hand through my hair. I'd stayed awake for hours as Jasmine leaned against me or Dario until he insisted on carrying her into the villa. He looked startled the first time she changed positions and laid her head on his shoulder but settled into it, and I smiled at the dumb look on his face. Jasmine touching Dario didn't bother me, but when I thought about her in that library with Lucas, I wanted to punch a wall or his face.

He claimed that Jasmine had sucked him off, but she was terrible at it, and he kicked her out of the library. I didn't believe it. Maybe that was stupid, but I just didn't. It pissed me off that he purposely turned the girls against her like he was trying to ice her out or make her vulnerable. I wasn't letting Lucas do something fucked up to her. If that meant I had to follow her around, I would, no matter how much she complained. I didn't trust him.

Annoyed, I marched downstairs to get something to eat. Like the other mornings, the dining hall had a long buffet, and my stomach growled with the smell of fresh food. I went straight for a cappuccino and loaded it with sugar before chugging it down. How did my father drink this black? Looking at the selection, I grabbed some berries and circled the table like a bird of prey before shoving three bite-sized frittatas in my mouth. Then I grabbed a pancake and smothered it with jam. Folding it in half to take with me, I walked outside toward the field where the guys were playing football today.

I really hoped they didn't invite the girls to play, and I was looking forward to 'accidentally' tripping Lucas. Some guys were hanging out on the pitch, and I nodded in their direction but didn't see Dario.

My ass no sooner found the bench when a muffled scream shot me to my feet. I looked around for the source, searching the surrounding trees. I knew Jasmine's voice all too well. A group of guys stood outside the locker room, and I had a bad feeling as I jogged over.

"Let go of me," Jasmine said.

"Open your mouth, now," Lucas growled.

Like fuck this was happening. I shoved guys to the side as I pushed through the crowd. I expected to see Lucas with his pants down, not Jasmine pinned on the ground as Lucas tried to shove her shoe into her mouth.

She smacked at him and got him hard across the cheek. There was a collective gasp from the room. Lucas raised his hand, and as she closed her eyes and looked away, something inside me snapped.

Jumping at Lucas, I tackled him to the floor and rolled along the hard concrete.

"What the fuck are you doing Angelo?" Lucas pushed at me to try and get me off, but I braced my feet against the wall and punched him as hard as I could in the face. His head snapped to the side as my fist connected with his jaw. He'd been a dick to me my entire life, and enough was enough. I didn't care what the consequences were.

"Fuck!" He roared and punched me back.

We rolled around, fighting for dominance as our fists, elbows, and knees connected wherever possible. There was cheering in the background, but I ignored it until someone grabbed me from behind and dragged me off Lucas.

"What in God's name is going on," my father said, and I realized that was who had me.

Don Giovanni stepped into the doorway, and most of the guys scattered as Lucas pulled himself to his feet. Blood trickled from his nose and split lip, but it wasn't enough. I wanted to rip his heart out.

"Answer the question, what happened," Don Giovanni asked as he glared at his son.

Lucas held his hand out to me. "Don't look at me. Angelo attacked me out of nowhere."

Don Giovanni looked at me. "Is that true?"

My father let me go, and I felt my lip for blood. It stung, but there was no red. "Yes, it's true."

Don Giovanni placed his hands on his hips, looking ridiculous wearing the black and white ref shirt. "Why?"

"Because he deserved it," I said, glaring across the room at my nemesis.

"Can you be more specific?"

"Ask him. I'd love to see how he's going to swing this," I said and crossed my arms.

"I wasn't doing shit. You attacked me for no reason as I was getting changed."

"Bullshit." I stepped in his direction, and my father grabbed my shoulder.

Don Giovanni looked like he was ready to blow. His face was red, and his eyes livid as he looked back and forth between us.

"I want the truth right now," Don Giovanni growled.

"He was trying to shove my shoe in my mouth," Jasmine said as she stepped into view. She was still missing her shoe, and I spotted it across the room.

"I did not, you lying little bitch," Lucas snarled.

My mouth fell open in shock as Giovanni stormed across the room and punched Lucas so hard that he fell to the ground, holding the side of his face.

"You do not disrespect a Don's daughter. She is a child. Why were you touching her in the first place?"

"Father, I swear...." Lucas stopped and held his hands up as Giovanni raised his fist.

"Do not lie to me, son."

"Okay, fine. Yes, I tried to shove her shoe in her mouth. She was being a bi—rude and needed to be taught a lesson."

Jasmine scoffed, and Lucas glared at her. I again took a step forward, but my father kept a tight hold on my shoulder.

"Do you have something you'd like to share, Ms. Falcone," Giovanni asked.

Jasmine walked past Lucas—and the evil stare he gave her—and grabbed her shoe. She pulled it on and sighed.

"I just want today to be over. If Lucas leaves me alone, I'll leave him alone. If he attacks me again...." She looked at Lucas, and my heart pounded harder with the look in her eyes. She really was a tiger, and she was mine. "I'll have a few things to tell you then."

Giovanni's brows lifted, his lip curling up. "Very well. You heard her. Stay away from her, and she won't bother you. Do you think you can handle that, son?"

Lucas stood and looked at his father, Jasmine, and finally me. I knew I had a target painted on my back from now on.

"Understood," he said.

Lucas and Giovanni left, and Jasmine looked at me. Her eyes searched my face, confusion shining back at me from their depths. Without another word, she walked out, and I was left alone with my father.

"You want to tell me what happened?" I turned to face my father.

"No."

He poked me in the chest, his eyes narrowed into a glare. "Don't embarrass the family and leave Lucas alone. I don't want to see you look in his direction the rest of the week. Do you understand me?"

"Why am I getting in trouble when he is clearly the asshole."

"That is debatable, but the reason is because he is still the Don of

Don's son. Keep your distance. One day, he will be your boss, and you need to be on good terms with him, or he could ruin the family. I have worked too hard to have that happen."

I fucking despised that Lucas could hold that much power over me, but I nodded. "I get it. I'll stay away from him."

"Good."

My dad marched out, but I needed a minute to cool off. I closed my eyes and took a deep breath. Things had gotten so confusing, and I wasn't even sure when it happened.

"Hey."

My eyes snapped open, and Jasmine was right in front of me. She cleared her throat as she smoothed down her t-shirt.

"I'm not sure why you did that, but...thank you." Grabbing my arm, she raised up on her toes and kissed my cheek. My heart hammered, and blood pounded through my body. Her hand felt like it burned a hole through my skin where it rested. At some point, Jasmine had poured liquid wax on my heart, and she'd just stamped it with the softness of her lips.

I stared into her honey-colored eyes, but in a blink, she was gone, slipping out the door and disappearing.

I touched my cheek and knew that when the time came, I'd find a way to make her mine. The whys of how this happened didn't matter. Jasmine Falcone would be my wife. I was sure of it.

Chapter Eight

JASMINE

SEVEN YEARS LATER

AGE 18

ALL I COULD SAY WAS THANK God he didn't pick me. Lucas had been loud and obnoxious all night, and although Rosa smiled the entire time, I saw the worry on her face and the uncertainty in her eyes. She was a year older than me and had tied herself to the most notorious cheater around. But Rosa knew what she was getting into. She had even fought for him. We'd hardly spoken in seven years, but she had become more ruthless each time I saw her. Gone was the shy girl I once knew.

The only other guy that came close to Lucas in his womanizing ways was Angelo.

I looked away from the wedding party at the head table and found Angelo and Dario talking to four girls who were all flirting with them. Why I thought things would be different between us when we left the villa that one summer, I couldn't say. But Angelo had gone right back to being the asshole. Not quite as bad as before, but he still took his potshots when he could, and Dario went back to ignoring me. Temporary insanity was the only thing I could chalk it up to.

The only time Angelo was kind was when my mama passed away two years ago. He'd hugged me like he had at the villa, and I hated to admit that I missed those few blissful moments between us.

I couldn't stand sitting here and staring at them any longer. "Do you want to dance?"

Ciro sat his wine glass down. "Are you talking to me?"

I tilted my head and blatantly looked at the empty chairs at the table. "Who else would I be talking to?"

"Good point. Sure," Ciro said.

He looked around as we walked to the dance floor, and I leaned in and whispered. "Marcus isn't here."

"How did you know?"

"Please, I know you so well, and the look you give him says it all," I said, nudging Ciro's arm before he twirled me out on the dance floor.

"Fair...okay, spill, why isn't he here?"

"His cousin from Australia passed away, and he's gone for the funeral." Marcus was Papa's personal assistant, and Ciro had been eyeing him up from the moment he laid eyes on the red-haired, blue-eyed Scotsman.

"Dammit, I was hoping to get to know him better tonight when it would look normal for us to be socializing," he said as I spun back into his arms. Ciro was a year older and an amazing dancer. The only reason I learned a single move was because of him.

"He'll be back, and I'll even cover for you."

"I can't keep asking you to do that," he said, but his eyes were all puppy dog and hopeful.

"Of course I will. I'm pretty sure you have nothing to worry about. He seems pretty interested in you, too," I said, smiling at my friend.

We'd always been close, but that was the one thing that had changed since the villa. We were closer than ever, and Ciro was over almost every day after school. When my mama passed away, he became more protective. Saturdays were our romcom night, and he would sneak into my room to watch movies until the sun came up.

"What about you," Ciro asked, spinning us around so I could see Angelo at the bar. He didn't look happy as he glanced my way, but that was expected when it came to him.

"What about me?"

"When are you going to start dating?" Ciro motioned with his eyes toward Angelo or maybe Dario. Heck, it could be both knowing him.

"That is never happening."

"Never say never. I've seen how Angelo looks at you. He wants you." Ciro's eyes shined with as much mischief as the glittering little lights hanging around us.

"He looks at me like he wants to kill me. That is not the kind of want I'm looking for, thanks."

"You're missing out. Angry sex is the best."

My face flamed red, and I shook my head at him. "Trust me, I never think about him like that."

As the song ended, he dipped me low and whispered. "I think you protest too much."

I wanted to smack him and wipe the smug smile off his face, but he bowed and wandered toward the bar. If he expected me to follow, then he had another thing coming. I walked over to the table where my papa was sitting. He was slowly swirling his drink glass but didn't seem to be looking at anything.

I squeezed his shoulders. "Are you okay?"

He patted my hand. "Just missing your mama. She loved weddings. She was always so excited to plan yours."

My chest constricted, and I bit my lip to hold the tide that wanted to burst free.

"I see her in the twinkling lights, the music playing, and the smell of the fresh flowers, Papa. She is on the dance floor right now and will be here with us when I get married, too." He looked up at me, tears in his eyes, and that broken look shattered my heart.

"Mia Bambolina, you are an incredible daughter. Thank you, you are right. She lives on in every moment we remember her." He stood and hugged me before he excused himself to get another drink. I looked at the half-full glass on the table and sighed.

I didn't feel like rejoining the party and escaped out the side door to the gardens. The summer was exceptionally hot, and even the nights didn't seem to cool off this year. A couple sat among the decorations near the fountain. They looked like a pair of love birds as they rubbed their noses together.

Not wanting to disturb their private moment, I veered onto the path of tall bushes that led down to the roses. During the day, they were magnificent. Not paying attention, I rounded the last corner and screamed as someone grabbed my arm and tugged me through a narrow opening in the thick bushes.

Before I could fathom who held me, my back was pressed against one of the large decorative pillars, and lips latched onto the side of my neck. Angelo's cologne filled my nose, his hands holding me tight as he nipped at the skin over my racing pulse.

"What the hell are you doing," I asked, but I sounded pathetic even to myself.

"Hello, Tiger," he growled, biting my ear.

Even though everything in me screamed to hit him or push him away, I didn't. My head tilted to the side to give him better access as my hands curled into the fabric of his shirt. It was as if his touch had put a surge into my blood as it raced through my body, making my heart pound hard. He had grown up so much. His shoulders were broad, his muscles were taut, and I couldn't stop my body from responding to his touch.

"You're so fucking beautiful," he whispered against my neck, and desire bubbled inside me. My breath caught in my throat as he slid his hand up my torso and rubbed his thumb over my nipple. "Every time I see you, you take my breath away."

That was certainly a lie.

"What are you...." The rest of my concern was swallowed down as he kissed me. It was the first kiss we had shared since the villa, and he commanded my mouth this time. Unable to help it, I moaned and opened my mouth for him, tasting the dark whiskey flavor on his tongue.

Every nerve ending came alive, and all my problems and worries flew away as the jittery excitement and passion soared around my body. Angelo made it hard to think. I should be objecting, and yet I couldn't remember why.

My back pressed harder into the pillar as he deepened the kiss, and my bones felt like they were liquifying throughout my body. I was lightheaded when he broke away and bent down. I gasped and swatted at him as he stood, but his hand was under my long dress, pulling it up.

"Stop it," I argued and put my hands on his chest, but his finger rubbed over my panties, and I shuddered.

"You don't really seem like you want me to stop. Tell me, Tiger, has anyone pleasured you before?" No mirror needed—I knew I was blushing from the tips of my toes to the tops of my ears. My cheeks flamed so hot that I wished I had a fan to wave at myself.

"I'm not answering that," I said. I'd never been kissed, let alone what he was talking about.

"They better not have," he said. His voice was growly, like he was pissed off, as he continued to run a finger between my legs. Staring into his eyes wasn't a good idea. It was like being hypnotized by a snake charmer.

"Angelo...." I protested feebly, but he captured my mouth again, and my heart pounded faster. I hated that I hoped he wanted me. It made me feel weak that I still wanted him after everything he'd done. I was no better than Rosa.

With each passing second, he made it more difficult to put a single thought together, and my legs shook as he swirled his finger. I'd touched myself late at night, but this felt different. His strong fingers pressed right where I liked, and a little moan tumbled from my mouth.

"Fuck, I've missed you. I want you so bad, Tiger," he said. He'd graduated a couple years before me, and it had been blissfully bully free. Which was why I couldn't understand why I would stare at his vacant seat and wonder what he was doing. I'd secretly grown fond of our battles of wits and wills.

An entire storm of butterflies took flight in my stomach, but the image from the bar was rooted in my brain. I knew he'd started dating and having sex several years ago. Girls whispered tales of how good he was, and every time I heard it, another pin of pain stabbed me through the heart.

"You miss me? Just like you've missed all the other girls you bed," I said and turned my head to glare at him.

His blue eyes had only gotten brighter as he got older, and they were now the color of the ocean on a sunny day. The hungry look in them made my heart race faster.

"Who I sleep with is not your concern."

"Oh, but it is when you pull me into the bushes to assault me like this." I pushed the arm between my legs away and was surprised he let me. My long dress fell to the ground once more.

"Please, you've been looking at me all night," he said, and I came very close to kneeing him in the balls. But instead, I smirked.

"You are mistaken. I wasn't looking at you. Dario has really filled out," I said, and he narrowed his eyes, his lip pulling up into a snarl.

"You're mine, Tiger. I will marry you, so you better get used to the idea."

I did shove him away with that comment. "Ha, I'm not property, and that is not likely to happen, my papa will make sure of it." I glared into his stupid blue eyes that made my heart race. "I will never marry you." I marched for the opening, but he grabbed me again and pulled me back against him. His hard chest pressed into my back, and I felt his breath on my neck, a shiver racing down my spine.

"Yes, you will."

"No, I won't."

"Why are you so stubborn?"

"Why are you such a whore?" I glanced over my shoulder as he chuckled. "I wasn't joking."

"I love your jealousy," he said, kissing softly along my skin.

"I'm not jealous."

"You're lying. I can feel the heat under your skin. You've always belonged in my arms."

Summoning all my strength, I pulled away, and he let me go. Yes, he was sexy, and I found him attractive. I couldn't deny that I wondered what it would be like to sleep with him. I secretly hoped things were different between us, but as I looked him up and down, I knew it couldn't happen.

"Whether I'm attracted to you is irrelevant. I won't be your stay-at-home sloppy seconds begging for attention like poor Rosa. We both know she will end up angry and bitter. Eventually, she'll take a lover at great risk to herself before becoming a shadow of who she was. Nothing more than a bitter version of the woman she could've been." I shook my head. "I want something different for my life, which doesn't include becoming one of the laundry list of girls that have rolled around in your sheets." I smoothed down the front of my dress. "No, I will not be marrying you, Angelo, because I want someone who will love me for more than the powerful son I can offer them as a princess—someone who will want all of me and only me like my papa did with my mama. Pick someone else. Dozens of others lust after you and would fall at your feet, but I'm no one's puppet." I turned away and looked back. "I'm honestly confused why you'd lie and say you want me. You made it perfectly clear our entire lives how you feel. Stick with that, we are much better off staying away from eachother."

I marched away, deciding it was safer at the party where more eyes could see me. No matter what, my mind would never be able to forget that kiss. It was my first real one, and my lips still tingled from Angelo's touch. So did the spot between my legs that only my fingers had ever been.

No, I couldn't let Angelo crawl under my skin and get into my head. He was dangerous to my heart.

Chapter Nine

DARIO

FUCK, we shouldn't be doing this. I leaned against the wall and glowered at the floor like it had insulted me. This was all Angelo and his stupid ideas. Jasmine didn't want anything to do with me, and why should she? I'd never given her any reason to trust me any more than Angelo had, but we were both hopelessly in love with her.

I could at least admit it to myself, but Angelo was still in denial. He thought it was lust that plagued him, but it wasn't. I saw it in the way he looked at her. It was the same look that I held hidden away in my heart.

So many years, so many stupid comments and jokes that, looking back, were not funny. Each one drove a wedge between us and Jasmine. I'd lost count how many times Angelo insisted on seeking her out on a weekend or summer holiday only to do more of the same crap. The one thing Angelo had gotten right was calling her Tiger. Those bright honey eyes were as intelligent and cunning as any tiger. Shit, I felt sick, I should leave.

"Dario?" I jerked at the sound of my name on Jasmine's lips.

I stared at her as she slowly walked down the hallway toward me. I allowed myself to soak in how stunning she looked tonight. The shimmering gold gown hugged every curve, and the color accented her eyes and midnight black hair that reminded me of a raven's wing.

"Are you okay," she asked, and I opened my mouth, but nothing came out. She eyes filled with concern, and her brow knit together. "Here, let's get you sitting down."

Why couldn't I make my voice work?

She fumbled with the key to her room and opened the door before grabbing my arm and helping me like I was injured. It felt like that. I was a soldier, a nobody, really. Why would a princess from a prominent family ever want me? I was far from insecure, yet she made me question everything about myself. Panic gipped me. What if someone saw me come into her room and called her father?

"Sit here. I'll get you some water."

"No, I...I...."

I grabbed for her hand but missed as she dashed across the room and poured a glass from the pitcher on her table. She held up her dress and jogged back, her hand going to my forehead, and I couldn't take it. Taking the glass from her hand, I set it aside and pulled her onto my lap.

"Oh." Jasmine's eyes went wide as she sat like a cat perched on the back of a chair, ready to leap off at any moment.

"I needed to see you," I finally got out.

"What's going on, Dario? Is something wrong?"

"I'm an asshole."

"Oh...um...okay. Have you had too much to drink?"

"I wish. Shit. I don't know how to say this." Her eyes searched my face, but at least she'd relaxed and didn't look like she wanted to run away.

"It's okay. Take your time." She laid her hand on my chest, and I was sure she could feel the pounding of my heart under her fingertips.

"I want to apologize for all the shit I stood by and watched happen to you." I smoothed back the loose waves around her face. "And I hated that I laughed and participated in bullying you."

A soft smile played along her lips.

"Thank you for saying that," she said, as her fingers fiddled with the front of my shirt. Her breath hitched as I slid my hand down her leg and leaned closer. She didn't jump up and run screaming, so I took the opening. I intended on keeping the kiss soft, but the moment our lips touched, I had to have more. I'd been starving for her touch for too long. I'd lost count of how many times I dreamed of improving my position and wondered what it would take to be considered worthy in her father's eyes.

Every muscle flexed and hardened, wanting to be inside of her. The physical attraction was there the moment I understood what a girl was, but it was everything else about Jasmine that captivated me. She wasn't like the other princesses. She was kindness and humility personified, yet strong and sure of herself. I loved how she stuck up for others even when outnumbered. I loved how she hummed under her breath when she was thinking hard and the little wrinkles she got at the corner of her eyes when she laughed. I loved how her smile lit up a room, and her sharp tongue never held back what she was thinking.

Her fingers raked into my hair, and I groaned, needing to get control before I threw her down on the bed. Breaking the kiss, I laid my forehead against hers.

"We never deserved you," I said, my pulse pounding in my ears. "We still don't, but we want you."

"Dario, you're not making much sense. Who is we," she asked, just as the long sheers covering the entrance to the balcony blew to the side, and Angelo looked like a cat lounging as he leaned against the arched opening.

"Me," Angelo said, and Jasmine jumped from my lap.

"What is going on? And how did you get up here?"

Angelo shrugged as he walked across the room. "I climbed. We weren't done with our conversation down in the garden."

"Oh, I'm pretty sure we were done." Jasmine crossed her arms over her chest, glaring at Angelo and then me. I hated that guarded look.

Standing, I marched to the door and locked it before turning around. Jasmine's eyes were angry, but under it was fear. "We're not going to hurt you," I said.

"Then why did you just lock my door?" She swallowed hard and started to back up but bumped into Angelo. Running across the room, she grabbed a letter opener and held it up. "Both of you stay away from me."

I grabbed Angelo's shoulder and nodded that I would talk to her. We'd spent so many years together that he knew what I was saying and nodded back. I stepped toward Jasmine cautiously and held my hands up.

"I said stay away from me." Her voice had a tiny growl, and I had to roll out my shoulders as the sound traveled down my body like her hand was stroking my cock.

I held my hand out for the sharp weapon. "I may not have always stood up for you, but I've never hurt you." Her hand wavered. "Do you remember the night at the villa when you sat on the bench between us with your head on my shoulder?"

"Yes."

"I carried you inside, and we sat with you all night to keep you safe. I held you close to my chest. Do you remember?"

"Yes," she said, her voice softer this time.

"You trusted us then, so trust me now. Give me the letter opener, and we can talk."

She licked her lips, and it took everything in me not to take my chances right now and kiss her again. My fingers ached to touch her. I was not as bold as Angelo and had known my place in the pecking order. It had taken me a long time before I stood up to Angelo, and it was only after I became his guard that I told him I'd never take part in bullying Jasmine again. We lived on top of one another, and I had to find my voice.

"You promise me?"

“I swear to you on my sister Lolita’s grave that we will not hurt you.”

Jasmine’s hand lowered, and she set the letter opener down. I kept my hand out but didn’t make another move. She eyed me cautiously, and I could see her questioning what was happening, but she eventually laid her hand in mine. Her hand looked so small, and I couldn’t imagine her marrying someone like Lucas. She had no idea how close she’d come to being forced into marriage with him, but Angelo and I had taken care of that.

A breeze came through the open balcony, and the loose strands from her updo blew around her face, and my breath caught in my throat.

“I don’t understand what is happening here.” Jasmine looked up at me and then peered around my shoulder to Angelo, who I could feel pacing behind me.

Stepping in close to her, I loved how she lifted her chin and stood her ground. I was willing her with my eyes to be okay with this...to be okay with me. Releasing her hand, I pushed the wild strands away from her face.

“I’m going to kiss you again,” I said, shocked when she didn’t snatch the letter opener and hold it to my throat. Desire flared and seared my blood as my lips brushed hers. She was sweeter than I could ever imagine. “I’ve wanted to kiss you for so long. Being in this room with you feels like a dream,” I whispered.

My kiss was soft and coaxing, whereas Angelo would throw her up against a wall. I didn’t think we were going to get anywhere with that tactic. There were too many old wounds that needed to heal first.

Her eyes fluttered closed as I laid soft kisses along her cheek and down her neck. Jasmine shivered as she let out a little gasp. She gripped my dress shirt, but I wanted to feel her hands on my skin. Grabbing the front of the shirt, I gave it a hard tug, and all the buttons scattered across the room.

Jasmine’s eyes widened, but she didn’t try to run off as I took her hands and placed them on my chest. They were cool against my heated skin, and I shuddered as she moved one to sit over my thumping heart. It had been going crazy since I walked up to her door.

"You two are confusing me. You hate me. Why are you doing this? Is it so you can say you checked another princess off your list? I know the two of you have shared many."

"No," Angelo barked out and stomped over. Jasmine immediately bristled as he got closer. "It's not like that. I was serious down in the garden. I want to marry you. I've wanted to marry you since we were kids."

She scoffed. "You have a remarkably stupid way of showing it," she said, and Angelo smirked.

"Well, picking on you was fun. I loved how you gave as good as you got," he said, walking around behind her. I didn't move as she turned to face Angelo and backed into me.

It took every fucking ounce of control not to wrap my arms around her. Even if Angelo didn't care or couldn't see it, I knew we were on a high ledge. Jasmine could push us off and make a run for it at any time, and I didn't want that. Tonight was supposed to be special. It was supposed to be the start of something new for all of us.

"I am sorry for almost all of the things I've done," Angelo said, shrugging out of his suit jacket and tossing it on a nearby chair.

"I'm sure." She crossed her arms.

"It's the truth."

"Fine, then tell me truthfully, what is all this about?"

The usual arrogance that Angleo held up like a shield melted away. "I love you," he said shocking me. "I don't know when it happened, but I've been waiting for the right moment to tell you." He cupped her face, and her body pressed closer to mine. "You said you want something more. I am promising you right now if you choose to marry me...I will never touch another woman other than you. I cannot deny my past, but I needed to wait until you were of age before your father would listen to an offer of marriage."

"You're serious?"

Angelo lowered himself down onto one knee. "Say you accept, and we will forever be yours."

"Why do you keep saying we?"

Angelo looked up at me, and Jasmine followed. "Like...marry both of you?"

It was my turn to chuckle. "No, your father would never let you marry a soldier. I'm Angelo's bodyguard. I don't have the right money, power, or connections to move up, you know that." She nodded slowly. "But I would be in the relationship if you'll have me. He knows how I feel about you."

Jasmine stepped around me, and I let her go. Angelo rose to his feet as we watched her pace the room with her hand on her forehead.

"This is crazy. I've spent my entire life wondering when the next prank will be or what embarrassing and mean thing you'll decide to insult me with. Now you both say you love me and want to marry me?"

"Yes, that's what we are saying," Angelo answered.

Jasmine laughed. I should've expected that response, but I was hoping for a different result. She marched across the room, pulled open the sheers and shook them out, then got down and looked under the bed.

"Where is it?"

"Where is what," I asked.

"Where is the camera?" She pulled open the dresser drawers, then walked to the closet and whipped the doors open. "Because I don't believe one word of this."

"We are not playing you," I said, but she snorted.

"I don't believe you."

Angelo stomped across the room and had her pressed up against the wall, kissing her before she could start another lap of the room. Walking to the bed, I removed my ruined shirt and kicked off my shoes before pouring glasses of wine from the complimentary assortment.

"I love you. No jokes. No lies. No pranks. No insults. This is me, the me that only Dario and now you see. I want to marry you. Say you'll marry me, and I'll speak to your father and make it happen. But if you say yes, I plan on devouring you tonight. I've waited too long already to claim you."

Jasmine looked between Angelo's intense expression to me and licked her lips. It was subtle, but I could tell she was thinking it over and not just planning her escape.

"And you're not just doing this to better your family holdings," she asked as her eyes scrutinized Angelo's face.

"I don't need to marry a Falcone to better my fortune. It helps speed up the process without you having a brother to take over the throne, but that's not why I want to marry you. I'm telling you the truth." Grabbing her hand, he placed it over his heart, much like I had. "My heart is yours."

She lifted her chin and stepped in close to Angelo. "Why do I need to make this decision tonight?"

"Because there are things you don't know about. Things that will force you to marry someone not of your choosing."

"My papa wouldn't do that."

"But, he did. He was going to broker an arrangement with Lucas." Jasmine's mouth fell open.

"No way."

"Way, but Dario and I stopped it," Angelo said.

"How?"

"The how isn't important. What is important is that my father and yours have never seen eye-to-eye. More recently, my father has lost favor with some of the other Dons, which would make an arranged marriage between our families more difficult."

"I'm not sure what to believe. I can't picture my father agreeing to anything that involved Lucas."

"It's true, every last word," I said and pulled out my phone. I played a short clip of Jasmine's father speaking to Giovanni about an arrangement. She looked skeptical right up to the very end.

"So what say you, Sergio? Are you willing to give up what is most precious to you," Giovanni asked.

"You promise that your son will take care of my Jasmine?"

"I do."

"I will give it serious consideration. You'll have my final decision in three days."

Jasmine's hands went to her mouth as the clip stopped. "I can't believe it."

"We have wanted you for years. Let's ensure your father will be reluctant to make an arrangement with anyone else?"

Her eyes flicked from Angelo to me. "You're using tonight as another chip to make sure my father says yes, aren't you? If you take my virginity, he will demand you marry me to protect my honor."

"Always the smartest in the room. Yes, that is the plan. I will tell your father of my undying love. I will give him a chance to say yes, and if he doesn't, I'll tell him of our time together and how I suspect you may be pregnant. He will question you, of course, and you can confirm we are together." Jasmine chewed her lip. "Your father will not disown you. He will order me to do right by you and marry you, which is what we want."

Jasmine was quiet as she looked down to the floor, and I held my breath. "I don't want him to know right away. I want to make sure this is real between us first."

Angelo looked ready to argue, but the firm look in her eyes had him nodding. "Fine, we can wait a few months and hopefully you really will be pregnant. That gives you time to see we're serious and me an iron clad position to argue for your hand."

Angelo didn't move as Jasmine thought it over. She gave her answer as she slid the shimmering dress off her shoulders, letting it pool at her feet and left her standing in lace panties.

"Fuck you're beautiful, Tiger," Angelo said as his eyes roamed over her body at the same time mine did. My cock was already hard, but now it ached to be set free. "You won't regret this."

"I will agree to marry you, but if you're playing me...Angelo, I swear...."

"I'm not," Angelo said, interrupting her before she could come up with a colorful way to kill us.

Relief bathed me, and the heaviness that had been sitting on my chest as I waited for a response flew out the balcony door. Jasmine never said she loved us, but it was now my mission to make her fall hopelessly in love.

Rising from the bed, I walked over with the wine glasses. Cupping her chin, I tilted her head up and stared into her honey eyes.

"Playing you will never happen." A blush crept across her cheeks, and I knew that no matter what was to come, she would forever hold the keys to my heart.

Chapter Ten

ANGELO

I HADN'T REALIZED how nervous I was that my Tiger would say no until the relief rushed through my body with her acceptance. Now, I just needed to convince her father, but I had backup plans just in case. One of those was happening right now. I watched her lips as she sipped the wine. I needed all of her tonight.

Dario took our empty glasses, and as soon as my hands were free and before she could think to kick us out, I brushed my thumbs across her soft cheeks and dropped my lips to hers. The world felt alive with color when I was near her. The feel of her lips and her sweet flavor mixed with the wine on my tongue was enough to drive a man insane.

Jasmine's small gasp made me deepen the kiss, and a moan that was sweet, sensual candy on my tongue was my reward. I wanted to feast on every part of her body and planned to do just that. I knew when Dario stepped up behind her. Jasmine pressed closer to my body, her muscles tensing. He growled, and I smirked as she shivered in our hold.

She was frozen, trapped between us. She looked up into my eyes, and I saw fear in those golden orbs.

"What's the matter, Tiger?"

The delicate pink on her cheeks turned a vibrant shade of red. "I... I...um...."

"I know you don't," I said, saving her from having to say she had no experience. I wasn't planning to tell her I paid handsomely to ensure no one touched her. Anyone who gave her a second look or lingered a little too long was never seen again. I kept tabs on any dates that dared to ask her out through a few of her guards—including one of the women her father insisted on. No man ever entered her room. I knew because I snuck in and watched her sleep everynight and had been tempted to make my move sooner. Age alone kept me at bay. I was ruthless when it came to getting what I wanted, and she was what I wanted.

"How do you know that?"

"I'm a guy, we just know," I said, the corner of my mouth lifting in a lopsided grin as she scowled back. "I just do." I shrugged. "But I plan on us being your first and your last."

"We'll be gentle with you," Dario whispered as his lips grazed her skin.

Jasmine's lips parted, and her eyes fluttered closed with a soft moan. I was done. You could only put so much pressure on a rope before it broke, and whatever had been holding me back from taking what I craved all these years had just snapped.

Cupping her face, I dropped my lips and tasted every inch of her mouth. She wiggled, and I could feel the nervousness running under her skin, but I didn't care. By the time we finished, she would be begging for more, and I was happy to give her what she wanted all night long. We had two nights left at this villa, and if she did get pregnant now, all the better.

I felt Dario slip his hand between me and Jasmine and knew exactly what he was doing when Jasmine gasped and moaned in my mouth.

"You're already wet for us, Princess," Dario growled. "You going to come all over my fingers?"

Her whimper made me push them both backward until Dario's

back was pressed against the wall, trapping Jasmine between us. I wore too much clothing and needed to feel her skin against mine. Panting, I broke the kiss and stepped back to watch Jasmine squirm in Dario's arms. I fucking loved to watch, and she was quickly coming undone, but the fabric of her thong was in the way of my view. Grabbing the sides I pulled down, forcing her to step out of them. Standing I stuffed the underwear into my pocket to keep.

"Fuck, that is better," I said, as Dario's finger disappeared inside of her.

"Spread your legs further apart," I ordered as I undid the buttons on my shirt.

Jasmine's eyes opened and locked with mine. Her legs shook as she stepped wider, giving Dario easier access. He was sucking on her neck, which would undoubtedly leave a mark, while his other hand held her tight to his body. A second finger was added to the task as his thumb rubbed at her clit. They were fucking intoxicating.

"Oh, dear god," Jasmine panted, her breathing ragged and eyes full of lust as she watched me slowly undress.

"Does that feel good, Tiger?"

Jasmine's mouth hung open, but no words came out as I pushed my pants down, and my cock was freed. It had been begging for this all night. I'd watched her dance with Ciro and wanted to rip his throat out for touching her. Luckily for him, I knew they were only friends, and he hadn't made a sexual move on her. Otherwise, I would've found him in the men's room and helped him understand the situation.

Jasmine's eyes locked on my cock as I stroked it from base to tip and back again.

"Do you see how much I want you?"

She nodded, not looking away. Her heated stare felt like a touch as I walked toward her.

"It's rude not to answer a question, Tiger. Do you need me to spank you?" Her passion flared to anger and was just as sexy. The dark look in her eyes made me want to tie her up and see what she did when I pressed all her buttons, but that would have to wait for another night.

"You wouldn't?"

Gripping her chin, I forced her to look up at me as she tried to fight off the climax building within her.

"Try me, and I'll tan your sexy ass until it is bright red." She pressed her lips together as she fought not to say something sarcastic. "Dario, stop and let her lick your fingers clean."

He did as ordered, and Jasmine huffed as his fingers slid from her body. She stared at them as they got close to her mouth.

"Have you ever tasted yourself," I asked, my hands gripping her hips.

"No."

"Do it, and I'll taste you. Lick his fingers clean."

Jasmine swallowed hard but opened her mouth, and Dario slipped them in one finger at a time. I groaned at the sight of her lips wrapping around his finger.

"Such a good kitty," I said, dropping to my knees in front of her. Before she could ask what I was doing, I pushed her thighs wide and feasted on her sensitive folds.

The sudden inhale of breath and swear words that freely tumbled from her mouth made me smirk. My tongue pushed deep inside of her, and she moaned. She tasted better than I imagined. Glancing up as Jasmine's body jerked, I was rewarded with the sight of Dario playing with her tits, the dark buds rolling between his fingers. Sucking on her clit hard, she cried out, her legs giving way, but Dario kept her upright as her hands went to my hair and pressed my face deeper into her pussy.

"Yes, that's it, let the passion guide you," Dario said, his voice deep and soothing. "Come for us. Come all over Angelo's face."

I felt the moment she lost her control. Her hips rocked back and forth along my tongue, and I groaned, stroking my cock as she came. Her body tensed, and I licked faster to drink down what she offered.

Licking the inside of her thighs and then up her body, I stopped to suck on one of her nipples as she whimpered.

"Tell me, Tiger, did you like that," I asked, my lips hovering over hers.

"Yes," she panted.

"Are you ready for more?"

Eyes as wild as any tiger and as golden as the most exotic cat looked up at me from under thick lashes. I was lost to this woman. As much as I fought it when we were young, she'd claimed me. I now understood that I was doomed from the start.

"Yes," she said, and I pulled her to me.

"Good, because I'm going to claim every inch of your body now, and if anyone other than myself or Dario lay a finger on you, I will cut their hands off before I rip their heart from their chest. You are ours and only ours, do you understand?"

She licked her lips, goosebumps rising on her skin. "Yes, I understand."

"Right answer." I kissed her and gripped her lush ass as I pulled her up my body.

I'd never wanted anything as much as I wanted her and had planned everything right down to this moment to make sure she was mine.

Chapter Eleven

JASMINE

I'D NEVER BEEN shy about my body, and the hungry look in Angelo's and Dario's eyes had me rubbing my thighs together. I kept expecting to be scared and figured it would be natural my first time, but fear was pushed aside for raw need. I wanted them. All the fantasies I'd never spoken to anyone about stepped out of my mind and into my bedroom.

Of course, my brain screamed that I should push Angelo away and take off out the door like I did the first time Angelo kissed me. But my body and the hope in my heart had a different idea.

I'd secretly wanted Angelo and even Dario over the years, thinking about them as I touched myself late at night before falling asleep. I hated them for making my life miserable, yet there was something so addictive about them that I found myself walking into the line of fire for more. Maybe even inciting the confrontations.

Here I was, placing my trust and my heart in their hands. Was it stupid? Most likely, but I wasn't going to stop. If I was going to marry anyone, I wanted it to be someone I chose, someone who made a fire burn in my belly and challenged me. Was it crazy to want both of them, to be okay with two men in my life? I didn't know, and at the moment, I could not have cared less what the gossipy other women would think.

The heat burning in my gut and the feel of Angelo's skin made me shiver as my back touched the cool sheets. He settled between my thighs, and the sliver of fear that I was really going to go through with this vanished as Angelo kissed me like I was his whole world.

Dario was suddenly there, his muscular chest like a wall beside me.

"Touch me," he whispered in my ear as I trembled under Angelo. Angelo broke the kiss only to suck on my neck in almost the same spot as Dario. My heart felt like it would pound right out of my chest as I stared into Dario's soft brown eyes.

Removing my hand from Angelo's flexing shoulder, I laid it on Dario's hip, but he pushed down until my fingers brushed his hard shaft. He felt impossibly large, and I timidly wrapped my hand around his girth. He sucked in a ragged breath and groaned in my ear as he squeezed my hand tighter.

"Just like that, Princess, that feels incredible," he whispered. I followed his lead as he guided me up his stiff cock and back down. The sounds of his pleasure drove me wild.

As much as Angelo unnerved me, Dario calmed me. The two of them together were like a strong drink that had a hard bite but a smooth aftertaste.

I pressed my hips up into Angelo, and he rose above me like a great snake. He looked deadly as he stared down at me, his chest and arms lined with muscle. This man was a far cry from the boy I knew growing up, and I abruptly realized how small I was compared to either of them if they wanted to hurt me.

"Have you ever fucked yourself with anything bigger than your fingers," Angelo asked as he rocked his hips against me. I blushed so hard that it felt like my entire body was on fire.

"What do you mean?"

Angelo smirked. "I meant a toy, but anything really. Could be a carrot or a cucumber, maybe a little zucchini action."

I smacked my hand off his chest, and he laughed. "No, I haven't."

"Not a big deal, but this is going to hurt at first, so grip my shoulders again so you don't unintentionally hurt Dario." I did as he said, and my pulse pounded harder. He rocked forward again, and this time, I felt his tip spread me open before pulling back out. "You ready?" I nodded, then screamed as Angelo drove into my body in one powerful thrust.

Dario muffled my yell as he kissed me, but I could only whimper and shake as my nails dug into Angelo's shoulders. No amount of warning could've prepared me for the sharp pain that lanced through my stomach right to my back.

"Fuck, you're so tight," Angelo said through clenched teeth. "God dammit, you make me want to come already." I felt his body shaking, and the sensation traveled right up his cock.

"It's okay," Dario said, his voice soothing. He kissed my cheek, and I realized tears were running down my face. "It always hurts at first. It will ease. Just try to relax." He smoothed my hair back and pressed his body against mine. I turned my head and buried my face into his chest. I hated tears.

He was right. The sharp pain eased to a dull ache, and as Angelo rotated his hips around in a circle, it began to feel good.

"You like that, Tiger?"

"It doesn't hurt as much now," I said, sucking in a deep breath as Angelo pulled out and slowly slid back into my body, groaning.

"Fuck, you feel like heaven." He repeated the action, and this time, I moaned with him as he spread me wide. I arched my back as he did it again, and my body not only began to accept the intrusion but welcomed it.

I yelped as he gripped my legs and wrapped them around his waist. The new position pushed him deeper, and I cried out, but not from pain. He was touching something inside of my body that felt indescribable.

Dario's cock brushed against my hip, and I instinctively reached down and wrapped my hand around him once more. He groaned in my ear, and the sound traveled through my body, making me shiver.

Angelo pulled my attention as he pushed himself onto his knees and took the lower half of my body with him. I now had a perfect view of him pulling out and disappearing inside me, and the climax pushed higher in my body.

"Oh," I cried as Dario dropped his head to my nipple, swirling his tongue around my sensitive, hardened peak. His hips bucked as fast as Angelo, his cock sliding through my hand. It felt so wrong and so right to be doing this with them.

Angelo growled, and I looked up to see him staring at Dario, sucking on my nipple. His hips picked up the pace, and my eyes rolled back in my head.

"You're a fucking bad girl, Tiger. Look at you enjoying two cocks for your first time."

I would've answered if I could, but the pleasure wiped out all other conscious thoughts as our bodies came together. The sound of slapping skin, moans, and the rustle of sheets filled the room with hypnotic music.

Suddenly, I was cresting the peak of my orgasm, but it was like nothing I'd ever experienced. Dario kissed me hard as I screamed into his mouth, releasing him to claw at the sheets.

"Yeah, that's it, Tiger, come all over my cock. Fuck that feels incredible, you're so unbelievably tight." Angelo groaned, slowly slipping out of my body, but my climax was only partially over. I cried out, not wanting him to stop. "Don't worry. We are far from done."

He looked to Dario. "She's loosened up for you," he said before slipping off the bed and heading to the washroom. I watched him go, confusion clouding my mind.

Dario blocked my view as he stood and picked me up. He sat right back down and placed me on my knees, straddling his stomach. I stared down at his cock trapped between our bodies.

"I...um...I don't...." Swallowing hard, I looked up, and Dario was smiling. There was a playfulness to the look. "Will that fit?"

"It will. Rise and put me inside you."

"You want me to?"

He put both arms behind his head, and I couldn't help but stare. They were as thick as my legs and cut with muscle.

"Don't be afraid. You're in control," he said.

Dario's cock almost sprang straight up at me when I lifted into position. I gripped him and still didn't think that something I couldn't get my hand around would fit, but I slowly lowered myself down. I gasped and moaned as he filled me, and the stifled climax rushed to the surface. Panting hard by the time I had him fully buried inside me, it only took a few gentle thrusts from Dario to topple over that edge, and I cried out as the orgasm slammed into me.

Shuddering as I came, I closed my eyes and placed my hands on his chest to keep from falling over.

"Oh my god," I said, my arms shaking. I should've been long done, completely spent, but as Dario laid perfectly still, I craved more.

"You ready," he asked as my eyes met his.

"Yes," I said, moaning as he gripped my hips and pushed up. I was bouncing on him and collapsed forward from the force of his faster pace.

"Ah! Oh, Dario, I...." I yelled as his hands squeezed my ass hard, and he drove himself up into me. I could hardly hold myself still.

"Fuck you weren't kidding," Dario said, his voice strained.

"Told you she was tight."

I looked over at the sound of Angelo's voice. When had he walked back into the room? He was sitting in the large chair, eyes focused on us. The heated stare was intense, and I felt trapped. He was stroking himself, and I couldn't look away if I wanted to.

"Roll her toward me," Angelo said, and with a quick move, Dario flipped us to our sides. His chest pressed into my back as he grabbed my leg and pulled it over his hip. I felt him nudging me until he was back inside and spreading me impossibly wide.

"You are so sweet, Princess, like a drizzle of honey. I want to lick every last inch of your body," Dario growled in my ear. His hand slid up and tweaked my nipples, making me cry out before wrapping around my throat.

"Yes, that's it. Fuck her hard. Make her scream, but don't let her," Angelo ordered, and I shivered.

The sensual thrusts turned into a hard pounding, and just as Angelo said I would, I screamed as the pleasure split and turned into pain. It felt glorious. Dario's hand tightened around my throat and dulled the harsh cries.

"Don't panic. Enjoy the rush," he said, whispering and nipping at my earlobe. I was a whimpering mess in his grasp and felt no stronger than a ragdoll as my body bounced in his control. "Fuck I could do this all day," Dario said softly, his words contrasting with the arm-sized piston hammering my pussy. I wasn't going to be able to walk tomorrow, of that I was positive.

The reduced air made me lightheaded, and as if sensing it, his hand loosened, allowing me to get a breath into my searing lungs.

"Are you close?" Angelo growled.

"So close," Dario answered.

"Remember what I said."

I didn't know what they were talking about, but I didn't care at the moment. Releasing my neck, Dario slid his hand down my stomach, and I bit my lip, trying to hold back the wail of pleasure as his finger rubbed my clit.

His thrusting quickened, and my mouth hung open as he groaned in my ear. I couldn't tell if I wanted to moan or scream or both.

"Shit," he said, and with a sudden roll, he was on his back, and I was on his chest. His cock slipped out, and Dario reached between us to stroke it. "Fuck, yes."

His chest rumbled, and his body shuddered as a spray of hot

liquid shot from the tip of his cock and landed on my stomach. I stared at the white line and watched in fascination as more flew out and, this time, landed near my boobs.

"Fuck, feels so good," he said as three more lines of come landed on me before he finally fell still, breathing hard beneath me.

"Now that was a show."

My head rolled to the side to watch Angelo slowly stand like a great predator. His eyes were fierce as they bore holes into me. I shook at the sight of him. He may not have been as tall or large in every way as Dario was, but he was in control and promised pleasure or possibly pain. It was hard to tell.

"Try it," he said, stepping toward the bed.

"Try what," I whispered, past my sore throat.

"The come. Taste." I looked down at my chest. "Run your finger through it, suck on it, and tell me how it tastes." Tentatively, I ran my finger through the warm liquid and brought it to my mouth. My tongue flicked out, but Angelo growled at me. "I said suck your finger."

Staring into his blue eyes that could've passed for the devil at this moment, I sucked my finger into my mouth and tasted the saltiness of Dario's come. It didn't taste terrible. I kind of liked it and cleaned off the bit that had landed close to my nipple and repeated the action until it was all cleaned up.

"Would be good with tequila and lime," I said and he smirked.

"That's a good Tiger, much better." He held out his hand. "Give me your hand."

My heart hammered hard, and my body shivered with anticipation for what would happen next. As I placed my hand in his, Angelo pulled me to my feet, and I almost collapsed as my legs didn't want to work properly.

Angelo kept me on my feet as he slammed his mouth down to mine like an animal feasting and not a man. He bent my body back, and I gripped his shoulders hard, my nails digging into his skin.

"I'm going to claim you properly now," he said, his lips gently touching mine while commanding my submission.

"You hadn't...you know...before?"

He smiled. "No, I didn't come before, but I took your virginity, and if anyone is getting you pregnant, it's me. Understand?"

Goosebumps rose along my body, but my aching pussy clenched tight at the thought of him coming as Dario had, only inside of me. Pregnancy was a terrifying notion, but if we were married, it would be the first thing the families expected of us, so what did it matter?

I nodded, and the smirk deepened and darkened. "I want you to know that I can come multiple times a night, and I plan on staying in here and taking you again and again. Even when you beg me to stop. Even when you say you can't take anymore, I will fuck you. So cry all you want, scream all you want, but I will have you all the ways I desire tonight."

The pounding of my heart from the prick of fear made my blood whoosh as I contemplated what I'd agreed to.

"One more thing before we get started." He gripped my chin and lifted my head, his eyes burning into mine. "Do you consent to non-consent?"

"I don't know what that means," I said.

"I will have you anywhere, anyplace, anytime, and however I want, and you can't refuse me. So if I visit you in the middle of the night, I will fuck you. If I find you sitting in the library, I will bend you over the couch. If I find you wandering in the garden, I will take you up against the statue, and you won't argue. If I see you walking through town, I will drag you to the car and fuck you before sending you on your way. You are mine in all ways, at all times, whether you want to be or not." He kissed the side of my neck as I contemplated what he was saying. "There will be one word that will stop me if something is too much for you. It will be, honey. You say honey and I will stop, but not for anything else. That goes for anything we do from now on. Understood?"

"It can't be anything in front of my Papa or anything else that will degrade or embarrass me. You've done enough of that over my life," I said.

"I wouldn't anyway, but I promise."

What he said should've terrified me. I could only imagine what he had planned, and I was sure there were already a hundred more ideas than the ones he mentioned, but I couldn't seem to say no.

"Yes, I consent." I heard myself say. What the hell was wrong with me?

"Excellent. Then get on all fours and put your face on the mattress." He let go of my arms, and I turned and stumbled onto the bed, every muscle complaining and shaking from the physical exertion.

I whimpered as his hands grabbed my ass, and he once more slipped his cock into my sore pussy. I couldn't picture him doing this multiple times, but I didn't open my mouth and say no. This was the most alive I'd ever felt.

Sweat trickled off my body, and tears of joy and pain fell from my eyes as Angelo didn't hold back. I yelped as his hand smacked my ass. It didn't hurt, but the shock made me lurch forward. He yanked me back into him and slapped my ass again.

He fisted my hair, and I cried out as he yanked me up so my fingertips touched the bed, and I bowed back, looking at him. "Bad Tiger. Don't jump away from me."

I was vaguely aware of Dario sliding under my raised body, and I shivered as I felt his hot tongue swirling on my clit as Angelo fucked me hard. This much pleasure was impossible for the human body. It had to be. My legs spread wider, sinking down until I rested my clit in his mouth.

"Oh no, I can't come again, oh God, ah," I screamed as the climax ripped from my body.

"Yeah, come on me good, Tiger. Fuck yeah." Angelo slammed into me harder. "You ready for me to claim you?"

"Yes," I yelled. "Claim me, make me yours."

"Fuck, fuck, fuck, yes." Angelo pumped into me one more time, then held still. I could feel him coming, and the sensation caused another small climax. He groaned as he pulled out and pushed in again. "Damn, Tiger. You were worth the wait."

I had no words left and collapsed on Dario as Angelo pulled from my spent body. "Oh, I hope you don't think we are finished for the night," Angelo said as he walked to the small table and picked up the bottle of wine. I couldn't move my body, but my eyes tracked his movements. He picked up the open bottle and didn't bother with a glass.

"Now lick my cock off like a good kitty while you rest. I'll give you fifteen minutes and some water, then I'm taking you again."

What the hell had I gotten myself into?

Chapter Twelve

JASMINE

FIVE YEARS LATER - PRESENT DAY

I NODDED to the guards as I walked down the hall, my feet not making a sound with the soft-soled shoes. I'd learned that I could find out more secrets if I moved around and didn't have the clicking of heels that the other women in the house wore. My mother passed away when I was sixteen, and my father decided that his duties as Don took up too much time and he needed to ensure positive influences around me. Ever since then, women have followed me around like ladies in waiting. It was more like ladies were annoying if you asked me. I was capable of peeing on my own.

I heard my father laugh, his warm voice cheery, which was rare for him lately. Ever since our family heirloom was stolen, my father had been more guarded with his dealings and protective over me. Sometimes, I really wished I was born a boy or had a brother. Then maybe there wouldn't be so much put on my shoulders. I would end up ignored like all the other princesses. As long as they were happy and didn't interfere with their Don's dealings, they could do whatever they pleased. I was not so lucky.

My father's office door was open, and the two guards standing on either side didn't glance at me as I stopped and softly knocked on the wooden frame to announce myself.

"Jasmine, my beautiful daughter. Come in, come in," my dad said, waving me in. His cheeks were pinked from laughing and what looked like brandy in his glass.

Stepping into the room, I saw the sitting area and smiled at Ciro and his father. Ciro was still my best friend. On the list of things I shouldn't do, sneaking Ciro into my room was at the top. Our parents thought we would end up doing something. But, it had never been Ciro they needed to worry about. I'd made that mistake with two people who had stolen my heart and then made a fool of me. Ciro had a front-row seat to the fallout of my decisions and had been there to help pick up the pieces of my broken heart.

My father greeted me in the middle of the room and gripped my shoulders as we kissed one another's cheeks.

"Father, it is good to see you smile," I said, and he beamed a little brighter.

Ciro winked from behind his father's back in greeting, but his hazel eyes seemed worried. I had a crush on my best friend at one point, but I realized what I loved about him was the ease with which we spent our time. We loved the same things right down to shopping, bad romcom movies and our lattes with extra cream. I was ten when Ciro admitted that he had a crush on a boy, and it became crystal clear why it felt so easy between us. I'd been keeping his secret for him ever since. I'd gone so far as to feign a date with Ciro as the chaperone when really I was the third wheel and found ways to sneak off, giving them privacy.

I didn't mind. His parents were very old-fashioned, and Ciro was the only heir in his family. Meaning he must produce a son to take his place one day. To come out to his father, the Don of the Caruso family, the second most powerful family next to the Don of Dons, would mean certain banishment. I wasn't a huge fan of Bruno Caruso, and the fact that Ciro was scared to talk to him about who he was pissed me off on a whole new level, but it wasn't my fight. Ciro needed to be the one comfortable with the knowledge being out there.

"Come have a seat. I need to speak to you." The office door closed, and I realized the four women following me stayed in the hall.

The hair stood on the back of my neck as an unsettled feeling fluttered in my stomach. What was happening that no one other than the five of us could hear? Jacopo, my father's underboss, stood silently in the corner, failing miserably at being a statue. I didn't like him any more than I liked Bruno, and despite keeping my feelings about him to myself, I kept my eyes peeled. I was a target, and I knew it. Jacapo had made not so subtle advances toward me more than once but, I quickly shot him down.

My father sat down beside me and handed over a glass of wine. It wasn't unusual for my dad to offer me wine, but ten in the morning seemed suspicious.

"Papa, what is going on?" I asked, looking at Ciro, but he wouldn't meet my eyes, which worried me more than anything else. Whatever this was, it was bad. My heart thumped harder, and my pulse spiked. The sound of blood in my ears reminded me of the whooshing sound of the tide. Except this time, it wasn't calming.

"Nothing bad, mia Bambolina," he said, patting my hand. "Don't look so worried. This is a celebration."

"A celebration? For what?"

My father was practically brimming with excitement.

"Your marriage into my family," Bruno jumped in and said.

I swallowed down the bile that rose in my throat. "Who am I to marry Papa," I asked, horrified that I was being married off to Bruno. Ciro's mother passed away when he was a baby, or so everyone believed, but I figured something far more sinister had happened to her. That was a horrible thought but Bruno wasn't much better than Jacapo on my creep-o-meter.

"To Ciro, of course. Who did you think you'd be marrying?"

I looked at Ciro. He finally looked up at me, and I could see his silent plea to keep quiet. There were far worse fates in the world than to marry your best friend, but there would never be any romantic love between us. Our love would never be more than what it was right now, and we would both be trapped forever in a loveless and sexless marriage. Except to have a child, and I cringed at how awkward that would be.

"What?" That was all I could get out. The shock had stolen all pleasantries from my mind as my gaze swung in Bruno's direction.

"Is that how you speak to your father-in-law?"

My mouth fell open as I stared at his smug face.

"Come now, Bruno, she is clearly in shock."

That was an understatement.

"Father, please. I knew about this, but Jasmine did not," Ciro said, and I shot him a 'What the fuck are you talking about' look.

"You could've fooled me with all the sneaking around the two of you do. I'm surprised she's not already pregnant," Bruno said, waving his hand at us. I gripped the material of my dress so I didn't jump up and smack the man across the face.

My papa jumped to his feet, his hands balled into fists as he glared at Bruno. "What did you just say about my daughter?"

"No offense meant." Bruno leaned back on the leather couch and crossed his ankles. "Just simply stating that we all know how much time they spend together. I hardly find this shocking news."

My teeth ground together as I glared at Bruno, but he ignored me and stared at my papa.

"That better be all you meant by that statement. If you are trying to tarnish my daughter's image, I will have Jacopo show you the door."

Bruno rolled his eyes. "Sit down and stop being so dramatic. No one is here to hear my joke, but if it makes you feel better..." Bruno finally looked at me. "I'm sorry for insinuating your intimacy or lack of intimacy with my son." He picked imaginary lint off his black pants, and I wanted my papa to shoot the man. "Happy?"

Papa sat down and laid his hand over my clenched one.

"You don't look happy, mia Bambolina. I thought this would be exciting news. You're twenty-three now, the perfect age to settle into a new life and family. You and Ciro seem like the perfect match, and I know how much Ciro loves you."

I could read between the lines. Papa had a limited understanding of what happened with Angelo. He was aware I had sex with him, but nothing about Dario. Part of his outburst was him ensuring my indiscretion remained secret. He wanted me looked after like the doll he called me. I didn't want that.

"Papa, I mean no disrespect. You know Ciro and I adore one another, but I hadn't considered marriage. Do you not want me here with you anymore?"

"What? Of course, I do, but I will not live forever. You are a princess but will never inherit the family business or, head seat or wealth. I have a cushion set aside for you, but you deserve so much more. Bruno and I have come to a mutually beneficial agreement to protect both our children for years to come."

"So, to protect me, I need to be married off? Like a burden?"

"In some countries, you would be considered a burden," Jacopo said, and I glared at him. "Worth no more than a couple of cows." Papa glared at Jacopo, but he was staring out the window as if he hadn't just called me worthless. "Your father only wants what is best for his beloved. I would happily take Ciro's place if you prefer?" Jacopo said, glancing back toward me. An evil smile curled his lip. I almost threw up in my mouth at the thought of him crawling into bed with me at night.

"You are my third cousin, Jacopo, that is revolting." His dark eyes twinkled, and goosebumps rose along my skin. I knew he was picturing me without the layered dress. The servants who had accepted an invitation to his bed whispered about his peculiar tastes and feared to sleep with him again. Some were given the choice, others not so much. Some never came to work again.

"I'm just saying that it is an option if you don't want to accept

Ciro," Jacopo said. My father opened his mouth, but Ciro jumped in before he could reply.

"Jasmine does not need to find a new fiancé. We have been friends and courting one another for years. It brings me great joy to announce that our families will join," Ciro said. I was tempted to stand, slap him, announce him as a liar, and storm out.

Instead, I chugged the wine, not caring if it was ladylike. Smiling, I sat the glass down on the table with a clink and stood with a flourish.

"Well, it seems that all of you men have my future planned out, and I might as well leave you to discuss the details that I will also have no say in. If you will excuse me, I have women's things to attend to," I growled sarcastically.

How was it that we lived in a modern world, yet I was treated no better than a breeding bitch to be sold off? I knew my papa had tried to arrange a marriage for me once before, but I thought that was past us. Apparently, I was wrong.

"Jasmine," Ciro said, rising to his feet.

He looked mortified and apologized with his eyes, but this was asking too much of our friendship. I would lie and cover for him forever, but now my life—quite literally—was tied to his and his bed. I would never know passion or true love from someone who viewed me as their whole world. I would not give up my chance—slim as it may be—at happiness to keep his secret.

My father grabbed Ciro's arm as I stomped past the couch. "Let her go, she will come around."

"She is like a high-spirited horse and needs to be trained with a hard crop. You've been too soft with her," Jacopo said.

"Agreed," Bruno chimed in.

They were lucky I was unarmed, or I would've cut off both of their dicks and fed them to them.

"Jacapo watch yourself," Papa snarled, but I didn't stick around to see what happened next.

"Like hell, you'll train my princess ass," I growled under my breath.

They did train one thing into me...never trust a man. Every man I trusted had betrayed me.

I flung the door open and stomped out, pointing at the four women waiting.

"Do not follow me unless you want me to shave your heads bald, tattoo penises on your faces, and not pay you for a year." Their eyes grew wide as I marched down the hall, leaving them, the guards, and the two men I thought I could trust in this world behind.

Sorry Ciro, but I'd rather live penniless on the streets than sell my soul to the system that would condemn us both. It was a good thing I already had a backup plan.

Chapter Thirteen

ANGELO

"UGH," Enzo grunted as he came all over my realtor's face while Dario rammed her like a fucking bull from behind. She would've been screaming if it weren't for the ball shoved in her mouth. Instead, her cries and moans were reduced to throat noises and soft whimpers.

There was nothing soft about Dario. Quiet and grumpy was his normal, but he'd changed over the last five years. Since all the shit went down and we lost Jasmine for good, he had gotten colder, harder.

I'd already fucked her and was now sitting back bored with the show. She was an okay lay, not great, but okay. She took this instead of payment for services rendered, always kept my name off the paperwork, and moved my shell company's names around to keep me well hidden. She was good at her job, and so was the lawyer I hired. Luckily, he was a man and preferred cash over sex.

Picking up the decanter, I filled my glass and stared at the dark brown contents. I was extremely proud of this recipe. I'd always wanted to try it, but my father wouldn't hear of changing our signature whiskey.

This whiskey recipe has been in the family for five generations, son. You don't mess with perfection.

I hadn't realized until I was kicked out of my home how much I needed the boot in the ass to finally make my way and step out from the shadow of my father. Banishment sucked, but now that we'd settled on the outskirts of Sin Haven and Beastville—two small towns loaded with heathens and underground business—we were thriving. Between the realty and construction business as well as my highly coveted whiskey distillery, we made money hand over fist.

I clenched my hand and glared at the family rings I still wore. They were a constant reminder of what I lost and what I planned on taking back one day.

Dario grunted, and I looked up just in time to see him rip off the condom and unload all over Mrs. Sherwood's ass. She flopped on the leather bench, her body heaving and shimmering with sweat. Standing, I wandered over to the woman who had become a monthly staple despite her husband.

Polishing off the whiskey, I rolled the flavor around my mouth and stared down at my realtor. Her normally neat hair was a mess and stuck to the side of her face. Her green eyes rolled up to mine.

"I assume we are paid in full for another month?"

"Mmmhmm," she mumbled through the gag.

"Excellent." I looked at Enzo, flopped in a chair, his head back and cock limp. "Get dressed and show Mrs. Sherwood out."

I left the room feeling empty despite decent sex and my business success. Being on the run had held a certain thrill and adrenaline boost. Building my empire was exciting. Fucking my way across continents to bury my emotions, not so exciting. Now—it all felt old.

"Do we need to do this again? Aren't you sick of following me around like a lost dog?" I glared over my shoulder as Dario walked behind me, his pants and gun in hand and a scowl on his face.

"Do I need to remind you that I don't give a fuck what you think?"

"Suit yourself."

I hadn't thought Dario could get any more doom and gloom, but holy shit, it was like the guy had a storm cloud following him around all the time. He was the best at what he did. I never feared for my safety, but would it hurt for him to crack a smile? I mean, he just got laid, and by the look on his face, you'd swear his dog just died.

I got it. I missed her too. I wanted Jasmine back, and I always kept options to make it happen at the front of my mind. But shit...if I walked around like that all the time, I would get nothing accomplished.

I walked into my bedroom, and he took up his post by the door, completely naked. "I'm going to shower. Do you want to use one of the other shower heads? At least then, you're clean and not smelling up my room."

Dario's eye twitched, and his lip curved up just a little. It was the only sign that he was amused. "What? You don't like the smell of old, dried-up pussy?"

"Not hers anyway," I joked, and he snorted but pushed away from the wall and walked into the bathroom with me.

The bedroom I'd converted was double the size of my bathroom back home. One whole wall was a shower with a long bench and four shower heads. There were two sinks, a private toilet area, and a large jacuzzi that looked out over the backyard. But my view was always ruined by Dario's ass in my face. He insisted that the large window was an easy sniper target and refused to move from in front of it.

"The house has been rented. The person knocked the price down a little, but they wanted to sign a year lease to start, and you know how much I hate Mrs. Sherwood coming around any more than needed."

I turned the brass knobs, and the warm spray was immediate and made me sigh. This was my second favorite room in the house. My favorite was the small library and reading nook on the top floor.

"I assume you voiced our issues about the last tenant to Mrs. Sherwood, and this one won't be a problem?" I titled my head back under the spray.

"She assured me this tenant is a model citizen and has already paid the first three months in cash."

"Excellent, and a little suspicious. I'd keep an eye on whoever this is." I didn't need the extra income from the old farmhouse on the far end of the property, but why have it sitting there doing nothing? That didn't make any sense. "Any word from back home?"

"If by any word you mean about Jasmine Falcone, then I heard she is betrothed to Ciro Caruso."

My teeth ground together so loud that my jaw cracked. Jasmine was mine. She was the reason I stole the egg, why I even came up with the plan in the first place that got me banished. It also explained the extra dark scowl on Dario's face.

"I didn't say I wanted to know about her."

"You didn't have to. I doubt very highly that you give a shit that your father has lost ten pounds, won a cool quarter mill in a poker game, and is still our largest competitor in stores."

"Who says I don't want to know about those things?"

I didn't care. Dario was right, but I wouldn't admit that. It was bad enough that he knew, without me saying, that I was still pining as badly as he was over her.

"Keep lying to yourself, but you don't fool me," he said.

I grabbed the soap and palmed it as I contemplated throwing it at his head. Dario turned his back, and the massive gorilla tattoo looked like it was roaring at me. Appropriate. The image suited his large size, fearlessness, loyalty, and chest-thumping personality.

"Fine, you're right, that pisses me the fuck off," I sighed. How had shit gone so wrong? "Just fucking tell me about the latest sales projections," I said and lathered up the soap.

As Dario droned on about the numbers, I pretended to listen, but my mind was somewhere else—more specifically, on someone else. With just a single mention, my Tiger once more plagued my thoughts. I would never forget those honey-colored eyes that captured my heart. I remembered every touch we shared and the feel of her body. Nothing could wipe the sound of her voice from my mind or how her laugh made me smile. I'd never been a soft or kind man, but when I held her close with her head on my chest, I wanted something different.

What was worse than remembering the sweet moments was being unable to forget how broken and sad she looked when I told her I was going to America for a few months and Dario had to come with me.

It was three years later that sheer desperation to cling to Jasmine had driven me to steal the egg. It had backfired, and now she was marrying Ciro. My hand clenched into a fist on the tile wall, and I was tempted to punch through the black ceramic.

The rage that filled me was unearthly in its potency. I hated Ciro. I didn't really know him, we didn't hang out unless forced, but I didn't care. If he were standing before me, I'd shoot him in the head and take what was mine.

"You didn't hear a word I said," Dario said, and I realized I'd turned around and was glaring at the far wall.

"Shut up and start over. I'll listen this time."

Sighing, I pushed all thoughts of the beautiful Jasmine Falcone from my mind. I needed to move on. But deep down, I knew it would still be her face I saw no matter who else came into my life.

Chapter Fourteen

JASMINE

KEEPING the cloak tightly in place with the hood up, I stood at the railing, watching the land that had once been a speck slowly grow larger. This was the second most exhilarating and terrifying thing I'd ever done. I didn't linger on the one that still took the top spot in my mind. There was no point in looking back and hoping for things that would never be.

I rubbed at my locket, a gift from my papa for my nineteenth birthday. The golden piece was stunning in its simplicity. It had a decorative design of our family crest and a picture of my parents inside. I hadn't taken it off for a single day since. Tucking it into my sweater, I felt terrible about leaving the way I did. No goodbye or warning. The argument with Papa about how I needed to be taken care of as a woman boiled me to my core. I was done being a princess in a mafia family. I wanted passion and love. I wanted children and to wake up not feeling like I had an axe of patriarchy pressed against my throat.

Even though I knew Papa meant no harm with his words—it was the world we lived in—I still hated it. I didn't need a man like a pet needed an owner. I was perfectly capable of working and taking care of myself. Our fancy home was nothing more than a cage made by a man many generations earlier. They wanted me to look and act like the perfect accessory, and now that I was old enough, I would be moved to someone else's home to birth babies and start the process again.

There was nothing wrong with having a family, but it shouldn't be part of your job description as a woman. I had dreams, and if I'd learned one thing from my fiasco with Angelo and Dario, it was to marry someone who truly loved me and couldn't live without me. Angelo and Dario said all the pretty words, but when it came down to it, they never cared. They played me and broke my heart.

My recent fight with Ciro was worse. He snuck into my room just like old times, but the tension between us was palpable. It was the only time in our lives that we'd fought, and I hated it.

"Please, Jasmine, I'm begging you to marry me," Ciro said.

"What for? So that we can have awkward sex in hopes that I get pregnant. Then you'll feel terrible and ignore me because that's what you do when you feel guilty and can't handle difficult situations. It's what you've always done. You couldn't even look me in the eye when you took the last cookie while watching a movie."

"That was years ago."

"Fine, what about when you started dating Marcus and didn't want me to feel like a third wheel? You ignored me for months. I'm your biggest supporter. Why would I ever have a problem with the two of you? I'll tell you why. You couldn't handle the idea that I might be upset that you had a life and I...well I didn't."

"I've changed and grown up. I promise I won't do that, I swear it."

"And even if you don't...let's pretend you are a perfectly doting husband, we both know it's a pretty lie. You'll still have Marcus, and I will resent being in a marriage where I am nothing more than a breeding commodity for you to hide who you really are."

"I can't tell my father. He will disown me or worse," Ciro said. "You're the only one who knows. You can sleep with whomever you want. You know I won't care."

I narrowed my eyes and would've smacked him if he hadn't stepped back and held up his hands when I growled at him in rage.

"Oh yes, please, let me become the family whore talked about in all the shadowed corners and family dinners that I cannot attend because it is a boy's club. Don't even deny it. I have friends among the servants. I hear the whispers." I put my hands on my hips, the anger potent in my gut. "Yes, please let me become the woman that suddenly every Don, on down the ranks, figures they can get a piece of because I'm that kind of girl. The one they can fuck and then go home to their wives. Why wouldn't I want a loveless marriage and be considered a slut on top of it? And all the while, you'll have Marcus warm in your bed every night, and no one would dare say a word." I rubbed at my belly for effect, and his eyes followed the movement. "As long as I give you a child, no one cares where you stick your dick."

Ciro stomped across the room. "I have always had to live in the shadows and hide who I am. I'm asking for a few years, and then we can get divorced if you want and take half of everything as payment. Am I so unbearable that you couldn't spend a couple of years with me to save me from a life of ridicule?"

"Do not guilt me," I snarled, my hands clenching. "And do not think money drives me like I'm some common whore or typical princess worried about what dress I can buy that week or what spa I can attend. I've been your friend for years, happily kept your secret, and you've never had to worry that I would turn on you, but here you are in my bedroom, turning on me."

"It's not like that." He held out his trembling hands, and I did feel for him. This life we lived was not an easy one, and Bruno was a mean bastard. As long as Ciro produced a son, his father didn't care if he had ten women or men in his bed at night. I would never be so lucky.

"You would so easily cast ridicule on me for your own sake? Do you even see how what you are asking is no small favor? To save your own skin, you wish to ruin my name, body, reputation, and my heart. All with the misguided hope that, in the end, I will be free to find love again. I'll be a used-up commodity no one wants. Worse than all of that combined, I

know our friendship wouldn't survive this. So not only do I lose my choice of what future I want, but I would also lose you. This is what you ask of me, and I'm supposed to be your best friend?" I shook my head and stared at him in disbelief.

"But you offered to have a baby for me and Marcus," he said. "I thought you would be pleased."

"Yes, I did offer that because that is the kind of friend I am. I would've happily snuck off on a so-called vacation, had your child with the help of medical professionals, and given the child to the two of you. That was my offer, my choice, and I could've kept my reputation intact. You know as well as I do that in this world, my reputation is all I have. But if I enter into this marriage with you, I'll either end up a slut for sleeping around or a princess who couldn't keep her husband. I might as well sign myself into the nunnery right now for all the luck I'll have in finding a decent man after that."

"I'm a better option than Jacopo. He will only hurt you or kill you. I can't determine what he wants from you, but it's not good."

"That's your selling line? You're nobly saving me from Jacopo? Get out, Ciro. I can't talk to you right now." I was so angry that tears started forming, and I refused to cry in front of him.

"Jasmine...."

I glared, my eyes narrowing as my body tensed. "I said to get out," I whispered harshly. "Go talk to Marcus about what you've asked of me and see what he says. I still can't believe you not only asked this but requested it of my father. I really thought we were friends." I pointed to the window. "Go. Before I find something to throw at you."

Was I being selfish to want my own life? I didn't think so, yet I couldn't help the guilt in my stomach.

All I wanted was to live free of the servitude this life wanted to press upon me. It shouldn't feel like I was asking for the stars. I thought my Papa was different, that Ciro was different, but now I wasn't sure they weren't as brainwashed as the rest.

"Isabella?" I turned at the sound of my alias. It was my mother's name and my middle name. I missed her every day and thought it was fitting as I embarked on this journey. "We will be pulling into port shortly."

"Thank you, Captain. I will need to arrange transportation. Where should I tell them to pick me up?"

"This is Port Hook, and you can wait at the guard station of Croc Docks. Wendy will take care of you with some coffee, and you won't have to stand out in the rain while you wait."

I nodded and used the large cloak to hide the envelope of money I was handing over. "If you should need me again...." He gave me a mischievous smile.

"I know how to reach you, thank you."

The captain whistled as he wandered the massive deck of the Lost Boys. I found the name fitting for the freightliner. I wasn't a boy, but I did feel very lost and a long way from home.

This was my new beginning. I was out from under the thumb of the families and the watchful eyes of my four ladies. I didn't have guards hovering around, and the best part was that I could do what felt right to me. I didn't know what that was yet, but I was excited to find out.

Chapter Fifteen

JASMINE

"I HOPE you're not paying a lot for it." I looked at the driver and then back out the window to the house I'd chosen to rent. To say it was a fixer-upper would've been the understatement of the century, but it was still my place.

"I think it's beautiful," I said, feeling defensive.

"I guess if you like the run-down, crack house look." I turned my glare on the driver, and he swallowed hard. Fifer hadn't been the friendliest driver, and I wasn't sure why I expected anything different now. "It does have a quaint look," he quickly added.

"Here." I handed him the cash and got out of the vehicle. He scampered out of the driver's seat and yanked my suitcase out of the trunk. I hated to think this, but he reminded me of a pig. He was short enough to make me feel tall, with a robust build, a round face, small ears, and an upturned nose. But it was the snorting as he laughed that sold it for me.

"Good luck, you're going to need it," Fifer said as he got in the car and drove away without another glance.

Fifer was right. I was paying way too much for this place. It looked rough in the ad, but it was worse in person. That was fine, though. I needed to learn to care for myself and some projects to occupy my time. Getting this place fixed up was a great way to do that while I figured out what to do next.

The stairs up to the front door squeaked loudly as the suitcase thumped against the old wood. Lifting the welcome mat, I found the key where the realtor said it would be waiting for me. My hand shook a little as nervousness set in. A gust of wind lifted my hair from my neck, and I shivered with the sudden blast of cold. Mama used to tell me that it was the boy in blue blowing his horn whenever the wind suddenly picked up like that.

"Moment of truth," I mumbled as I pushed open the door. It creaked so loud that I almost turned around and walked away. It felt like I was walking into the middle of a horror movie of my own making.

When I poked my head inside, the house was shrouded in shadows, and I expected the power not to work. Shockingly, the lights flicked on, and everything instantly felt more inviting.

"This is as good of a time as any to get started. So what do I start on first?"

The food and cleaning supplies I requested were in the kitchen, which seemed an excellent place to start. Leaving the suitcase out in the hall, I stripped down to my traveling pants and shirt, rolled up my sleeves, and grabbed the bucket.

It was getting dark when I finally decided to stop and have a snack. A distinct rattling sound when I walked into the kitchen made me pause and listen hard.

I searched the room to figure out what was in here with me. When the bag of potato chips moved on the counter, I squealed and jumped back. The noise scared my little thieves because three mice ran out of the bag, knocking it to the floor, and scampered along the counter.

"Get back here," I said, running after the tiny creatures. I managed to capture one as it ran between my feet, and when I picked it up, I couldn't find it in me to hurt it. The little white mouse was blind and had no tail, as if someone or something had cut it off.

"Poor little thing, were you hungry?" It didn't squirm in my hold, and instead rubbed it's head on my hand like it wanted to be pet. I decided to keep him as my thumb stroked back the soft white fur on it's little head. I couldn't put him outside, and allowing him to wander in and out of my food was so not happening.

I had seen an old empty fish tank in the living room and placed the mouse in his new temporary home before setting off to find the other two. They proved to be more challenging, as I ran up and down the stairs chasing them and just missing them when they ran under furniture or into a hole in the wall.

"Gotcha," I said, jumping off the couch like a cat. The mouse was far faster than it should've been for something that couldn't see where it was going. "Don't you get all squeaky with me. I think I'll call you Dick," I said teasingly, lowering him into the tank with his friend.

Squeak. I jumped as the third mouse ran over my foot and took off down the hallway. I would've sworn this was a game for them. The chase was on, and we must have sounded like an entire herd of elephants with the number of times I thumped through the halls and flipped over furniture.

He rounded into the dining room, and instead of chasing him, I waited in the hall. Getting low, I was ready as soon as his little white nose poked out of the room. I made my move and jumped for him.

"Yes," I cheered as someone knocked at the door.

I stared up at the entrance from where I was lying on the floor. It was impossible, but I couldn't help thinking my father or Ciro had arrived to drag me back.

"Who is it?"

"Enzo," came the male voice with just enough gravel to be sexy. "I'm one of the owners. I came to greet you and make sure you're settled in."

Jumping up, I didn't even think about what I must look like as I opened the door. At least I didn't until Enzo's mouth fell open and he looked me up and down. I turned to stare at my reflection in the small piece of glass in the door and realized my hair looked like a bird had nested. I had dust and grime smeared all over my face, and there wasn't a single inch of my body that wasn't dirty.

Embarrassment flooded me as I stared at the handsome man outside my door. He had sandy wavy hair that fell messily around his eyes. His eyes were an exotic silverI'd never seen on a real-life person before. He held a small basket with plastic on it, and for the life of me, I would never understand why I held the white mouse up like it was a prize.

"I got him. He's blind, and someone cut off his tail, I think, but I'm going to keep him, so don't hurt him," I rambled. "His name is Dock."

"You named the random mouse in your house?"

"He's not random anymore. Dock and his friends are my pets." This argument didn't make me sound any saner.

"Okay, well...I wanted to bring you this welcome basket," he said, and I stepped back into the hallway.

"Come on in, let me just put Dock with his friends." I put my pesky little roommate in the fish tank and made a mental note of all the items I needed to fix it up for them. "I made a list for you. The rent for this place is highway robbery, but I know how you can make up for it. Follow me," I said and expected him to follow.

Not having servants at my beck and call would take some getting used to, but Enzo followed without question.

"Thank you for the basket," I said, taking it from his hands. Our fingers brushed briefly, and a thrill ran up my spine. He smirked at me, eyes mischievous under his thick lashes, and I cleared my throat. Although I wanted to hold the basket like a shield, I set it aside and walked over to the kitchen table to pick up my long list.

"That's the list?"

"Sorry it's quite long, but several things need to be done around here. I don't mind the labor. But I need supplies, and I don't feel I should have to pay for the items when I'm bettering the property. You can rent or sell it for more in the future." Enzo looked at the list and said nothing, but his expression was baffled. "I'm sure there will be more. This is only from the first level."

"I see. Well, I'll take this to the other property owners, and we will see what we can do."

"Please do so. I want to get started tomorrow if possible."

"Tomorrow?"

"Yes, of course. There is no time like the present. Oh, do you happen to have a map of the area? I'd really like to find the grocery store. How far away is the closest town? I don't have a car, so I hope it is close enough to walk. Darn, taking a taxi whenever I want to go to town will be expensive. I really should've looked into that before I decided to rent." I blathered on like a fool, but Enzo just smiled.

"The town isn't that far. A thirty-minute walk at most, and I have an old map at home. I can even mark an *X* on all the best stores. I'll bring it to you tomorrow."

Sighing, I smiled. "Great."

We stood there staring at one another, not saying anything until I finally looked away. "Um, would you like a drink? I had orange juice brought in."

"No, thank you, I'd better get going. But it was nice meeting you...." Enzo held out his hand.

I slipped my hand into his, and my body warmed with the contact. "Isabella."

Walking Enzo to the door, I blushed as he turned around, looked at me, and smiled but didn't say anything further.

"Thank you again," I called out as he got into the black SUV and waved.

Closing the door, I leaned against it and fanned at my heated face and neck. Maybe everything was going to be okay after all. I now had three roommates and an extremely hot landlord. Things were looking up.

Chapter Sixteen

ENZO

HOLY SHIT, that girl is incredible. Despite looking like she'd been dragged through the house by her hair, she was fucking hot. I really shouldn't have put that image in my head. I'd pull her hair. She had an accent that reminded me of back home, and her smile reached into my chest, captured my beating heart, and made it race. My jeans were uncomfortable suddenly, and I needed to adjust myself.

The last two years on the run had been difficult, but we were finally on the right path. Angelo had spun his words like magic, and before you could even say real estate, we owned ten different properties that were all making money. Then, like he'd thrown fairy dust on us, we found the perfect location for the distillery, a supplier for all our other needed items, and voilà our whiskey was brewing. I didn't really understand why Angelo called it *The Genie's Jinn* when it was whiskey, but our slogan was *Magic in a bottle*, so it fit. More importantly, it sold like it had real magic inside. So fast, in fact, that we could hardly keep up.

On the far side of the property, I pulled into the driveway and drove down the long lane of trees that reminded me of home. My family loved having trees, and I'd helped plant the saplings that lined our property when I was just three. By the time I took off with

Angelo and Dario, they were tall and shadowed the drive just like these. I wondered what they would look like if we were ever allowed to go home.

I liked it well enough here, but there was no place as sweet as home. Dario was outside smoking a cigarette when I pulled up. I couldn't see him, but the red, glowing dot gave away his location in the shadows. I'd never met someone who could blend in with the darkness like Dario.

"Hey man," I said, getting out of the vehicle and heading for the front door. "Angelo inside?"

"Where else would he be?" Came the gruff voice, and I shook my head, not bothering to answer. Dario was like a thundercloud. He had a brooding personality and followed you around quietly, and when he spoke, it was always with a grumpy rumble, like you'd pissed on his shoe. I would've said he was angry about us having to leave and be on the run, but Dario was like this long before that night.

"Hold the door," Dario ordered as he finished his cigarette and stepped out of the darkness. He looked like a Navy Seal, with his six-six frame of solid muscle, short hair, all-black attire, right down to the cargo pants, and boots that could crush my skull with one stomp.

"Why are you in such a good mood," Dario asked, and my smile fell.

"Why are you in such a bad one?"

"Who said I was in a bad mood?"

"This is your happy face?" I countered, and he glowered at me. "Okay, that was your happy face."

"Hysterical."

"I might as well tell the two of you together." I kept replaying Isabella holding out the mouse to me. She was fucking adorable.

Angelo was on the phone when we walked into the office. I poured us all a drink and sat one on Angelo's desk as he spoke. Dangling a glass between my fingers, I held it out for Dario and got a grunt when he took the glass. I understood why he never dated or, more accurately, why no woman alive would want to put up with his attitude.

"I'm looking forward to doing business with you. Have a good evening." Angelo put the phone down, then slammed his fist off the desk with a bang as he cheered.

"Fuck," I grumbled as I jumped and spilled my drink down my shirt. Dario chuckled, and I glared at him from the corner of my eye.

"That was Mr. Rhodes," Angelo said, a smile spreading across his face.

"The jerk you mentioned earlier," Dario asked. "The guy you said acted like he was a gift from god?"

"Riker Rhodes, that's him. He is more demon than angel if you ask me. The way he does business, fuck, I need to learn to be as shrewd as him. His ability to get you to agree to deals is mindblowing. He had two other calls on the go while I was on the phone with him." Grabbing his drink, he wandered around his desk and sat on the edge. Angelo looked like he could take on anything and anyone. When he got like this, watch out.

"So, did he agree to sell you the building and equipment," I asked.

"Yes, he did. He's still asking for a little more than I'd like to pay, but he assures me that the distillery took good care of their equipment."

"You're not going to take his word for it, are you," Dario questioned. He was the most wary and untrusting of the three of us.

Angelo waved his hand. "No, I wasn't born yesterday. We have a meeting set up for a month from now and I can do a tour before then." He looked at his phone. "The meeting is on a Wednesday."

"Are we flying to New York," I asked, hopeful to see the big city.

"No, since the building is in Sinhaven, Riker and his wife Minetta are coming here. We need to impress him. This deal could take us to the next level in production. Should I take him out or have a feast here in his honor?" Angelo sipped his drink as he smiled.

"A feast? What is he a fairytale prince?" Dario snorted as he swirled his drink, and Angelo rolled his eyes.

"Enzo, did you stop to meet the new tenant?"

"Yes, and she is...she is beautiful," I said, unable to keep the smile from spreading across my face. "Like holy fuck stunning. Oh, and she gave me this." Pulling out the list, I walked over to Angelo and handed it to him.

"There are like twenty things on here," he said. "Who the hell has time to figure all this out in a few hours."

I shrugged. "I don't know, but I'm telling you right now that I couldn't have been more shocked."

"Yes, well, I'll take your word for it. The last thing we need is to get involved with our new tenant. Besides, I have too many other things to concentrate on."

"He's grumpy because Jasmine Falcone is marrying someone else," Dario said, and Angelo shot him a glare.

"Oh, so you're happy about it?" Angelo shot back.

"You two are obsessed with this girl. One day, I need to see what she looks like. She has to be something pretty special."

"Don't bother yourself with it. Who she was to us is in the past." Angelo pushed away from the desk and dropped the list in Dario's lap. "Tomorrow, go pick up what's needed on the list, call HD Services, and get Eggbert out to the house to fix the leak in the ceiling."

"Why me?"

"Say stupid things, win stupid prizes," Angelo said. Dario mumbled "Asshole" under his breath.

"I'm going to bed before you have more dickish ideas." Dario marched out the door and disappeared as Anglo snickered and flopped down in the chair.

"Is he right?"

"About?"

"That Falcone's daughter is getting married. Is that true?" Angelo's eyes flicked down to the drink he was holding.

"Apparently. Nothing I can do about it. I can't go back without being killed, and what the fuck do I have to offer her?" He rubbed at his eyes. "She must know about the egg by now, and she hated me before that fiasco. It doesn't matter anymore, that was another life."

"You really should meet Isabella, maybe she can get Falcone's daughter out of your mind," I offered, and Angelo shrugged. "We could share her, give her a good ride."

"I'll think about it, but..." He stood and marched over to his desk. "I have work to do. You can show yourself out."

And just like that, he closed the door on any talk of emotions. How did I get stuck with two emotionless jerks?

"Okay, boss," I said and walked out, a smile tugging at the corner of my mouth. It was his loss, less competition. I would make Isabella mine, and he would be sorry.

Chapter Seventeen

JASMINE

MY MUSCLES SCREAMED as I lifted the blanket. I didn't think I could get out of bed. Everything hurt so bad. I'd never been one to shrug off responsibilities, but I'd never had to tend to an entire house before. My admiration rose a dozen more notches for all those back home who looked after the mansion daily.

There were no drapes on the windows, and I stared out at the grey, overcast sky. I couldn't help wondering what my father was doing. Was he angry or sad that I was gone? No, I couldn't look backward if I wanted to move forward.

Even though I had no job to go to, I forced myself to toss off the blankets, quickly made my bed, and wandered into the shower as I ignored the limp. The water sputtered and spurted when I turned it on before it began to flow. Trickle was a better description. I would've had better luck standing outside in a rainstorm or someone spitting on me, but it was all I had. I grabbed my soap and stepped under the meager ice-cold spray. I'd hoped this was just an issue last night when I was washing up. Apparently, I wasn't so lucky.

Tipping my head back, I wet my hair and shampooed, and then the water stopped.

"Shit." Soap ran down my face, and I groped for my towel,

keeping my eyes closed. "Oh crap," I swore, remembering I didn't bring any. I left home with the bare minimum and didn't arrange for any to be here, expecting something as basic as towels to be supplied.

My eyes stung and burned as I felt my way out of the shower. I used the door to stand without falling and swung my hand toward the sink. Why was this so hard? I turned on the taps with a squeak, but nothing happened.

"Are you kidding me?"

I slapped my hand on the wall and slid it around until I found the small towel and wiped my face. Stumbling out to the bedroom, I aimed for the bed but got myself turned around and stubbed my toe on the reading chair instead.

"Ow!" I dropped into the chair and held my now throbbing foot up as I pressed the towel to my eyes. There were water bottles in the fridge. I just needed to get there in one piece. Standing, I winced on my toe and had to feel around for my sweater that I had left on the chair. I pulled the cardigan on to stop the shivering and put my arm out as I tried to find the door. I managed with one eye open enough to know I was heading the right way. With a death grip on the banister, I took one stair at a time. I was proud of myself when my feet touched the lower-level floor, but my victory was short-lived as something sharp stabbed the bottom of my foot.

"Ah, fudge biscuits," I growled. I hopped to the side to avoid landing on whatever was stuck in my foot again but smashed my shoulder into the wall.

A whimper trembled on my lips as I leaned there. As an added insult to injury—a hard knock sounded at the front door, and I glared down the hallway.

"Coming," I called out as I limped on one foot and my heel to get to the door. It was a win to reach the handle, and not bothering to look or care anymore, I opened the door to find Enzo on my doorstep.

His eyes ran from my face down my body, and I realized my sweater was partially open and I wasn't wearing anything underneath. I quickly grabbed the front in my free fist, and my skin warmed with his heated, sexual stare. I swallowed hard as his eyes found mine again.

"Um..." he said, licking his lips.

"I'm kinda having a bad morning," I said, closing my eyes and covering my mouth with the hand towel to try and hold back the tears. "I'm sorry, I shouldn't have come here. I don't know what I was thinking." Leaving the door open, I hobbled toward the kitchen.

The door closed, and I heard his boots following me. What was wrong with me? I hardly knew him. I could've just let a murderer into my house for the second time, and the way my morning was going, it was a distinct possibility.

My reason for getting to the kitchen in the first place escaped me as I sat down at the table and put my head in my hands.

"I'm a mess. I'm not cut out for this," I said as a warm hand gripped my shoulder, which only made me want to cry harder. I was thousands of miles away from everything I knew. Breaking away from the family and the overpampering sounded like freedom, but here I was on my second day, already falling apart.

"Hey, don't cry. It's going to be okay." Enzo squatted in front of me. I felt humiliated. "Tell me what I can do. How can I help?"

"I was in the shower, but the water stopped working, and I have soap in my eyes, and then I stubbed my toe and stepped on what I think is a splinter." I held up a strand of my wet, sudsy hair. "I have shampoo in my hair."

It all seemed so trivial, said out loud, but it felt like the world was crashing in on me, and to make matters worse, I was bawling in front of my sexy new landlord. Could I make a bigger fool of myself?

ENZO

The good Lord was testing me. That was all I could think of as Isabella opened the door and stood there looking like the sexiest creature I'd ever seen. My heart was beating so loud that I couldn't hear anything else. My cock stood at attention like a soldier ready for duty as my eyes raked down her body. The inch gap in the sweater wasn't near enough. I wanted to rip it open and take her up against the wall. I was no slouch when it came to women and had been called a ladies' man on more than one occasion, but I'd never felt a rush like this.

"I'm kinda having a bad morning," she said, closing her eyes and covering her mouth with a small grey towel. "I'm sorry, I shouldn't have come here. I don't know what I was thinking." Isabella hobbled toward the kitchen, and I was left with the option of closing the door and leaving or closing the door and following her.

There was no option. I followed her. Fuck, I would follow her anywhere she wanted to go. My body sang with just the sight of her.

"I'm a mess. I'm not cut out for this," Isabella cried. I gently gripped her shoulder, but it only made her cry harder.

"Hey, don't cry. It's going to be okay." I squatted in front of her and immediately knew that was a terrible idea. "Tell me what I can do. How can I help," I asked, trying to remain professional, but the sweater rose up her thighs when she sat down. It covered just enough that I couldn't see anything but another half an inch, and I would have the whole show.

Thank God she didn't notice how I couldn't peel my eyes away from the small triangle of her partially spread legs.

Licking my lips, I tried to listen to what she said, but the hard cock pressing on my jeans made it very difficult. The word 'splinter' registered, and I quickly stood and grabbed her a bottle of water, setting it on the table before going on the hunt for tweezers.

I had to put some space between the two of us before I did something wildly inappropriate. Yanking open the cupboard door in the downstairs bathroom, I found the small kit I'd seen in here before.

I returned to the kitchen and found Isabella dampening the towel and wiping at her red and swollen eyes. I felt horrible. Part of this was my fault. I knew there was an issue with the water and had called in, but I hadn't followed up and totally forgot about it.

Grabbing a chair, I sat it in front of her and patted my lap.

"Give me the foot with the splinter."

"You're going to pull it out?" Everything she said sounded sexual. My brain was permanently stuck in the gutter.

"Yeah, I have the right tool for the job," I said, holding the tweezers. Yet, that wasn't the tool my brain conjured. I tried to rein in all the images of Isabella on the kitchen table as I made her feel better in a whole other way. She put her naked leg on my lap, and once again, I knew this was a bad idea.

I gripped her smooth calf and bit back the groan from my chest as my entire body shuddered.

"Is everything okay," Isabella asked. I couldn't get a word out and didn't dare look up, or I really would spread her legs and kneel between them. This attraction wasn't normal.

I nodded and forced myself to focus, lifting her delicate foot a little higher to see the bottom.

Her toenails were painted bright red, a devious color for someone who seemed so innocent. Maybe she had another side hiding under the sweet exterior. I gently ran my finger up the sole of her foot, and she giggled and squirmed in her seat. Ticklish, good to know.

The sharp point was easy to see. The old, darkened wood stood out against her fair skin. I smirked as I nabbed the piece and pulled it free.

I held it up. "There it is. That should feel a lot better now."

"Thank you. I cannot even imagine what you must think of me."

"I think you're beautiful," I blurted out, and she just blinked at me.

Clearing my throat, I put her foot down and went to the garbage. I couldn't believe I just said that. Was I trying to scare her off?

When I turned around, she was standing, and a fucking knit sweater had never looked so sexy. She held it closed, but doing so molded the fabric to her body. Damn, she was all up in my head, and my blood sang.

"Are you getting a good look?"

My eyes snapped up to hers. I swallowed and nodded and then shook my head. "Sorry, shit."

I closed my eyes and tried to be calm. "I'm going to get the parts to fix the water tank."

The tension between us grew as I marched forward. My feet stopped before Isabella despite my internal protest. Her head was tilted, her eyes still red but firm with a regal air. She reminded me of the princesses back home. There was no way I was good enough for a woman like Isabella, but fuck me, I was determined to win her over.

"I'll be back," I said, forcing myself to walk away. My blood was like alcohol burning in my veins, and she'd lit a fire to the high-octane accelerant.

Glancing back as I opened the door, my eyes locked with hers, and I knew I was in trouble. She was trouble.

Chapter Eighteen

DARIO

HOW THE FUCK did I get suckered into this? I stomped out of the hardware store and looked like a damn pack mule. I guess I could've gotten a buggy, but the list didn't look that bad. That was until every asshole I spoke to upsold me on all the other parts I needed to make the one I wanted work properly. What the hell was up with that? Why did I need ten packages when I only came in for one?

I always parked at the back of the lot so that some dick for brains wouldn't hit my truck. Getting arrested because I smashed the fucker's face into the hood of his car wasn't a great idea when you're trying to remain hidden. It didn't stop me from being tempted, though.

Lifting the bags above my head, I squeezed through a tight opening between two vehicles and growled at the poor parking job —case in point. Walking up to the bed of my truck, I swung all the bags over the side and slipped off the plastic that was cutting off the circulation in my arms.

Mid-turn, I spotted Enzo's SUV parked beside my truck. What the fuck? He was supposed to get started on the crap in the house while I went and got supplies. Why the fuck was he here rather than there? Stomping around the back of my truck, I realized he was still in his vehicle.

"Son of a bitch," I snarled. Enzo's head was back like he was sleeping, but his hand furiously stroked his cock. "You have got to be kidding me."

"What the fuck are you doing?" I bellowed as I yanked open his passenger door.

"Ah!" Enzo yelled and jumped while he gripped his cock, and the thing unloaded like a gun, making a mess all over the inside of his windshield. "Fuck, man." He grimaced and hunched over, nursing his dick that was still making a mess of his car.

"Disgusting. This is why you can't have nice things."

"I was fine until you scared me," Enzo complained as he shot daggers at me with his eyes. "Now look at the mess. I had napkins ready. Dammit."

"Yeah, it's my fault you're yanking your wanker in a public parking lot. You're fucking shampooing this bitch before anyone else gets in, and don't think I won't tell Angelo if you don't."

"Such a fucking asshole." Enzo leaned over and opened the glove compartment, grabbing another thick wad of napkins, but a drop fell from the ceiling onto his knee. "Shit."

"Why the hell are you here stroking your meat? You're supposed to be working on the house."

"She was like half naked and...."

"Half naked? What was she wearing?"

He licked his lips. "A button-up cardigan, but it was fucking hot, man, and I had to touch her foot."

"You're a disgrace to the male race. Get yourself cleaned up. I have a few more stops to make, and then I'll head to the house. Do you think you can handle that? Or are you planning on playing a little more tug and spray?"

"No, I'm sore now. I almost pulled my shit off because of you."

"I guess you learned your lesson then. Better me than a cop." I was about to slam the door when Enzo called out my name. "What?"

"Can you get this stuff too?" He reached for a piece of paper on the passenger seat, but I swiped it before he could touch it with his hand.

"Fucker, don't touch shit that I have to touch with your dirty cock hand." I glared at the list and growled. "Are you kidding me? You want me to go back in there?"

"I was going to, but I needed to relieve myself first."

"What you were doing is not called relieving. Taking a piss is relieving yourself. That was a public display of indecency. Asshole." I slammed the door and stomped back into the hardware store to be raped for more money.

An hour later, I pulled into the driveway, hopping mad. I had to go to two other hardware stores to get all the parts needed to fix the water tank. Then, just to be on the safe side, I bought a brand-new one and had it strapped down in the back, too.

We hadn't fixed anything in this place since we purchased it, so why we had to start now for some chick was annoying as fuck. Grumbling, I pulled the bags from the truck bed and marched for the door. I left them there and headed back to the truck for another load.

Carrying the second load of bags, I marched up the steps. I raised my hand to knock but heard laughter and peered through the living room window instead. My heart stopped, and my breath froze as I soaked in Jasmine. She was like a breath of fresh air, and I sucked in a deep lung full, feeling alive for the first time in years.

This couldn't be real. I thought her name was Isabella. My heart remembered how to beat and pounded like a hammer inside my chest as my blood whooshed through my body. I pulled back from the window and closed my eyes as I listened to them talking.

I couldn't make out the conversation, but as she laughed, I shivered. That was definitely Jasmine. I peeked through the window again, careful not to get caught.

My gaze raked over her features but settled on her unusual honey-colored eyes that looked like they were touched by gold. No one else had eyes like her. It had to be her. I would know them anywhere. Her black hair was tied up and showed off the delicate features of her face. I wanted to bust open the door but was sure all that would accomplish was getting myself punched in the face.

She still seemed so delicate. Every movement, right down to how she held her hands and tilted her head up, screamed that it was the woman I loved. How did Enzo not see she was a princess? She was no commoner. This was the daughter of one of the most powerful Dons in Italy. If she were here, even by some strange twist of fate, her family wouldn't be far behind.

My heart pounded hard, thinking we would have to run again. But I didn't want to. I never thought I would see Jasmine again, and there she was, no more than twenty feet away.

"I could've sworn I heard another vehicle pull in." I heard Enzo say, and I ran for his SUV.

Yanking open the door, I paused as I stared at the steering wheel and seat. "Shit."

Memories of this morning in the parking lot came rushing back. It didn't smell clean, and I cringed as I got behind the wheel. He always left the keys on the visor, and I started the vehicle just as the door opened. I floored it, spraying rocks on my truck as I backed out of the driveway like a fucking bat out of hell. I couldn't let her see me. She didn't know Enzo, but I could only pray he didn't say my name.

Shit, this could be a trap. What if she was the distraction, and they were collecting Angelo right now for execution? Did she hate us that much?

I hit the road and dared to glance at the front door to see a confused look on Enzo's face. I peeled away and drove far too fast around the back country roads to our home on the other side of the property.

Pulling out my phone, I sent Enzo a quick text message.

D: Whatever you do, do not mention my name to our new tenant. I'll explain later.

E: You're fucking weird, but fine.

Dropping my phone in the cup holder, I grabbed the wheel. "Fuck, you asshole. I'm going to kill you. I will slit your throat while you sleep." I swore a blue streak as my hand stuck to the steering wheel when I tried to lift it. I was going to piss in his shoes. That was what I was going to do to him.

There were no unusual cars in the driveway, but I still pulled my gun, left the SUV running, and ran for the front door. The door slammed against the wall as I burst inside and ran in and then turned down the hallway to Angelo's office, almost colliding with him as stepped out.

"What the fuck?" Angelo stepped back as I pushed past him and looked around the room. "What the hell are you doing?"

Panting, I slumped over on my knees as relief that Angelo was okay washed over me.

"Dario speak up, you're freaking me the fuck out."

Slowly standing up straight, I looked him in the eyes and couldn't believe I had to tell him this. We were doing great here. For all my bitching, this was the first place to feel like a home again. But he needed to know so we could plan. I couldn't think about winning her back. That seemed too much like a fantasy that would never happen, but we had to find a way to get her to leave, or we would be found for sure.

"Boss, we have a problem. Like a big fucking problem, and God help us, I don't know what to think."

Chapter Nineteen

JASMINE

I HELD out the tool that Enzo needed next. I couldn't get the SUV peeling down the driveway out of my mind. It was like the man was running away, but Enzo shrugged it off and said he got a text about an emergency at another property. It seemed plausible, but I couldn't help worrying that it was one of my father's spies.

"Isabella?"

"Hmm?" I was startled and looked down at Enzo. "I think that's it. Did you want to go try the water and see what happens?"

"Fantastic, I'll be right back." Jogging up the stairs from the basement, I went to the two-piece bathroom and turned on the tap. It sputtered, and then water began to flow. A smile spread across my face.

"Shit! No. Turn it off," Enzo yelled up the stairs, and my smile fell. "Dammit," he swore as he stomped up the stairs. He was wiping his hands, but his shirt was soaked and sticking to his body. Once upon a time, it had been white, but now it was a disgusting mess. The wet material clung to the muscles of his cut chest and highlighted the tattoo that covered his arm and half of his body.

Enzo reminded me of a rock climber—I'd met a few—and how they were all fit and muscular but not bulky. It didn't make him any less sexy, and I had to peel my eyes away from the sight of him. I didn't have the freedom back home to spend time with men like this, and now I knew why. My father was afraid that I would fall into sin again. I wiped that image from my mind before it could take root. Too many nights, I'd cried over Angelo and Dario. Too many nights, I berated myself for ever thinking they loved me.

"I think you're going to need a whole new one," Enzo rubbed at his wavy, wet hair, and I crossed my arms and looked away.

"How long do you think that will take?"

"A couple of days to install. I don't know, I've never done something like that, but I'll figure it out. I like to build things."

"Okay." I looked down as I thought.

"You can use our shower tonight. At least then you can get the shampoo out of your hair," Enzo said just as his phone dinged. He pulled it out and glared at the screen. "Actually, my co-owner said to take you to our hotel for a few days so we can fix the water and the leaking roof before you return."

"Oh wow, I don't want to trouble you," I said.

"No trouble at all. When the boss calls for extra care for our clients, take it."

I smiled, and even though I wasn't sure this was a good idea, I nodded. "I'll take you up on that. Thanks." Pointing down the hall, I asked, "Is the greenhouse in working order?"

Enzo's shoulder lifted and dropped casually. "Honestly, I have no idea. I couldn't keep a cactus from dying, so that should tell you all you need to know," he teased, the joking making me blush.

"I hate to impose on you anymore, but if I make a list, would you take me to a store where I could buy dirt and seeds? I think I want to grow some vegetables, maybe some fruit."

"For sure. You make a list of what you want, and I'll change my shirt."

Before he could turn away, I reached out and grabbed his arm. His skin was hot under my touch, and his flexed arm felt amazing. He looked at my hand, then up into my eyes, and butterflies filled my stomach. I quickly let go of his arm as the strange tension that filled like a balloon swirled around us.

"I um...I just wanted to say thank you. I was ready to give up this morning."

Enzo stuffed his hands into his pockets, the shy smile pulling at the corner of his mouth, making his dimple stand out.

"That would've been a shame. I'm glad you're feeling better. You should make that list so we can get to the store before they close."

"Yes, of course. Closing time, I should've thought of that." He chuckled as I walked away and pulled out my phone to make a list in the notes. It didn't take me very long, and it wasn't like I really knew what I needed. I had a basic idea of how to garden, and I always loved the flowers back home, but everything seemed so new. It was like learning how to speak a whole other language.

Walking to the front door, I opened it just in time to see Enzo with his shirt off, and the sight stole the air from my chest. His perfectly tanned skin was sun-kissed, and the tattoo I'd seen through the T-shirt looked like the intricate patterns on the Persian rugs my father loved to collect. All too soon, the show was over. As he turned in my direction, I closed the door and locked it.

"Do you need a purse or anything," Enzo asked, and my cheeks flushed hot.

"That would be helpful. My head is all over the place. I'll be right back."

"No, no, that's okay. You can pay me back. I mean, I do know where you live," he teased.

"Thanks, Enzo. I feel like I should say that every few seconds."

"And it looks like Da...Maurice knew that we might need a whole new unit," he slapped the tank in the back of the pickup truck.

"That's great. I will have to thank Da...Maurice," I teased.

"It's just Maurice. My brain is fried," he said and blushed, which looked so cute on him.

I slipped into the passenger seat of the truck and buckled my seatbelt.

"What music do you like," he asked as we pulled out of the driveway.

"Do you like *Peter and the Piper*? I love them," I said.

"Coming right up. I have all of their albums. The percussion one with the howling wolf they did as a Christmas song is one of my favorites."

"Yes," I said, excitement filling me to find someone else who loved the same eclectic music. "My favorite is *Home Again Home Again Jiggety Jig*."

It was amazing how easily we slipped into conversation and jumped from one topic to the next. I was hysterically laughing by the time we pulled into the parking lot of the massive greenhouse. The sign at the end of the road read, Jack's Stock.

There were a few other cars in the lot as we parked, and it seemed odd to go someplace and not see someone I knew. Back home, I couldn't walk into a shop or a restaurant and not be treated differently. Some of the other women loved the special service, but I'd never enjoyed being catered to like that. I loved feeling normal, and the thought of doing something like growing my own food or starting a business was thrilling.

"Do you know what you want to grow," Enzo asked as we stepped through the doors to a place that felt like a fairytale.

"No, maybe a little of everything. I'm just not sure." I picked up a basket as a man who reminded me of a walking leaf came over. Everything he wore was green. Even his boots were a shade of green.

"Good evening. Did I hear you say you aren't sure what you want to grow," he asked, his voice as soft as a whisper. I looked around, wondering why he talked like that and felt compelled to do the same.

"Yes, you heard right. I could really use your advice. I'm new to gardening and have no idea what I need, but I'd love to grow vegetables."

"My name is Jack, and I have just the thing for you."

Enzo and I followed behind Jack, who seemed a little peculiar as he continued to whisper. He tossed in a how to book and then so many packages in my basket that it was getting heavy. Without asking, Enzo took the full basket and handed me an empty one.

"Lastly, you will want this." Jack held up two bags. "This is my secret fertilizer blend, and I promise it will make all your seeds grow like magic. The beans especially love it. I'll have one of the staff members load everything into your vehicle."

"Thank you, Jack." I waited until he walked away before looking at the load we carried and then glanced outside at the pile growing beside the SUV. "I didn't expect to spend so much."

"Don't worry about it. You can pay me back, and just so you know, cherries are my favorite." He held up the package with cherries on the front, and my body flushed so hot that the tips of my ears burned.

"I really shouldn't. You've already been so nice to me. I feel like I'm taking advantage of your kindness now."

We both looked out the window at the sound of roaring motorcycles. Enzo screwed up his face at the sight of the bikes.

"You don't like them?"

He shrugged. "I'm not a fan of any of the MCs in the area. That's the Royal Bears. Their prez is Zayde Sinclair, stay away from them, they're bad news. They tend to sell things that never belonged to them. If you get my drift?"

The sound of the motorcycles faded, and we headed to the register to pay for the supplies. The total almost made me fall over, but Enzo didn't blink an eye as he handed over a wad of cash.

There wasn't a spot left in the truck bed or back seat. It was so full that the hummingbird feeder I got was sitting on my lap. I'd always loved the little birds back home. They were a highlight of my day when they came to the garden. The drive back was much quieter as the sun set.

It felt like I had a solid plan, yet I was terrified and hated being so sheltered that the world felt foreign. We passed dozens of unique shops and signs for things I'd never heard of before.

"Here we are," Enzo said.

I looked up at the small hotel's bright blue sign, *The Glass Slipper*. It was an unusual name, but there seemed to be a lot of oddity in Beastville.

I got out, and Enzo walked us toward the side of the small building. There couldn't be more than a couple dozen rooms.

"This is a tiny hotel."

"Yeah, I guess it is more of a motel, but we keep the place exceptionally clean, and the room service food is five-star." Pulling a key out from his pocket, he unlocked a door on the main level, and I was shocked when I walked in.

Everything looked like it was made to mimic being at the seaside. The walls were a pretty blue, and sea shell pillows lined the massive bed in the center of the room. A kitchen was off to one side, and a couch by the window looked toward a park. It smelled fresh and clean.

"Maurice was already by and put some food in the fridge, and the bathroom is in perfect working order. There are complimentary fuzzy pajamas on the bed and a change of clothes in the wardrobe."

"How did he know my size?"

"I don't ask those questions. I just do what I'm told. Your house should be fixed in a couple of days. Did you want me to come by tomorrow and show you around the town?"

"If it's not too much trouble?"

He smiled wide, and it reminded me of a devilish cat. "No, of course not. We can do lunch. I know a great spot." He nodded toward the truck. "I'll take everything back to the house and drop it off."

"I really feel like I'm imposing on you," I said, looking up at his handsome face.

He stared at me for so long that I blushed and looked away. I'd forgotten what it was like to flirt with someone and felt rusty.

"Trust me. I want to." Enzo held out his hand. "Here is the key to the room. There is a fantastic coffee and sweets shop no more than a two-minute walk down the road." I took the key, and he stuffed his hands in his jeans pockets. "I'll be by before lunch to take you out, say eleven-thirty?"

"Sounds good. Thank you."

"Goodnight, Isabella. I enjoyed spending time with you today."

The corner of my mouth lifted in a smile. "Same."

Backing out the door, he closed it, and I flicked the lock. I watched him pull away from the window and bit my lip as I held back the smile. Day two had started terribly, but it ended up being amazing.

I needed to grow tougher skin to remain in this world without a safety net, but first, I needed a hot shower.

Chapter Twenty

ANGELO

IT WAS REALLY HER. No two people could look that much alike. Could they? I watched her from the darkened window of my car as she stepped out of the truck, and Enzo escorted her into the hotel.

It was definitely her, and if she were a mirage made of my mind's longing, then I never wished to wake up. There was nothing in this life I desired more than her. From the first touch we shared as children, I knew deep down that she was mine. I hated her because she made me feel. Jasmine made me hope for something different than what my parents had. It took me a long time to understand that, but the moment I let the reality of my love for her sink in, I was done for.

I'd tried three times to broker a marriage when I got back from America, and each time her father turned me away before my ass could touch the chair. Hell I never made it inside the gates. The rage I felt at the insult was so great that my first thought had been to kill Don Falcone with my bare hands and take what I wanted. Jacopo was the reason I didn't act. If he took control of the family, there was no telling what he would do with Jasmine. So, I came up with another plan.

The question was, why was she here if she was betrothed to Ciro?

The better question was, did I care about the betrothal? No, I fucking did not. I would march across the parking lot, kick down the door, and fuck her against the wall right now. Fuck that wasn't a terrible idea. The fact that my pants were suddenly uncomfortable confirmed it.

"I told you," Dario said, his voice as hopeful as I felt.

"I just don't understand why she's here."

"Neither do I." Dario looked over. "Do you think they know we are here and are using her as bait?"

It was something to contemplate, but I didn't think so. "She paid cash and is using a different name. Jasmine is running from something, maybe even her fiancé. She may even be looking for us. I mean what are the chances that we'd end up in the same town?"

"Or all of this is Don Falcone's doing to rook us in, and he is waiting to pounce."

"Possible, but why not storm our house already?" I shook my head as Enzo stepped out of the room and slipped into the truck. "No, I think our Tiger has secrets she is trying to hide, which works well for us. She doesn't want to be found either. No matter what, I'm willing to take the risk to find out."

I pulled out of the shady hiding spot and followed the truck.

"What are you planning?"

"I'm not sure yet, but I have hoped for a moment like this since shit went down. I'm not passing up this opportunity to reclaim what is mine."

"Ours," Dario said, and I glanced over at the man who looked ready to kill.

"Yes, ours."

"What about Enzo? I don't think he'll just walk away."

"You mean without killing him?" Dario glared at me, and I shrugged. "I'll think about it. I've never had a problem sharing Jasmine with you, but Enzo is still new. Faceless, annoying women are one thing. My Tiger is another."

"I suggest we talk to Jasmine, tell her what happened and let her choose what she wants," Dario said.

"If I did that, we would have bullets in our skulls. No, we need to be more devious than that. I'll come up with a plan."

The moment we all got home and inside the house, I pounced on Enzo like a fucking cat. Grabbing his T-shirt, I pushed him up against the wall. The more I thought about him touching her the more pissed off I got.

"What the fuck?" Enzo complained.

"You can't have her. She's mine," I growled, and the shock on Enzo's face evaporated.

"Oh, now you want her. I told you to meet her, and you had no interest," Enzo argued.

I could feel Dario as he walked through the front door. Even before I looked over my shoulder, I knew what I would see. His face rarely changed. It was either resting dick or fucking you up. Right now, he was in rest mode.

"I've always had an interest in her." I let Enzo go and stepped back. "Her name is not Isabella. It's Jasmine Falcone. I don't know why she's going by Isabella, that was her mother's name, but that is her."

Enzo crossed his arms. "Well, in that case, she technically belongs to that guy you mentioned...Ciro." I glared at Enzo, not liking where this was going. He shrugged. "I want in. I know you two had a thing with her, and if you're making a move, then I want in on it."

"Are you fucking kidding me? You've known her all of two days. I've known her my entire life."

"Yes, and why aren't you running over to the hotel and bursting through the door to profess your undying love? Oh, that's right, you can't because she's pissed at you or hates you."

Grabbing Enzo, I slammed him up against the wall again. "Watch your fucking tone with me."

He held up his hands. "Look, the point is that for the first time in a fucking long time, I feel something, and she is the cause. I'm not letting that go just because you say so." I growled at him, and my fist flew before I could stop myself.

"Fuck," Enzo yelled as I connected with his jaw. Dario gripped me from behind and hauled me away from Enzo.

"Knock it off," Dario said, his voice calm, considering.

Enzo dabbed at his lip. "I can't believe you fucking hit me."

"I should cut your dick off and feed it to my piranha. Consider yourself lucky it was only my fist."

"Fuck, man. Until I got mixed up with you, I had a good fucking life. I should've stayed in Chicago. Instead I follow your ass and one favor later, I'm on the run. I've been nothing but loyal since we met. The least you can do is loop me in, or I'll just move out and pursue her myself."

I growled and lunged in Dario's arms.

"Enough! Both of you shut up. No one is taking anyone."

This couldn't be happening. I was finally free of the family constraints, she was on the same fucking property, and now my friend wanted to try and take her from me. What kind of nightmare was this?

Dario let me go but moved to stand between me and Enzo.

"Both of you go sit down," Dario said, pointing to the sitting room. It was a good thing he made me leave my gun in the office before we left the house, or I would've been tempted to use it on Enzo.

I marched into the room and poured myself a drink before sitting down in my usual chair.

"Angelo, you know I love you like a brother and respect you as my boss, but...shit. Times have changed. We're fugitives and have done some dark shit together, and we don't have the family's honor hanging in the balance anymore." Enzo leaned forward on the couch, his eyes sad and distraught. I knew that feeling. I'd felt it every day for years, and it didn't just go away. She'd infected him with her smile and gentle touch, just like me.

"What are you trying to say?"

He leaned back and crossed his arms. "Just that, we have all grown into more than an underboss and soldier dynamic. I really like her, and whether I have her to myself or with you two doesn't matter to me."

I looked away as I thought about a solution. "I'm not letting her go. I've waited too long for this chance. Fuck, the entire reason we are even out here is because of her. That is how much I wanted her. How much I want her and love her," I said. My drink shook as I squeezed the glass tighter.

"We," Dario piped up.

I rolled my eyes in his direction. "Fine. How much we want and love her," I said, not wanting to argue over grammar. "Enzo, you hardly fucking know her."

"One second was all it took. Call me a hopeless romantic all you want, I know enough that I want her," he said. "I also have an in with her, and I am your electronics guy. You need me if you want her bugged, tracked, or watched. Which, I'm sure you do."

Storming to my feet, I walked over to the large window that looked out at the gardens. I knew that Jasmine would love walking in them when they were in full bloom.

"Okay, I'm just going to say it. We've been sharing women for two years. What's the difference now if Jasmine wants all of us? At the end of the day, it is her choice. It doesn't matter that you think you claimed her," Dario said.

"I did fucking claim her. You were there," I said, spinning around to glare at Dario, my hands balled into fists.

"Yes, and I was there when we left for Chicago and ended up losing her." Dario marched in my direction. "You think the memory of that shit doesn't bother me? Do you think adding someone else is what I want? But Enzo is right. She likes him and trusts him. If we want find out why she's here and protect her we need a way to get into the house consistently, and Enzo has proven himself to be loyal. If he wants her and she wants him, we don't have a say anymore. We lost that right."

"Fuck! I never should've lost her. This never should've been a fucking argument," I yelled. "I love her, Enzo, but Dario is right that you've been loyal. So let me make this really fucking clear. If you try to take her from me, I will shoot you between the eyes, cut you up into little pieces and feed you to my fish. I won't even lose a single night's sleep, know that. Jasmine is everything to me...everything."

"Understood, and hopefully, she isn't here to meet Ciro. If he comes and claims her, we're all out."

Enzo's words hurt. He was right that Ciro could show up any moment, and then what? We'd be left with our cocks in our hands and an ache in our chests. I'd gotten used to that longing, but to taste her lips and then give her up to Ciro felt impossible. No I wouldn't allow it.

"If Ciro comes here to claim her, I'll kill him with my bare hands and smile as the light fades in his eyes. I can't get anymore banished than I already am, and I sold my soul a long time ago," I said, turning to look out the window, dismissing the conversation.

I couldn't let her go again. Her coming to this small town in the middle of nowhere was a sign. I felt it.

Chapter Twenty-One

ANGELO

THE ROOM WAS DARK, and even though I knew I should, I couldn't stay away. If Jasmine woke up, it would scare the crap out of her, but I'd spent too many nights wondering. I never thought she would fade into the background without me in her life—she was too strong for that—but I wondered if she thought about me as much as I thought about her.

Slipping my key into the lock of the adjoining room, I turned it as softly as possible. Stepping into the bedroom, it was like time had never lapsed. Jasmine was on her back, black hair fanned around her, and one arm over her head.

After I returned, and her father wouldn't agree to a union, I was feral with anger. I snuck in and watched her sleep every night without her knowing, just like I had before she agreed to marry me. I'd been tempted to kidnap and take her away until her father agreed to let me have her. She made me insane.

Lowering myself into the seat in the corner, I watched the sheet rise and fall with her steady breathing. The world had seemed so much simpler five years ago. I had a plan to get the girl and everything else I wanted, and nothing was going to stop me...until it did.

• • •

My phone rang, and I quickly answered it, slipping from the bed.

"Father?"

"Angelo, good. Did you get my text messages?" I looked at the time. It was four in the morning.

"No, it's only four. I was asleep," I said and sucked in a shuddering breath as arms slipped around my waist. I looked down to see a pair of mischievous, golden eyes staring up at me.

My heart pounded harder just looking at Jasmine. It may have only been a couple months that Dario and I had been sneaking into her room at night, but it felt like forever, and only a single day rolled into one. This was where I was always meant to be. No matter how we got here, I knew this was right.

"Where are you? You weren't in your room."

"Does it matter?"

"No, I guess not," he said.

I wasn't telling him about Jasmine until I spoke to Don Falcone and we came to an understanding. There was no way in hell I was letting my father near that negotiation.

Lifting my arm, she stepped underneath to hug me from the front. I closed my eyes and sighed.

"What did the messages say," I asked, annoyed to be pulled from her warm bed for whatever my father wanted.

"I need you to fly to North America and run the Chicago side of the family business."

My mouth fell open. This was what I needed to prove myself, but it couldn't have come at a worse time.

"What happened to Roberto?"

Jasmine kissed my chest, and I smoothed her long hair, loving the feel of the silky texture running through my fingers.

"He had to be dispatched. He failed me one too many times, and that is something I cannot tolerate."

"When do you need me to fly out?"

"The jet is set to leave in two days, that should give you enough time to

sort who you want to take and pack. I need you on the ground before anyone realizes we are missing our El Chapo and decides to take advantage."

How could I be filled with so much excitement to take the position and panic over leaving Jasmine behind at the same time?

"Alright, I'll be ready. How long will I be gone?"

"As long as it takes for us to find a new replacement. I have a few people in mind," my father said. "Be ready, and don't screw this up." He hung up, and I tapped the phone on my bottom lip.

"What's going on," Jasmine asked, her voice as airy as the breeze coming in the window.

"I have to leave in two days for the United States," I said, and she pulled back, staring at me with a guarded expression only she could pull off.

"For how long?"

I lifted my shoulder and let it drop. "I'm not sure, but I don't think it will be too long. It's just until some business is sorted." I smiled at her as she bit her bottom lip, which always made me want to ravish her. "Don't worry, it shouldn't be more than a few weeks. I thought you said you'd never miss an ass like me," I teased.

"Who says I'm going to miss your arrogant ass?"

I looked over my shoulder. "It's a nice arrogant ass."

"Oh, shut it." Jasmine swatted my arm and rolled her eyes at me.

"Oh, you did not just roll your eyes at me?" Grabbing her around the waist, she screamed as I tossed her over my shoulder and marched for the bed.

"What the hell is going on?" Dario sat up straight, his hand on his gun sitting on the bedside table until he saw it was just us.

"Someone is being sassy and needs to be taught a lesson."

"Don't you dare," Jasmine said, squealing as I smacked her ass and tossed her on the bed.

. . .

I'd never forgotten her fiery look or how we laughed and rolled around in a ridiculous fight that ended with the three of us panting and once more satisfied. My eyes lifted to the sleeping woman who was in my blood. For two and a half years, I stayed in Chicago. It had been my greatest ambition, but turned into a jail cell.

Days stretched into weeks and then weeks into months with no end in sight, and each day, as hard as she tried, I heard the longing in her voice. When my father said I might never be coming home, I did what I thought was best and called Don Falcone. I asked for Jasmine's hand in marriage, but he wouldn't hear of his daughter moving that far away and declined the offer. I tried every day to convince him for weeks, and when he stopped taking my calls, I did the only thing I could and cut off all contact.

I didn't think Dario would ever forgive me. Maybe he shouldn't. I never forgave myself, but I couldn't string her along for years, not knowing if I would ever get to come home. I couldn't tell her that her father had refused my offer without turning her against her only living parent. So why was it that it didn't seem noble? Why did it feel like I'd chopped off my arm?

Jasmine stirred, her soft whimper cutting my heart like a sharp knife. Her brow was tense as she tossed her head back and forth.

Drawn to her, I stood and stared, wanting so badly to touch her. "Shh, my Tiger. I'm here now, and I will never let you go." I brushed some hair from her face and let my finger trail along her cheek.

"Angelo," she said, her voice thick in her dream state. My name on her lips confirmed that her here in this town was no coincidence. She was here for me, and nothing and no one would take my second chance away.

"I'm not a good man, Tiger. I have done terrible things, and my soul has hardened into stone. To keep you, I will do my worst. I will kill whoever I need to. I will lock you up and throw away the key if necessary, but I need you. I hope that one day you'll understand that whatever I choose to do next will be because I love you."

Picking up her cell phone, I pried off the case and put a tiny dot tracker inside before putting it back where it was. Forcing myself to step away, I slipped through the door to the adjoining room, the beginning of a plan already formulating in my mind.

"Every room," Enzo asked.

"Where the fuck is he?" Dario yelled in the background. I knew Dario was pissed. I snuck out of the house without him, but his following my every step got old a long time ago.

"Yes, of course, every room, including the bathrooms and closets. I don't want a single space in or outside of the house that I can't see her." Dario growled something else in the background. "Tell Dario if he's a good boy, I'll bring him home a fresh plum pie." Enzo relayed the message, and I smirked as I heard Dario yell, "Go fuck yourself."

Driving him crazy was always a highlight of my day. Just then, the hotel door opened, and Jasmine stepped out. Or it had been a highlight until this moment.

"Make it happen. I have to go."

I hung up on Enzo before he could argue with me and slouched inside the sports car as I watched her walk along the sidewalk. She wore a simple pair of blue jeans with running shoes and a knit sweater with her hair tied up, exactly how I remembered. I wanted to take it out of the cute little twist and let the waves blow in the breeze.

She was heading toward the heart of Beastville. There were many cute shops and places to sit, but trouble also lurked in this quaint town. She wandered into Miss Muffet's Whey coffee shop and emerged shortly after sipping a hot drink and nibbling on something in a white bag. My guess was a hot macchiato latte with half cream, a dollop of whipped cream, and a sprinkling of cinnamon. The muffin would be something fruity, blueberry or blackberry.

Jasmine would want a spot to sit near flowers, and sure enough, she angled toward the small park with benches and flowers still in bloom. It was late in the year, and soon, not a single leaf would be on the trees.

I kept my eyes peeled for any danger hanging around, looking for an easy target. My hand rested on my gun, the metal calming me from marching over and dragging her into my car for safekeeping. Irrational? Maybe. But, after all the shit I'd seen, I preferred to lock her in a tower and throw away the key.

When she finished eating, she moved on and continued toward downtown. I waited until she entered a flower shop before starting my car and pulling out of my hiding spot. It was more challenging to hide downtown, but I wasn't letting her out of my sight. Traffic was picking up, but there was an open space on the main street, and I quickly parallel parked, watching the flower shop door from my side mirror.

She stepped outside with the owner, smiling as she held a small bundle of all her favorites. Cracking my window, I heard her laugh, and my heart sputtered. I was a fucking crime boss. I should march over there, drag her into the car with me, and that would be the end of it, but Jasmine was different. She was the fierce tigress, and that would only flare her well-known stubborn streak.

Then again fucking her in my car while she was spitting mad was a hell of an image, and my cock hardened in my pants. Shit, this was going to be a long day.

Jasmine waved goodbye and continued walking but paused as she stared at the lingerie store.

"Don't you dare go in there," I growled under my breath. "The only person you're buying sexy clothes for is me." She smiled a devilish little grin and yanked open the door. "Son of a bitch." Who the fuck did she want to impress? If Ciro was coming here or if this was for Enzo, I might kill them both. I tapped my finger on the top of my steering wheel. "Shit."

Stuffing my gun in my holster under my suit jacket, I stepped out of the car and marched across the street.

"This is a dumb idea." Mumbling, I glanced in the large glass window and saw Jasmine head to the changing room with an armful of items. Nothing could've stopped me from opening the door and walking inside. The shop had flowers everywhere, soft music playing, and smelled of sweet perfume.

"Good morning. How can I help you? Are you looking for something for someone special," the saleswoman asked as she walked over with a smile on her face.

"Actually, I'm looking for my girlfriend. She just walked in here. I plan on buying her whatever she wants. In fact, here is my card..." I pulled out the fancy platinum card I had for the business. "Make sure that anything she wants is taken care of, but don't let her know it's me. Say you are having a sale or something." The saleswoman smiled wider.

"She's an independent woman and likes to care for herself?"

"Yes, exactly," I agreed. "It makes it so tough to do sweet things for her when I only want to give her the stars." I busted out my best million-dollar smile, and she blushed.

"We need more men like you in the world."

No, you really don't, was all I could think as a memory of screaming flooded my mind. My hands were so coated in blood that they would never be clean.

"Do you think I could sneak back there? I know she wants to keep it a surprise...."

The saleswoman looked around and then whispered. "I never saw you."

Glancing at her name tag, I smiled. "Thank you, Allie. I'll grab my card on the way out."

Marching past her, I poked my head in the women's changing

room and heard Jasmine humming. The sound made me shiver. There were several rooms, but the floor-to-ceiling curtain at the far end was where I quietly headed. It was storage for extra boxes and was perfectly dark. I cracked the curtain just enough to see the mirrored doors.

My heart stopped beating as one of the doors opened, and there she was in a black lace number that left very little to the imagination. It hugged every curve, and my cock went from hard to painfully wanting out of the constrictive dress pants. I could see her dark nipples pushing at the fabric, and my mouth watered. Jasmine slipped on a pair of heels, and as she did, she bent over. I had to bite back a groan as the teddy slid up her ass, giving me an unobstructed view.

I rubbed at my cock as she stood and walked like a model on a runway toward the mirror closest to me. She was so close I could've reached out, grabbed her, and dragged her into the dark. Fuck, I was tempted. Her hands slid over the lace, accentuating the sexy allure of the piece.

When she disappeared inside the changing room again, I unzipped my pants and pulled my aching cock out. I didn't give a fuck where I was and stroked my hand along my shaft as I waited for the next show.

She stepped out a few moments later in a shimmery dark blue negligee that made my mouth run dry and my hand move faster. When she reached the mirror, she pulled the sash, and her nipples hardened with the cool air. She turned in a circle, giving me a better view, and I could feel the orgasm building. I would've paid any amount for her to sit on the small bench, spread her legs, and finger herself for me.

I was panting hard by the time she walked away. I leaned my hand against the wall and jerked off to images of Jasmine's fingers disappearing inside her body as she moaned my name.

My eyes snapped open at the click of the door, and I stared out my slim view once again. This time, she wore red with thigh-high stockings, garter belts, and crotchless panties. The top was just as provocative, and as she stepped forward and turned in a circle, the first shot of come flew from my cock. She slipped her hand down her body and struck a sexy pose, and I was unable to hold back and unloaded.

My mouth hung open in a silent yell as the release gripped me with staggering force. Jasmine looked at the curtain, and I didn't care if she whipped it open. I held still, gripping my cock, begging for more even as I came all over the back of the curtain.

Shrugging, Jasmine walked away, and I slumped and took a ragged breath. She was not wearing that shit for anyone other than me and Dario...maybe Enzo, but I wasn't prepared to say that definitively yet. I stuffed my cock back in my pants, ignoring the fact that it was still hard. I strode out of the changing room and approached Allie, who was waiting behind the cash register.

"Do you have what you need?" I asked, nodding toward my card.

"Yes, I do." She handed it over, and I stepped away before turning and smirking at her.

"I would clean the black curtain back there. Charge my card for it. I may have made a mess."

"Oh...." Her mouth dropped open, her face flushing a deep red.

"Or you can lick it off if you're into that sort of thing." Her eyes darted toward the changing room, her tongue wetting her lip. I had a feeling she was a little freaky and wouldn't be surprised if she ran back there the moment I stepped out the door.

Smiling, I marched out and back to my parking spot but growled under my breath when I spotted Dario sitting in the passenger side of the car.

"Fucker."

Chapter Twenty-Two

JASMINE

I WOULD SWEAR that Beastville had eyes. Everywhere I went, it felt like someone was watching me. But I never saw anyone or anything out of place. It was probably the fact that I was hiding. Was it normal to always be looking over your shoulder? It wasn't like I'd ever been on the run before.

I walked down the main street toward my hotel and smiled when I saw Enzo's vehicle in the parking lot. I pushed down my excitement and gave him a courteous nod as he stepped out of the SUV to greet me.

"Sorry I couldn't meet you earlier. I had some work to do, but the good news is that the plumber was out earlier, and the roofer will be out later. So, hopefully, we will have you moved into your house in a day or two."

"That is fantastic news." I held up one of the bags I was holding. "I have a roasted chicken pasta and salad for lunch. Would you like to stay?"

He rubbed at his ear and mumbled something under his breath. "Unfortunately, I can't, but I brought you the map you asked for, and I thought you might like this."

Enzo held out a pink pastry box.

"Thank you. Are you sure you don't want to stay? I don't know anyone else and it would be nice to have company."

He looked over his shoulder. I also looked but didn't see anything.

"You know...I can spare a few minutes before I need to get back to work. My boss is a real asshole, and I'm sure I'll hear about it, but how can I pass up lunch with such a beautiful woman?" My cheeks heated with the compliment and the playful glint in his silvery eyes. "Just give me one second."

Enzo opened his vehicle door, and the sun's glare made it hard to see inside, but I would've sworn he was talking to someone and pulled something out of his ear. That was ridiculous. Only spies, the Secret Service, and bodyguards did something like that. What if he was? What if he secretly worked for my papa and relayed everything I did and said to him? What if he was on his way? Worse what if he was the FBI or some other agency and they were looking to get to my papa through me?

Okay, I was acting crazy. I'd only been on the run from my family for a week and acted like everyone was after me. I saw eyes among the bushes and drapes moving in the windows when no one was there.

"Would you like me to take a bag," Enzo asked.

I handed him the food and a bag with decorative knickknacks but kept the bags of sexy clothing tightly in my grasp. Just holding the bags with Enzo so close made me flustered, let alone if he looked inside. I still couldn't believe everything in the store was ninety percent off. I bought almost everything, even things I would never try on. It was a huge waste of money that I couldn't afford to spend, but I felt so naughty and something entirely for me wearing them and couldn't resist.

The stupid dream about Angleo last night had to be the cause. I hated that I still missed him and Dario. They'd branded themselves on my heart, and I feared I would never be free of the memory of our time together.

Unlocking the door, I held it open for Enzo and followed him inside. "You can put that on the table, please," I said as I hid my bags in the closet.

I placed the pastry box on the counter as Enzo pulled out the food containers that luckily came with plastic knives and forks, but I had no plates.

"Oh…" I opened the cupboards, hoping that some would magically appear. "I don't have anything to eat on." I turned to face Enzo, my hands on my hips.

"I don't mind sharing…with you," he said, leaning closer. His wavy hair fell forward, casting his eyes in shadow. I gripped the edge of the television stand behind me. All around us, the energy in the room felt charged, and my earlier unease washed away as I breathed in his cologne. He reminded me of the ocean.

"Um…as long as you're sure," I said as he reached out and grabbed the container and the baggie of utensils.

"Oh, I'm sure," he said, his arm brushing against mine as he stepped back.

Damn, I was going to need a cold shower after this. I fanned my face as I followed Enzo to the tiny table. He popped the lids off the containers, and I couldn't help staring at the muscles working in his toned forearm. I traced the tattoo on his arm with my eyes. The 3D detailing was exceptional. I was sure the carpet would fly free if I pulled on the pattern.

"You like it?" I was startled and looked up into Enzo's eyes. He was calmly staring back. "The tattoo. Do you like it?"

Clearing my throat, I nodded. "It's stunning."

"Thanks." Enzo took the lid and filled it with some food for himself, giving me the bottom of the container. I couldn't help feeling mildly disheartened that we weren't eating out of the same one.

"Why a Persian carpet pattern? Seems like an unusual choice."

"It's a family thing. My great-grandfather made carpets, and so did my grandfather and my father. I'm the only oddball in the family who chose a different path, but I couldn't help taking a little of the legacy when I struck out on my own."

"I love that. So what exactly do you do besides being a very gracious landlord?"

Enzo smiled, a dimple appearing on his cheek that made my heart flutter. I watched him eat a piece of chicken and wanted to know if he kissed as methodically as he ate. I blinked and shook my head. I wasn't in this town to find a man. I was here to strike out on my own and prove that I didn't need my family or a man. The voice in my head kept saying, 'Yeah, but that doesn't mean you can't have some fun along the way.'

"Electronics and sales, I have the gift of the gab," Enzo smirked, and I imagined he used that exact smile to get what he wanted many times. "So, what brought you to Beastville?"

"Oh...um...." I held up my finger and finished chewing to give myself an extra second to think. "I just needed a fresh start."

"Family or boyfriend issues," Enzo asked, and my body heated with embarrassment. Did I have it plastered on my forehead?

"I guess a bit of both." I stood up, needing to move away from his intense stare. "Did you want a bottle of water," I asked. Any topic other than me would be great.

"Sure."

As I stepped between our chairs, my toe caught, and I screamed as my knee twisted and I fell forward. Enzo snaked his arm around my waist, pulling me back, and I ended up frozen on his lap, staring into his eyes.

"Are you okay?"

"Yeah, I think so," I said, feeling stupid. When had I turned into such a klutz? Enzo moved in a little closer, and I was sure he would kiss me, but his phone rang. He closed his eyes and swore. I tried to stand, but Enzo didn't let go of my waist. His phone stopped, and he moved in, only to have it start again.

"I'm going to get up, and you better answer that. They seem insistent," I said, standing as he sighed and let me go.

Enzo growled a litany of profanities as he dug out his phone and answered it. I watched him stomp across the room and stare out the window as I pulled water bottles from the bar fridge.

"Boss?" His voice was tight with anger. "I'm having lunch. I am entitled to lunch." I couldn't hear the other side of the conversation, but Enzo's face slowly pulled into a dark scowl. "I see. I guess we need to talk about it when I get there. Yes, I'm leaving now."

He ran his hand through his hair and put the phone away, collecting himself before he spoke.

"I'm really sorry to cut our lunch short, but I need to get going."

"Wow, you weren't kidding about your boss being an ass," I said and he chuckled.

"Oh you know it. Listen, I had a great time. I'll let you know when the house is done." He came toward me, and with each step, the fluttering in my stomach increased until I felt like sprinting off. I had no idea what to do with my hands other than hold out a bottle of water like that was why he was walking across the room.

Enzo took the bottle, but his fingers lingered on mine. "Thank you." He turned and walked away but stopped when he reached the door. "Would you like to go on a date sometime?"

"Um...I...."

"You don't have to."

"No, it's not that. You know what...yes. Yes, I would." Enzo smiled wide, and I smiled back.

"Great, I'm looking forward to it." He left the room, and I flopped down into the chair at the table, my heart beating faster than a hummingbird's wings.

"What are you doing? You're not here to date," I scolded myself. But going five years without sex is a long time, and it was about time I did something just for me. Enzo seemed like he would be very interested in getting me back in the saddle.

I shuddered as images of riding him crossed my mind. It had to be the air here. Whatever it was...I liked it.

Chapter Twenty-Three

DARIO

"I'M GOING TO KILL HIM," Angelo swore as he stomped through the house. I finished sanding the drywall that needed to be replaced from the leak and wiped my hands off on a rag.

"Why?"

Angelo stopped mid-stride. "What do you mean why? I gave him a direct order, and he disobeyed it. I should shoot him in the head."

I rolled my eyes as a vehicle pulled into the driveway, and Angelo took off out of the room.

"This ought to be good," I said, grabbing my drink to watch the show. The yelling was almost immediate, and then there was a loud crash. I whistled as I wandered down the stairs. Spotting a loose board with some wood sticking up, I pulled the sandpaper from my back pocket to fix it.

"Fucker," Angelo growled as he and Enzo rolled through the hallway into the living room and back again. Exchanging blows like kids in the schoolyard.

"I'm allowed to fucking spend time with her," Enzo said.

"No, you're not."

I ran my hand over the wood, happy it was smooth, and Jasmine wouldn't get a splinter. There were so many other issues I never paid attention to before, but I wanted this place perfect for her.

"Yes, I am."

There was another loud crash, and I shook my head as I stood to break up the childish argument.

Walking into the living room, I sat my drink down and grabbed Angelo by the back of his T-shirt and jeans before heaving his ass onto the couch.

"Hey!" He growled as he glared at me with his gun in his hand.

I picked up Enzo and pushed him backward until his ass found the chair on the opposite side of the room.

I pointed at Angelo. "If you point that thing at me, you better use it." He narrowed his eyes but lowered the gun.

"I wasn't planning on shooting you, just him." Angelo nodded at Enzo, who was dabbing at the blood dripping from his nose. I tossed the rag his way.

"Fuck you, Angelo," Enzo snarled.

"The pair of you are idiots who both look stupid. If Jasmine were in this room right now, she'd leave disgusted."

Enzo glared at Angelo. "He started it."

"Shut up. You're not making this any better. How did I end up the fucking voice of reason?" I flopped down onto the couch beside Angelo.

"Do you really want to shoot him," I asked and picked up my drink.

"I want him to keep his hands off what's mine. That's what I want."

"She's not a thing. She's a person and, therefore, cannot be yours. You aren't buying a bottle of alcohol off a shelf," Enzo argued.

"Enough. Holy fuck, you sound like ignorant ass wipes, and you're making my head hurt." I rubbed my forehead. The headache these two caused made me want to choke them both.

"Angelo, is Enzo your friend or not?" I asked, trying for reason.

"I'm not sure anymore."

"Just answer yes or no," I said.

"Fine. Yes."

"Enzo, is Angelo, your friend?"

He crossed his arms and looked away. "I thought so."

"Oh, for fuck's sake. Just answer yes or no. This is not that difficult," I growled.

"Fuck...yes, he's my friend."

"Great, then let's set some ground rules. Angelo, you go first."

He growled under his breath and stormed from the room.

"I'm not doing this," he said, stomping out of the room and slamming the front door behind him.

Enzo shook his head. "He's impossible."

"Didn't I tell you to shut the fuck up?"

"But..."

Grabbing my knife from my boot, I whipped it at Enzo. It cut off a tuft of his hair as it whizzed past his head and lodged in the wall behind him.

"Geezus fuck," he swore and looked over his shoulder, his eyes wide.

"Now, let's have a little talk, and just in case I wasn't clear, I'm doing the talking, and you're going to sit there and listen." I relaxed back on the couch and stared at Enzo.

Did I classify him as a friend? I guess I did. I had considered Angelo my only friend until we were forced to go on the run together. After my sister died, I had a hard time letting anyone in, which was what made Jasmine so special. She never tried to heal me or pity me. She never looked down on me from the pedestal I placed her on. Jasmine treated me with kindness and compassion even when I didn't deserve it. I had finally gotten her to whisper 'I love you' in my ear, and then Angelo and I broke her heart. She made my heart beat. I didn't feel dead inside with her, and the need to fix what was stolen was so strong that it took everything I had not to storm that hotel room and grovel at her feet. I understood Angelo even if I didn't fully agree with how he treated Enzo now.

"You will not antagonize Angelo about Jasmine. You're also not going to go all cowboy like you did today and do whatever you want."

"But...." Enzo shut his mouth as I pulled the second knife out of my boot.

"What did I say?"

Enzo slowly leaned back in the chair.

"You won't do either of those things out of respect. Regardless of the situation we find ourselves in, Angelo is still the son of a powerful Don, and if he ever finds a way to restore his power, we are nothing but soldiers once more. Do you understand that?"

Enzo sighed and nodded.

"Good. I know you like to think we are all equal, but we're not, and Jasmine could never marry either of us, her father would never allow it even if she wanted to. Jasmine Falcone is a princess. So if you want to have a shot at this long term and not just a fly-by-night fuck, you had better start showing Angelo and his love for Jasmine a little respect. Or you will find your throat slit, and if Angelo doesn't do it...." I stood up and stared down at Enzo. "I will."

He swallowed hard. "I just don't want to be cut out, and I know Angelo doesn't want me involved. I have never wanted anyone like this before. She is...I won't walk away."

"I will speak to him and make sure that doesn't happen, but when you purposely try to get under his skin like today, you're only making shit worse. I can't believe I have to say this but grow the fuck up."

"You really are a miserable prick sometimes," Enzo grumbled.

"I am, but I also know this will only work if we are all on the same page. So get on the fucking page and stop trying to re-write shit. You have no idea what Angelo and I went through to get back to Jasmine. The things we did would make your skin crawl. If I have to have this discussion with you again...."

He held up his hands. "I'm not going to stop poking at him, it's way too much fun, but...I will get on the same page. I don't want to lose Angelo as a friend, I think of him as family. I really do like her though."

"Yeah? Try pining over her for five years and tell me how you feel then." Marching out the door, I slammed it behind me. I found Angelo looking out over the pond at the far edge of the property. "You good?"

"I can't lose her again," Angelo said.

"We won't."

Angelo slowly turned around, and there was a hint of something I rarely saw in his eyes...vulnerability.

"I hurt her so bad...Enzo is a fresh slate. What if I can't overcome what happened?"

"Fucking stop saying I. We were both involved, and we both left. We didn't come back, and we both stopped taking her calls. We broke her heart."

"Dario, don't fucking try that with me. You would've gone back if you weren't such a loyal fucker to me. We also know you had no choice but to go, and you hated cutting off contact." A flock of black birds took flight, and we watched them soar overhead, their wings flapping as they squawked about something.

"That doesn't matter, we're in this together."

"I am not an insecure man, but fucking Enzo...he's her type. He's a decent guy. She deserves someone like that in her life. What can I offer her now?"

"Have you ever stopped to consider that she never wanted to marry you because you were the son of a Don?"

"You're right, but talking her into it so she didn't have to marry someone else doesn't bode well either."

I didn't give it a second thought before I pushed Angelo hard in the chest. He yelled as he flew backward off the grassy edge and splashed hard in the stagnant water. Sluggish green crap hit my legs a second before he completely submerged.

Angelo slowly stood up with green algae hanging off his shirt and jeans and a lily pad sitting on his head. For the first time in years,

I laughed. I laughed so hard that tears trailed down my cheeks, and I had to sit down.

"You fucking asshole," Angelo said, but there was no heat to his voice, and a second later he laughed as well.

He flicked the lily pad off his head, and I held my stomach, laughing harder. One squishy footstep at a time, he walked up the bank and plopped down beside me.

"I guess I deserved that," he said once we'd quieted down.

"Don't ever fucking doubt yourself again. It doesn't look good on you," I said as I pushed myself to my feet and held out my hand. "Now let's get you cleaned up, you fucking stink like swamp water."

"Asshole." Angelo smirked and slapped his hand in mine. "I do have an idea, but I don't think you'll like it."

Maybe I liked him better when he was unsure of himself.

Chapter Twenty-Four

JASMINE

A WEEK HAD PASSED since Enzo moved me back into the rental house, and I'd hardly seen him since. When he did drop by, there were no lingering glances or flirting like before. Well, there was a little bit, but it was strange now. It was almost like he thought I would bite him or something. How had I managed to scare him off so quickly?

I wiped the sweat off my brow with the back of my hand and rolled out my shoulders. I looked up and down the rows set up in the greenhouse and smiled. I followed everything exactly how the book said, and it was starting to really take shape.

And bonus, at least I couldn't make a fool of myself with the plants. Then again, maybe they would shrivel up and die to escape me.

"Stop that," I scolded, patting the dirt softly over the last seed I planted. "That's not why you came here, and I won't allow moping."

I placed my little card in the dirt that indicated this line was cucumbers and decided that was enough for today. Humming, I tugged at the gardening gloves. I needed a small radio to hang in here. I missed the extensive music selection on my phone. Hours were spent creating playlists of my favorite music or from books I loved, but there was no way to bring my phone with me. I didn't dare open an account, even under a fake persona. I was born into the mafia and knew just how far their reach went. I couldn't take that chance. So a cheap pay as you go burner was all I dared to have.

Opening the door to the house, I paused and looked over my shoulder at the neatly manicured boxes and smiled. There was something so satisfying about doing this. I still had a ton of work to do, including building a roadside stand, but first, I needed the fruit and veggies to grow.

I grabbed water and cheese from the fridge and a small handful of crackers for my little pets. The tank now had a nest of fabric, straw, and wood chips.

"Hey there, Hick, Dick, and Dock." I chimed sweetly in a soft voice.

It was a little creepy whenever the large nest moved like the ball was alive and breathing. Dock poked his nose out first. It was easy to tell them apart once you got to know them.

Reaching in, I poured some water into their dish to top it off, then broke apart the crackers into tinier pieces and did the same to the cheese. By the time I finished, all three were out and happily eating.

"I know I need to get you some proper food. How about a wheel? I hear they are all the rage. I smiled as they looked up at me but continued eating. "Okay, fine maybe not, rough crowd."

A car rumbled past, and I looked out the window, but the sound faded after the brief flash of headlights. I didn't think I could get any lonelier than back home, but I was wrong. It was a different kind of loneliness in Italy. There were people to say good morning to or share a cup of coffee with, but here, I only had my thoughts to keep me company.

"Night, guys," I said to my little roommates, flicking off the light as I wandered to the stairs. I wasn't a chicken, but it was dark here. That was something else I wasn't used to, and after the first night of complete exhaustion, I hadn't slept well. I had a sleep aid, but I hated taking it. The medicine caused strange dreams and made me sluggish the next day.

Stepping into the bathroom, I opened the cupboard and pulled out the Absolem bottle. I needed sleep, and I could feel myself getting irrational and jumpy over nothing. Sitting the bottle aside, I quickly stripped and hopped into the shower. Tomorrow was a new day with new challenges, and I was determined to meet at least one new person in this town. Stepping out of my comfort zone was my new motto.

ANGELO

Fuck me, she was stunning. Enzo had set up an entire wall of monitors to watch Jasmine's house, and pathetically, I hadn't moved from this room since Enzo dropped her off days ago. I took my business calls, ate, and slept on the couch while watching her every move and only left to shower. I'd even turned the storage area into a small closet. I was officially losing my mind.

I watched her now as she slipped out of her adorable jumper and t-shirt. With each layer she removed, my cock grew harder. This was torture. Jasmine was giving me the worst case of blue balls.

"You watching her," Dario asked as he walked in and set the mail down on my desk.

"Yup."

"Jesus, is she naked?"

I could hear the heavy breathing from across the room and knew Dario was as captivated as I was.

"We shouldn't be watching this. It's pervy."

Ignoring Dario, I shivered as she tilted her head back under the shower and pressed her tits up in the air. I licked my lips, remembering how she tasted. My Tiger was as sweet as fresh honey drizzled on strawberries.

"Angelo?"

I jerked at the sound of my name and realized I'd leaned in until my face almost touched the screen.

"What?" I growled, not bothering to look at my friend or acknowledge the disgust I knew was on his face. "If you're going to tell me to stop watching, you can forget it."

"Fine, whatever."

Jasmine stepped out of the shower, the water droplets like tiny gems on her skin. She picked up a bottle by the sink, and the corner of my mouth lifted as she drank two spoonfuls. Yes, this was what I'd been waiting for. While in her room, I'd taken the opportunity to look around and see if I could find any clues as to why or how she ended up here. I'd not only stolen myself a pair of her underwear—that was in my pocket, and I rubbed them like they were a fucking stress ball—but I also noticed she had Absolem. This was the first time I saw her take it, and the excitement grew in my chest as she changed and slipped under the covers.

"Tonight is the night," I said.

"For what," Enzo asked as he walked into the room, eating out of a bag of potato chips.

I'd hoped to get out of here before Enzo returned, but no such luck. "Tonight, Jasmine starts to fall back in love with me."

"Us," Dario and Enzo chimed together, making me grind my teeth.

I waved my hands at them. "Yes, us."

"What exactly are we doing? You've been very secretive all week about your plan," Dario said, crossing his arms over his chest. I knew he would hate this idea, but I didn't care.

Striding to the closet to change for the night's activities, I opened the door and stared at the clothes I'd stashed in there.

"We are going to go over to Jasmine's house and make sure she has an amazing dream about us," I said casually.

Dario narrowed his eyes at me, looking too much like the judgmental portrait on the wall. I made a mental note to get rid of the thing. I never liked it to begin with.

"And how exactly are we going to do that?"

I glanced between Enzo and Dario, then shrugged.

"It is as easy as it sounds. We go over there and pleasure Jasmine in every way possible."

The two men looked at one another and then back at me.

"Just like that? Knock on her door, convince her to have sex with us, and poof, like magic, she'll be in love with us again. Forget all the baggage and hurt and her fiancé?"

"Don't be ridiculous, Dario. We aren't knocking. We're taking what we want."

The monitors showed her still awake, but she was yawning, and I knew it wouldn't be long until she was under the power of the sleeping medication—my little godsend.

"What? Oh, hell no. I'm not raping her," Enzo said as he glared at me. "And neither are you, that's just fucked up."

"I can't believe you'd even suggest this," Dario said, shaking his head at me in disgust.

I went to my desk and opened the top drawer to pull out three simple black masks similar to those worn at a masquerade ball. I tossed one at Dario and then Enzo.

"You can either come with me or stay here, but I'm doing this."

"Angelo...." Dario balled his fists. "We can't do this to her."

Marching to my best friend, I got right up in his face, the rage in my gut overriding everything else.

"Do not fucking tell me what I can and cannot do. Jasmine was my fiancé first, and she consented to non-consent. You were there to witness it and neither has been rescinded. She is still mine until she is married to someone else, and I will do whatever I need to, whether you think it is ethical or not. So, either get on board or stay here and watch the show. I don't fucking care." I turned around and walked to the door. "Are you two coming or not?"

"Fuck me," Dario grumbled and tied the mask on his head. "I'm pretty sure there is a statute of limitations on consent. I mean it's been five years."

"Says who?" I grabbed my gun and shoved it into the back of my jeans. "You don't make the rules. Jasmine Falcone handed herself over to me, and I'm not standing by and letting Ciro steal her from under my nose. Not when she is this fucking close. She needs to remember how much she wanted us and loved us. I'm telling you this is our second chance, and you're either going to take it with me, or you're going to stand here and jerk off while watching me do what you couldn't."

"Is he telling the truth? Did she agree to CNC?"

I rolled my eyes as Enzo pointed at me but spoke to Dario.

"Yeah, he is," Dario answered. "I still can't believe we're doing this, but yeah, I'm in. If for no other reason than to make sure you don't go overboard with this stupid plan."

"Well, shit. You're not leaving me out, but I do have one request," Enzo said, tying his mask in place.

"What's that?"

"I want to help her at the house tomorrow and take her to dinner. You might not be

able to show your face, but I can. Before you say no, think about it this way. It's better that she is with me and not someone else from town. I can maybe even find out more about why she's here."

I couldn't stand that he had a point. "I'll think about it. Now that's settled, let's get the fuck out of here."

Our boots thumped along the marble foyer in time with my racing heart. This was stage one of my plan, and by the time we moved on to stage two, we would be all that Jasmine thought about.

I smirked and felt like my old self as we stepped out into the night.

You'd better get ready, Tiger. Your real fiancé is coming to claim you.

Chapter Twenty-Five

ANGELO

UNLOCKING THE DOOR, I pushed it open, careful not to make a sound. I knew this house like the back of my hand. When we first moved here, this was where we lived until I got the distillery going and offered the owner enough cash to move away. We took over the main house and started renting this the moment his ass was out the door.

The only sound was the soft shuffle of feet of the men behind me. We slipped up the stairs like ghosts, our shadows slinking along the walls from the soft glow of the hallway nightlight.

I clenched my hand into a fist to try and push away the nervousness as we reached her bedroom door. As quietly as I could, in case Jasmine was not yet sound asleep, I twisted the old brass knob. When the door opened, I held my breath as my heart tripled, thundering like a million galloping horses.

The past flashed before my eyes as I stared at her sleeping form. Her black hair was spread across the pillow, and her eyes were closed as she breathed deeply. Stepping into the room, I couldn't look away from my Tiger. I could watch her like this every night and feel content.

My shirt was off and tossed to the wall before I reached the bed. Grabbing the blankets, I pulled them down her body and smiled at the adorable sleep outfit. The flowy tank top and matching shorts were as sexy as any skimpy lace, but she could wear a fucking paper bag and turn me on. Time apart had not diminished any feelings I had for her.

"You sure you want to do this?" Dario whispered.

"There is nothing I want more." Leaning over Jasmine, I breathed in her fresh soap and shampoo scent. "I've missed you, Tiger," I said.

Her brow furrowed, and she moved her lips, but no sound came out. I could only imagine what she would say if she woke up. A punch to the face would be the first thing that happened, and I would kiss those knuckles and still fuck her.

"Do you miss me, Tiger?" I whispered in her ear. "Do you still touch yourself when you think of me?"

She made an adorable growling sound, and a mumbled, annoyed version of my name fell from her lips.

"That's right, I'm here."

I slid my hand under the flowy top, and as soon as I touched her warm skin, I knew I would kill anyone who got in my way again. I didn't give a fuck who it was. I would put a bullet between their eyes. Her father included.

"You're so beautiful." My thumb ran over her nipple, and it hardened at my touch. I wanted to rip her clothes off and fuck her in every position I could think of, then hold her until she woke up. I needed her sharp nails and angry words, and then I would fuck her again.

I grabbed the front of her top.

"Stop," Dario hissed at me. I turned my head to glare at him. "Do you want her to have a pleasant dream of us or a nightmare? You can't rip her clothes off. She's going to freak out. You can't leave a bruise on her body or anything out of place. This must be covert, yes?"

I snarled at my friend, then took a steadying breath. He was right. I was acting crazy. I blamed my father. He sent me to America without instruction or warning of what was expected of me, and it was a bloodbath. I tortured and killed over a dozen people in my first week. It had changed me, and not for the better.

My eyes focused on my clenched hands, and I slowly let go of her top, ready to move away before I did something else stupid, but my Tiger laid her hand on mine. I stood frozen. Would she wake up? Did I want her to?

"Take her shorts off," I ordered, but Dario didn't move. I looked over at him, but he wasn't staring at me. His eyes were transfixed on Jasmine's face. The bitter, hard lines I'd gotten so used to seeing were gone. "Dario. Shorts. Off. Now," I whispered harshly, and he jerked as his eyes refocused on me.

He knelt on the bed and gently lifted her hips to remove her shorts. My brow raised when he stood and folded them neatly before laying them on the dresser. There was no point in saying she wouldn't notice a wrinkle. He'd always been like this when it came to Jasmine. He could crush a man's skull—I'd seen it with my own eyes—and yet, with her, he made me look like a barbarian.

"Now what," Dario asked, crossing his arms over his chest.

I pointedly looked at my hand. Jasmine had now linked our fingers together. "I'm stuck, so you pleasure her."

"I don't feel right doing this," he said.

"For fuck's sake, Dario, would it make you feel better if it was an order? I'm ordering you to make her come. Happy now?"

"I think I hate you," Dario growled as he got on the bed and slowly spread her legs.

"What do you want me to do," Enzo asked.

"Lay beside her," I said, and Enzo crawled along the bed until he could stretch out next to her.

"Mmmm, she smells so good," Enzo murmured. I lost sight of his head as he buried it into her neck, and she moaned softly.

Mirroring his position, I nuzzled my Tiger's neck and sucked on the sensitive spot I knew so well. Her hand tightened in mine.

She moaned louder this time, and I glanced down to see Dario swirling his tongue between her legs. Aching did not accurately describe how badly I wanted to be inside her. I needed to find a way to make her forgive me.

"You still want me, don't you, Tiger?" Her mouth opened, and her back arched slightly. Taking advantage, I kissed her lips but let her take the lead. A shiver ran through my body as she kissed me back. For just a blink, I could pretend that nothing had changed.

"You want me to fuck you until you pass out, don't you," I mumbled against her lips. "You've been dreaming of the day we are reunited. You've always been mine." She whispered my name, and I growled against her lips. "Yes, Tiger, you'll never be rid of me. I'm never letting you go again."

Her chest heaved as her breathing quickened, and unable to help myself, I lifted her top far enough to get at her breasts. I almost growled at Enzo when he took the opportunity to suck on the one closest to him. Dropping my head to her other nipple, she squeezed my hand tight.

"Oh...."

Jasmine's eyes were still closed, but the whimpers were getting louder as Dario continued to coax the climax from her.

"That's it, Tiger, let go. Come for us, like the naughty girl I know you are." Jasmine moaned loudly, her body softly bucking up into Dario's face. "Come in Dario's mouth," I said, cooing to her. I nipped at her ear lobes and whispered every dirty thing I wanted to do to her. "Scream, like you used to."

With a small cry, she came, and Dario groaned as he furiously licked until her body slumped against the bed. He slowly sat up, and I smirked at the drunk look on his face. No matter how much he protested, he wanted her as badly as I did.

"Should we get going," Enzo asked, and I shook my head no.

"We'll let her rest for a bit, and then it's my turn to make her come," I said, slipping my fingers out from Jasmine's lax grip.

"But what if she wakes up?"

"She won't, not for a few hours yet. Plenty of time for all of us to make this a dream she will never forget."

Pushing myself up from the bed, I wandered over to the large chair in the corner and sat down as Dario took the spot I left vacant beside her. I needed to get control before I pushed shit too far, too fast. Pulling out my cock I stroked it hard and fast, the sound loud in the now quiet room.

"Fuck, you drive me crazy," I growled as I came all over my chest. "Fuck Tiger, you made me make a mess of myself."

Dario snorted. "Not the first time."

"Shit, I need to do that too," Enzo said and swapped spots with me as I walked to the bathroom.

"Don't get a single drop anywhere," I snarled at him. I was still butt hurt that he could do something that I couldn't, and that was show my face. If Jasmine didn't already hate me for leaving and cutting off contact, she hated me for stealing her family heirloom.

I quickly washed off my chest, not that it mattered. I would come again before the night was through. She'd always made me come more than once.

Opening the medicine cabinet, I looked through all her items, to see if there was anything new. I didn't find much when she was at the hotel, but now that she was back, I found what I needed. I immediately picked up the package of birth control.

"Oh, we can't have this," I mumbled. I looked under the cabinet and found a year's supply tucked away in a simple paper bag. Checking the brand name, I knew just who to call to get a placebo made. Maybe my old plan would work after all. Don Caruso would never let his son marry a princess pregnant with another man's child. Especially a fugitive shunned from his own family.

I glanced out to the bedroom as Enzo groaned, but he didn't hold my attention. Dario lay on his side and read the book from her nightstand aloud. How was he so calm? He flipped the page and continued reading, and I envied his resolve.

I quickly put everything back the way I found it before walking out to the room and kneeling on the bed. Using my tongue, I drew long, wet lines along the inside of her thighs until I reached my prize.

Some would call me an asshole, I called myself morally broken. Whichever I was didn't matter as long as Jasmine Falcone was mine.

Chapter Twenty-Six

JASMINE

GASPING, I sat up straight and looked around for Angelo, Dario, and Enzo while my heart pounded. I lifted the blanket and stared down at my body, but I was still fully clothed. Jumping from the bed, I stared at it before running my hands over the sheets, but they were dry and clean.

"What the hell?"

Leaning down, I sniffed the pillow, but it smelled like the fabric softener. I turned in a small circle, my eyes searching every corner and shadow like they would suddenly step out from the walls.

"That felt so real," I whispered, and then got down and looked under the bed.

Realistically, I knew that all three of them wouldn't fit under here, but I'd never had a dream like that. Pushing myself up, I looked for any sign that I wasn't so desperate for a man that I conjured three of them in an erotic dream. There wasn't a hair or a single speck of dirt on the floor.

At this point, I wasn't sure if I was impressed with my mind or horrified that I dreamed about three men taking turns pleasuring me for hours. Walking to the bathroom, I looked in the mirror but saw no marks on my neck. When I lifted my nightshirt, my breasts looked as unmarred as before I went to sleep.

Opening the medicine cabinet, I pulled out the Absolem and decided it had to be a bad batch, tossed the bottle in the garbage, and walked out to get dressed. Dammit, why did I have to dream about Angelo and Dario? I could see how Enzo was on my mind, but not the two men that broke my heart. Leaning on the dresser, I gripped the edge until my knuckles turned white as the old emotions tried to poke their head from where I'd stuffed them. I couldn't do it again. I couldn't go back to longing for them and going to sleep every night, hopeful they would walk through the door and explain what happened.

I'd already had to face the reality once that I meant nothing to them. Why was I so ready to torture myself all over again? Closing my eyes, I took a deep breath.

"It was just a sexy dream. Everyone has them. You just chose to think about the only three men you've ever had those kinds of thoughts about. That was normal. Why would you conjure a stranger?"

Talking out loud seemed to help, and the anger and sadness simmered. Yanking open the drawers, I tossed my clothes on the bed. I quickly changed, and even though it was crazy, I could still feel their eyes on me. A thought occurred to me, and I ran to the bed and picked up the book, but it was where Dream Dario had left off reading. I remembered reading before falling asleep, but didn't think I got this far. Did I?

"Wow, you're losing it. Dario did not sneak in here to give you the best oral sex and then read you a book. Like hello, fairytale land," I mocked, slamming the book down.

I stomped out of the bedroom and then stopped and closed my eyes. Stepping back, I stared into the bathroom, and it felt like the bottle of Absolem was staring back, taunting me and telling me that I was a chicken.

"Shit," I grumbled, fishing the bottle out of the garbage. I didn't have a doctor yet, and this was not easy to come by. It could've been a combination of the long day, what I ate, all my fears, and the sleeping meds. That was plausible. I set the bottle in the cabinet and quickly scanned the room, but everything was in place.

"Get a grip, Jasmine, it was just a dream. A hot dream, but just a dream," I scolded myself as I stomped out the door to make breakfast. I'd never baked, but I was determined to learn and follow the biscuit recipe like it was the word of God.

I had just put them in the oven and was whipping together eggs for an omelet when there was a knock. Poking my head out of the kitchen, I stared at the door. I had no idea why. It wasn't like it would announce who was there.

"Isabella?" Enzo's muffled voice came through, and I quickly sat the bowl down, panic racing through my body. I glanced down at my flour-covered shirt and groaned. Why did I always look a mess when he showed up?

Dusting myself off as I walked the plank to the door, I opened it just as Enzo had reached the bottom step.

"Hey," I said, my cheeks flooding with heat as he smiled.

Please, dear God, I didn't want the fact that I had an erotic dream about him to show on my face. I had enough issues.

"Hey, yourself. Is this a bad time?" Enzo glanced at my sweater, and I wiped at it a little more as my embarrassment ratcheted up to the likes of which I didn't know possible.

"I was baking. If you're brave, you can be my first victim," I said, forcing my hands to stop fidgeting.

"Do you have coffee?"

A smile spread across my face. "Colombian or Peruvian?"

"Oh fancy, I like it." He stepped up to the top step, and I quickly looked away from his eyes as I pictured them between my legs. Holy hell, what was in the water at this place? "Did you need me to help you?"

My mouth fell open as the words, *Let me help you feel good, beautiful*, drifted through my mind.

Enzo pointed toward the kitchen. "I think I smell a pan burning."

"Oh shit, the eggs." I bolted for the open doorway and stupidly grabbed the metal handle of the smoking pan and hissed, dropping it as it burned my palm. "Ouch!" I shook out my burnt hand.

"Shit, are you okay?" Enzo flicked off the stove and guided me to the sink.

I turned on the cold water, but he grabbed my arm before I could stick my hand under the tap. "Never use cold, only lukewarm." His face was calm as he adjusted the temperature and helped ease my hand under the spray.

I bit my lip hard as I beat back the pain throbbing up my arm. "Why am I such a mess lately? I went from being a boss lady and in control to this."

"You're still a boss lady. You're incredible."

I turned my head to look up at Enzo. His eyes seemed so sincere, the silvery depths filled with compassion. My gaze dropped to his lips, inches away from mine. The heat from his body spread and reminded me why I was so flustered. Luckily, the buzzer on the oven went off, breaking the building tension.

"I'll get that. You keep your hand under the water." I heard the squeak of the old hinges behind me as I closed my eyes to steady myself. The pain in my hand was not the worst I'd ever experienced. That pain wasn't visual and wasn't something that ever went away. The loss of my mother to cancer had been crushing and almost destroyed my papa.

I stared at the swirling water and understood his need to try and protect me. Maybe he was right. Perhaps I couldn't be out here alone and make it. Tears stung the back of my eyes. I wouldn't cry in front of Enzo again.

"Here, let me look at your hand." I blinked back the tears and faced Enzo as he turned off the water. "I found this in the first aid kit in the greenhouse." I looked down. Between the strange dream last night and another embarrassing display, I just couldn't look him in the eyes.

"My Nonna used to call me Birichino. I was always doing something crazy and reckless," Enzo said as he dabbed disinfectant onto my hand.

"You think I'm reckless for coming here when I so obviously don't have a clue about anything?"

He stopped dabbing on the cool liquid. "No, of course not. I think just the opposite. As I got older, I stopped taking big chances, but you are striking out on your own and doing something new. I think it's brave."

"How do you know I've never lived on my own?" I narrowed my eyes at him.

"Oh...I...just the way you talked, I just assumed that...shit. I'm sorry, I shouldn't have said anything." He sat the liquid down and picked up the cotton wrap.

"You're not wrong. I'm just pissed that I seem that pampered, is all."

"You don't seem pampered," he said, and I gave him a don't be ridiculous look. "Okay, fine, maybe a little pampered." As our eyes met, we both started to laugh. It felt good to laugh again.

"Oh my god, I'm pathetic. I can't even cook eggs without hurting myself. I mean, who does that?" I pointed at the stove, caught sight of my biscuits, and groaned. They looked terrible.

Enzo followed my line of sight. "They look worse than they taste. I mean, they taste good," he quickly added. He finished tying the bandage on my hand and smiled. "How about I take you out for breakfast, and I can give you that tour I promised?"

"Fine, but only if I can pay for something this time. You were way too generous last time, and those caneles de bordeaux you left at the hotel were amazing. How did you know they are my favorite?" I smiled as he blushed.

"Just a guess. I love them, too. Come on, let's get some breakfast before you burn the house down."

"Rude," I said as we laughed. Normal had no meaning to me. When you were born a princess in a mafia family, there simply was no such thing, but if I had to picture what it was like, then this would be it. I liked it.

ANGELO

Swearing, I slammed my fist into the dash of Dario's pickup truck.

"Hey man, knock it the fuck off," Dario growled as he shot me a dark look.

"Fucking guy, I swear I'm going to kill him. *I think you're incredible*," I mocked. "*Why don't I take you out to breakfast*." I glared out the passenger side window, trying to control the rage taking over my body. When that happened, people died.

"You sound like a fucking child pouting over having to share your toys." He shook his head at me, and if we weren't traveling a hundred miles an hour down an interstate, I would've punched him in the face.

"Do it, and I swear I'll stop at the first bridge I come to, drag you out, and throw you over," Dario said. I snarled at him with a few choice words but looked away.

"I'm not like you. I can't sit by and watch Enzo do all the things I want to do and can't."

"You think I'm okay with it?"

"Well, you sure as fuck don't seem worked up about it," I said as we passed a cluster of old run-down farms. If they weren't so far away from the other property, I would look at buying them up, but we were already forty minutes outside of anything I would entertain.

"I just don't let myself get all worked up over something I can't control. I wanted to punch you in the face every time you bullied

Jasmine, but I didn't. I wanted to date her, but my status would never allow it, so I didn't. I had no interest in leaving Jasmine behind when you got the call from your father, but I went. I've spent my entire life knowing that I'll end up doing shit that I don't want to."

Looking at his profile, I saw the tension in his jaw return. The angry lines at the corner of his eyes were once more in place.

"I guess I never looked at it that way," I said.

"Why would you? You were born never having to worry about what you wanted until you set your eyes on Jasmine. Until that moment, anything you desired was at your fingertips. Even now, you attack everything like it is owed to you, but Jasmine won't jump when you snap your fingers. She may even bite them off," Dario said, and even though he was serious, I couldn't help but laugh at the visual that popped into my head.

"You're right about that. Tiger has a killer instinct." I didn't doubt that she would try to rip out my throat if she found out about my night excursions. But watching her jump from the bed and look underneath was priceless. Fuck, I loved her, and last night had done nothing but make me crave her more.

"So you're saying I was born with a silver spoon in my mouth?"

"I'm saying that we view the world and our opportunities differently." Dario glanced over at me. "Enzo's involvement pisses you off because lines are blurred. He is here because Jasmine likes him. I don't piss you off because I've always been at your beck and call."

I opened my mouth to argue but snapped it shut. Fuck he was right. I hated it when he was right. Dario had been by my side from such a young age that he grew into the role of best friend and bodyguard. I trusted him with my life and, in this case, Jasmine. Enzo was my friend, but I didn't know him as well, and Jasmine's interest in him made me feel out of control. I didn't do out of control.

"Fuck. I still don't like that Enzo's taking her out, no matter the reason."

"Then be mad. I don't care, but don't punch my fucking truck," Dario grumbled as we pulled off the interstate.

I could see the condo building I owned in the distance. It wouldn't be open for another seven months, but once it was, it would be extremely lucrative and would help me move around some of the not-so-legal money from my underground casino.

We pulled into the parking lot and saw men up on the scaffolding working and walking across the steel beams. My father never thought I would amount to anything without him, but I made a shit ton of money and did it on my own, keeping pretty much everything legal. I was fucking impressed with myself.

Matt, my head contractor, was leaning over a table looking at blueprints when he spotted the truck. I watched him closely as he spoke to Nicolas, my foreman on the job sites, before walking over. I made it my business to know everyone who worked for me. I knew their names, family, criminal history, and where they liked to spend their time and money. You never knew when that information would be useful.

"Mr. Esposito, what a pleasure to see you today. As you can see, the building is coming along right on schedule."

I gave him a small smile for his effort. "Indeed it is. Why don't you hop in the back? We are going out for breakfast," I said casually, but Matt hesitated and swallowed hard. A single stream of sweat trickled down the side of his face despite the cool breeze today.

"I really should stay and work," he finally said.

I lowered my sunglasses and gave him the full weight of my stare. "Get in the fucking truck, or I'll consider it disrespectful, and that will anger me. You don't want to anger me."

"No, no, of course not."

Matt yelled to Nicholas that he would be back and hopped into the back seat. Unfortunately for Matt, unless I liked the answers I got from him, he would never be going home again.

"What's the special occasion," Matt asked as Dario pulled out of the parking lot.

"I don't discuss business on an empty stomach. Do you like waffles, Matt?" I didn't wait for him to answer. I didn't give a fuck what he said. “I do. I like them cooked golden brown and loaded with fresh fruit, and I know just the place.”

“Sounds great,” Matt said, then sat back and didn’t say another word, like a scolded child.

“Great, indeed,” I mumbled.

Chapter Twenty-Seven

ANGELO

I PULLED the knife out of Matt's shoulder, and his scream echoed along the walls of the abandoned warehouse—a stark contrast to the sunlight that pooled in the windows.

I owned everything in this shit part of Beastville. The area had become rundown with time, weather, fire, and abuse. While others saw it as nothing more than a place for the homeless and drug dealers to hang out, I saw it as a prime opportunity. The land was practically given away and was only a ten-minute drive from the city's main hub. With money and some TLC, I planned on turning this into an upscale shopping district with a hotel to rival anything in New York.

Beastville was a smaller community, but the tourism was prime and ripe for the picking with nearby attractions, beaches, and nightclubs. It also helped that there was a rampant number of motorcycle clubs and mobsters looking to spend and launder their money. Which, of course, gave me the perfect excuse to move my underground and very illegal casino above ground.

"You know, Matt, I was really hoping you would tell me I was wrong, and we could've avoided all of this." I slowly waved my hand up and down to indicate his badly beaten body.

"Please, please," he begged.

I rolled out my shoulders while sweat dripped down my back. I looked over at Dario, who hadn't moved from his post by the door, watching for anyone who came this way. He looked like a fucking statue. I didn't even know if he blinked.

Walking over to Matt, I cast my shadow over his body. He blinked out of the eye, not swollen completely shut, as he rolled his head up to look at me.

"Please," he blubbered again, blood and spit dripping from his mouth to join the tears trailing down his cheeks.

"This would go so much smoother if you would answer the question. Where is my money?"

He cried and said please repeatedly, which was really starting to piss me the fuck off. Like I needed one more thing in my life to piss me off?

My knuckles cracked across his jaw, the sound of my large rings connecting as loud as his wails. His head fell forward as he blubbered. I stomped away and picked up the folder of paperwork that held the evidence against him.

"I asked you a fucking question," I growled as I squatted before him. Smacking Matt across the face with the folder seemed to startle him, and he lifted his head to look at me. "I know you've been stealing from me. You've been padding the invoices and taking the extra money. I will let you live, and you can scurry off to be with your family as long as you move very fucking far away. But I want my money. No money, no living. Do you understand?"

"I don't have it," he said so softly I hardly caught the words.

"Say that again? I thought you just said that you don't have three-quarters of a million dollars anymore. I couldn't have heard you properly." I chuckled as I gave him a fake smile, but his split bottom lip quivered as he shook his head back and forth.

"I don't have it," he said again. "Please don't kill me, I'll get it back."

Standing, I walked over to the steel bench and slammed the folder down with a thud.

"What did you do with my money?" I was quickly losing my patience.

"I spent it."

"Well, I gathered that. What did you spend my money on," I asked, picking up my knife as I turned to face Matt. His eyes focused on the sharp blade I'd used to stab him multiple times in places that wouldn't kill him but would hurt like a son of a bitch. Blood pooled on the floor around the chair he was tied to, but I would drain him dry until I got the answer I was after. If this idiot bought a boat or a fancy car, I could re-coop some of my money, but if he snorted it up his nose or went on trips, I had no way of getting any of it back.

"I went on a cruise and got divorced. I needed the money to pay off my wife," he said. "She was trying to kick me out of the house." He broke down again, and I almost felt sorry for him. Not that I'd ever been married, but I knew what crazy things love and hate could make you do. The difference between me and Matt was that I never intended to keep what I stole for myself. I'd only taken it as a part of a ruse to get what I really wanted.

"Pay off your now ex-wife." I grabbed the handkerchief from my suit pocket and cleaned off the bloody blade. "And why was she divorcing you, Matt?" My curiosity was dragging this shit out.

He cried harder, and my control slipped. Stomping the short distance, I let my fists fly until he slumped in the chair, knocked out. I pulled out smelling salts from my pocket and held them under Matt's nose. With a jerk and a gasp, he sat up and looked around. As soon he realized he was still tied up, he whimpered.

"Please, let me go. I'll earn your money back. I'll work overtime or do something else as well as my day job. I swear I'll get you your money."

"Answer my question, Matt, before I really get pissed off and have Dario come over to rip your arms off your body." Matt's head turned to where my best friend stood and shivered when Dario looked his way.

"I...." He stopped and licked his lips. "I cheated on her," he said, his head dropping. "With her best friend."

"So what you're telling me is that you cheated on your wife...of how many years?"

"Sixteen."

"Of sixteen years, with not only another woman but her best friend. You got caught, and she wanted to take you for everything. So you decided it would be better to steal from me to pay her off?"

He nodded his head.

"I'm sure you hear a tragic story of your life, but this is what I hear. You made a commitment, broke your vows, and cheated, but not just with anyone, someone who would crush her. This went on for however long until she caught you, and I'm assuming you begged for a way to make it all okay. Then, in your wisdom, you lied, stole, and broke my trust. This Matt is what we call a pattern. A pattern is where someone repeats behavior when put under pressure or temptation. You don't know which way your asshole is facing anymore, let alone your morals. So why would I trust a single word from your mouth?"

"I swear, I swear I will. I'll put it in writing. I'll sell a kidney. I'll sell my house."

My ears pricked up at that one. I had no interest in entering the black market for organs, and putting it in writing was no better than Matt pissing on my shoe and wiping it off, but a house I could sell. I placed my shoe on the chair between his legs, leaning on my knee. Matt swallowed loud as he stared at my foot.

"Tell me more about your house."

"It is just outside of downtown on Mockingbird Lane. It has four bathrooms, and...."

I cut him off. "I don't care about that. How much land is it on?"

"Two acres."

"And you own it outright now? No leans, loans, or ties to your ex?"

His lower lip began to tremble again. "Not quite," he whispered.

I pressed my shoe down on his family jewels, and he cried like a baby. "Explain now, or I swear I will cut your dick off and shove it up your ass so you know what it's like to be fucked over by you."

"Once the divorce was final, I moved my girlfriend in," he stammered.

"You mean your wife's ex-best friend?" He nodded. "Fucking classy move there."

"I…I…I…."

I pressed on his weasel dick harder. "Spit it out already."

"I put the house in her name so my ex couldn't come after me for more money."

That was it. Matt had just hammered the final nail into his coffin. I straightened up and shook my head at the pathetic excuse for a man. I put my knife away and walked over to where my shirt and suit jacket hung.

"Please, I'm begging of you, I can get her to sign it over to me. I know I can. I have other stuff like my car and some jewelry."

Ignoring him, I examined the blood on my knuckles and remembered all too well the last time they were this red.

Even though it was a quiet night, the water was loud, like a siren's call. Chains and cement blocks were in place, and all I needed to do was give Kristof a shove, and the last of the traitors would be dead.

"Please, Angelo, don't do this. I swear I didn't cheat your father out of any money. Neither did Roberto. He is mistaken. We have always been loyal to your family. I'm the third generation that has served the Esposito family." Kristof knelt before me, hands behind his back and his face a mask of red.

When I arrived, Roberto was dead, killed by my father's soldiers. It took me a week of killing everyone I could get my hands on to flush out

Kristof. His story had remained the same for the last hour as I tortured him, and I'd held nothing back.

"Then why do we have evidence that you sold out my family to the fucking street gangs? We've lost millions in product," I growled, gripping his chin.

He didn't cry. He stared me in the eyes, which unnerved me. All those I tortured to find Kristof had cried and wouldn't look me in the eyes, but he was cut from a different cloth, and I respected that.

"I cannot explain the forged documents, but while I was in hiding..." He looked behind me to the group of soldiers on the pier. "Can they move back," he asked, lowering his voice so only the two of us could hear.

I was going to refuse, but something in my gut told me to hear him out. Looking over my shoulder, I barked at the men.

"All of you, but Dario, get off the pier and wait by the trucks." They hesitated, looking at one another. "Are you hard of hearing? Fucking move. Now," I said, swinging my gun up level with the group.

That did the trick, and they all marched away except for Dario, who remained as still as a statue. Except for his eyes...they searched the dark.

"What did you need to say?"

"I took the video footage and the voice recording to a specialist. At first, he didn't see anything, but I only ever use the best, and after a few hours, he finally confirmed they were faked. They were such amazing copies that you could never tell unless you had top-of-the-line equipment, and it would've cost a fortune to create. I don't know who made them...yet. But someone set Roberto up and everyone else who was implicated in those records. I think someone wanted your father to order all of our deaths." When I didn't hit him he continued. "Then I took all the documents to our forger to have them analyzed, but he was already dead. The body was weeks old. Blood coated the table where the fingers off his left hand had been cut off. Someone had forced him to make something and then shot him in the head. I believe the documents sent to your father were made under duress. I called in a favor, that took almost every cent I had, but it's confirmed...they are fake as well."

"Why didn't you fucking lead with that?"

"Because I don't know who to trust or who is watching. I swear to you, Angelo, we never betrayed your family."

"What do you want me to do with him?" Dario's voice yanked me from the memory. I hadn't seen him move, but he stood beside Matt, who was still begging to be set free.

"Call Nicolas and have him come here when he's done work. It's time he got his hands dirty." Dario nodded. "They are pouring concrete tomorrow. Wait until dark and bury him alive in the floor of the new building. I don't care where," I said as if I was talking about economics and not murder.

"What? No, no, no. You can't. Please."

I ignored the man as he thrashed around on the chair bolted down to the floor.

"I'll take the truck and head home for my next meeting." Grabbing a bottle of water off the table, I poured some on my hands and used my handkerchief to dry them before pulling on my dress shirt.

"What do you want me to do with his car?"

"Call Mike's Garage and talk to the Castenella boys. They'll know what to do with it."

"And how exactly do you expect me to get home," Dario asked, as we both ignored Matt, who was screaming hysterically at the top of his lungs.

"Text Enzo. He can cut his date short." There was no hiding the annoyed look as he narrowed his eyes at me. "Yeah, I'm being petty, and no, I don't fucking care," I said, taking the truck keys.

"Whatever," Dario mumbled as I walked for the door. "Hey, do I have to keep him conscious?"

"Only while you bury him. The rest of the time, I don't give a fuck. It was a pleasure while it lasted, Matt. I hope you enjoy your dirt nap." I glanced over my shoulder and gave Matt a parting smirk.

The screaming got louder, and then all was quiet. My feet crunched over the gravel of the large, crumbling parking area. I fucking hated that Matt reminded me I was no longer a good man. I pretended I was. I smiled at people walking down the street, and I was polite on the phone, but if pressed, I would eat a fucker's heart for breakfast, move on, and never think of them again.

Just as I got into the truck, my phone rang, and I recognized the burner cell I'd given Kristof before I left Chicago. I let him live but ensured everyone thought I'd killed him. He'd been working for me ever since to find out who set up Roberto and set the wheels in motion that kept me in Chicago for two and a half years. I answered but didn't say anything.

"It's me. Would you like a poison apple?"

Chuckling, I started the truck. "You have a name for me?"

"Oh, I have a name alright, and you're not going to like it," Kristof said.

Chapter Twenty-Eight

ENZO

I WAS TRYING REALLY hard to be a gentleman, but fuck, Jasmine made it difficult. She bent over as she finished putting things away under the sink, and no threat would've stopped my eyes from tracing the shape of her legs up to her sexy ass.

As she stood up straight and turned toward me, my eyes snapped to hers, but luckily, they were closed as she fought with the messy bun on top of her head. It was off to the side, and strands of her wavy hair had escaped. That was all it took for my control to snap, and before I realized I was moving, I was in front of her.

"I've got this," I said.

"Thank you. It is always unruly, but the air here has given it a life of its own. I feel like Medusa."

"You're too beautiful to turn anyone to stone," I said, gently removing her hair from the colorful scrunchie so she didn't struggle with her injured hand. Jasmine made a little snorting sound but didn't say anything. Her eyes clearly said she didn't believe me. "You think I'm lying to you?"

"I think you're being a flirt and would say anything to make me blush."

She wasn't wrong there. She was sexy as hell when she blushed.

"Why can't both things be true?" The back of my knuckles trailed down the soft skin of her cheeks.

"Well, I um...I...."

I loved watching her stammer with nerves. The fact that I could fluster her made me feel like a Don.

"You have a little powdered sugar on your face," I said.

"Oh no, where?" She went to turn away, but I held her face in my hands and rubbed my thumb over the corner of her lips and the imaginary white powder.

"Right here," I whispered, touching my lips to the spot.

"Oh...I see," Jasmine said, her voice airy, and my heart sputtered that she didn't move away.

"We can't have that," I said, moving over a little and touching my lips to hers. I kept expecting her to shove me away. Dario was right. I didn't deserve to be in her presence, let alone touch her for any reason. But to get a kiss—a kiss that she willingly gave—felt like winning the lottery.

Her exotic golden eyes fluttered closed, and I took what I hoped was an invitation and kissed her. Everything started soft and sweet regardless of my out-of-control heart, but the moment she moaned, I was done.

I needed to taste every inch of her mouth and drown in her sweet flavor. She still had a hint of the fresh strawberries and cream we shared at lunch on her lips. Groaning, I deepened the kiss and shuddered as her hands touched my waist. I didn't care if it was too forward and grabbed her ass to pull her up my body.

She let out a startled gasp but moaned as I pressed her back into the wall. Everything strained, and I wanted her in every way possible. A tiny spark of guilt ignited in my gut as I thought about her moaning for me last night. I was tempted to tell her, but Dario's warning ran through my head. *Angelo will find a way to one day go back home, we will no longer be equals, and Jasmine will forever be a princess out of our reach. Remember your place, Enzo, or you'll end up out of the race altogether.* The memory kept my mouth shut, and instead, I deepened the kiss, not wanting this moment to end.

I growled as my phone rang, my lips pausing on hers as I contemplated my choices. If it was Angelo, he was most likely watching, and if I didn't answer, I was a dead man.

"I'm sorry, I have to take this," I said, easing Jasmine onto her feet before fishing out my phone.

It was Dario's number, but that didn't mean it was him. "Hey, what's up?"

"I need a ride."

"What happened to your truck?"

"Boss took it. Meet me at the new building in an hour. You can help me clean up."

I glanced at Jasmine as she fixed her hair into a ponytail and knew the moment was lost. Angelo could be anywhere if Dario was alone. Pinching the bridge of my nose, I nodded even though Dario couldn't see the action.

"Okay, I'll be there soon. Do I need to bring anything to help clean up?"

"Nope, I have all of that taken care of," he said, and I could make out muffled screaming in the background. I swallowed hard. That would be me if I pushed Angelo too hard. I knew it, and yet...as I glanced at Jasmine, I couldn't help wanting to push every one of his fucking buttons.

"See you soon." I hung up the phone and turned to face Jasmine. "I'm sorry, Isabella, but I have to go. Work is calling."

"You work very strange hours," she said, and I smiled.

If she only knew.

"Yeah, a landlord's job is never done, but I had a great day and a lot of fun."

"Me too," she said, looking up at me as I cupped her cheek. Placing a chaste kiss on her lips, I walked out of the kitchen before I forgot all about Dario.

"Don't forget to put more antiseptic on that burn," I said and nodded toward the bandage on her hand. Jasmine followed me out into the hall, and each step I took felt like my boots were weighted. "Also, lock your doors. You never know who is around at night." Granted, it was me, Angelo, and Dario sneaking in at night, but I still wanted her to be safe.

She smiled, and my heart skipped a beat. "Okay, Dad," she said, and I paused with the door open.

"You can call me Daddy if you want," I said. Then I wanted to bang my head off the door. "Sorry, that was...." Her shocked expression fell as she burst out laughing. "I'm going to go before I say anything else wildly inappropriate."

"Goodnight, Enzo."

"Goodnight, Little Mess," I teased and closed the door as she whispered, "Jerk." I waited until the door clicked with the lock before jogging down the steps to my SUV. Clean-up duty sucked—worst part of the job. Dario seemed completely comfortable with the blood and gore, but I hadn't grown up like Dario and Angelo. My hands hadn't gotten dirty until I became an official member of Angelo's group.

The shock of seeing someone shot in the head for the first time was something I would never forget. Now, it didn't faze me, but I tried to hang on to that first experience for fear of turning into a heartless monster. Angelo toed the edge of that line. I could see the dead stare in his eyes, and I never wanted to fall that far.

Three hours later, I pulled into the house driveway. Dario hadn't said two words the entire drive. He was a broody fucker at the best of times, let alone after burying a man alive. I grabbed his arm before he could get out of the car, and the glare I got would stop another man's heart.

"If you're about to ask me to share my feelings, I'll punch you to make myself feel better."

"Um...no, but good to know." I let go of his bicep before he decided to do it anyway.

"What do you want to talk about? I could feel you wanting to talk all the way home, fucking annoying energy you give off when you're nervous."

"Jesus, are you clairvoyant now?"

He grabbed his pack of smokes and put the window down. "No, and just get on with it."

"Fine. Are you really okay with what we did last night?"

"Does my fucking face look like I was okay with it? Of course not." He lit up and blew the long stream of smoke out the window. "If you want to try and talk him out of it again, be my guest, but it will be your body I bury next."

"Why don't we just tell him no." Dario snorted. "I'm serious. She is sweet, and she trusts me, and here I am sneaking into her room at night and licking her kitty."

"You didn't just say that?"

"Fuck off, you know what I mean. Angelo will bump it up, and I don't know if I can fuck her like that. It's wrong. I mean, it's fucking hot...no, no, it's wrong."

"Who exactly are you trying to convince here?"

I glared at him, not that he cared. "I'm not sure why I bother trying to talk to you."

"Honestly, I don't know why either." He took another pull on the smoke, pinched the end like it wasn't a little flame, and put it back in the pack. "Look, let me ask you this. What do you think will happen if we both march inside and tell Angelo that we don't want to go along with his plan?" He leaned against the door and stared at me. Even though the car was dark, I could feel his gaze on my face.

"I was hoping we'd convince him not to do it."

"Sure, and Lucifer is a saint," Dario said.

"I'm serious."

"So am I, Enzo. Let me try to make this clear. You have choices here, but two of them will end very badly. The first choice is to go in there and try to talk Angelo out of whatever he has planned for Jasmine, and Angelo tells you to fuck off. If you pursue it, he will order me to kill you. I like you, and I'll give you a head start, but I will do what he says."

I swallowed at the hard edge of his tone.

"Your second option is to tell Jasmine who you are and what is happening and maybe even convince her to run off with you. Angelo will use every ounce of his ability and power to track you down and then order me to kill you, most likely in front of Jasmine, to make a point."

That one was worse than the first, and I could picture Jasmine screaming as I bled out on the floor. Not good.

"Third choice is that you can out him to the Falcone family, but the first thing Angelo will do is tell Don Falcone you have his daughter...I'm sure you can already picture how well that will go over considering your family status."

He paused and just stared at me. "I'm sensing you want me to say something," I said.

"Very observant. What is your last option," Dario asked.

"To go along with what he wants," I sighed.

"Great. Tell me why."

"Can I tell you how annoying you are instead?" I growled at him.

"You can if it makes you feel better. I couldn't care less," Dario said.

"Fine. I go along with it because I'm a carpetmaker's son, not an underboss or anyone with power or authority within the mafia families."

"Very good. We will go back home, and when we do, you are just a soldier like me. So go ahead, propose, and run off with her if she agrees. Do whatever you think you must, but at the end of the day, either Ciro is marrying her, or Angelo is, take your pick." Dario opened the door and got out but leaned in and looked at me. "Personally, I like to use the little bit of influence I have to point Angelo in a direction that doesn't cause Jasmine distress. Besides, this will blow up in his face, and he will have to grovel." Dario smirked. "I'm dying to see that happen. She's going to kick his ass." Dario closed the door, and I smiled. He had a point.

Hopping out, I followed him to the house. We could hear Angelo on the phone and walked down the hall to his office.

"Don't tell me to fucking calm down. I'm going to gut the fucker, pour salt in the wound and lower him an inch at a time into a tank of piranhas so they can eat him slowly. He's dead," Angelo yelled as we walked through the door.

He slammed his cell down and, in the next breath, pointed his gun at me. "Oh fuck man, what did I do?"

"Did you have a nice day," he asked, his hand never wavering.

I glanced at Dario as he casually leaned against the fireplace mantle, and something in his eyes told me to say no.

"Um...no?"

"Is that what I'm going to find if I look at the video footage of Jasmine's house?"

I cleared my throat. "Probably not...."

Angelo moved his arm slightly and fired. I ducked as the bullet whizzed past and shattered a statue on the table behind me. I looked at the mess and then back at Angelo.

"Have you lost your fucking mind?"

"Don't whine. I didn't shoot you." He sat his phone down as Dario chuckled.

"The two of you are fucked up," I said, pissed off.

"Agreed, but we have an issue. Kristof found the snake who set up Roberto. and sent us on a two-and-a-half-year wild fucking goose chase." With a yell, Angelo pushed everything off his desk. "I'm going to kill him. I'm going to string him up by his cock until the weight of his body pulls it off."

"Creative. Mind sharing who it is?" Dario drawled.

"Fucking Jacopo."

“What?” Dario snarled, and his entire demeanor changed as his furious energy filled the room. “If you don’t kill him, I will. You know what it has to be about, right?”

“Jasmine,” they said together.

I hated being out of the loop. I knew the name, but no more than that. I wasn’t from the same part of Italy as Angelo and Dario, and only met them for the first time in Chicago. I didn’t know all the players in their inner circle, and we were forced to run not long after returning home, so I didn’t have much time to learn all the pertinent family politics. “Can someone fill me in?”

“I’m going to do you one better,” Angelo said as he walked around his desk. “Learn as much as you can about him. I want to know everything Jacopo has done over the last ten years, right down to where he buys his socks, what color he likes, and who he’s been fucking. I want it all. That piece of shit is mine.”

Angelo marched for the open office door. “We leave in thirty to visit Jasmine. Be ready to go.”

“You still want to try and talk him out of doing this?” Dario laughed as he walked out of the room.

“Prick!” All I got in return was more laughter. “Hey, what is Jacopo’s last name?” No one answered and I grumbled as I flopped down at my laptop. “Never mind I’ll figure it out myself.”

Chapter Twenty-Nine

JASMINE

I SPENT a good fifteen minutes arguing with myself over whether I should take the Absolem, but in the end, the dirty little angel on my left shoulder won out. If it was a one-off dream, so be it, but if it wasn't....

"I shouldn't be doing this," I mumbled as I downed the second spoonful. "It could be laced with something." Even as I said the words out loud, it didn't dull the urge to see if it would happen again.

Shame at the thought of seeing Angelo, Dario, and even Enzo like that again burned in my gut. I hated Angelo so much for still infecting me after all this time. I should've purged him from my system when he cut off all contact and never looked back. Now, I had taken a sleep aid that created a ghost effect in my mind. I had issues, but it was too late now. I glanced at the toilet. No, I couldn't do it. I hated being sick. I would rather deal with the emotional fallout of taking the Absolem.

Walking over to the bed, I sat down and picked up my latest book. How I talked myself into reading a romance about a serial killer when I now lived in the middle of nowhere was beyond me. But there was something about this Cain guy that I loved.

Settling back into my pillows, I picked up where I left off. It wasn't long before I couldn't hold my eyes open and didn't have the strength to put the book on the nightstand.

I was floating in a sea of darkness. Hands were on my body, and I moaned as they traveled up my legs and back down again.

"Hello, my Tiger, did you miss me?" Angelo's voice filled my mind as if whispering directly into my ear. He touched my face and moved my hair out of the way, and I wanted to cling to him.

Here, in my mind, it was safe to want that. More hands were on me, and my head lolled to the side. I smiled at Dario, loving his warmth pressed against me. My breath hitched with the feel of his hard body, and I remembered curling up in his arms and how safe I felt.

"Do you want me, Tiger," Angelo asked.

Anger and sadness didn't exist here, and I reached out to touch Angelo, finding his chest naked and hard. My sleep shorts were suddenly gone, and I felt wanton as his hands slipped between my thighs, touching me. The sensation was so familiar that I pushed up, wanting more.

"Yes," I said.

"Say it again. Say you want me to fuck you and make you scream. Make sure you say please."

I licked my lips, and everything felt slow. "Please...fuck...me," I said and moaned as Angelo growled against my neck. The moment he moved, someone else took his place beside me. My body shifted on the bed, and my legs were spread wide.

"You want Enzo's cock in your mouth, don't you," Angelo asked, and I nodded, agreeing to anything he said. My body was hot as Dario nuzzled my neck, his hand playing with my nipples.

"You want me to stick my cock in her mouth," Enzo asked.

"Yes," I answered.

"Tiger says yes, and Tiger gets what she wants. Cock in her mouth, now," Angelo ordered, and I squirmed, listening to him. I loved it when he got all commanding. I wanted to tell him no, just to see if he would spank me, and my ass tingled at the old memory.

Angelo turned my head to the side just before a cock touched my lips. I opened my mouth, moaning as Enzo slipped inside.

"Sweet fuck, this should not feel so good," Enzo said, which confused me. Should my mouth not feel good? Did he not think I would feel good? I didn't like hearing that and sucked harder, my hand wrapping around his shaft. "Oh my god, this is not fair. I'm such an asshole," he said.

"But you're not going to stop, are you," Angelo asked as his weight blanketed me.

"No," Enzo said, gripping my hair and quickening his pace.

"That's it, Tiger, suck him hard, make him come," Angelo encouraged, and I moaned and sucked harder wanting to get a good girl out of him.

"Shit, oh fuck those lips. So fucking beautiful, I'm so sorry," Enzo said and groaned as he came. I had no idea why he was apologizing. He was confusing me. I swallowed him down and sucked until he pulled himself from my mouth, leaving me squirming in frustration.

"Such a good girl." I smiled, happy that I got him to say it. It always sounded so sexy and naughty. "You love to suck cock don't you," Angelo asked, and I nodded, shuddering as his hips pressed into me and his cock nudged my pussy.

"Yes," I said, wrapping my arms around his warm, tightly flexed body. My fingers danced over the dips and planes of his back, and I cried out as he pushed into me a little more.

He felt the same, and it was just another night they snuck into my bedroom as if no time had passed. Maybe it was. Maybe everything else was a figment of my imagination, and this was my reality. I wanted that to be true.

"Fuck Tiger, you are tighter than I remember. How is that possible? Shit, don't wiggle like that. You'll make me come too soon." I loved hearing him say he was losing control. Nothing gave me as much joy as making him lose his tightly wound control.

"Angelo," I said, arching into him as he filled me.

"Yes, Tiger, I've got you. I love you, and I'm never letting you go." He paused and nipped at my ear. "Are you ready?"

"Yes."

"I'm going to fuck you hard, Tiger."

"Yes." I bucked under him, wanting him to move.

"I'm going to fuck you and make sure this time you get pregnant, Tiger." He pulled back and thrust into me, and I wanted to cry. It felt so good.

"Yes," I screamed, wanting more and agreeing to have a family with him. I'd always pictured multiple kids with him and Dario, and I loved the idea of adding Enzo. My relaxed mind and body were on the same page, and I felt the climax quickly rushing to the surface. I clung to his shoulders as he fucked me hard, and with each thrust, he whispered something else dirty in my ear.

"Tell me, Tiger, did you dream of my cock at night? I bet you touched yourself thinking of me."

I cried out as the climax hit, and the waves of pleasure washed over my body. I jerked and whimpered with the feel of two mouths on my nipples as Angelo picked up the pace until every thrust made me scream.

"You." *Thrust.* "Are." *Thrust.*" Mine," Angelo said, pounding into me and yelling my name as he came. I never wanted to wake up from this dream. I slumped, panting hard. "I love you, Tiger, remember that. I never stopped loving you."

He slipped from my body, and I felt empty all over again. I didn't want the dream to end. I wanted to take as much of this feeling as possible and hang on to it.

"No, please. Don't go," I said.

"Amorina," Dario said softly, kissing my cheek, and I almost cried with joy that he was still here. I loved it when he called me his little love. It had been so long since I heard that name. My chest warmed, and my stomach tightened with the single word. Angelo talked dirty, but Dario made me feel like a princess. "Do you still love me, Amorina?"

His fingers trailed along my body in lines that made me shiver. "Yes," I said, rolling in his direction and grabbing his face. I never wanted to let go of the calm he brought to my soul. "I missed you."

"Shh, don't cry." His arms wrapped around me, and I wished I could see his face in the dark. "I'm never leaving you again. Do you hear me?" I nodded, but the tears still fell as I held him tighter. I loved Angelo, but I could be vulnerable with Dario, and he wouldn't judge me. "I love you so much."

"I love you more."

He chuckled, and the rumble made me warm all over. "That's not even possible."

DARIO

Pulling the blankets over us, I cuddled Jasmine as close as I could and let her cry. I shot the odd glare at Angelo, who was sitting in the chair watching. My loyalty ran deep for him and his family, but my resentment had grown over the last five years. I'd pined for her before we were together, but I knew she was always out of reach. Once we kicked that door open and I had her, I wanted to hold onto her forever. Leaving her had ripped out my heart. To feel her crying in my arms broke me all over again.

She lifted her head, and I dropped my lips to hers, kissing away the salty tears. No matter what happened from this moment on, I would never let her go. They would have to pry her from my cold, dead body before I let anyone come between us.

Jasmine deepened the kiss, her hand running down my side as she pulled me closer. I wanted to have her like Angelo, but I also wanted to tell her to stop and wait until she was awake and wanted this. Fuck, she was making it very difficult to do the right thing.

I tried to pull out of her grasp slowly, but she whimpered and held on so tight that there was no way I was going anywhere. Rolling us over, I settled on top of her and slid her devious hands above her head. She gripped onto mine, and my heart pounded hard behind my ribcage.

"I shouldn't do this," I whispered, rubbing my cheek against hers.

"Please," she said and slipped her legs around me.

Every muscle tensed as my entire body screamed to be inside of her. She mumbled and wiggled beneath me, and still, I refused.

"Dario, please." Her hands squeezed mine, her labored breathing pushed her breasts against my chest, and I shook with a carnal need .

"Just do it, Dario," Angelo said, and my head whipped in his direction.

"Fuck off," I growled, and his eyes went wide. "Don't push me tonight."

"Fine, do whatever you want, but we only have about twenty minutes left before we need to clean up." Standing, he marched out of the room.

"I'll give you some privacy," Enzo said, but I didn't look at him as he closed the door. All my attention was on the woman beneath me.

"Dario," she repeated my name, and it sounded like she was in pain. Her begging was my undoing. I was an ornery fucker, able to rip out another man's heart or tear him into pieces with my bare hands, but a single touch from my beautiful Amorina and I caved to whatever she wanted.

"I'm a terrible person. I shouldn't be doing this to you." Closing my eyes and breathing in her scent tore me in two. But the decision was made for me when she bucked up with her hips, and the tip of my cock slid into her.

"Yes," she panted and pushed up again. Her hips moved me deeper, and that was all I could take. She cried out in pleasure as I pressed the rest of the way inside of her.

"I'm going to hell for this, but fuck...I love you. Let hell swallow me whole, if it means I get one more night with you." I nipped at her ear and slowly pumped. The little whimpers were so familiar, and my body lit up and recharged like she was what I had needed to sustain me for so long and had been missing.

"Yes, please, oh god, Dario." Jasmine's body tightened, and the walls of her pussy gripped me. She was close, and I wouldn't be far behind. Releasing her hands, I reared up and pulled her with me until she sat in my lap with her knees straddling me on the bed. Wrapping Jasmine's arms around my neck, I grabbed her ass and bounced her on my cock. She cried out, her body shuddering. I knew all of her favorite positions with me.

"Oh please, don't stop." Nails ran across my shoulders.

Growling, I bounced her faster and held her up until she screamed and came. Her back arched away from me, but I held her firm and let her ride her release. Her dark nipple was too enticing as her breasts pushed up into my face. I sucked the hard peak into my mouth and groaned when I felt her soak me as her muscles clenched my cock.

"Fuck, yes." Closing my eyes, I thrust up into her hard as I came. The release seemed endless as I held her tight. I wanted to collapse to my side and take her with me.

"I love you," she said, her voice wavering and soft.

"I love you, Amorina," I said, kissing her neck.

"Did you just come in her?" I turned my head to glare at Angelo. I had no idea if he just walked in or watched.

"I fucking did, and you're not going to say shit to me about it because I have been by your side, protecting your ass, and ended up a fugitive because of you. I will be loyal until I take my last fucking breath, but you are not giving her to me in half measures anymore." He cocked a brow at me.

"Is that so?"

Standing, I lifted Jasmine and cradled her in my arms like I had when we were children. Marching toward him and the bathroom door, I stopped and stared at my best friend.

"Yeah, it is. Would you really deny me this?"

His jaw twitched, but he looked away and unclenched his hands. "No."

"Good, then we aren't going to have a problem other than seeing who can get her pregnant first." I smirked as Anglo's eyes flared with the challenge. "Also, I'm cleaning her up. You two can do the room."

"Why do you get to choose," Enzo asked as he walked into the room eating a sandwich.

"Because you're too weak not to fuck her again and scare the shit out of her if she woke up, and Angelo would probably drown her in the tub by accident. I'm not trusting either of you to do this." Using my foot, I slammed the bathroom door behind me. Fuck that felt good.

Chapter Thirty

JASMINE

KEEPING MY EYES CLOSED, I slid my hand to the far side of the bed, but it was once more empty. I knew the room would be perfect and the doors and windows locked, yet I could feel their hands on my body and smell their scents in my nose.

I was slowly losing my mind. Every night for the past week, I argued with myself about perpetuating this obsession by taking the Absolem. Ultimately, I was weak and gave in, needing to feel their touch. I was in love with the ghosts in my mind, and it scared me, but I didn't want it to end.

My eyes fluttered open, and I stared at the plain white ceiling with age cracks and knew that if I kept this up, one day, I would end up just like this house. Old, alone, and practically forgotten among the tall, young trees.

I swung my legs out of bed and quickly re-made it before doing my morning stretches and getting ready for the day. When I got downstairs, I fed my little mice roommates first, then went to check on my vegetables.

The nightlights were still on, and I flicked them off as I walked in. My mouth fell open as I stared at the rows. It was like magic how quickly everything was growing. They had doubled in size over the last few days, and the room was filled with the sweet scent of fresh fruit, vegetables, and herbs. They were much larger than the book, I bought from Jack. said they should be, but they looked close to ripe.

Plucking one of the bright red strawberries, I popped it in my mouth and moaned with the sweet flavor. They were delicious, and that little morsel put a smile on my face.

I wanted to be a badass woman who could do something worthwhile on my own, and this was the first time my new life felt real. Picking up my growing bible, I looked at the images and read the description and according to it, the vegetables were a couple of days away from being picked. Now I needed a place to sell them.

Jogging into the kitchen with a revived spring in my step, I put on a pot of coffee and grabbed a granola bar and yogurt for breakfast. Fishing around in the kitchen cupboards, I found a thermos and poured my coffee into it to take outside.

It was a beautiful, late summer day, and I breathed in the morning air as I stepped out the door. The first thing I needed to scope out was a location to sell my wares. Not having a car was an issue. Reaching the end of the driveway, I looked both ways and sighed. This wouldn't work if no one knew I was here. The small country road ran in either direction for too long a distance for anyone to see my stand from the main roads, but I also didn't want to drag everything a mile away.

Inspiration hit as I stared at a faded sign leaning against what looked like a tool shed. It was weathered for sure, but still in decent condition. All I needed to do was paint it and put stakes on the back so it would stand in the ground.

I was pulling things out of the shed when I heard a vehicle pull in and turned to see Enzo's SUV. It was hard to keep the smile from consuming my entire face as he stepped out and waved. Butterflies soared at the sight of him even though he came to me every night in my dreams, and we did far dirtier things than the soft touches and kisses we'd shared so far.

"What do we have going on here," Enzo asked as he stared at the piles of wood.

I sipped my coffee to keep my hands from reaching out and touching him.

"I'm building a roadside stand to sell my produce and making a sign for the end of the road so people know I'm here." I smiled wide, and he rubbed the back of his neck as he gave me a less than enthusiastic look. "Did I do something wrong? Was I not supposed to touch anything in there." I pointed my thumb at the shed. "I just thought I would reorganize while I was at it, but I'm sorry if…."

Enzo wrapped his hands around my waist, and whatever words I would say were lost to the breeze.

"No, it's not that, although I think that the nickname Little Mess really suits you," he said, and I narrowed my eyes and swatted his arm. Retaliating, he tickled my sides, making me squeal as I jumped away. He laughed, and I loved the sound that, for whatever reason, reminded me of gingerbread cookies and hot chocolate. It was a silly comparison, and yet I felt like I could drink down his laugh, and it would be as sweet and rich.

"You're in so much trouble," I said, pointing at him.

"Oh yeah? Why don't you come back here and get me in trouble then?" His eyes filled with heat and mischief, and the sweater, jeans and sneakers I was working in suddenly seemed like way too many clothes.

"Nice try."

He stuffed his hands in his pockets as he gave me an innocent look that never reached his eyes.

"Fine. I was just thinking that it will still be hard to get anyone's attention without a bigger sign and maybe one for both ends of the road."

I looked down at the wood that I planned on painting and sighed. I didn't want to spend any more money than I had to. But how would I sell my produce if I couldn't get anyone's attention?

"I have an idea," he said, pointing to a stack of long wooden boards piled up near the house. "Those are left over from some of the renovations. Why don't I use them and build you two larger signs?"

"You can do that?" I picked up my coffee to take a sip.

"You'd be surprised what I can do with these hands."

The coffee I was swallowing proceeded to go down the wrong way, and I choked on it and his statement. I remembered very vivid dream moments showing me exactly how talented he was.

"Are you okay?" Enzo rubbed my back.

"Yeah, it just went down the wrong way." I was ruined because even that sounded dirty in my mind.

"I hate it when that happens." He left his hand on my shoulder, and an awkward silence fell as I stared into his silver eyes, but he didn't say anything back.

"Um...did you want to do that now? Why are you here again? I'm not complaining, but I figured you'd be busy with...whatever it is that you do."

"My job is to be here for you for the day. The bonus of a day off is that I get to choose what I want to do, and I enjoy spending time with you." He removed his hand and put it back into his pocket. "Unless, of course, you prefer I leave?"

"No, no, I'm happy to have the help, and I kinda like having you around."

"Just kinda?"

"That's all you're getting out of me for now," I teased and stepped into the shed to continue my clean-out. "Do you happen to know if there is a large table or a patio set with an umbrella? I need to make a stand for the end of the road."

"I think we have an old one at the main farm. I'll swing home and check. Do you need anything else like paint and brushes?"

I'd just picked up an old shovel when I turned to stare at him. The clouds picked that moment to shift and bathe him in a golden hue that took my breath away. It wasn't fair. These dreams made it feel like we were already together, yet I couldn't just walk up to him and kiss him or hug him like I wanted to. It was like I had one foot in a fantasy world and the other in reality.

"That would be fabulous if you have some lying around. Any color will do."

"Okay, I'll be right back."

"Did you need any help?"

"Nope, all good," Enzo pulled out of the driveway again before I could ask any more questions. Shrugging it off, I got back to work. By the end of the day today, I wanted my stand and signs ready to go. In a few days, I would sit and pray that someone came by.

Chapter Thirty-One

ANGELO

JASMINE DIDN'T TAKE her sleeping medication last night, and the disappointment of not getting those hours with her put me in a foul mood this morning. I'd woken up and glared at the screen, trying to figure out the best time to announce that we were real.

It was like Enzo had handed me the paint because I'd done a great job painting myself into a corner. I now knew she still wanted me. Hell, I knew she still loved me. It didn't matter what she said now. Her subconscious told me all I needed to know. So why wasn't I rushing over there and kicking in the door to reveal myself to her?

Pacing in front of the monitors, I watched her as she did some cleaning, then got changed and put on a jacket.

"What are you up to now?"

"I'm doing a crossword," Dario answered from across the room.

"Not you. Jasmine is getting ready to go somewhere, but where would she go without a car?"

"Maybe she just wants some fresh air and to go for a walk, or maybe she called for a ride to go to town," he casually said, and I turned around to face him as my earlier annoyance shifted into anger.

"Like hell that's happening." Stomping across the room, I opened my desk, pulled out my gun, and quickly swiveled on the silencer.

"What the hell are you doing?"

"I'm not letting her get into a stranger's car without protection. Do you have any idea what kind of weirdos are out there who would take advantage of her?"

He looked up over the crossword book and lifted a condescending brow in my direction. "You don't say."

"Sarcasm, I see. We're different," I said, stuffing the gun into the holster I always wore. I grabbed my suit jacket and tugged it on just as Jasmine walked out her front door.

"You're right, we're worse."

"I don't think I like your attitude," I snarled at Dario.

"That's fair. Half the time, I don't like you, so I guess we're even." He stood up and rolled out his shoulders. He looked like a fucking giant sprouting up from the ground. Dario cracked his neck as he stared at me coolly, waiting for my response.

"I don't have time for this. I need to go." Maneuvering around the desk, I marched out of the office and felt him following in my wake. "You don't need to come."

"We going to have this argument again? What I do is literally built into the job title. You're the body, I'm the guard. Bodyguard, see how that works?"

"You are so...fuck." I bit my tongue. Arguing with Dario was a waste of time, and he knew exactly what buttons to press to make me want to shoot him. I was more tempted than usual.

"Fine, you drive," I said, pulling out my phone and bringing up the monitoring app as we got in Dario's truck. I searched all the outside cameras and just about fainted when I saw Jasmine rolling out of the driveway on an old bicycle I didn't know we had on the property. "What the hell does she think she's doing?"

I held up the phone to show Dario just before she disappeared around the corner.

"It's a twenty-minute bike ride to town, and what if she gets hit by a car or someone tries to kidnap her or gets a flat tire? Hell, what if she falls off and breaks something?"

"Whoa, man, take a fucking breath. People have been riding bikes for generations, and Jasmine is a grown-ass adult, despite what you think. She traveled here from home and made it in one piece and has been in town before. Give her a little credit."

"You're right," I said, but my chest hurt, and my stomach was tied in knots. The panic was new. I didn't panic, not about anything, but the thought of Jasmine being injured or losing her again made me want to throw up.

"That's all you're going to say?"

"Why, do you want me to argue with you?" I glared at the side of Dario's head as he pulled up to the stop sign that would take us to Jasmine's house. "Wait here until she turns onto the main road. We don't want her to see us."

"I think I know how to tail someone," Dario said, but I ignored his annoyed tone and watched the little flashing light on my phone.

"Okay, she just turned, let's go." The stupid, anxious feeling wouldn't leave me even though, logically, I knew there was no need for it. Reaching the corner, I looked down the road and saw her off to the side, peddling for town. A red sports car whipped by where we were parked and shook the truck. I held my breath as the asshole blew past Jasmine, and she swerved onto the gravel.

"Fuck," Dario said, his eyes wide as he stared at the almost fatal moment.

"That fucker almost hit her, and you thought I was overreacting." The weight of my gun pressed into my side, and I wished I'd shot the fucker as he drove by.

"Fine, you weren't overreacting, at least where cars are concerned," Dario said and pointed down the road. "We should wait til she is past the next sideroad, then drive there, turn in, and watch until she passes the next. I really hate following people in broad daylight."

I just nodded, never taking my eyes off her blue jacket, growing smaller with each passing second. Dario did as he said, and it worked well, so we continued all the way to town. By the time we were there, I was ready to kill every driver on the road.

She hopped off the bike and parked it in a stand in front of Charlotte's Hand Woven Baskets. I had no idea how a basket shop made enough money to stay in business unless they were a cover for something else.

"Where is a damn overcast sky when you need one? Take me to the alley between those two buildings and drop me off."

"You're going to get caught, and I don't care if you do. Jasmine should know we are here, but I'm just warning you."

"Talk about not having any faith. I stalked and killed dozens of people in Chicago," I said as he pulled into the alley. "I'm all stealth."

"You're something alright." He rolled his eyes at me and I really wanted to punch him. "None of them were Jasmine Falcone and you're...." He waved his hand in my direction. "You're not exactly yourself at the moment."

I had no idea what that meant, but I was sure it was an insult, so I just glared at him before hopping out of the truck.

"What do you want me to do?"

"Stay in the truck until I need you. I have a feeling there will be a few bodies to clean up."

"Fuck me," Dario swore as I slammed the door.

Waiting until he backed out, I moved to the shadowed east wall and peeked around the corner. Pulling out my phone, I snapped photos as Jasmine came out of the store with an armful of small baskets. She loaded them in the large front caddy of the old bicycle before pulling it away from the rack.

I slipped back into the darkness and held perfectly still as her shadow drew nearer. What would she do if I stepped out of the alley in front of her bike? Seeing the expression on her face made it worthwhile, but scaring her in public and her trying to kill me was not ideal for staying off the news feeds these days.

As she walked past my hiding spot, I caught a whiff of her shampoo, and a shiver raced through my body as goosebumps rose on my arms. It took more self-control not to drag her into the alley and kiss her stupid than it did for anything else in my life. Just her breathing pushed my buttons. Dario might be right, and I wasn't myself, but I sure as fuck was never telling him that. I watched as she stopped and wandered into the flower shop.

Beastville may seem quaint, but you had to keep an eye over your shoulder and a weapon close at hand. It wasn't that I didn't trust Jasmine to take care of herself, like Dario thought. She was new here, and this place had pitfalls and dangerous spots everywhere. It was like sending a lamb into a lion's den and not telling it of the danger that lurked.

I kept an eye on the door and stood up straighter when the same fancy red sports car that almost ran Jasmine off the road parked in front of the shop. The engine's roar was loud, and whoever was driving gave it some gas, rattling the windows before he turned it off. Fucking show-off. I rolled my eyes. The only men who did that were those with cocks smaller than their bank account.

She gave him her patented, courteous smile—that I'd seen her flash a million times—before grabbing her bike and continuing along the sidewalk. The man looked to be around my age and held the door open as he blatantly stared at her ass when she walked away.

"Hey, excuse me," he called after Jasmine.

Letting go of the door, he marched after her. Without a thought, I pushed away from the wall and stalked after him.

"Excuse me," he called out again. Jasmine was mid-turn when I grabbed the man and yanked him into the next alley. "What the...."

I pressed the barrel of my gun under the soft part of his chin. "I wouldn't yell if I were you."

"Do you want my car?" Hands shaking, he held up the fob for the fancy car.

"You almost hit that woman on the bicycle when you drove into town." He swallowed, and the bottom of his throat pressed into the barrel.

"I didn't…."

"Shut up," I ordered. "Don't bother denying it. I watched you and her as she almost fell into the ditch."

"I'm sorry," he mumbled, and at one point in my life, I might've cared, but that part of me was long dead.

"I don't care." Moving the gun so it was pressed into his stomach, I glared into his terrified eyes. "You almost killed her. No one hurts my Tiger and lives."

The muffled sound of the gun firing and the shocked look on the man's face made me smile. Pushing him off to the side, he landed on his knees and stared at his hands as the red dripped through his fingers.

Pulling out my handkerchief, I wiped off the muzzle and waited until he flopped over before grabbing his key fob and covering him in cardboard. The Castanella boys were going to love this car.

"Thanks for the ride," I said, checking for Jasmine before walking to the car. Fuck I felt so much better. I didn't even feel like murdering Enzo in his sleep anymore. Who said killing wasn't good for the soul?

Chapter Thirty-Two

JASMINE

I WOKE up with a spring in my step, and not because of any sexy dream. Put it down to a successful night of sleep without the Absolem and no fantasies about what-ifs.

Dashing around, I dressed and grabbed an armload of baskets to set up. I spent all last night sitting at the table, working out where each item should go to best utilize space.

On my way out the door, I glanced at the television, remembering how weird yesterday was. Going into town was a great way to learn about the area. I got some shopping done, and other than almost being killed by a sports car, it was a great day. Until I saw that same car everywhere I went, like it was stalking me. The strangest part was that I kept catching glimpses of Angelo. His reflection in a window or walking down the street, but the next moment, he was gone. That was the final straw and reason for me to stop the sleeping medication. I couldn't have those nighttime fantasies turning into daytime visions as well. It was bad enough that I thought of him at all.

Enzo had acted strange last night as well. He had turned on the television to the local news reporting on some shootings in town and how they were looking for a suspect. Every time I moved to look at the screen, he moved to block my view, and we ended up in a strange dance with him apologizing. When I got around him, the character sketch was gone, and he left without an explanation. If he hadn't been waiting for me when I got home and finalizing my signs while I was gone, I would've sworn he was the person of interest. I really liked him, but there was something about him that reminded me of everyone back home. There were always agendas, half-truths, or things omitted from stories for personal gain. I hated the politics of it all, even if I understood the necessity.

The sun was cresting the tops of the trees as I placed the last of my produce out. There was quite the selection, and as I stared at the large table, I couldn't keep the smile off my face.

Lettuce, cucumber, tomatoes, zucchini, sweet peppers, and radishes lined most of the table, but I had some strawberries, figs, and peaches tucked in. I had never been so proud in my life. I produced something from what felt like nothing, and hopefully, someone would enjoy the fruits of my labor. Literally.

A vehicle approaching made my heart jump at a possible customer. I was only mildly disappointed when I recognized Enzo's black SUV.

"Wow, this looks incredible," he said, pulling up.

The elated smile on his face sent butterflies whipping around in my stomach. "You think so?"

"You really pulled it all together. Let me go park, and I'll hang out for a little while." I watched him the entire way into the driveway, then mentally scolded myself and turned around.

The crunch of his boots on the gravel drawing closer made the butterflies swarm.

"I brought you these," Enzo said, pulling out a massive bouquet of flowers from behind his back. "It's a little congratulations for all your hard work."

"Oh my god, they're beautiful. I took the flowers and closed my eyes as I breathed in the delicate scent of lily and jasmine. "Lillies are my favorite."

"I know," he said.

"You do? How do you know that?"

His smile fell as he rubbed the back of his neck. "I'm not sure. You must have said something," he said.

I couldn't say why I didn't believe him, but before I could push, the sound of a vehicle slowing down caught my attention. I turned to see a fancy black car.

"Hi there, so nice to meet you," I said, setting the flowers down.

"This is incredible. How long have you been here," the beautiful blond woman asked as she picked up a tomato and took a bite like an apple. She moaned as some of the juice ran down her chin. "Wow."

"This is my first day open. You're my very first customer." I smiled as she ate the tomato.

"Well, I'm going to be your last."

My smile fell. Was the tomato terrible? I tried one and thought they were delicious.

"Oh, I'm sorry you don't like it. You don't have to pay," I said, and the woman paused mid-bite and then laughed.

"No, I mean, I'm going to clean you out. I'm buying it all." She held out her hand. "My name is Gina, and I own Athena's Palate."

"Isabella." I shook her hand and it was warm and firm, like we'd just signed a contract.

"I've eaten there. The food is exceptional," Enzo said, as he came to stand by my side.

"Thanks, but with fresh produce like this, it will be even better. My brother only wants me to buy from certain suppliers, but if you don't tell him, I won't." She winked at me. "Do you grow anything else?"

"Not yet, but I could try," I said, baffled. Was this even real? For a brief second, I wondered if Enzo had put her up to it, but the shock on his face seemed genuine.

"I'm after herbs and could use garlic and carrots. We have a few signature dishes. I'll give you the ingredients, and let me know what you can provide. Is this all you have?" She pointed to the whole table.

"Yes, but more will be ready in a couple of days, and I can always grow more. I have a greenhouse."

"So you can grow all year? That is excellent news."

Gina didn't say anything as she walked to her car and returned with a large handful of cash. She counted out enough for everything on the table and a handsome tip. "I mean it. I will be your only customer. I want first dibs on anything you have for sale," she said, handing over a business card for the restaurant.

"The cellphone number is my direct line. Call me as soon as you have more, and I'll come get it."

"Wow, Gina, thank you. I don't know what to say." I stared at the business card in bewilderment.

The corner of her mouth curled up, and she struck me as the type of woman used to giving orders and not taking any shit. I loved that about her aura.

"Nothing needs to be said. Just make me your first call."

"You got it." I was brimming with excitement at the thought of truly building my very own business from the ground up.

"Do you have a business name yet?"

"Oh...um...maybe Jas's Jams," I said. "I'm planning on making my own real soon and having them be a show stopper." I smiled, at my little sales pitch.

"I love that idea, I'd definitely be interested in those as well. Any reason for Jas's Jams and not Izzy's Jams?" I swallowed hard with my slip up and could feel Enzo's eyes on the side of my face.

"My mother's name, it holds special meaning for me," I lied and hoped it didn't show all over my face.

"Parents are very special, I love that," she said, her eyes softening.

"Here, let me help you put the stuff in your car," I offered.

Between the three of us, we loaded the back seat and trunk in no time. Gina smiled just before she got in.

"You two make a cute couple. Have a great day." I didn't even open my mouth to correct her, and she was off. I watched her car leave and then slowly turned to look at the empty table and then up at Enzo's face. His expression looked just as bewildered as I felt.

"I'm sorry she called us a couple. I should've corrected that," I said, staring at the empty table.

"Don't be sorry about that." Taking my hand, he pulled me in close. The earlier jitters that had disappeared with Gina's arrival were back. "I don't come over because I love the old house." Enzo's eyes filled with mischief as he smirked at me.

"I thought it was because of Hick, Dick, and Dock. They've taken a real liking to you."

"The mice have?" He chuckled. "Just the mice," he asked, tilting my head up.

"I'm a little harder to convince." He smiled at my cheeky response, but whatever I was going to say next floated away in the wind as his lips met mine. The kiss was soft, but there was nothing soft about the look in his eyes.

"I like a challenge," he said, nipping at my lower lip.

"Is that so?" Stepping back, I gave him a playful smile and grabbed my flowers before walking around him. "In that case, do you know how to make pancakes?"

"If I say yes, do I get to drizzle the syrup on you?"

"Um...ah...." I blushed as I stammered over my words.

"I'm joking. Kind of," Enzo said, wrapping his arm around my shoulders. He was so easy to be around that I forgot we had only known each other a short time. Even with the nervousness, I felt comfortable with him touching me.

Flirting had become foreign to me, and I had no idea if I was doing it right. Was there a right way? I'd dated very little, not finding any interest in anyone after Angelo and Dario until now. Enzo was different. I didn't know what it was exactly, but he made my heart race and my blood run hot. I could picture him drizzling syrup on me, and I wanted him to. I would hand him the bottle. I had no idea what had gotten into me.

ENZO

Containing myself around Jasmine was getting harder every day we spent together. She was so beautiful that I wanted to get down on my knees the moment I saw her. I would worship her anywhere. But she was more than her stunning beauty. She was kind and made me laugh. She was strong, and living without her family's protection was brave. Especially, when I knew it was all she'd ever known. Then there was the fact that even though I wasn't supposed to know, I knew she was passionate and loving. She was everything I ever dreamed to be worthy of in my life. I didn't care about who her father was or what her political standing could do for me. At one point that was me and I would've happily taken the edge to move up. Not with her.

"I'll get out the ingredients," Jasmine said, but I grabbed her hand before she could walk away and, with a little tug, wrapped my arms around her.

"Oh..." Her face turned as red as her ripe tomatoes. She had a sweet innocence but shocked me as she grabbed my face and kissed me hard.

Groaning, I picked her up and walked into the living room, laying her on the couch without breaking the kiss. Jasmine didn't let go and shuddered as I settled on top of her.

"I barely know you," Jasmine said, her voice husky, when I broke away and nibbled on her neck.

"I know," I said, but I didn't stop.

"Tell me this first." I stared into her eyes, worried she would ask me about the late-night dreams. "You don't have a girlfriend, or married with a family or anything? That's not why you keep running off all the time?"

I smirked. "I really want to tease you and say yes just to see what you would do, but the answer is no. I don't have anyone special in my life... other than you." I loved how she looked away, her expression so vulnerable for someone so powerful. I had to taste her again and dropped my lips to hers just as my phone rang, and I closed my eyes with a heavy sigh.

"Don't answer it," Jasmine said, and fuck I was tempted. "You said it's your day off. They can't call you into work on your day off, can they?"

"My boss can. He is really fucking annoying like that." I glared up at the hidden camera in the room and decided I needed to switch off my phone the next time. It would totally piss Angelo off, but it would serve him right.

The phone stopped ringing but immediately started again. Annoyed, I pulled myself up and grabbed the cell from my pocket.

"Boss?"

"What the fuck do you think you're doing," Angelo growled into the phone.

"Trying to enjoy my day off."

"I fucking see that. I said keep an eye on her and keep her safe, not fuck her on the couch."

"I'm capable of doing both at the same time. I multitask well," I said, and knew I was pushing my luck.

"If you make me come over there, I will bury you six feet under, and Jasmine can visit your grave instead."

"Fine, I will come into work for a little while." I hit end and wanted to throw the phone, but that wouldn't stop my frustration with the situation. Angelo needed to lighten up.

"You need to go," Jasmine said as she slowly stood.

"Duty calls. How about I make it up to you and take you to dinner tomorrow night?" Cupping her face, I wanted to give Angelo the middle finger, but I didn't trust him not to shoot me. "The Pond has great casual pub food and an easy-going atmosphere. The bartender, Lucky, has a huge personality. You'll love it there."

"So, an official date without a phone?"

"Not a single phone call. I'll even turn it off."

Her smile lit up the entire room. "I'd love that."

"Great, then it's a date." I gave her a quick kiss and let her walk me to the door. Lingering on the threshold, I kissed her again, and she moaned. "See you tomorrow."

Grumbling the entire way, I reached the main house in record time and slammed the front door as I marched inside.

"Are you fucking kidding me," I yelled as I stomped toward the office. Angelo was pacing in front of the monitors when I walked in, but Dario was nowhere in sight. That wasn't good. If we really got into it, there was no one to break us up. "What the hell was that?"

He wheeled on me, and I braced for him to charge across the room. "I told you. No fucking her on your own?"

"We were only making out, and what the hell is your problem? We're supposed to be in this together, but the moment I get close, you pull the plug."

"You can get close without fucking her, and don't deny it, I know that was next." He tapped the gun sitting on his desk, and I shook my head. "Your job is to protect her."

"Oh, you mean protecting her by following her around town and killing five people while it's her face that the authorities plaster on television, calling her a person of interest?" Angelo looked away.

"I took care of that."

"Yeah, after the fact. I looked like a fucking idiot hiding the screen from her," I growled. "I'm surprised she didn't call the cops on me with the suspicious look she gave me."

"You mean idiot is not your norm?" Angelo smirked.

I pointed at him. "Fuck you. I'm taking Jasmine to dinner tomorrow night, and you're not stopping me." He narrowed his eyes. "And if she wants to have crazy car sex, then I'm going to make sure it's a ride she doesn't forget."

"Don't you fucking dare," Angelo snarled and stepped toward me.

"Whoa, what is happening in here?" Dario walked in carrying takeout bags.

"You talk to that asshole, but I'm taking her out tomorrow night, and nothing other than a bullet to the head is stopping me." I stomped out, my heart pounding in my chest. That was the first time I'd stood up to Angelo, and it felt good.

Bang

I ducked at the sound of the gun and patted down my body as I whipped around to see a hole in the drywall. The bullet had missed me by a foot and hit the opposite wall.

"Stop fucking shooting in the house. You're going to kill someone," Dario yelled.

"That's the point."

"Crazy fucker," I yelled back, then ducked and ran just in case he decided to take another shot.

I was falling for Jasmine, and it was the most dangerous and stupid thing I had ever done. But I didn't care. She was worth fighting for.

Chapter Thirty-Three

JASMINE

I THOUGHT I couldn't contain my excitement yesterday, but I jumped out of bed like I was shot out of a cannon. Not only had I managed to withstand the allure of the Absolem once again, but today, I was turning over the unused beds in the greenhouse, readying them for seeds. I'd made enough yesterday to pay for half of a month's rent, and if I could do that three times a month, I could pay for the house and essentials without having to dive into my reserve.

I also fell asleep thinking of Enzo and our date tonight. It was hours away, but adrenaline coursed through my body with the thought of finally being alone without his phone ringing. His boss really did seem like a jerk of the first order. If I ever met him, it would be hard not to give him a piece of my mind.

Dressed and ready to face the day, I jogged down the stairs and made a quick breakfast of scrambled eggs and a smoothie. It was still dark outside when I stepped into the brightly lit greenhouse, but I wanted to start early on the rest of the beds. By my calculation, if I could get the grow cycles down, I would have fresh items every week. Filling the rest of the greenhouse would take a lot of work, but I was determined to do it.

Taking a sip of my smoothie, I sat it down on the edge of the first bed and grabbed my tools. I was looking down when a flash of something caught my eye. A cool trickle of fear traveled down my spine as I stared at my reflection. I couldn't see outside, but it felt like someone was watching me. My eyes strained to see if anything moved. Nothing did, but was that better or worse? My gut screamed worse.

I lived in a world of betrayal and ruthlessness, and from a young age, I'd learned to trust my instincts. The sound of my breathing was loud as I held perfectly still. My eyes darted back and forth, looking for any threat while hoping it was nothing more than an animal.

Thump, thump, thump.

My heart beat louder than a drum in my ears, and I reached for my phone, but it wasn't in my pocket. I was starting to think I had overreacted when I looked down to the bottom of the glass, and there, among the darkness, was a hand. A blood-curdling scream lodged in my throat as my gaze traveled back up, and a set of eyes stared in at me.

I stood frozen, like a rabbit caught in headlights, as my brain caught up to the fact that someone was really there—a man in a mask. Bolting for the house, I pushed through the door just as the outside entrance to the greenhouse smashed. Screaming, I turned and fumbled with the lock, hating that I hadn't gotten Enzo to fix it, too. I just got it bolted as not one but two men slammed into the door, and it groaned and cracked.

Weapon and phone were the only words running through my mind as I ran for the kitchen. My blood ran ice cold with a crash. Glass shattered, and the only door separating me from the intruders broke apart. Yanking open the knife drawer, I grabbed the first handle I could as boots thumped closer.

All my life, I'd prepared for a moment like this—a time when someone broke in and wanted to hurt either my papa or me—when I would need to fight back to survive, and yet now that the moment was here, my hand shook with fear. Even though I always knew it could happen, I never believed it would.

There was no way to get to the stairs or my phone now, but I darted out of the small kitchen that would act like a trap and ran for the front door, switching off the light as I did.

"What the fuck?" The one guy growled. His voice was familiar, and yet my brain couldn't place from where.

"Get her," the second man said, but he'd altered his voice, making him sound like a robot.

The darkness slowed but didn't stop them. I stuffed one foot in a sneaker as they reached the light switch. The second one didn't want to go on, but I didn't care. I was running out of precious seconds and unlocked the front door as the light came back on.

I glanced over my shoulder and wished that I hadn't looked. The men were tall and dressed all in black, including a mask that covered their faces. They had to be wearing contacts because their eyes were bright red like demons had just crashed into my house.

Holding up my weapon, I fumbled with the door handle. They hesitated, giving me a glimmer of hope.

"Get out of my home," I ordered, getting the handle turned.

"Love your fire. I'm going to have fun taming you," the one with the robot voice said.

I smirked. "Not likely."

"I know you're nothing more than a common slut, and you'll soon be our whore to play with."

I glared. "You've got the wrong girl, I'd rather cut your fucking cocks off."

They chuckled. I needed to get out of here. The door released, but I had to step closer to them to get it open, which would put me within arms reach. I took the chance and swiped at them as I opened the door. The large knife glinted as I yelled and made them jump back.

Swiping at them again, I cried out as the guy with the robot voice moved fast and grabbed my wrist. He shoved me hard, and we crashed back into the wall.

"Let go of me," I snarled as I hit and kicked at him. I got him across the face with a punch, but he twisted away with the lower half of his body, avoiding a hit to the balls.

"Bitch," he growled, the mechanical sound making the hair stand on the back of my neck.

I felt like a ragdoll as he yanked my arm forward and slammed me back hard over and over until the knife clattered to the floor. Spinning me around, he pushed my face into the wall. His hot breath on my skin made me twitch, but as he licked the side of my neck, I thought I would be sick.

Hick, Dick, and Dock were freaking out in their tank, their little screeches loud like they were trying to call for help, but no one was coming. I needed to get out of this on my own.

I swung back wildly with my elbows, and a grunt was my reward.

"Bitch, you'll pay for that."

His fingers dug into my arms as he pulled me away from the wall, knocked my feet out from under me, and threw me down onto the floor. My cheek hit the wood hard. I could see the stairs, and with a burst of speed, I lunged forward, but a boot came down on my back, pinning me to the ground. My heart pounded so fast that my chest hurt, and my lungs burned. Adrenaline made me shake, but I wasn't giving up and swung my arms at any body part close enough to hit.

"Close the door," the robot guy said, and as I heard the door close with a bang, my stomach dropped. "Good, now grab her hands."

"You fucking grab her hands. I don't want to get punched," the guy with the familiar voice said.

"Don't be a fucking pussy, grab her hands."

"Fuck you, you don't tell me what to do. I tell you what to do. You grab her fucking hands, and I'll fuck her first."

As the boot lifted from my back, I flipped over, screaming like a banshee and kicking out at whatever I could as I pushed myself backward along the floor. There was no plan. I didn't know where to run, but I needed to put distance between us. Maybe if I could last long enough, the sun would come up and scare them off, or Enzo would stop in with coffee, and his car pulling in would chase them away.

"Fuck you're annoying. I want you to scream, but only when I'm ripping your ass apart," the familiar voice said.

"Fuck you, asshole. If you need to scare and rape me to get off, you're nothing but a pathetic excuse for a man." I kicked hard and got him in the knee. He swore and bent over as the robot man chuckled.

Taking advantage of the distraction, I rolled over and ran for the stairs. My foot touched the bottom step, and I screamed as I was yanked backward by my hair.

"Where do you think you're going slut? You have nowhere to run," the robot man said.

This time, he pushed me down onto the floor and put his knee on my stomach, making it hard to breathe. I punched at his leg, but he laughed as he leered down at me, an evil smile showing under the black ski mask. The red contacts were even more terrifying up close, and I felt my eyes water.

He pulled hard on the front of my shirt, and my tears fell as the material tore. I came here for a new life, a new beginning, and a chance at a happy future, and in only a few weeks, I was attacked in my home. I never thought I would miss the mass of guards that wandered Papa's mansion, but I did now.

"Grab her arms," the robot man said.

"What the fuck did I say to you? You grab her arms."

"For once, just fucking listen to me."

"Fine." Familiar guy stomped behind me, and I glared at him as he kneeled on the floor by my head. As he reached for my hands, I went feral and scratched at his arms. He swore as my nails found skin and dug a long red line.

"Cunt," he growled.

My small victory was only that, as robot voice backhanded me across the face so hard that my ears rang. Rough hands groped at my chest as mine were forced over my head. The yoga pants I wore were no match for the knife that robot man pulled out, and with a quick slice, the material snapped apart, leaving me exposed. I couldn't believe this was happening.

"Spread your legs," robot man snarled as he grabbed my chin and squeezed.

"Fuck you," I said, seething and crossing my feet at my ankles.

"This was fun, and I was going to make this pleasurable for you, but now you're just pissing me off," he said.

"Good. Go to hell," I said, and my cheek stung as he smacked me again. Tears continued to flow from my eyes, but I refused to give in. If they thought I would roll over and be a compliant little female, they had another thing coming.

He grabbed my underwear, and I prepared for him to rip them off my body, but he never got that far. The front door banged, the wood making a cracking sound. *Bang*. It slammed open like a battering ram hit it, splintering and falling off its hinges. I couldn't see who it was, but robot man jumped up and yelled to run.

Everything happened so fast. It was like my fantasy dream and living nightmare clashed together as Dario ran past me and tackled one of the men to the ground. Angelo stepped through the door, his gun drawn, and I rolled over and covered my head as shots flew in all directions. Glass shattered, and debris fluttered to the floor as the bullets lodged into the drywall.

"Fuck," Dario snarled, and I looked to see the man he'd been fighting running toward the greenhouse doors. He had left a knife stuck in Dario's shoulder.

I didn't know if this was happening or if my brain was trapped in some crazy dreamscape, but I crawled across the floor to where he'd propped himself up.

"Stupid knife. I should've seen that," Dario said as he glared at the blade like it insulted him.

Hand shaking, I touched his face, and his eyes shifted to mine and warmed. "Oh my god, you're really here," I said, and he smiled.

"Amorina," he said softly, his hand cupping my cheek.

"Oh, my god," was all I could come up with to say. "What do I do? Do I pull it out?"

"Enzo, make sure they are off the property," Angelo ordered, then squatted beside me. I watched Enzo jog past, gun in hand, and looked at Angelo as all the little pieces of the last few weeks fell into place.

I stared at him with my mouth open. "It was really you, wasn't it?"

He looked at me and then at Dario's shoulder. "We need to talk, but let's wait until we're out of here."

"That wasn't a no." He smirked. "Oh my god," I said again, my brain reviewing everything since I arrived at this house.

"I'm fine." Dario waved off Angelo's help. "I'll drive myself to St. Prince's Hospital. Doctor Morales still owes me a favor."

"You're not driving yourself," I said.

"You were the one attacked and telling me what to do?" He lifted a brow, and I remembered that I was practically naked. Pulling the sides of my torn top together, I glared at him.

"Yes, I am."

"Jasmine is right. You can't drive yourself. I'll get Enzo to drop Jasmine and me off, then take you to get stitched up."

"I'm not going anywhere with you," I said. Even though I knew I couldn't stay here, the thought of being alone with Angelo anywhere pissed me off. My emotions were slowly catching up, and the shock was quickly replaced with anger.

"They're gone," Enzo said, his boots crunching as he walked through my destroyed greenhouse doors.

"You were in on this? You knew all this time who I was," I said, and he swallowed hard and looked away from my eyes. "I don't believe this."

"We can argue about it later. We should go just in case there are more," Angelo said.

"More what? They were robbers, looking to take advantage of a woman alone."

It had been so long since I'd seen Angelo's arrogant eyebrow lift, and I still wanted to smack it off his face. "That was no robbery. They were here for you and you alone. Now let's go."

He had to be kidding. The thought of going anywhere with him had the same appeal as an STD. Angelo grabbed my arm, and I went to yank it away, but I screamed when he stood, picking me up as he went and tossed me over his shoulder.

"You asshole. What is it with men?" I tried to ignore his muscles under my hands and his ass flexing in a sexy pair of jeans within grabbing distance. How he could still make me think of him like that after two men attacked me made me hate him even more.

Not in my wildest imagination could I picture my morning going like this, and the moment Angelo put me down, I was punching him in the face.

Chapter Thirty-Four

ANGELO

"FUCK," I growled as I rubbed my jaw. She still had a hell of a hook.

"I can't believe you did this to me. The audacity!" Jasmine fumed as she marched around the massive bedroom. "You disappear for five years and then randomly swoop back into my life. You don't tell me and instead sleep with me when I'm drugged and let me think I am going crazy? What the hell is wrong with you?"

She turned her furious golden eyes on me, and I almost crumbled to my knees with the need coursing through my body. Holy fuck, she was sexy. Not even my vivid memories could compare to the real thing. Jasmine was yelling at me and pointing, but I couldn't concentrate on a single word with her shirt hanging open and nothing but her lace bra and underwear on.

"Are you listening to me?"

"Of course I am," I said, and she glared as she crossed her arms over her chest. "Okay, I have no idea what you said."

"Unbelievable." She grabbed a book off the bookshelf and hurled it at me. I stepped out of the way and watched it smack into the wall. Good arm.

"That was a first edition," I said, smirking as she yelled and grabbed two more. Shit. I ducked as one sailed over my head, but the other grazed my side.

"You asshole!" She roared and snatched a small statue on the shelf. I jumped out of the way as it smashed into the wall. "I hate you! You're nothing but a common monello!"

"Ouch, that hurt. I'm not a street rat," I argued, shocked that she would hit below the belt like that. "Oh shit." Jasmine grabbed the bronze paperweight and threw it at me like a quarterback. It crashed into the picture behind me, all the glass shattering on impact. She snatched the antique hand mirror and looked like she would throw it but stomped toward me.

"Whoa, what are you doing with that?"

With a yell, she took a swing, but I sidestepped her attack. "I think you're overreacting," I said.

"Overreacting? Are you kidding me?" She took another swipe at my head, and I jumped back.

"You enjoyed every second of it." I thought I'd seen Jasmine angry, but she looked ready to eat me alive and spit out my bones as she two-handed the long decorative handle of the silver weapon and swung at me like she was playing baseball.

"You were just attacked, and you haven't even said if you're alright." I tried to derail her rage before she destroyed the entire room.

"Of course, I'm not alright, but not because of those two jerks. Night after night, you snuck into my room!" She swung again like it was a sword, and I did not doubt that in her mind, she was cutting me open with one.

"Okay, enough of that. We need to have a civil conversation so I can explain," I held up my hands as Jasmine stalked me across the room.

"Civil, my fucking ass," she growled, and it was the sexiest thing I'd ever heard.

"I'm all for fucking your ass," I said, my lip curling up as I pictured her on all fours with her ass in the air.

“I’m going to kill you.” She lunged at me, and I pushed her arm away and stepped out of punching distance.

“Put the mirror down,” I ordered, but she swung at me again instead. “Do it one more time, and I’m using the mirror on you,” I threatened.

“Screw you,” she said, her eyes all fire as she took another shot at my face.

Grabbing her hand, I yanked the mirror out of her hold and spun her around, using her momentum to push her over the arm of the massive reading chair.

“Get off of me, Angelo.”

“I warned you,” I said, grabbing her flailing arms and pinning them behind her back. Fuck she was a sight with the adorable blue strip of lace running down her cheeks.

“You wouldn’t dare,” she said, glaring over her shoulder at me.

“You know me better than that.” I ran the rounded tip of the handle up and down the fabric of her thong. She wiggled back and forth, and I smirked. “See, I knew you liked it.”

“It’s called trying to get away,” she said, but she couldn’t hide the softer look in her eyes. If I let her go, she would still try to kill me, but I had no intention of releasing her hands until my Tiger was a moaning mess.

“Is that what this is called?”

Using the handle, I moved the thong out of the way while she was still trying to kick me, but I knew she would try. Standing between her legs and keeping them spread, I was safe from her wrath. Bending over, I nipped at the soft skin of her ass cheek.

“Knock it off, and let me go.”

“I’m never letting you go again,” I said, and I meant it. “If I have to lock you up in this room forever, I will, Tiger.” Unable to resist, I licked a line up her pussy, and she growled, making my cock throb inside my jeans. “Fuck, I missed this pussy. You taste so good.”

“I swear to God, Angelo.” Jasmine’s breathy voice gave away how she really felt. I groaned and thrust my tongue into her and didn’t miss the gasp she let out. She was already soaking wet. I wasn't surprised. She always got wet when she was angry with me. Angry sex had been on the menu more than once while we were together. Apparently I had a habit of pissing her off...admittedly, I liked it.

"No, you're mine." I couldn't get enough and swirled my tongue deeper.

"I...said...." She didn't get a chance to finish the sentence as I sucked her harder. Slipping the mirror handle into my mouth, I got it good and wet before I pushed it into her pussy. Fuck, it was sexy watching it disappear one inch at a time. "Angelo, don't you...ah fuck...you're not actually fucking me with a mirror?"

"Does it feel good?" I pumped it in short, fast strokes, and her legs shook. "All those ridges and the round head rubbing all the right places, making you want to come."

"No," she said, but it ended on a moan.

"You lying to me, Tiger?" I loved teasing her. Jasmine didn't answer, but she didn't need to. I switched positions and released her hands, smiling when she didn't try to jerk them away. Kneeling behind her, I fucked faster with the mirror and resumed my treat as I sucked on her hard clit. "I think you're lying and don't want me to stop. I think you want me to fuck you all day."

"No...ah...oh fuck."

"What's that? I couldn't hear you." Getting her riled up had always been my favorite pastime. I dreamt of seeing that look in her eyes again. "Did you say you want to come all over the mirror like a good girl?"

"No," she said, but the heat in her tone was completely gone.

I pumped the silver mirror faster, her legs flexing, and I knew she was close. "That's it, Tiger. Be a good girl, and let me watch you come." Her muscles tightened around the handle, and as she screamed, I thought I would erupt along with her. The sound of her pleasured wail as I licked faster at her pussy was a slice of heaven I'd missed for too long.

Jasmine thrust back harder and shuddered as she came again,

and I had to have her. She slumped on the arm of the chair, her body going lax, as I pulled the mirror out. I moved into her line of sight and sucked the long handle into my mouth, sucking off her juices. Her eyes flared with anger but also passion.

I finished licking off every little bit and turned the mirror so she could look at herself. "Look at how sexy you are."

Her eyes found mine. "I hate you."

"See, I know you're lying. I know you still love me as much as I love you." Standing, I put the mirror down and picked her up before she got any more ideas about finding a weapon to try and kill me.

"What are you doing," Jasmine asked as I laid her down on the bed.

"I plan on fucking you all day or until you pass out." She opened her mouth, and I knew by the look in her eyes that she wanted to tell me off. At my peril, I placed my finger over her lips. "I know I hurt you, and I know I have to explain. You can swear at me, throw things at me, and tell me off all you want tomorrow. But for today, I'm asking you to leave it at the door."

"You let me think I was dreaming."

"I know...I figured that was the only way you'd ever want me again."

Her fingers trailed down the side of my face, and I leaned into the palm of her hand and closed my eyes. The heaviness in my chest eased slightly from that single touch. I'd gotten so used to the empty void where my heart was that I'd forgotten what it was like to feel whole.

"You're really here."

"Yes, Tiger, I'm really here."

"You know I'm still going to kick your ass no matter what happens," she said, and I smiled, kissing her hand.

"I wouldn't expect anything less."

Her hands slid around my neck. "I shouldn't say yes. I should shoot you with your own gun and walk out the door." Her eyes glanced to my gun laying on the nightstand.

"You definitely should do that if you ever want to leave again." Dropping my head to her neck, I breathed her in and had to contain my rage at the sight of the bruise forming. I would find those fuckers and kill them slowly.

"What happens if I say yes?" I loved the breathless sound of her voice as she turned her head to give me better access.

"You'll be stuck with me forever." She looked at me, and I could see the doubt in her eyes. I hated that she looked at me like that. I hated that she didn't trust me, even though she had every reason not to. "I'll explain what happened. Just know I never wanted to leave or stay away." Those beautiful eyes of hers searched my face.

I couldn't take the chance that she might say no and dropped my lips to hers. It was unfair, but I would do anything necessary to keep Jasmine. If that meant I needed to play dirty, I would do it without feeling an ounce of regret.

She tasted like I remembered, and as hard as I tried to keep the kiss sweet, it didn't last. I groaned when her arms wrapped around my neck and held me tighter. Sheer desperation had me ripping my T-shirt off. Next was her bra and the tattered shirt. The kiss was feverish, our hands roaming each other's bodies as I undid my jeans.

"Fuck," I growled, pulling away to get rid of the rest of our clothing.

I remembered the first time she was laid out before me like this. I never forgot the moment when I realized my feelings ran far deeper than lust alone. Stroking my cock I loved that she watched my hand and blushed as I groaned.

She was so beautiful, squirming on the bed, covering herself with her arms. How she could still be shy was a mystery to me, but I loved this softer side as much as I loved the strong woman who would punch me in the face. Her eyes remained on mine as I crawled between her legs. I kept expecting her to tell me to leave, or I would wake up like I was the one drugged all this time, and she was once more a a fantasy that my desperation had created. A memory that tortured me the moment my eyes closed.

I sucked her lush bottom lip into my mouth, and she kissed me as I pressed into her. It felt like the first time all over again...no this was better. Being forced apart made me miss her on a level I couldn't explain with common words. Only ballads of love and sonnets of longing could come close, and even then, it paled in comparison to being held and loved by her.

With her arms wrapped around me and her soft moans filling my ears, my control was ready to snap. Thrusting into her, she clung tighter, and my sanity sailed out the window like an arrow.

I had to be gentle and hold back when we snuck into her room, but not anymore. Capturing her lips, I pounded into her the way I'd dreamed of and swallowed every one of her screams down.

"Come on, Tiger, be a good girl and come all over my cock." She moaned and nipped my lip as her nails dug into my shoulders.

Sliding my hands under her ass, I pulled her tighter into my body as I pressed into her. I couldn't get deep enough even when there was no more cock to push into her. It would never be enough. She made me crazy. Her whimpers grew louder, and nothing else existed other than her. Breaking the kiss, I sucked her earlobe into my mouth, and she shuddered, wrapping her legs around my waist.

"Fuck me, Tiger. You make me feel alive," I softly growled in her ear. "Let go, come for me. Scream my name." I nipped at the soft skin on her neck and groaned as she clawed at my back, my name echoing around the room as she came. "Fuck, yes."

My fingers dug into her ass as I let go and didn't hold anything back. Fucking her as hard as I could, I growled like the beast she made me.

"Oh fuck!" I gritted my teeth as I came so hard I thought I would black out. Panting into the side of her neck, I felt her heart pounding as fast as my own. "I missed you so much," I said, kissing her neck. "I hate that we were separated."

I looked up as she turned away and realized she was crying. Even as she covered her eyes, I could see the tears traveling down her cheeks to her trembling lip.

"Don't cry, I've got you." I pulled her in tight as I rolled to my side, and she buried her head and let it all out. "I've got you." I rubbed her back, hating that this was what we'd become. "Shh, it's okay."

"It's not okay. You ripped my heart out and left me when I needed you the most, so no, it's not okay." Jasmine pulled away and gripped the blanket to her chest as she cried.

"I know I have so much to make up for, but I never wanted to leave you."

"But you did, and you cut off all contact with me. Why? Why did you do that? I tried to reach you so many times. You wouldn't respond, and then you blocked me. Do you have any idea how much that hurt?"

I couldn't stand the look in her eyes. The guilt already eating at me swirled to the surface and grabbed me by the throat. Looking down at the bed, I remembered all too well how hard it was to block her number and delete her from my phone. It felt soul-shattering to cut her off, but it needed to be done.

"I tried to broker a deal with your father to marry you, but he wouldn't listen to reason. When I realized we could be years, I couldn't stand talking to you, knowing that we might never come home. It wasn't fair to anyone." As hard as it was, I met her eyes, and she was shaking her head. "Please, Jasmine, try to understand. I asked him so many times. He wouldn't take my calls anymore. I had no leverage, and I couldn't string you along."

"You don't understand." She stood from the bed, and I got up to follow her, but she pushed my hands away as I touched her shoulders. "Don't, I can't. I'll fall apart all over again if you touch me."

I grabbed a large hoodie from my dresser and handed it over. Jasmine looked so damn small in it as she pulled it on. I loved this look. I loved her in all my clothes, but my dress shirts with ties had me on my knees.

"What don't I understand?" She hugged herself and squeezed her eyes tight. "Please tell me. I want us, and I want to fix this."

"You can't fix what happened," she said, her golden eyes shimmering with more unshed tears. "You had your leverage, Angelo. At least you had it for a time." I stared at her, not understanding what she was talking about. Jasmine sighed and sucked in a deep breath like she was collecting herself for a blow. "I was pregnant," she said, and my heart thumped harder. Her eyes roamed over my face. "And then I miscarried and...I had no one I could trust other than Ciro, but I was too embarssed to call him and ask for help. I was in so much pain, and there was way too much blood." She covered her mouth as a sob wracked her body.

I sat there, not moving, just staring at her. I couldn't have heard her right.

"The bleeding wouldn't stop and I knew something was wrong. I was growing weaker by the day, and I finally had to unlock my door and find my papa. A guard had to help me to his room, I was...so scared. I found out I was pregnant, and you cut me off. I was going to keep our baby...." She stopped and choked back a sob. "I was going to keep our baby. I wanted our baby, but fate had other ideas, and everything was ripped away from me."

The guilt and sadness twisted in my heart like a knife. Standing, I wrapped Jasmine up in my arms.

"I'm so sorry," I said, my throat closing. Not only for what we lost, for what I caused, but for what she went through alone. "I'm so, so sorry." I could only imagine what her father thought of me. The anger and disgust I saw in his eyes all made sense now. I'd felt so many horrible things about him, contemplated killing him, and then he caught me stealing a family heirloom. I closed my eyes, all my mistakes and wrong turns biting my conscience and infecting it with a venom I knew I would never be free of.

"I never meant to hurt you. I love you, Jasmine. I swear to you if I'd known...." I couldn't get the rest out. My heart felt like it was in a vise. Of all the anger she could and should hurl at me, this blow took me to my knees. But, as she sobbed and held me, I knew this was what she needed, what she needed when I hadn't been there to help her through. Forcing my emotions down, I picked Jasmine up and walked back to the bed.

"I've got you now. I swear I'll never let anything come between us again, and I'll always be here when you need me." Grabbing the comforter, I pulled it up and kissed her head, holding her tight.

How could I expect her to forgive me when I wasn't sure I would ever forgive myself?

Chapter Thirty-Five

ANGELO

THE REST of the day was an emotional mess. There was no other word for it. I made love to Jasmine three more times, and in between, we talked, or she broke into tears. Fuck, I hated feeling useless. I felt her pain gripping my heart as surely as her hand with each small whimper that passed between her lips.

It was dark when she fell asleep, and I slipped from the bed walking into the bathroom. Closing the door, I turned on the light and stood there as emotions I didn't understand and couldn't contextualize flooded my system. Regret, rage, fear, and sadness swirled in my gut, but leading the pack was guilt. I hated leaving for Chicago, but worse, I hated that I cut off contact with the one person I loved. I wasn't there when she needed me the most.

My knees gave out, and I fell to the floor as I silently screamed. My child, I lost my child, and I wasn't there. The thought of Jasmine writhing in pain and begging her father for help tormented my mind. Crawling to the edge of the tub, I leaned against it and hung my head as I let the tears fall. I'd only cried once in my life, and it was when I blocked Jasmine. The irony that what brought me to tears then brought me to tears now was not lost on me.

I didn't hear the door open. I didn't even see Dario walk in until he sat down beside me. He didn't say anything and waited for me to speak. I'd never let anyone else see me like this. The son of a Don wasn't allowed to feel in front of others. It was a life of suffering in silence.

I stumbled over the words like an infant learning to speak as I revealed what Jasmine told me.

"This was all my fault. It was my idea from the start, and it was my idea to cut off contact." I shook my head as Dario wrapped his arm around my shoulders. "What have I done?" Looking at my friend, I watched a lone tear slide down his cheek. What a pair we made. "I don't know how to fix this."

"You can't fix the past. You made choices that, at the time, you thought were the correct ones. If we could see the future, how much easier life would be," Dario said, and I knew he was right, yet it didn't make me feel better. It didn't make any of this better.

"I hurt her. I told her I loved her and told her I wouldn't leave. I told her I would protect her, and when she needed me, I wasn't there." I stared at my hands, which had seen a different kind of blood, and it was like the stains had reappeared. "I always have a plan, but with this...how do I ask her to forgive me?"

"I don't have that answer, but I wish I did, for both our sakes."

Pushing myself off the floor, I locked eyes with my reflection, but the man in the mirror didn't seem to have the answers either.

"I've spent my entire life working to be worthy, and in the end, it was by my hand that I was unworthy. I should cut her and Enzo loose and let them find happiness, but I can't let her go. I'm a selfish asshole Dario, and I love her too much not to try and put the genie back in the bottle."

JASMINE

Angelo flooded my mind as my eyes fluttered open. Turning my head, I knew he wasn't in here with me. The bed was cold without the warmth of his body. If it weren't for the fact that I was not in my bed, I would have sworn everything that happened yesterday was a dream.

Every part of me ached as I pushed myself up and took in the massive bedroom I was too angry to appreciate yesterday. It suited Angelo with the masculine colors and large furniture, but what intrigued me were the paintings on the walls. I recognized most of the places from back home and smiled when I spotted a picture of the café that Angelo, Dario, and I had gone to many times growing up. I remembered all too well him throwing struffoli honey balls at me and them getting stuck in my hair. I also recalled when he went and got me my favorite desserts and brought them to me one night after everyone had gone to bed. We stayed up all night fooling around and eating the treats. Enzo knowing what to pick up at the bakery now made sense. I'd stared in the pink box, impressed with his choices, but he had help.

Annoyance settled back in. Angelo had explained some of what happened but still chose not to announce himself. He snuck into my room and sent Enzo to...I didn't know what his ultimate plan was there.

I stretched as I slipped out of bed and couldn't say that I didn't like the aching, but I would keep that to myself. Angelo didn't need another reason for his head to turn into the Goodyear blimp.

The shower was large and had more heads than people who lived here. It took a minute, but I figured out all the controls and knobs and stepped under the hot spray. Washing myself with his soaps and shampoos felt dangerous, like I needed another reason to be reminded of him all day.

Rinsing off, I searched for clothes and found a large duffel bag open by the closet with some of my things piled on top. The entire bag was full of my stuff. Someone had raided my house, and while normally this would piss me off, considering what else I was angry about, clean clothes were low on the list.

It was stupid, but I was more pissed off that he left me to wake up alone after everything Angelo and I shared and talked about yesterday. Shaking my damp hair, I was ready for another fight and figured I would find him working.

The house was massive, and it took me a second to find the stairs, but as I trotted down, I heard music and talking along with the amazing smell of breakfast. My nerves were getting the better of me, making butterflies flit around with the sound of their voices as I stepped closer to the kitchen door.

There they were: Angelo, Dario, and Enzo. I really wanted to be pissed as they smiled and laughed, but they were all half-naked and wearing aprons as they cooked. It was not helping me stay angry. The shirtlessness was distracting. I didn't care what people said about being above the physical. When you had three sculpted men cooking in front of you, your brain misfired. I owned that.

"Hey," I said, and they stopped and stared at me.

Dario slowly smiled, and the look in his eyes tugged at the soft, squishy parts of my heart. Of all of them, I understood him and the position he was in the most, but that didn't mean I wasn't still hurt and going to give him a piece of my mind.

"Fuck you are a vision. I can't stop staring," Angelo said, and I cocked a brow at him.

"Flattery will not get you back in my good books." Crossing my arms, I shot him a stern glare.

"How about flattery and a lot more sex?"

I rolled my eyes at the teasing comment but was tempted to grab the spatula and beat him with it.

"He's not wrong. You take my breath away, always have," Dario said, setting the mixing bowl down and coming around the island. The closer he got, the faster my heart pumped. Dario stopped in front of me, and I stared up at his handsome face. He looked much more rugged than when they left for the US, but it suited him. He was undeniably sexy.

"I'm going to smack you," I said.

"I deserve it."

I smacked him across the face as hard as I could, and it echoed loudly in the quiet room. I shook my stinging hand while his head hardly moved.

"Do you want to do it again to the other side?"

"Tempted, but no, that hurt."

Dario grabbed my hand and brought it to his mouth to lay soft kisses all over the reddened area that was still sensitive from me burning myself.

"Don't worry, Amorina, you could slap me every day, all day, for a thousand years, and it would never equal the agony I felt losing you. I didn't think my heart would ever heal, yet seeing you here is like a balm to my aching soul."

"Wow, who knew Dario was all...like that?" Enzo said, but Dario ignored him.

I knew. My body heated with his pretty words and intense stare. Dario was a poet and loved to paint, but no one ever saw that side. To the world, he was a bodyguard who would kill you in the blink of an eye, but with me, he'd always been different.

"I'm still angry, and I don't know when I'll get over you sneaking into my room. Or letting him." I stuck my thumb in Angelo's direction.

"I know."

I knew it was Angelo's idea, but Dario didn't throw him under the bus. He didn't even look his way. His loyalty to those he loved was something I cherished.

"You know I haven't decided to take you or Angelo back?"

Angelo made a disgusted sound, and I glared in his direction, but he continued to cut up fruit and didn't look at me.

"I do."

I nodded.

"How's the shoulder?" I touched his arm near the bandage, and he shrugged, not looking away from my face.

"I'll live. Can I hug you?"

I nibbled my bottom lip and knew every touch I shared was another step closer to falling down the rabbit hole to a strange world once more. It didn't matter. I nodded and fell into his warmth. It felt like no time had passed as I wrapped my arms around Dario and closed my eyes.

"I've missed you," Dario whispered in my ear. "Can we talk privately later?" I nodded into his chest as I held back the tears.

It wasn't fair to have had them in my life for such a relatively short time, and yet they had plagued me ever since.

Kissing the top of my head, he pulled back, and the corner of his mouth turned up. "I'm making pancakes just the way you like. Would you like a coffee?"

"That would be great."

Angelo popped a berry into his mouth and winked at me but said nothing else. There had to be a country where his sexy arrogance was criminal, and I could have him locked up.

I looked over at Enzo, and he cleared his throat. "Are you going to explain yourself? Was any of what happened real, or were you playing a part for Angelo?"

"No, I swear that's not how it happened...I...."

I held up my hand and stopped him from continuing. "I don't want to hear about it right now."

"What? But...."

"No," I said and bit back the smile at the distraught look on his face. It served him right. He spent the last few weeks with me almost every single day and had earned my trust. I thought he genuinely liked me, and even if he actually did, I wanted him to suffer a little.

"Why do they get to apologize?"

"She's not playing," Angelo said. "You better walk away and get some air before you piss her off even more." I didn't know the dynamic between them, but the smirk only I could see told me he was having way too much fun antagonizing Enzo.

Enzo glared at Angelo's back and then threw his hands up. "You did this. This is all your fault." He stomped out of the room, and there was a certain satisfaction to pissing him off and making him feel as in the dark as he'd kept me.

Angelo leaned on the counter and smiled at me. "It's nice not being the only one in deep shit for a change."

"Maybe, but you're still in the deepest." I crossed my arms as he pushed away from the counter. Picking up a strawberry on the way to me, he smiled, and I squirmed.

"Are we still talking about getting me in trouble or something else that I get deeper?" Leaning in, he ran his lips up the side of my neck, and goosebumps and shivers raced along my skin.

"Do you think your charm will work on me?" I managed to sound unaffected, but my insides were turning to mush.

"Maybe." He held out the strawberry for me to bite before slipping the rest into his mouth. The fruit was sweet and exploded with flavor on my tongue. I squealed as he grabbed my waist and sat me on the large island. "Maybe I lay you out on the counter and have you for breakfast instead."

"Didn't you get enough yesterday?"

Wrapping his hand around my throat, he turned my head slowly from side to side, a dark, predatory look in his eyes. "I could never get enough of you."

Anger flared in my gut and I glared at him. "Is that so? So tell me, is that why you paraded around with models and American princesses for the world to see, because you couldn't get enough of me?"

"I didn't want any of them."

I narrowed my gaze as the tension in the room grew. My jealousy was as volatile as any volcano, and I'd destroyed a few expensive items over the last five years.

"Yet, I'm sure you had them."

"You're free to kick his ass, but can we have a nice breakfast first. I already have cannoli made, and the saccottino will be done shortly. I'll happily help you later. Would you like me to shoot him? You're the only one that I would shoot him for."

Angelo released my neck and glared at Dario, who'd managed to defuse the room, but it wouldn't last. Angelo and I had a lot more to work through if we would ever have a chance. That was if I even took him back, took any of them back, for that matter.

"At least I know where the line is on your loyalty."

Dario smirked. "It's in the same place it's always been."

"I can live with that. I'd hate to ruin a great breakfast," I said, and Angelo huffed and wandered back to the fruit salad he was in the midst of making.

Slipping off the counter, I took the coffee that Dario held out to me and found it made perfectly. He gave me a shy smile before returning to work, and my heart sighed. I didn't want to let them in again after all the sadness and anger, but standing here with them felt like no time had passed at all.

Would Angelo even let me go now that we were in the same space? I had a feeling that would turn into another fight. The number of things we needed to argue about was growing. How did this even happen? How had I escaped my past only to run right into it all over again?

Chapter Thirty-Six

DARIO

THE ENTIRE BREAKFAST was a tennis match of insults and retaliation. I would've laughed at Jasmine and Angelo if it weren't over such serious topics, but the tension was growing out of control.

"Don't tell me what to do. I am going home, and that is that," Jasmine said. She gripped her fork so tightly I thought she might use it as a projectile to throw at Angelo's head.

"No, you're not," Angelo growled.

"Yes, I am."

"No. You're. Not."

"I'm not staying here with you," Jasmine said, and it hurt to hear, even though she had all the reasons in the world not to want anything to do with us.

"Yes, you are. Whether you like it or not." Angelo stood from the table and slammed his plate down on the island.

"I'm not your prisoner, Angelo. You can't keep me here like I am."

"What part of not safe, do you not understand?" He placed his hands on his hips, and Jasmine rose to her feet and leaned her hands on the table.

"I can take care of myself."

"Oh, is that what you were doing when we stormed your front

door? Taking care of yourself? Were you waiting for them to get you fully naked before you threw them out?"

With that comment, all the air was sucked out of the room, and I pinched the bridge of my nose. I had no idea how Enzo looked so calm. In fact, he seemed to be enjoying the endless drama.

"Well, at least with them, I knew they were trying to rape me. I had no idea you did," Jasmine said through gritted teeth.

Angelo laughed, but it was a maniacal sound, and I could feel this conversation going sideways at a lightning-fast pace.

"Ha! You agreed to marry me, and you consented to non-consent, and...you never rescinded either. Technically, it's on you that this happened. I'm still your fiancé, no matter whose dick you tied yourself to while I was gone."

"I'm going to kill you." Jasmine lifted the bowl of fruit salad off the table. I grabbed it from her before it got hurled, and there was a huge mess to clean up. "He is impossible. How do you not shoot him in the night?" Jasmine turned her furious eyes on me.

"I ask myself that same question daily."

"Ugh. Screw you, Angelo. I need some air." She stomped out of the kitchen, and I knew the fight would resume. Neither of them would back down. I'd seen them lock horns before, and it only got worse until there was an explosion.

"Don't wander too far, Tiger, or I'll hunt your adorable ass down," Angelo yelled back.

"Do it, and I'll claw your eyes out," Jasmine yelled before the back door slammed shut.

"If she wants to get her things, then you two go with her and don't let her out of your sight. Bring her straight back here and keep an eye out for anything suspicious. I don't trust her not to try and take off, and we have no idea who they were yet or why they wanted to hurt Jasmine." He shook his head and stomped out of the kitchen. The room plunged into silence except for the sound of Enzo chewing.

He had a piece of bacon hanging out of his mouth and another in his hand. I'd never seen someone double-fist bacon until now.

"Are they always like this," Enzo asked as he took another bite.

"They can get pretty volatile, but this is next level." I sat the bowl of fruit down and decided to follow Jasmine to try and make her see that staying here was the safest decision, even if she didn't want to see our faces.

"It's fucking awesome." Enzo smirked. "I've never seen Jasmine like that. She's always so...non bloodthirsty." He shrugged. "But, it's fucking hot, and I'm not going to complain that Angelo is making me look good."

"Unbelievable."

Marching out of the kitchen, I found Jasmine sitting in the gazebo facing the small pond. She looked just as she had the night before we left for Chicago. Jasmine hadn't wanted us to see her crying and had slipped down to the beach in the middle of the night. She had sat just like this, staring at the dark water with the same shrouded sadness in her eyes.

"Do you mind if I sit?"

"Are you here to take Angelo's side?"

"I'm here because I love you." She looked up, and the glare softened. She nodded, and I took the invitation to sit on the picnic bench beside her. I didn't say anything, letting her feel and sort through her thoughts.

"I know he's right, you know," she said, her voice barely louder than a whisper. "About staying at least, the rest...I may kill him. I'm giving you fair warning."

"I know." My mouth pulled up into a lopsided grin.

"I just hate the idea of him or anyone taking control of me all over again. I came here to...well, to get a fresh start and escape doing whatever the men around me wanted me to do. I'm building something, and I don't care that it's just selling fruit and vegetables from a roadside stand. The point is that it and all the decisions made since I left home are mine and mine alone. I just know he'll try to turn me back into the perfect princess on his arm."

I glanced down at the top of her head and so badly wanted to wrap my arm around her. “Did you really hate your old life that much?”

She sighed and rubbed at her face. “Not all of it. I miss my papa something fierce, and I loved it when the three of us were good. I saw a whole future, but we know how that turned out, and...I’ve changed.”

We lapsed into silence, and I wrapped my arm around her as the breeze picked up, and she shivered. I expected her to pull away, but she snuggled closer, and my heart swelled.

“I don’t think he’ll try to change you. Angelo has changed, too, and he loves your tenacity. You might be surprised.” She crossed her arms but didn’t say anything. “Why are you here? I know you’re engaged to Ciro,” I said, and her shocked eyes flicked up to mine. “News travels fast, and I still have friends I talk to regularly back home.”

That was a bit of a stretch. They wouldn’t call themselves my friends but people who owed me information. But that was beside the point.

“It was an arranged marriage. I didn’t agree to it. I love Ciro as a friend, but nothing more.”

“So you left?”

“I did. My papa thinks I need a man to take care of me, and I don’t think I need anyone,” she said, her voice was strong but sad.

“You never have, but I understand your father. We live in a different world than most. So, are they looking for you?”

She looked down at her hands. “Maybe. Most likely. I don’t know. I didn’t tell anyone I was leaving, so...I don’t know.”

Angelo was right about her not wanting to be found. I couldn’t help but also wonder if he was right that of all the places in the world to go, there wasn’t some push from a higher power to bring us back together. I really hated it when Angelo was right. He was utterly unbearable when he gloated.

“I want to say I’m sorry.” She lifted her head, and our eyes locked.

"I'm sorry we left, and for you having to run, this is not how things were supposed to turn out."

The breeze picked up, and Jasmine's hair blew around her face. The long, wavy strands reminded me of waves. Could a soul be hypnotized by another?

From the day we met, she'd held my heart in the palm of her hand, and with each passing year, her hand closed a little more until I was firmly in her grasp. I would never love another.

"I know you didn't have a choice but to go, Dario. I know how our world works." She lifted a shoulder and let it fall. "It's why I also knew I couldn't have a life with you without Angelo. I did love him... grudgingly still do," she grumbled. "Don't tell him I said that." I smirked. "But, he is just so damn...uh."

"I know. He is the son of a Don, and arrogant, and an ass, and thinks he always knows best."

"Exactly."

"Maybe I didn't have a choice about going, but I could've ignored Angelo's order to cut off all contact. Just because he thought what he was doing was right didn't mean I had to follow. But, I did what I was told because on some level I agreed with him, and I regret that." I held her tighter.

"Did Angelo tell you about what happened after the two of you left?" Her voice was steady, but the sadness was back, and I kissed the top of her head. My heart ached over what happened. Not being there for her was bad enough, but the fact she couldn't reach us and had to ask her father for help...we were lucky there wasn't a hit on us before we stole the egg. I couldn't even imagine what she felt or what that was like. All I wanted to do was pull her into my lap and hold onto her forever.

"Yeah, he did. He's putting on a good act but tearing himself apart."

"He could've fooled me." She drew little circles on my leg with her finger, and I smiled as she made the infinity symbol.

"You must remember what he is like. Emotions are not his strong suit, and what he feels comes out all wrong," I said, and she laughed.

"I don't know if I want to stay here with him, Dario. He hurt me, he really hurt me, and let's not even get started on his latest late-night escapades. I can't believe he did that." She leaned back a little, her eyes searching my face. "You didn't want to. I remember begging you."

I looked away as the complex emotions twisted together in my chest. "It wasn't because I didn't want to. Trust me, I wanted to. I've always wanted you." Her hand touched my cheek, soft fingers brushing against my jaw, and I closed my eyes, soaking in the caress. "No matter what happened while we were apart, I never stopped loving you. Neither has Angelo, but that is for you and him to sort out."

Jasmine's hand fell from my face, and I looked at her.

"Do you know how painful it was to hear the guys laugh and talk about the two of you? How they would talk about how well you were doing and making a name for yourselves? Lets now forget all the women? And if it wasn't the men, it was the women chattering. I couldn't escape it. I saw the social media videos and beautiful princesses draped all over Angelo and knew what would happen later. It killed me. I can't let him in like that again, Dario. If I do, then what? He will leave the next time his father calls, and I'll...I just can't."

I tilted my head and examined her expression. "You don't know?"

"Know what?"

"Angelo isn't speaking to his father. They had a falling out a couple of years ago. We've been moving around ever since. This is the first place we settled down. Angelo has businesses of his own that he built from the ground up." Her mouth fell open.

"Well...it's about time he got out from under his father's condescending narcissism. Angelo always deserved better and was never appreciated. It doesn't change anything, though. How am I supposed to trust him?"

"It's not just him that needs to build back your trust. Don't let me or Enzo off the hook. There is always a choice and, orders or not, we could've said no."

"And end up shot." She scoffed.

"True, but we still have to own our part in all this."

"How is it that you haven't changed a bit? You're still just as sweet as I remember." I smiled.

"I'm only sweet with you. The rest of the world can burn for all I care." I buried my nose in her hair and loved her laugh. She turned her head, but I didn't move, and my lips hovered over hers. My pulse pounded harder as I waited to see what she would do. Her golden eyes bore holes into my soul, making me want to confess every last sin and lay it at her feet to judge.

I didn't care about my healing shoulder as I cupped her face and gave in to the need. Touching my lips to hers sent a charge racing down my spine. Deepening the kiss, her hands gripped my shirt and held me tighter.

"Sorry to interrupt, but Angelo said we should get going to retrieve Jasmine's things and whatever is needed to create a new greenhouse here," Enzo said.

My lips lingered on hers, hoping he would disappear, but I felt him standing there. It made me want to hit him.

"He's not going to let me move back home, is he?"

I slowly pulled away and stood.

"No, he's not," I said. "And if I'm being honest, it's not safe, and I'd end up sleeping in your driveway every night."

"If it were Angelo put in that kind of discomfort, I'd think about it." I couldn't help but smile. Jasmine pushed herself to her feet, a sparkle in her eye, and I knew she had an idea.

"Enzo, did Angelo give you a limit to what I can spend on the new greenhouse?"

He shook his head no. "No, he just said go shopping if it was what you wanted.

Jasmine laughed. "Well, in that case, let's go shopping."

This seemed like a bad idea suddenly—a very bad idea.

"Give us a second," I said to Enzo and as soon as he was out of earshot I searched Jasmine's face. "Did you ask your father not to come after us?" She looked down and I knew the answer. "After everything we put you through, you should've had him send everyone to kill us."

"I couldn't do it. Call me weak if you want, but I loved you both, I wouldn't have been able to live with myself if my papa killed you because of me."

I tilted Jasmine's head up, wanting her to look me in the eyes. "I said it once, but I will say it again. We never deserved you, but I love you and I'm going to spend every last breath I have to prove that to you," I said. Laying my forehead against hers, I could only pray she let me into her heart again.

Chapter Thirty-Seven

ENZO

I THOUGHT I'd seen Angelo furious. But I'd never seen him as angry as when Jasmine refused to stay in his bedroom and locked herself in one of the spare rooms on the opposite side of the house.

Angelo swore as he marched past me and slammed the office door, closing him and Dario in together. I could hear him having a total meltdown, and I was honestly worried he would burn the house down around us. He was that angry.

Making a small plate of sweets and grabbing a bottle of wine, I decided that now was as good a time as any to try and apologize. It had been a while since I felt so out of place. I was the player, the happy go lucky guy, but it was my impulsive personality that had me hopping from one bed to the next. Which was great for a time, but there was a point when I realized I had no real relationships of any kind in my life. Everything had become a picturesque snapshot, but nothing more.

It was also the first divide between me and my family. My history with my parents wasn't terrible, but there was nothing quite as heavy as the disappointed stare of a father. Angelo and Dario became my found family, and I'd been comfortable until I saw Jasmine and realized I wanted more from life than being on the run and hiding among the shadows.

My knock seemed loud in the quiet hallway as I tapped my knuckles against the door.

"Go away, Angelo."

"It's not Angelo," I said and held my breath. I could hear her coming closer, and my heart thumped faster with each step. The click of the lock sent a jolt of excitement down my spine.

Jasmine looked up and down the hall. "I'm surprised you're alone."

"I wanted a chance to talk. I know you said you didn't want to hear what I had to say, but..." I cleared my throat. "I hope you changed your mind."

She leaned against the door frame, and the adorable, clumsy woman I'd met was hard to see now. Not that she was acting any differently, but I couldn't get images of her walking by her father's side and marrying a Don or Don's son out of my head. My family had worked for the families for years. I was close to this world long before being accepted into it. I knew my place, but I'd never been much for the rules.

Jasmine stood still as her penetrating gaze interrogated my soul without saying a single word.

"I promise I will only stay as long as it takes to finish this dish," I said, holding the plate of treats. Jasmine's lip curled ever so slightly before she stepped back and let me walk inside.

I'd never spent any time in this room. The walls were as blue as the ocean on a bright summer's day, and the accents were varying shades of yellow and white. Sitting on the small couch, I placed the desserts and wine down. Now that I was here, I didn't know where to start.

Jasmine stood on the opposite side of the table, her arms crossed. Even furious, she was sexy. Blue jeans and a cream sweater shouldn't be so bloody hot. The jeans hugged her legs and an ass that I was dying to get my hands on. Her sweater was flowy, and yet it could have been knit lingerie. Keeping my eyes on hers took way more effort than it should.

"Was any of it real? Or were you flirting with me and helping out because Angelo told you to?"

I held up my hands. "I swear to you, I had no idea who you were when we met, and I was awestruck from the moment I saw you."

"Oh, please."

"No, I'm serious. I will never forget you answering the door with dirt all over your face and holding out that little mouse." I nodded toward the tank she insisted on bringing with her that had the three little mice inside.

"So when did you find out?"

"You remember the day I was over helping, and I thought it was strange that Maurice, aka Dario, switched vehicles and flew out of the driveway like a madman?" She nodded. "He was bringing everything up to the door and spotted you inside, then took off to tell Angelo. I didn't know until I got home that night."

Sighing, she sat down beside me and grabbed a cannoli before turning to look at me.

"Okay, let's say I believe you. You still lied to me and pretended to be my friend, knowing that Angelo, Dario, and I had a history. You went along with Angelo and his scheme to sneak into my room at night."

Opening the bottle of wine, I poured a glass, but Jasmine shook her head, took the bottle from my hands, and downed a swig.

"I think I love you," I said as she chugged a few mouthfuls.

"I'm going to need a lot more wine than that to deal with Angelo daily."

I smirked and fought the urge to adjust myself, but all I could see were her lips wrapped around the mouth of the bottle and her tongue licking her lips.

"I could make excuses for everything and tell you that Angelo ordered me to do all of it, but that is only a half-truth. I wanted to see you. Angelo didn't want me involved with you, but I told him I wanted you, and we fought. So yes, I hated the lying and the sneaking into your room, but...I still did it, and I hope you'll find a way to forgive me."

Jasmine took another sip from the bottle and popped the last pastry in her mouth as she looked at the cold fireplace. Her eyes weren't on my face, and I shifted uncomfortably in the silence.

"I'll think about it. I really liked you, but now I'm not sure what to believe," she said, and my heart sank.

"I don't blame you." I picked up a brownie and took at bite. "But, as you can see my boss is a real jerk," I teased and nudged her arm making her smile.

"That I do believe. Tell me something, how did you all know I was being attacked?"

I choked on the brownie I was swallowing.

"Oh...um...well. Do you want some more wine? I can go get it. Or I can get you a book? Do you like movies? I can put on a movie," I rambled, as I scrambled to try and change the topic.

Only the Devil's stare could've rivaled the penetrating look in her eyes as she turned to face me. One elegant eyebrow raised, and sweat broke out all over my body. Fuck, that look did all sorts of things to me.

"I would love all those things, but tell me what I want to know first," she said softly, as her eyes commanded the answer. Fuck.

"So the thing is...the house has some cameras," I said.

Jasmine swore, and I couldn't sit any longer. Snatching my glass of wine, I drank it down.

"How many cameras?"

"Um...."

"Three?" I shook my head. "Five?" I shook my head again. "Ten?"

Oh, I would rather walk the red-hot coals of hell. Anything other than seeing the steadily increasing look of rage in her eyes.

"Maybe I should go for the night. It's been a long day. Oh, look at the time," I said and didn't get a single step toward the door before she was up off the couch.

"Don't you dare try to disappear. How many Enzo?"

Of all the questions I thought she would ask, this was not it. Why hadn't Angelo talked about this with her? Would praying to be swallowed by the sea help? Fuck I wish it would, but I didn't have that kind of luck.

Sighing, I sucked in a deep breath and met her angry stare. "Sixty-four. There are four cameras per room and over twenty outside."

"What kind of sick...you rent the house like that? What are you hoping to catch on film? Bunch of perverts."

"No, no, it's not like that. I only installed them after you arrived."

There were moments in life that most people wished they could go back in time. Generally, I didn't care about anything that happened and was here for the magical ride and whatever happened next. But this was one of those times. I stepped back as her mouth fell open.

"After I moved in?" I nodded. "Every room? Like every room?"

I was a dead man. "Um...yes."

"And you installed them?"

I couldn't hate myself more. "Yes."

"Let me guess. You were busy installing cameras and being a creepy stalker while also taking me shopping and to meals while I was at The Glass Slipper?" Her hands balled into fists, and I glanced at the door, my only escape other than jumping out the window. The window seemed safer despite the long fall to either my death or broken bones.

"Would it help if I said I never watched you shower and it was a direct order?"

"Ah!" Jasmine yelled and grabbed the bottle of wine.

"Oh shit." I ducked as the bottle flew past my head and crashed into the far wall. I prepared for another attack, but the door to the room flung open with a bang.

Jumping up, I followed her at a safe distance as she marched along the hallway.

"What's going on," Dario asked, gun drawn as he reached the top floor. "I heard a scream."

"I'm going to kill Angelo," Jasmine said as she jogged down the stairs.

"Oh, is that all? Okay." Dario put his gun away, and I shook my head.

He fell into step beside me, but he seemed a lot less worried than I was. I didn't give a fuck if Angelo was pissed that I said something. There I was like an idiot asking for forgiveness while telling her we'd all been watching her on camera for days on top of everything else.

There were very special seats in hell reserved for assholes like us.

Chapter Thirty-Eight

JASMINE

COMPARED to everything else Angelo had done, this was low on the list of issues, but it was like a burr under my ass. He'd been watching me like some crazy stalker since almost the moment I arrived. On the other hand, who knew what would've happened with those two men if he hadn't been watching? Never mind, that was beside the point.

"He's that way," Dario said, his mouth turned up in a lopsided smile as he pointed the way.

"I wouldn't look so smug. You knew about the cameras, too," I said, marching past.

Angelo's voice came from the room at the end of the hall, the door partially closed. I didn't care and pushed the door open with a bang as loud as a gun going off. Angelo looked up from the stack of paperwork on his desk, but I didn't veer toward him. I marched for the wall of monitors set up in the corner.

Enzo wasn't kidding. There were multiple views of each room, including my bathroom and bedroom.

"Are you kidding me?"

"I need to call you back," Angelo said, rising from his desk.

"So let me get this straight."

I turned in a slow circle to face him, my body shaking with anger. None of this should be sexy, but I really wanted to know what he did while watching me shower. I had a pretty good idea, but the implications of what that said about me were not something I wanted to explore.

"You've been watching me since I arrived," I said, pointing at the screens angrily.

"Of course I was. I wasn't letting you out of my sight," he said, sounding far too self-assured and sexy. "I mean, how did you think I knew about the men attacking you? I didn't randomly stumble on your house at six in the morning to find two men assaulting you."

Angelo's cocky as fuck answer had me grabbing a bronzed statue of a tiger off of the table. He unbuttoned his suit jacket as he sat on the corner of his desk, seemingly unaffected by my rage, which only pissed me off more.

"Put the statue down, Tiger. You know what happened the last time you threw a tantrum." His eyes traveled down my body, igniting sparks that made me shiver. "I don't think you'd enjoy me fucking you with the statue as much as you did the mirror." A wicked smile spreading across his face. "I'd choose wisely."

My blood boiled in my veins. Angelo had always been able to get under my skin and push all my buttons, but I thought I was past all that.

"Ever hear of invasion of privacy? You're a fucking stalker, and you want me to consider taking you back?"

I could feel the other men's eyes on me, but they wore completely different expressions. Enzo looked sheepish and like he might throw up, while Dario seemed happy as a pig in shit to watch the show. It was a stark contrast from breakfast.

"First, I've always stalked you, this should not be surprising. I followed you everywhere unless I was detained with work. Even in your home I would drag you into any dark corner I could find. I would climb into your room every night to fuck you, and if you were already asleep I'd stay and watch you until the sun started to rise." Okay that was way hotter than it should be. I had issues, and it was annoying that he had a point. I knew what he was like and capable of.

"This is not that same," I argued.

"Maybe, maybe not." He shrugged casually. "My sexy, wild tiger, you've already agreed. You just don't want to admit it to yourself. You've always been mine as I am yours. You can't just close your eyes and wish that away," Angelo said, and I hated how true that comment was.

Taking him back after everything shouldn't feel like the right thing. I should be angry for years and make them suffer for what they did, or not take him back at all and protect my heart. But that wasn't what I felt when I looked into his blue eyes. It wasn't what I thought about when Dario wrapped his arms around me. It also wasn't what first ran through my head when Enzo admitted to setting up the cameras. A part of me liked it, and the self-hatred ate at the corners of my mind.

"Don't you wish," I said, turning. I pulled my arm back to throw the statue at the monitors and destroy their setup, but Angelo gripped my wrist and pried it from my grasp before I could release it. His eyes dared me to test him. That look alone set me off, and I swung for his cheek. He gripped my wrist and stopped my hand just before I made contact.

Angelo's face never changed, his stare making my heart pound wildly.

"Let go of me," I demanded, but his smirk only grew. I yelped as he pushed me back, pressing me up against the wall.

Thump, thump. Thump, thump.

My heart sputtered and restarted as he molded his hard body to mine. My hands were useless above my head, and I felt like an animal backed into a corner. I wanted to growl at him to stay away but also scream for him never to leave again. The game of tug-o-war was alive and well in my chest as it heaved.

"I said you wouldn't like the statue. I didn't say I wouldn't use it on you."

A flicker of fear snaked its way down my spine at the thought of him bending me over his desk and doing what he threatened.

"I hate you." I glared at him, but the passion that burned bright in his captivating, blue eyes drowned the last of my resolve.

Jerking me forward, he spun me around and trapped me against the wall once more. His cock pressed against my ass, and I fought hard not to wiggle against him. Angelo's breath was hot as he kissed the side of my neck.

"Who are you trying to convince, Tiger?"

"Must you always mock me?"

"Not always. Only when you're being a bad kitty."

"I'm going to kill you when you sleep. You know that, right?"

He chuckled and rubbed his cock against my ass. "No, you won't, and I'll tell you why." He nipped at my sensitive skin and licked a line up my neck, and I couldn't stop myself from shuddering against him, making him groan. "You won't kill me because you still love me."

"No, I don't."

"Yes, you do. You told me when you were dreaming."

"That doesn't count. I didn't know what I was saying," I argued.

"Wrong, it counts more than right now. You spoke from your heart, the part of you that was hurt and locked away. You spoke without worrying about what you should say or do." He kissed my neck again, and I closed my eyes. It was worse that he saw through my anger to the fear inside. "I deserve all your anger, Tiger. I deserve every nasty word, slap to the face, and more, but know this...everything I've done has been for you. To marry you, to get back to you, to win your heart," he whispered in my ear. "Not a moment has passed that I haven't worked to be by your side and call you mine. I'm not letting you go, never again, and deep down, you don't want me to. That's why you won't kill me."

Releasing my hands, he pulled off his suit jacket and tossed it away, then rolled up the sleeve of his dress shirt.

"Do you see this?" He held his forearm out for me to look at.

I remembered he had a tattoo, but I was so emotional last night that I didn't pay attention to what it was. My eyes scanned over the stunning tiger that covered his entire forearm, but my breath caught when he rolled his arm to show me the underside. My name was mixed in with the black and orange stripes, but not my given name. It was my name, as if we were married. Elegantly scrolled from his elbow to his wrist was *Jasmine Esposito*.

"You are the ghost that haunted my soul, the fantasy that invaded my mind, and the only woman who has ever touched my heart. You are mine, Jasmine, and I'm crazy enough to do whatever I must to keep you by my side."

Tears welled in my eyes as my fingers slipped from the imaginary ledge in my mind, and I gave up trying to fight my emotions. His hand wrapped around my throat as he pulled my hair back, forcing me to look at him. I felt the pressure of each finger as he pressed hard enough to make it difficult to breathe. An old, dark passion bloomed within me.

"Do you remember your safe word?"

"Honey," I said, and he smiled.

"That's my good tiger. I'm going to fuck you on my desk, something I've dreamed of doing for a very long time, and then I'm going to watch as Dario and Enzo fuck your face before Dario, and I take you together." I swallowed hard, and he leaned in closer. "Maybe even the same hole. I remember how much you love two cocks in you. You'd like that, wouldn't you?"

I couldn't look away and didn't want to. "Yes."

"Good girl," he said. Kissing me hard and arching my back more, but I knew he wouldn't let me fall. Angelo didn't kiss. He consumed. He demanded, and I stopped fighting what I'd secretly dreamed of for years.

When he broke away, my lips were sore, and my body felt alive. I hadn't realized how much I missed his domineering aura. My sweater was pulled off and tossed away, and my bra followed suit.

Angelo turned me around, and I moaned as he sucked my nipple into his mouth while he undid my jeans. They were quickly yanked down over my ass, and his hand slipped between my legs.

"Mmm, look at how wet you are. Are you a slutty princess, Tiger? Do you want to be fucked and used? You want me to make you scream?"

"Yes," I cried out, my fingers gripping his hair as his fingers teased me.

"Good." He helped me out of the jeans and fisted my hair as he pulled me over to the desk, forcing me to sit down. I jumped as he smacked my breast. There was a sharp sting, but the pleasure was instant and roared through my body. "You're going to come on my desk, and every time you step foot in here, you're going to think about how you screamed as you came and begged me for more." The tearing of my underwear was loud as he ripped them from my body. "And from now on, no more underwear. If you put them on, you'll be punished."

I nodded as he lowered himself to his knees between my legs. I was called Tiger, but Angelo looked like a predator. The hair on the nape of my neck stood as he gripped my hips and pulled me to the very edge. Dario and Enzo sat together on the couch behind Angelo, and I loved that they watched us as they touched themselves. There was simply no world where I wouldn't find a man stroking himself unsexy.

My eyes locked on their hands as they traveled up and down, and I whimpered as Angelo swirled his tongue around my clit. Leaning back further, I soaked in the pleasure. His tongue flicked over the sensitive skin as he fucked me with his fingers, and I unraveled. Just as I reached the edge, ready to come, he stopped, and I wanted to hit him all over again. Angelo cleared his desk with a swipe of his arms, and everything crashed to the floor.

I watched him walk around behind me and squealed when he picked me up like I weighed nothing and turned me around to face him once more.

"Undo my pants," he ordered as he stuck his finger in my mouth to suck. I tasted myself and sucked hard, knowing he loved that. I was rewarded with a groan as his cock was freed from the confines of his pants. He curled his fingers inside of my cheek like I was a fish on a hook and forced me to follow him.

He opened the lid of a box on the bookcase and, one at a time pulled out the leather straps he used to tie me up and the tiger's head nipple clamps he had made for me. Gripping the items, he led me back to the desk and unhooked his fingers.

"Such a good girl, Tiger. Fuck, I've missed you." The straps were loud as he dropped them on the desk beside me. "Touch me." My fingers traced the lines of his defined shoulders, hard pecs, and ripped abs. Time had done nothing to lessen how sexy he was. "Good, now stroke my cock."

Wrapping my hands around him, I stroked him just the way he liked, and a thrill ran through my body as he growled and dropped his lips to mine.

"Say you're mine. Tell me you still want to be mine, Tiger."

This was my out. Angelo held the door open, and I could see the other side, but I'd lived there for the last five years and hated it. I felt empty without them. The loneliness had been unbearable at times, and as much as I wanted to make something that was mine, I didn't want to spend my life alone or in a loveless marriage. I wanted both things.

"Say it, Tiger?"

"I want to be more than your princess arm candy. I want to build my own business and not only be known as Jasmine Esposito. There is more to me than that. I can't say yes unless you agree to that first."

His eyes softened ever so subtly as he cupped my cheek. "Don't you get it? You were always more than that to me. If you want to build an empire, tour the world, and be worshiped for the woman you are, then I will happily stand by your side." He held up his finger. "But, only if we do it as a team and in the bedroom...." The impish grin spread across his face. "I'm still in charge."

My heart was pounding out of my chest as the old hope that had been burned to ash was ignited and burned brightly once more. I didn't even care how we reconnected, just that we did.

"And them," I said, pointing to Dario and Enzo. "I want them both."

"I already assumed that was a forever thing," he said and rolled his eyes, but there was no anger in his tone.

"Then yes, I want us back. I will still marry you. I'm yours." It was as if an earthquake shook the world when he kissed me. I hung onto his shoulders to keep from falling and felt his desperation and passion, but under it all, I felt his love.

No amount of yelling, hitting, or denying my feelings would make up for what happened between us. I was moving forward, but that didn't mean I wouldn't find other ways to make Angelo pay. I particularly liked the idea of kicking a football at his head.

Chapter Thirty-Nine

ANGELO

"SIT DOWN. HANDS BEHIND YOUR HEAD." Jasmine did as I said. I preferred this position for her arms instead of behind her back. If I wanted to fuck her doggie style or up against a wall, then her arms weren't in the way.

The relief I felt when she said she would be mine again made me want to sink to my knees and thank whoever was listening for the second chance. I would've kept her captive in a room until she agreed, but I didn't want to do that.

Picking up the custom, padded leather restraints made only for her, I quickly put on the wrist cuffs. Next were the straps that forced her forearms to stay up like she was being arrested. I'd never played like this with anyone else. She brought out this side in me, and we found a mutual passion. Right from our first time together, I knew and wasn't wrong.

Picking up the black diamond and amber encrusted nipple clamps, I kissed her as I secured them in place. Jasmine trembled, and I swallowed every shuddering breath and whimper. She tasted like heaven dipped in honey. That was why it was her safe word. I always felt like I was drowning in a pool of sticky golden liquid when I was around her.

I attached the cuffs to the arm straps to keep them in place, then stood back to admire her. I wasn't just hard. I was on edge and needed to calm the fuck down to make this last. Opening the desk drawer, I pulled out my plastic ruler, and her eyes widened, making me smirk.

"I'm not putting this in you," I said, and relief washed over her face as she sighed.

Holding the ruler against her leg, I smiled and watched her face as I pulled back on the plastic and let it go. She jumped slightly with the loud snap that left a red mark, but it was the flare of desire in her eyes that I was after.

"You like that, Tiger? You like being a little office slut?" Her cheeks pinked a deeper rose, but she bit her lip and nodded. "You want me to fuck you while I'm working?" She nodded again and wiggled on the desk. I snapped the ruler just below the first mark, and a soft moan left her lips. "You want me to fuck you while I'm on the phone? Maybe I'll keep you under my desk, and you can suck my cock all day. Would you like that?" Her eyes lit up, and I rewarded her with another snap from the ruler. "Such a good girl, Tiger, a good girl indeed."

My cock throbbed, the ache of genuine desire was an old friend. I snapped the ruler again and stroked my cock a few times. Jasmine licked her lips, her eyes following my every move.

"Lay down and hang over the desk. I want you to watch them as you come on my desk."

She bit her lip and wiggled to tip herself over backward. One glance at the dark look in Dario's and Enzo's eyes as they stroked themselves told me exactly what she looked like.

I wanted them to watch. I loved it, but more than that, I was a dominant, fucking asshole. They could fuck Jasmine and love her, but she was still mine. I was marrying her. My ring would be on her finger, and it would be my name she signed to paper. And I didn't give one flying fuck if that made me an inconsiderate prick.

As soon as she was in position, I used the ruler to tease her. The fact that she couldn't see it now was as good as being blindfolded, and she shivered as I drew a little design on her stomach. Lifting the ruler, I waited until I could feel her antsy energy. I wanted her nervous but excited about what came next. Placing it over her clit I gave it a little smack, and she jumped then moaned. With her legs spread wide and on display for my eyes to feast, she was getting wetter by the second.

I gave her three smacks on her sensitive clit, and she cried out, her body shaking. I was tempted to come all over her just from watching her writhe on the desk. I could see it so clearly but reined myself in. There was plenty of time to make a mess of my beautiful Tiger.

The sound of the ruler was loud as it hit off her leg, then her stomach, and then I used it like a little paddle and tapped it off her pussy.

"Oh, god, yes," she said. I stopped and walked around the desk so she could see me. Kneeling by her head, I held up the ruler, which was now glistening and wet.

"No, I'm not God." She watched as I licked the ruler clean. "Only the Devil would eat your pussy like I do."

Standing, I stared down at her. Her hair hung like a waterfall to the floor, and her tits heaved. "Make sure to scream my name next time."

Crawling on the desk between her legs, I gripped the edge of the hardwood, and she butterflied her knees wider so that she had my arms as support. I didn't want her to slip off the desk, and her trust in me made me smile. This was an awkward position to hold, and I wouldn't be gentle. Lining up, I thrust into her pussy, making us both groan.

"Fuck," was the only word I got out. My arms strained and flexed as my body begged for release, but I fought it back. I wanted Jasmine to scream the walls down so the neighbors miles away knew she was mine.

I was lost in the pleasure of each powerful thrust when I felt her coming, and she screamed my name. There was no sweeter sound than my name on her lips while she was caught in the throes of passion. Jasmine's body arched higher off the desk as she rode the last of the waves. Pulling out, I smiled at the mess we'd already made. The moment she walked into the room, I wanted her wet with anticipation from the number of times I was going to fuck her on it.

Pushing myself up and off the desk, I grabbed her before she could fall. I smiled at the satisfied look on her face. I held her in my arms until the light-headedness in her eyes was gone and the quivering in her muscles ceased.

Placing her on the floor, I looked at the other two men. "On your knees, Tiger. Both of you come over here." Gripping Jasmine's chin, I forced her to look up at me. "You like sucking cock don't you."

"Yes," her voice was soft and wispy, making me shiver.

"You want to feel those two big cocks sliding down your throat?"

She bit her bottom lip as she stared me in the eyes. "Yes."

Leaning over, I kissed her hard, our tongues lashing as I made sure she still had me on her mind. "Good, I like watching you suck cock. Your mouth and throat will be sore. You sure you can handle it?" The fire of challenge was in her eyes, and even though I didn't think it was possible, I fell harder in love with her.

"Yes," she said, her voice determined.

Dario and Enzo stripped the last of their clothes off and walked over to join the two of us.

"Stand here."

They stood shoulder-to-shoulder and stroked their cocks in front of her face. Grabbing her hair, I aimed her mouth toward Dario, and she opened for him. I controlled her head and how much or how deep he got. Pulling her off of him, I did the same with Enzo until the room was filled with grunting and slurping noises.

"Oh fuck," Dario groaned as I shoved her mouth down until he was in her throat.

"Good girl, Tiger, take him all the way." I pulled her back, and she gasped and sucked in a deep breath as I smoothed the hair from her face and moved her back over to Enzo.

"Are you going to make Enzo come," I asked her.

"Mmmhmm," she mumbled around his cock. I knew he was close when the muscles in his cheek twitched just before he came. Enzo wouldn't have made a good poker player. I picked up the pace, and he groaned.

I let go of her head and let him take over. Enzo's hands gripped her hair as he fucked her face hard.

"Fuck me," he yelled as he came down her throat.

"Good girl," I praised and pulled her away from Enzo to wipe away the reflex tears and let her rest. "Follow me," I said to Dario and walked over to the couch. "Sit down."

As soon as he was comfortable, Jasmine straddled him but faced me. Dario held her steady as her legs shook from the effort expended already. She slowly sank down, and Dario groaned like an animal.

"Oh God," Jasmine cried, and I smirked. She screamed and came again all over Dario as I undid the nipple clamps and held them out for Enzo to take. Breathless, Jasmine slumped back against Dario.

"Now you're good and wet for two cocks. Are you ready," I asked, getting into position and putting one foot on the couch. She licked her lips and nodded. I slowly worked my cock in beside Dario's, and she screamed. We'd only done this to her a couple of times before, so I took it slow to give her time to adjust. Once I was fully inside of her, I was panting as heavily as she was, my blood pounding in my ears as I remained still.

"Relax," I said, wrapping my hand around her neck and pulling her up so our lips met and I could suck her bottom lip into my mouth. "Relax, Tiger." I nuzzled the side of her neck and felt her pulse leaping under her skin. The tension slowly eased, and she molded into my body.

"You ready?" She nodded, but I shook my head at her. "Say the words."

"Yes, I'm ready." I held her neck firm and sucked on her pulse as both Dario and I found our rhythm. "Ah!"

Jasmine's yells filled the room. Her tits were pushed up, and her sensitive nipples rubbed against my chest with every thrust. She was always tight, but with Dario inside of her and his cock moving along with mine, it was a losing battle to keep from coming.

Dario picked up the pace, his grunts loud as he pummeled Jasmine's tight pussy.

"Fuck, you feel so good," Dario said, his hands gripping Jasmine's hips as he hammered in like a piston.

"Fuck me!" The extra speed pushed me over the edge, and I came hard. "Fuck, fuck, fuck." My muscles tensed against the sensation of Dario still going and drawing out my orgasm.

"Ah! I'm coming," Jasmine screamed, and I kissed her hard, loving that I could swallow her pleasure down like it was my own.

"Yes, that's it," Dario said and then thrust up hard and froze.

I felt his cock releasing inside of her as well, something that once I wouldn't have allowed, but time had changed so much. I slowly pulled out, and when Jasmine whimpered, I knew she would be sore. Dario held her up as she slumped into him. There were already red welts and small bruises forming on her skin, and as much as I loved the idea of her wearing my marks, I didn't want her in pain. She would need extra care tonight, and a different kind of possessiveness filled my chest with the thought of easing every one of her aching muscles.

I undid the straps and cuffs, laying them aside before picking her up off of Dario. She was utterly spent and tucked her head in the crook of my neck as I marched from the office and through the house up to my bedroom.

Dario walked into the bathroom right behind me and, reading my mind, turned on the water to the large bathtub and set out a tub of arnica cream.

"I'll grab some water and pain meds to be safe," he said, disappearing.

Stepping into the tub, Jasmine winced as the water touched all the sensitive areas. “Easy, I’ve got you,” I whispered, smoothing her damp hair. Nothing could’ve prepared me for how I would feel having her back in my life. Or the panic I felt that her father or Ciro would find us and try to steal her away from me.

Jasmine was sound asleep when I finished washing us clean, massaging her sore body, and rubbing the cream into her skin.

Walking out to the bedroom, Dario was in bed and lifted a brow at me in challenge when I opened my mouth to order him out. Sighing, I conceded that Dario, Enzo, or sometimes both would end up in here from now on.

Dario pushed the blankets out of the way so I could lay Jasmine down and crawl in beside her. She curled into me and placed her head on my heart as Dario cuddled her from behind. For the first time in years, I felt peace. It scared me. Nothing good in my life ever lasted long, but I refused to lose her. Not ever again. I would kill anyone who tried to come between us and take my happiness away.

Chapter Forty

JASMINE

"PSST," *I jumped at the sound of Angelo's voice. Whipping my head around, I saw he was standing on my balcony, just like every night since I first said yes to marrying him. He looked so handsome in his black jeans and T-shirt. Hand shaking, I put down my hairbrush and stood from the vanity to meet him across the floor.*

"You have to stop sneaking in like this. We're going to get caught," I whispered, but Angelo just smiled and pulled his hand from behind his back with a single lily between his fingers.

"I had to see you."

I tried not to smile at the sweet gift, but it was impossible. Plucking it from his grip, I sniffed the fragrant flower and lifted my eyes to his.

"You just saw me this morning." I started to walk away, but I screamed as he picked me up, forcing me to wrap my arms around his neck.

"Shh, you're going to get us caught," he said, his lip curling up.

"You're such an ass," I said, but I loved that he couldn't stay away. He'd been sneaking in at all hours of the night and day and even hunting me down and dragging me into rooms all over the house to catch a few moments alone. It had become a game, and I now peeked around every corner and door, never knowing where he might appear.

A knock sounded at the door. "Mistress Jasmine, is everything okay? I thought I heard a scream," the deep voice of one of my papa's guards called through the thick wood.

"Yes, I'm fine. I thought I saw a spider. Sorry to worry you," I said, and Angelo snickered into the side of my neck, making it hard not to laugh.

"You're sure everything is okay?"

"Perfectly fine. I'm off to bed. Have a good night," I said and waited until the shadow under the door had moved on before giving in and cupping Angelo's face to kiss him.

"Mmm, it's been way too long," he mumbled against my lips as he lay on the bed and settled between my legs. His hands traveled along my body, and I shivered from his heated touch.

"Working for your father just not as exciting?" I teased.

"Not even close. I never want to see him in a silky bathrobe," he said, and I covered my mouth as I laughed.

"Shh, Mistress Jasmine, you're being far too noisy this late at night," he said, kissing the side of my neck, making my heart race. "You always smell like heaven. I want to bottle your scent and take it everywhere with me."

"Did you ever see this happening when we were kids?" I loved watching his shoulders flex under my fingers as I raked them over his muscles.

He lifted his head to stare down at me. "Are you kidding? I hated you." I looked away. It was stupid, but Angelo saying that hurt. He kissed my lips and forced me to look up at him. "I was a stupid boy who didn't understand that I hated you because I liked you. The more sass you fired at me, the more I wanted until it was never enough. I'd become completely addicted to a look from across the room or a touch from your finger. When I close my eyes, it is your face I see. You're my angel, Tiger. My heart has always been yours, even when I didn't realize it."

"I love you," I said and blushed, shocked that I finally said the words I'd been holding back.

"Sei la vita mia," Angelo said, his lips capturing mine.

• • •

My eyes fluttered open, and I turned my head from side to side, but I was once again alone, and the warm fuzzy feelings of the memory slowly faded away. Pushing myself up, I winced and wanted to flop back down.

I looked up as the door to the bedroom opened, and Enzo stood there with a tray of breakfast, looking far too sexy in his plaid shirt and ripped jeans.

"Good morning," he said, with a smile that could make any woman trip over their heels to get another look.

I pushed myself up, holding the sheet to my chest. "Good morning."

"I made you breakfast, and don't worry about Gina. I already picked everything ready to go and gave it to her. I also told her you'll be able to supply more items, and she was thrilled." He smiled as he sat the tray over my lap.

"You already did all that? What time is it?" I looked around for a clock.

"It's just after eleven, but don't worry, I didn't mind. Dario said these are your favorites, and when you're ready, the guys will be arriving at one to start building the new greenhouse." Enzo smiled as he backed out of the room. "No rush, I have the blueprints to get them started. Oh, and Angelo just got the invoice." A wicked grin crossed his face. "I thought he was going to have a heart attack," he said and laughed. "See you soon."

I opened my mouth to tell him to stay, but the door closed before I could get another word out. He was like a whirling dervish. Picking up the coffee, I took a sip and moaned as the rich and creamy flavor hit my tongue. It was perfect. Enzo, being on his toes, had some perks. Lifting the tray lid, I smiled at the thick waffle with berries and whipped cream.

"Okay, I can get used to this," I whispered, cutting into the golden goodness.

I ate every last bite and then worked through my morning

stretches despite being sore. If last night were any indication, I would need to stay limber. Wandering out of the room, I went in search of Enzo, but when I reached the bottom floor, I heard Angelo yelling and quietly made my way to his office. The door was open, and I poked my head inside to see him standing by the window, his arm braced on the frame.

"What do you mean you won't give me the money? This is a solid business investment," he said. "No, of course not. I need to expand to make more." He drummed his fingers on the wood. "It would take too long to sell one of the other properties. I need the money available for Wednesday. I could sell one after Wednesday if you're wanting it as collateral." He hung his head, and I could see the stress on his face. I suddenly felt terrible for spending so much money on the fancy greenhouse. I didn't know what this deal was, but it seemed important to him. "You know I'm good for the money. This will more than double my productivity. Did you even look at the sales projections?" His hand curled into a fist. "I'm not high risk. Look at the numbers again." He shook his head, and I could see just enough of his eyes in the reflection of the glass to know he was contemplating murder. "Mr. Rhodes is not a patient man. He'll back out if I don't have the money. That means it will take me twice as long to pay the lenders back for the loan. Fine."

"Fucking Cogsworth," Angelo growled as he hung up the phone and spun around like he was going to throw it when he spotted me. He froze, and the look in his eyes softened.

"Good morning. Sorry, that was a business call. I hate banks and investment companies. Despite what they advertise, they are all useless." He smiled and came around his desk to meet me as I walked further into the room.

"Is this because of the greenhouse? I only got one that big to annoy you," I said, and he laughed.

"I figured that. It was either that or you decided to grow something illegal." I blushed as he teased me. "No, the greenhouse is not the issue. I need much more than that, but I'll figure it out. I always do." Angelo wrapped his arms around my waist, and the lingering memory from my dream flooded my mind. Hugging him back, I laid my head over his heart. "Not that I don't love it when you're spitting mad, but it's nice not to worry about you stabbing me."

"Oh, I'm still thinking about it," I said, and he chuckled, the rumble deep under my ear.

"I have a dinner meeting on Wednesday, and I'd love for you to come with me. I could give you a tour of my business first."

"What do you do?" I asked, and he smiled wide, reminding me of the mischievous look he got when we were younger.

"I'll let you taste." I lifted an eyebrow as I eyed him suspiciously. "You have to close your eyes."

"Hmm, I remember you doing this once before, and it ended badly for me." I crossed my arms, remembering the spider he put in my hands. I'd never screamed so loud as I ran for a teacher while I heard him laughing like a hyena behind me.

"No spiders, I promise. In fact, no insects at all." He smiled as he went behind his desk and pulled out two shot glasses.

"No reptiles either."

"Nothing living, I swear."

"Okay then." I took a seat on the couch and closed my eyes.

"I'm going to give you two shots to drink. I want you to tell me which one is better," he said, his voice getting closer.

"What if I choose the wrong one?"

"Well, then I'll have to spank your ass until you can't sit down, then fuck you until you pass out. I mean, that seems fair."

I wiggled on the couch and cleared my throat as the thought of him doing that crossed my mind. "Then, I better choose wisely."

"Or not...." I could hear him smirk as he poured liquid into what I assumed was a shot glass. "This is the first one." Holding my hand out, he sat the little glass between my fingers, and I brought it to my nose to sniff.

"Whiskey. Smells elegant and floral and has a note of nut." I took a sip, and it was rich but burned all the way down, and I could feel it in my belly. "Good flavor, but burns a little too much for me."

Angelo handed me a glass of water, and I rinsed my mouth.

"Now, this one."

I repeated the process and took a double take on the scent, it made me want to smile and buy a bottle without even trying it. "This is very rich with a sweetness like honey, cinnamon, and notes of vanilla. It smells incredible. I could picture cooking with this." I took a sip, which was just as smooth as it smelled. "Wow. It has all the traditional whiskey flavor, but it's smooth and has no bite or harsh burn. I can taste the hit of cinnamon, but it's not overpowering." I opened my eyes and looked at the dark liquid. "This is delicious."

Angelo was smiling so wide I thought he would break out in song. He cupped my face, his excitement contagious as he kissed me, his tongue invading my mouth and licking at the whiskey on my lips.

"I guess I chose the right one, or was it the wrong one? Hard to tell with the punishment threat," I teased as he grabbed two bottles off the table. I recognized his family's whiskey right away. His father prided himself on the secret recipe passed down for generations.

"This was the first one you tried. I'd been trying to get my father to create another whiskey line for years, but he wouldn't hear of it." He held out the second bottle and smirked. I stared at the black and gold label, *The Genie's Jinn*. It was so like Angelo to go against the grain, and I loved it. "I made this one when I left Italy for good and settled here." He knelt in front of me. "It tastes how I remember your sweet lips tasting on my tongue. This is you in a bottle."

I searched his face, my throat clogged with emotion. "You really thought about me all this time?"

"Getting back to you is all I ever thought about, but I lost hope. It seemed like nothing I ever did would be enough. I've done so many things I'm not proud of and need to make up for, and I hate that I hurt you. There is so much I still need to explain, like the other women you saw...." I placed a finger on his lips to stop him from saying more before tracing the angles of his face.

I leaned in and kissed him softly, trying to express what this meant to me. If I was going to move on, I couldn't wallow in the memories of the pain. It only drummed up anger and frustration. I didn't want to feel those things anymore. I just wanted to start on a clean slate from this moment on.

"Don't. I don't want to know why. The why isn't going to change what happened and I honestly can't think about it or the anger and sadness consumes me. If we want a future, we must move forward. If I think about those women or the loneliness anymore, I will never forgive you, and I want this to work. I want for all of us to work." His eyes filled with tears, and he turned his head. He blinked them away, but I saw the raw emotion he rarely showed. My heart was once more tumbling downhill without a safety net, and it was probably stupid, but I was going to let it roll.

I tapped the bottle. "Why the name?"

A shy smile lifted the corner of his mouth. "Because I wished for a way to be with you again, and I figured I would need a little magic to make it happen. The Genie's Jinn was my ticket home to you."

I couldn't find the right words to express the churning of emotions in my chest. Wrapping my arms around his neck, I pulled him down on the couch and poured everything in my heart into the kiss.

Chapter Forty-One

DARIO

I GLANCED over at Jasmine as she stared out the truck window, her hands in her lap, hidden behind the center console. I badly wanted her to move so I could hold them.

"I know the perfect store," I said, and she turned to look at me. It was unbelievable that after everything, she was here. "You didn't catch what I said, did you?"

Jasmine blushed, her eyes dipping down. "No, I'm sorry, I was thinking about...well, everything. It seems crazy."

Smiling, I held out my hand. "I was just doing the same thing." She placed her hand in mine, and I hung on tight. "I just said I know the perfect store for you to find a dress."

"Why is it that doesn't surprise me?"

Smirking, I tore my eyes away from her face and focused on the road before we ended up in a ditch. "Oh yeah? Why's that?"

"You always seem to make a point of knowing every store, restaurant, and great place to see the sights. Like that night we snuck out to have dinner with Angelo and wanted to get dessert, but everything was closed. Or Angelo and I thought everything was closed, but you knew one place that would be open."

"I can't believe you still remember that."

"Of course I do. I remember every moment we spent together." I brought her hand to my mouth and kissed her knuckles. "Where are we going?"

"A place on the outskirts of the city, the locals call it Trendelburg Tower because there is an old silo in the middle of the square of shops." There was also an old oak tree with benches and flowers that I knew Jasmine would love. "We can have lunch before heading back."

"I'd love that."

My phone rang as we cut off the highway for the back road I preferred to take to the market. The number was unknown, so I hit ignore. If it was important, they could leave a message. There were only three numbers I answered: Angelo, Enzo, and Nicolas. The one fantastic thing about being cut off from the rest of the families was the lack of drama. There was never a shortage of bullshit to deal with back home, and I'd never been very good at ass-kissing.

I glanced over at Jasmine. "Whoever it is can leave a message. I have more important things to do."

"You didn't have to do that."

"Yes, I did. I've spent enough time handling things I didn't want to. Spending time with you is where I want to be and what I want to be doing." Jasmine smiled wide, and my body warmed from head to toe.

It was busy for a Tuesday afternoon, and I had to drive around the side streets until I found a spot to park. It would be a bit of a walk, but I didn't mind. Every second I spent with Jasmine alone was a win.

Getting out, I walked around and checked the street for danger before opening her door. Despite the bright sun and colorful flowers, I searched every shadow and corner. I'd learned the hard way that danger lurked in the most beautiful locations.

Jasmine hopped out and stood beside me so I could shut the door and lock it.

"Is your shoulder bothering you," she asked.

"It's a little stiff but healing quickly. You don't need to worry about my ability to protect you."

Jasmine's brow pinched as she stared at me. "Dario, I don't care about you guarding me. I'm worried about you." She laid her hand on my shoulder. "You were stabbed."

I placed my hand over hers. "I've also been shot twice, but the pain from all of that together pales in comparison to leaving you behind. Trust me when I tell you that I'm perfectly fine."

"You've been shot?" Shock was written all over her face as the color drained. "Twice?"

"Do you need to sit down?" I wrapped my arm around her waist.

"No, I don't need to sit down. I want to know who shot you." She clenched her hands into fists. "And you better tell me they are six feet in the ground."

Jasmine was getting herself fired up for a rant, but I didn't want today to be spoiled, so I cupped her face and kissed her before she could say anything else.

"Breathe, Amorina," I said and nipped her bottom lip. "Let's not ruin this beautiful day with talk about this."

She took a shuddering breath and nodded. "I wasn't shot, but I missed you every day, too," she said and blushed before stepping back.

"Come on, let's get you a dress for dinner tomorrow."

Linking my fingers with hers, we walked in a comfortable silence. The closer we drew to the square, the busier it got. There were buskers on every corner, and Jasmine would stop to listen before tossing money into their collection with a smile and warmth in her eyes. She didn't even notice all the looks she got or how people naturally bowed their heads.

We walked into the classic boutique, and it didn't take long for the woman working to help Jasmine to the dressing room with an armload of dresses.

"Are you coming?" Jasmine called out, and I turned from the display window. "I need your opinion."

"Even in a wet paper bag, you would look...." My mouth fell open, the words turning to dust and blowing away as Jasmine stepped out of the stall.

The glittering dress hugged her body like it was spun from gold just for her. From the deep scooping neckline and the sexy slit that showed off her legs right down to the matching strappy shoes, she was a work of art. I'd marveled at a thousand sculptures from around the world, yet none could rival her exquisite beauty or capture the kindness radiating from her soul.

"You are a vision. A goddess plucked from the heavens and placed before me."

Jasmine's face turned a bright red, and although she held her head high, her eyes darted to the floor. I lifted her chin, and my eyes traced the details that I'd committed to memory long ago.

"Never look down. You are a princess of one of the most powerful families in the world. It is I who should be on my knees before you."

"I never want that," she said.

"And that is why God has graced you with this power and the daunting responsibility to keep the rest of us humble."

"You've always made me sound like I am so much more than I am. In our world, I'm sought after for two things: to remain quiet but beautiful and to give whoever I marry a child. I'm a glorified breeding cow."

"Who said that to you," I asked, anger burning in my chest.

"No one had to say it. Just look around. Even my papa couldn't leave the family to me and planned on marrying me off to *keep me safe*." She made little air quotes. "I appreciate and love that you see me as more than a woman on the run from men you claim I'm better than, but the truth is far uglier."

Running my hand down her arms, I picked up her hand and laid it over my heart. "I'm going to tell you a secret. Anyone who thinks that is scared of how powerful you'd become. You can do whatever you set your mind to. You need only believe." I ran my hands down the shimmering material and couldn't help wishing I was taking her out in this dress. "The dress is perfect. You don't need to try another one if you don't want to. Angelo is a lucky man."

Jasmine softly poked me in the chest. "No, that's not happening. You can't give me that speech and not give it to yourself. It may be Angelo's name, I take, but I love you both equally, and truth be told, I liked you first."

I dropped my lips to hers, relishing in the moment.

"Did you need any help? Oh, I'm sorry, I didn't mean to interrupt. I'll leave you and your wife alone." The saleswoman disappeared as fast as she arrived.

"I guess her showing up was just as well. I was getting ready to pull you into one of the stalls," Jasmine said, making me laugh.

"Well then, I better step outside. I wouldn't want to give you too many naughty ideas. You might ruin the dress," I teased, making her giggle as she disappeared.

My phone rang, and I wanted to throw it. There really was something to be said for being completely off the grid. I pulled it from my pocket, but it was another unknown caller. I sent it to messages just as Jasmine walked out.

"Same number?"

"Or lack there of, but yeah, they didn't leave a message before. I think it's a telemarketer, but I really don't need my gutters or ducts cleaned."

"Is it normal to get calls like that?"

"Not often, but it happens."

"Hmm. If they call again, maybe you should answer it. If it's a salesperson, you can always hang up. But what if it's important?" Rising up on her toes, she kissed my cheek. "I'll pay for this, and then I'm ready to explore with you."

I glanced at the black screen to see if a message was left. Nothing appeared, but now I couldn't help worrying. Stuffing the phone into my pocket, I ran my hand over my hidden guns and took a deep breath to steady the uneasy feeling before joining Jasmine.

If anything happened, I would die to keep her safe.

Chapter Forty-Two

JASMINE

I HADN'T FORGOTTEN what it was like to spend time with Dario, but the memories had faded around the edges. His ability to make me smile and blush was at the top of the list. How he still knew all of my favorite things was endearing and unnerving at the same time. If I remembered half the things about him that he knew about me, I would be pleased.

We had lunch under a large tree that I knew would, in the fall, look like it was on fire with its leaves changing. He recited pieces of his favorite poetry from memory as we ate from the same dishes. The man was an enigma to me, yet I didn't want him any other way.

He never let go of my hand, and unlike Angelo, who glared at everyone we passed, Dario's presence moved the tide. Like the parting of the Red Sea, people in our way stepped aside at the sight of him, yet he never spared them a glance.

"Do you like this?" Dario lifted a scarf that beautifully mixed all the blues of the ocean.

"It's stunning. It reminds me of home."

"Me too." He held it out to the man selling. "I'll take this." Turning to me, he draped it over my shoulders, and I rubbed the soft material along my cheek.

"Thank you, it's amazing."

Dario opened his mouth to answer when a commotion across the way drew our attention. As soon as I saw what was going on, I was on the move, marching across the open court to the man who had just dragged a boy into his shop.

"Let me go," the boy yelled. "Help, help. Let me go, Mister."

I stepped into the store as the man raised his hand to slap the boy. He looked no more than eight or nine and very obviously lived on the street or in an impoverished part of town. The bare feet, shabby clothes, and dirty complexion gave it away. A small bag was at his feet with a few apples inside.

"Don't you dare," I said, and the man, who I assumed was the manager or owner, whipped his head in our direction. Dario's shadow loomed in the doorway behind me, but I appreciated that he wasn't interfering.

"He's a thief," the guy said.

"He's also a child."

Marching forward, I picked up the bag and looked inside before quickly grabbing other items to add until it was full. "I will pay for what's in the bag, but you will never strike him, or I will call the authorities on you."

"He and his friends are always in here stealing things. They are going to make me go broke. They are the ones that should be in jail."

"Ow," the boy said as the man shook his arm.

"Or you could offer him a job. Sweeping your storeroom or being a greeter at your door." I got close to the man and looked down at his hand. "Unhand him right now." Giving orders had never been my thing, but using any power I may hold for something like this felt right. "Or my boyfriend will ask you, and he won't be as nice as I am about it."

I heard Dario's phone buzz but kept my focus on the store owner, who seemed to be weighing his options.

"Hello," Dario's deep voice said from behind me.

"This works for this time, but what about all the other items he and his hooligan friends stole?"

There was a flicker of red light like a laser that cats played with, and then everything erupted into chaos.

"Get down," Dario yelled as he tackled me to the floor, his big body covering me and the boy as the window shattered. The gunfire outside the shop was loud, and I cringed and covered my ears. There was a loud thump, and I stifled a scream as the store owner fell in front of my face, blood dripping from the hole through his eye. It was like we'd been thrust into a horror movie.

There was yelling and the sound of more gunfire, but I couldn't tell where it was coming from. Blood seeped toward me on the floor like a red oil slick, and I lay there frozen and horrified.

"Let's go," Dario said, yanking me to my feet and pushing me ahead of him. There was a break in the noise, but my ears were still ringing as I ran toward the back of the building, guided by his hand.

I pushed through a pair of swinging doors that led to a storage area, and as if Dario knew the store like the back of his hand, we weaved through the rows until we reached the back door.

"The boy, I can't leave the boy," I said and turned to run back, but Dario grabbed me with one hand and nodded under his other arm. The child was curled up and hanging on to Dario's side, the plastic bag still tightly clenched in his small fists.

"Let me look first." Dario pushed open the door and looked out. "Okay, let's go."

Dario put the boy on his feet as we stepped into the alley.

"Hey, are you okay," I asked, looking him over. He looked at me and then Dario and didn't say a word before taking off down the alley. "Wait, come back," I called out, but he turned at the end and disappeared.

"He is probably heading somewhere safe. We need to do the same." Dario wrapped his arm around my shoulders and pushed for us to break into a light jog. He took us a different way back to the truck, but I could tell that was where we were heading.

Dario pressed his arm against my body, keeping me flush to the wall as he peeked around the corner. It was quiet where we were, but I could hear sirens in the distance and screams that seemed so far away now.

Holding out his fob, Dario hit the unlock button. There was a distinct rumble as it started, then a loud explosion. I screamed and ducked as Dario once more covered me.

He forced me to look at him. I realized as his steady hands cupped my face that I was shaking. “What’s happening?”

“I’m not sure, but we are the targets. We need to get off the street. Are you okay to run?” I nodded. He pulled his gun and grabbed my hand. “Then let’s go. I know a few hidden spots and have a couple of friends around here.”

Dario was fast, and I felt like he had to drag me along, but he didn’t seem bothered and never broke stride. I followed like his shadow, staying close and doing what he said. Many turns later, he had me stand back while he opened a random gray door and guided us inside. The scent of food cooking hit me, and I knew before we took another step that we were in the back of a restaurant. He pushed through another door, and a dozen line cooks turned to look at us as we walked through.

“Dario ga koko ni iru to Kenji ni tsutaete kudasai,” Dario said to the woman who rushed up to us as he pushed through the black door to the front of the restaurant.

She gave a little bow and rushed off. Dario pulled out his phone as he kept me close to his side, and I couldn’t figure out what to say or ask first. I’d been angry with the shop owner, but I didn’t want him to die, and yet I knew that his lifeless body was going to haunt my dreams.

“I didn’t know you spoke Japanese,” I said, but my voice sounded like it came from someone else.

“I know nine languages,” he said, rubbing his hand up and down my arm.

“Oh no,” I said, and Dario’s eyes roamed over my body as he

began patting me down. "I lost my bag." He pulled me in and held me. I felt cold, really cold. Did I get hit?

"Angelo, I'm at Kenji's with Jasmine. There was an attack. Yeah, but she's going into shock," Dario said. That explained the cold. If it weren't for his arm holding me up, I would've sunk to the ground. My head felt light and spun like I had too much to drink.

"Dario-san, kon'nichiwa." A handsome man, who seemed to appear out of nowhere, approached us. I opened my mouth to greet him, but my tongue was heavy, and my knees gave way.

Dario didn't let me fall as he picked me up into his arms, and I rested my head against his shoulder as he spoke. I couldn't understand what they were saying as we walked. Everything was slipping in and out of focus. My eyes were heavy, and I couldn't fight anymore. They closed, and everything went dark.

Chapter Forty-Three

JASMINE

I WOKE up wrapped in warmth.

Then, a flash of gunfire and a dead man crossed my mind. My eyes snapped open, and I gasped like I'd been jerked by an invisible line. I didn't know whose bed I was in, but I could hear Angelo's voice, too soft to make out what he said. I blinked a few times to get my bearings in the dark room. When did we get home? Or better yet, how? Everything was foggy after we reached the restaurant. Tracing the features of the man in front of me, I knew it was Enzo, and the arm wrapped around me from behind had to be Dario.

"Shh, it's okay. You're safe, and it is still very early. You might as well rest a little longer," Dario whispered.

"When did we get home?"

"It was late. The shock wore off, but you were still pretty upset and fell asleep almost immediately."

"That poor man, I didn't want him dead." Covering my mouth, I tried to wipe the image from my mind. I grew up in a family where death was as normal as eating Sunday dinner, but I'd never seen anyone killed before. Papa kept me from that side of his business.

I'd heard tales of torture rooms and knew that those who crossed any of our families found themselves hunted and killed. I wasn't completely sheltered from what happened, but nothing could've prepared me to be inches from a deadman's face. One moment, I was talking to him, and the next, I was staring into a hole where his eye had been.

"I know you didn't. You're a good person and would never want that." Dario held me a little tighter as he kissed my head.

"And the boy...he looked so scared. I hope he's okay. And your truck...were...were they after us?"

"Don't worry about that right now. Just go back to sleep for a few more hours. There is nothing we can solve at the moment."

I knew he was probably right, but I couldn't stop my mind from racing in circles like a windup toy.

"Dario?"

"Mmmhmm?"

"Thank you. You saved my life."

"You never need to thank me for that. I would happily lay my life down for you and die a happy man, but you are welcome. Now get some rest, and then we will talk."

Enzo shuffled closer, his hand reaching out and finding mine. I wasn't sure what led to Enzo being in bed with Dario and me instead of Angelo, but I linked our fingers together and closed my eyes.

"Fuck, I don't like this," Dario growled as he marched the length of Angelo's office. "We don't even know who it is, let alone if they will try again."

"I agree, but we can't show weakness. That is the surest way for someone to think they scared us. The three of you stay here, and I will go with the guards Kenji lent us. I guess it's time I looked at hiring my own team again. First on the list will be Kristof."

"No," I said, interrupting them before they continued arguing the point. Pushing myself up from the couch, I walked across the room to meet my men.

"No, what?"

"No, I am not staying here." Rolling out my shoulders, I straightened my spine and took on Angelo's stern stare. I didn't care if he didn't want me to go now. This was my new life, the one I chose, and I was going to dinner.

"Yes, you are. It's safer here," Angelo said as he poured a glass of his whiskey.

"And I don't really care if it's safer. I'm not staying here. How, why, or if another attack happens is completely irrelevant. I could be shot sitting in the garden. I could walk into my room, and it's booby-trapped." Angelo's face paled. "We are safer together, and you're right about acting normal. We should keep the plans to visit your distillery and then have dinner with Mr. and Mrs. Rhodes. Anything less will look weak, and I, for one, refuse to allow some asshole to scare me."

"I'm not sure I like that idea any better," Dario said. "Can't they come here instead?"

"No, they can't. Riker made it very clear that they had limited time before they needed to deal with a hell of an issue." Angelo waved his hand as if that would dismiss the comment. "No, he didn't mention what that means. If I'm going to make the deal, I need to meet him at the restaurant like planned."

"I can whip something up that will help," Enzo said, and we all turned to face him. "Obviously, I can't do anything with a gun, but I can get us all trackers, earpieces, and taser pens. I've been working on some smaller gadgets we can use daily."

"I don't know," Angelo said, leaning against the desk.

"Angelo, this is the smartest plan. I know you want to keep me locked up here where you think it's safe, but divided, we are weakened. We stick to the plan and take the men you mentioned like nothing has fazed us."

His hand clenched into a fist on the desk, and I thought he was going to keep arguing with me like all the other men back home would. No, that wasn't true. They wouldn't have allowed me in the room to begin with, but Angelo surprised me by nodding.

"Are you sure you're fine with this? You just had a very traumatic day yesterday."

I crossed my arms. "Spend a single day as a woman and then tell me yesterday was dramatic in comparison."

Angelo smirked. "Okay, fair. I...."

We all turned and froze when the doorbell rang. Dario pulled his guns as Enzo jumped up and hit a button to show the camera outside the door. I stared at the screen, frowning.

"Who is that?" I asked as the guys swore in unison. The woman on camera was a pretty blonde, who looked a little older but was well dressed in a skirt suit.

"I'll go get rid of her," Angelo said and left the office.

I crossed my arms as I looked at Dario. "Who is that? I want the truth."

He rubbed the back of his neck and looked uncomfortable, which was an easy tell that I wouldn't like the answer.

"That is Mrs. Sherwood," he said, and I raised an eyebrow.

"And?"

He cleared his throat. "When we first arrived here, we didn't have much money. We wanted to keep our business dealings as well as ownership secret and didn't have the shell corporations set up...so she...um...."

I sighed. "Let me guess. She took payment for keeping all of your names quiet in a physical manner?" Rage and jealousy mixed in my gut. The idea of this woman touching any of my men made my blood boil.

"Who is her husband, and what does he like?"

"Mr. Sherwood? His name is Greg, and he owns the real estate company where Mrs. Sherwood works. He is worth millions and plays golf at Hatter's Glen. Is that what you wanted to know?"

"It will do," I said and marched out of the room.

"Shit," Dario mumbled.

"As I mentioned, the deal is off. I will have everything drawn up properly next week, but we will no longer pay the way we were for the extra services performed."

"I don't care what you say. We had a deal," Mrs. Sherwood said as I reached the back of the foyer. I couldn't see her around Angelo and stopped as I thought about what to do. Angelo loved it when I was jealous, but that wasn't what I wanted. No, I had a far better idea.

I pulled my blouse off over my head, and Dario's eyes widened. My jeans and socks quickly followed, leaving me in my bra and thong. Angelo's order to not wear any underwear would take some time.

Bending over, I fluffed out my hair before picking up my clothes and pushing them into Enzo's arms. "Hang on to these, please."

"It's simply impossible," Angelo said.

"Well, I'm not leaving without a proper explanation," Mrs. Sherwood said.

With a dramatic flourish, I stepped up beside Angelo and smiled as I draped myself over his arm. "There you are, Shnookems. You said you'd only be a minute before meeting me in bed. I'm all for chasing you around the house, but I didn't realize we would have a guest."

I turned my gaze onto Mrs. Sherwood, whose mouth had dropped open. "Hi there, I'm Isabella. I'm Angelo's wife. Are you that sweet woman he's been fucking to help us out? I told him that would work, you know. You had that desperate housewife look to you when you first showed up here," I said, impressed that I could act like the girls I'd grown up with and a little disgusted with myself at the same time.

"No worries though, you'll be thoroughly compensated with money from now on, isn't that right, Sweetie Pie?" I looked up at Angelo, who looked beyond shocked as I teasingly ran my nails down the side of his face.

"Yes, most definitely," he said.

Mrs. Sherwood crossed her arms, her eyes narrowing until she looked like a shrew.

"What if I refuse?"

"Refuse what exactly?" I leaned against Angelo and placed my hand on my waist.

"To take this new payment or anything else." She huffed.

"Then, this is what will happen. The first call I make is to your husband." I paused and smiled. "I knew my husband was fucking you. We don't keep secrets from one another, isn't that right, hun?"

Angelo nodded, his face composed just enough that it was believable.

"And then, I'll send him the video footage of you being fucked like a stuck pig on Thanksgiving. You didn't think we weren't filming, did you?" Her eyes bugged out of her head, and I knew I had her. "You didn't. Oh, that is so sweet and innocent of you. I'm sure Greg would love for the video to be shown to all his golfing buddies at Hatter's Glen." She swallowed hard. "I bet you signed a pretty ironclad prenup too."

Her hands balled into fists. "What do you want?"

I crossed my arms over my chest and tilted my head. I'd seen the girls in school do this so often that mocking the pose had become second nature. "Me? Why I don't want anything." I gave her my best Wicked Witch smile. "Other than for you to transfer all the paperwork into Angelo's business names per his instructions. Then charge a reasonable amount with a lovely twenty percent discount, just because you're nice and we're amazing clients who will continue to use your husband's company." I wrapped my arm around Angelo's neck and ran my leg up his. "I'm sure that seems fair to you. It would be a shame for Greg to find out, and you lose that fancy car, clothes, and spa treatments." I looked her over. "I'm not sure you would hold up well, I'm afraid."

"Fine. I'll send the paperwork in the morning, but I want the copy of the tapes."

I laughed. "Oh no, I don't think so. Those will remain locked up in the bank box, where they will be kept nice and safe. Please don't play me for an idiot, Mrs. Sherwood. My husband may be the face of the company, but I'm the bitch that steers the ship. Understood?"

Nodding like some sort of puppet on speed, she stammered yes, then turned and trotted to her car. I raised my hand and waved as she left, but I glared up at Angelo as soon as she was gone.

His mouth hung open, and he stared at me like he was seeing me for the first time. It was good to keep him on his toes.

"I...."

"Don't bother. At this point, I don't even want to know. Do you think I can handle myself now?"

"I think you can more than handle yourself, that was fucking incredible." He smirked and reached for me, but I stepped away. I was still seething but purposely kept my face neutral.

"If we're going to be married, never mistake me for arm candy or a bored housewife to be seen and not heard. Or you will see how much of a tiger I can really be." It was hard to shock Angelo, but the raised eyebrow mixed with the dark desire in his eyes was close enough.

"I'll be ready to go in half an hour." I stepped away, then stopped and looked back at him. "Oh, and Angelo, please make sure anyone else you've paid with sexual favors never touches you again." I gave him the full weight of my glare. "Or I'll order Dario to shoot your cock off. Do you really want to test where his loyalties lie?" I looked at Dario, who was smirking before giving Angelo one last disgusted look.

I swayed away from him and grabbed my clothes from a stunned Enzo. "Pick your jaws up off the floor, boys. Today is going to be a good day."

Giving them all a disapproving glare, I marched up the stairs.

"Damn, that was the hottest fucking thing I've ever seen," Enzo said as I got to the landing.

I smiled because I was done with people, especially men, underestimating me. My politeness and kindness in the face of great challenge and stress had been mistaken for weakness. The girls I grew up with made sure to let me know I didn't fit in, while the boys bullied or dismissed me.

I'd grown up thinking something was wrong with me, but that was far from the truth. My parents had instilled a different kind of strength, one where I could rule with an iron fist but a heart full of compassion.

Even Angelo had underestimated me, but I wouldn't allow that to happen again. I would never be second to anything or anyone. Being kind and having manners didn't make me meek, and I would prove it, starting today.

Chapter Forty-Four

ANGELO

"AND THIS IS where the magic happens," I said as I held out my hand for Jasmine to step out of the SUV. It had been so long since I had black vehicles with guards following me around that it seemed strange to see Kenji's men parked around us.

My eyes scanned the neighboring buildings for any sign of danger. Jasmine slipped out of the vehicle, holding my hand, looking like the princess she was born to be. Strong and powerful, but with a grace that captivated everyone who looked her way. She said she didn't want to be treated like arm candy, and although I wouldn't have dared even before she threatened to remove my cock, I couldn't help but want to show her off to the world. I felt as tall as the largest building in the world with her by my side.

"We're not the largest yet, but I'm working on doubling the size. That is what the dinner meeting tonight is about. My real estate projects are at a standstill until I can make enough to build what I want."

"Is that why you were arguing with the investment place," Jasmine asked, and I nodded.

I had ways to get the money, but they would involve selling off items that at one time I thought about, but couldn't. There was no way I could look her in the eyes and sell off the things I'd stolen from her father. Even I had limits to being an asshole.

Dario and Enzo stayed close as we walked through the front doors. The entrance was rustic but charming.

"When I bought this building, it was falling apart, but I've completely renovated it and turned it into what you see now."

Jasmine smiled. "It's stunning, Angelo. I love the inspiration you've added from back home while keeping some of the local heritage," she said, nodding toward the wall with images of the area and buildings from over the last hundred years.

The office staff was lined up outside their doors, waiting to greet us like they were viewing a parade.

"We don't need to stop," I whispered, annoyed that they were all standing around rather than working.

"Nonsense, that is not how you treat people," she said, glaring at me before holding out her hand to the first employee.

Jasmine took the time to meet every single person, and they gushed over her as she asked their name and thanked them for their work. It didn't matter that she had no idea what they did. What mattered was that she made them feel special. Every moment I spent with her, I learned something new about her or myself. With one simple action, she schooled me in something that I'd been too blind in my ambition to see. I needed people as much as I needed space and equipment, and these people loved her. I could see it in their eyes as they spoke.

We pushed through the doors to where the whiskey was made. Every time I came in here and looked around at the tall metal vats, pride filled my chest.

"Mr. Esposito, it's so good to see you again," Tuck, my manager, said as he hurried over, smoothing back the little bit of hair he still had on his head. He zealously shook my hand with both of his while his round face glowed a bright shade of red. No matter how hard he tried, he could never find a suit to wear that the buttons weren't popping at the seams and ready to shoot across the room.

"Good afternoon, Tuck. This is my fiancé, Jasmine. Jasmine, this is Tuck, my head production manager and the best mixologist you will ever meet. We all call him Friar Tuck."

"Friar Tuck? As in..." Jasmine stopped herself from asking the question, her cheeks pinking as she looked up at me. I knew she was worried she was about to insult Tuck, but she had nothing to worry about.

Tuck laughed, and the jovial sound bounced off the metal. "Yes, ma'am, the one and only. I take pride in my nickname and my job. I love working for Mr. Esposito and love sampling the product even more."

Jasmine giggled even though it looked like Tuck was going to shake her hand so hard that her teeth would rattle right out of her head.

"Today is a perfect day to arrive. We have some samples we need to test after the tour."

I loved that Jasmine asked questions as we walked the floor and showed a genuine interest in every stage. While Tuck explained what happened during the fermenting process, I stepped closer to Dario.

"Any concerns?"

"Not yet. Kenji's men have searched the building and found nothing. There doesn't seem to be anything suspicious in the neighboring buildings, and no one unusual is hanging around."

"Good. I would never forgive myself if something happened to her," I said.

"You and me both."

"Um...how about all three of us? I'm still here, you know, and I can hear you," Enzo said, and I rolled my eyes at him.

It was bad enough that Dario corrected my grammar and reminded me that he was in our relationship, now Enzo. If I didn't like the guy or love Jasmine so much, I would be tempted to shoot him and put myself out of my misery. On the other hand, I recognized that Enzo was something I wasn't. He was still fun and spontaneous and didn't take everything so seriously. Too many parts of me had died in Chicago, and the darkness had forever tainted what was left. Even if Jasmine made me feel alive again, there were some things that might never heal.

"This is amazing, Angelo," Jasmine said as Tuck continued the tour, and we walked to the office. "I'm really very impressed. I always thought your father didn't give you the credit you deserved."

"Is that so?"

She looked up at me, and I wanted to melt into her golden eyes like I was throwing myself into a vat of whiskey.

"It's easy to see how hard you've worked, and I remember you coming up with so many ideas that he shot down. You tried to hide the disappointment, but I knew you would prove him wrong, and here you are doing just that. I love it." She smiled, and I wanted to tell everyone to go away while I pushed her up against the wall and lifted her little black dress to fuck her hard. "Honestly, I'm surprised I never heard about it. Your father is a complainer, and I figured I would've overheard him once when he was over," she said, shrugging.

I found the last statement strange, considering my father banished me from home. He would never want to talk about me. I was a stain on his reputation. Before I could ask the question, we reached the office, and Tuck dragged Jasmine inside.

"So, there are three new flavors we have created. Would you like to try those? You would be our first," Tuck said, pulling a chair out for Jasmine to sit.

"Yes, that would be incredible."

Tuck held up a bottle. "This one is called *The Charmer's Cache*." Tuck smiled wide. "Up your charm with one shot." He gave Jasmine a wink. "Experiences may vary. We are not responsible for black eyes, unexpected pregnancy, or getting locked up. Please drink responsibly."

Jasmine laughed as Tuck finished his sales pitch. He wanted us to make it a commercial, and I hated that it was kind of catchy.

"Let me explain the flavor profile of all of them first, and then you can decide which you'd like to give a whirl," Tuck said as Jasmine sat down at the desk.

I pulled out my phone and answered a few messages from Kristof, warning him of the strange message Dario had received from Giovanni. I still wasn't sure what the hell he meant by "*The cuckoo's nest is empty. Beware the snake.*"

All hell had broken out, and now I didn't know if the clue had something to do with what happened in town or something else. I even tried calling him on the secure line he'd given me when he and Dario had arranged our escape from Italy, but he didn't pick up. God, I hated riddles. Who was the cuckoo and the snake? Did I know them, or was it a new threat? My head hurt thinking about it.

Why he couldn't just tell me was frustrating. He still owed me as far as I was concerned. I could've sent him and Lucas to hell three times over with the shit Lucas did to four Dons' daughters. Giovanni wanted to protect his son, which I did and didn't understand, but he was still a powerful man, and I'd gotten myself into hot water and needed his help, so we came to an understanding. Lucas was a piece of shit, and as far as I was concerned, Giovanni should just put him down. But I still held an ace up my sleeve, one I hadn't shared with him and planned to use only in a dire situation.

I jerked my head up from my phone as a faint scream for help reached me. Dario must have heard it, too, because he immediately stepped outside the office door.

"Did you hear that," he asked softly.

"Yeah," I said as it came again, and Dario and I pulled our guns. I looked back at Enzo and signaled to stay put. He took out his gun and nodded. I didn't want to terrify Jasmine, so I closed the door.

"This way." Following Dario, my senses were on high alert. He marched fast, his eyes scanning every corner. "Over there." There was a thud, and he pointed to the taste testing room. We jogged and skidded to a stop when we reached the door and stared down at Carlos. He was our batch taster before the whiskey was bottled.

He lay on the floor with his hands wrapped around his throat, eyes wide as foam leaked out of his mouth. He was still jerking like a fish, but I knew that look, and there was no helping him now. Rage roared through my system. Someone wasn't just targeting me. They were targeting my business. I had no idea who it was, but I would have to pull back the latest shipment that had just gone out to be safe. Fuckers.

"He was definitely poisoned, so until we know by what, don't touch anything. I'll get a crew to come in and test. Sheriff Nottingham still owes me a few favors," I said and spotted the testing glass on the ground. I turned and ran back the way we came.

Sprinting across the floor, Dario was right beside me as I burst through the office door, making Enzo jump and turn his gun on me. Jasmine already had the glass to her lips, and with a maniacal yell, I charged across the room and smacked it out of her hand.

Jasmine screamed and jumped up as it smashed, her eyes wide as she stared at me. I grabbed her face and looked at her lips. They didn't seem wet, but I wasn't taking any chances.

"Don't lick." I pulled her into the small bathroom and turned on the water. "Rinse your lips just in case anything touched." Fear flashed in her eyes, but she did what I asked, and I handed her a towel. "Did you drink any of the others?"

"No, that was still the first."

My thundering heart slowed as relief washed over me. Grabbing Jasmine's hand, I marched back into the office to confront a wide-eyed Tuck.

"Sir, what is it? What's wrong," Tuck asked. He looked to be in as much shock as Jasmine.

"Who has been in this building that shouldn't have been?" I yelled at him, and he leaped back in surprise, his eyes going to the gun in my hands. "Answer me!"

"I...I...I don't know. I don't handle security unless someone says there's an issue. Gilles takes care of that," Tuck stammered, his hands going up.

"And you haven't seen anyone new, an employee you didn't recognize?"

"Um...there have been a couple of new hires for the delivery truck drivers, but not anyone on the floor. I interview them personally."

I grabbed Jasmine's arm and tucked her close to my side. "You sure you didn't drink any?" She shook her head no. My eyes lifted to Tuck. Right or wrong, I was going to blame him. He was the one in charge of the building.

"When was the last chemical analysis test done?"

"For this batch." He pointed to the table. "And the ones that shipped out today, about a month ago."

"And you test every batch?"

"Yes, of course. It's protocol, and I'm strict on it. Once Carlos says it's good, we test it, and I do a final taste to be sure it's the best quality. I never skip a step. Why, what's going on," Tuck asked, his voice shaking.

Jasmine touched my arm, and I realized I still had my gun pointed at Tuck. "Put down the gun, Angelo." Taking a deep breath, I slowly lowered the weapon.

"I want everyone out of the building and the security footage from the last testing until now." Tuck stood there staring at me. "Now!" I bellowed, and he ran from the room.

I pulled Jasmine into a hug, the terror of what might have happened taking over my anger.

"What's going on," Enzo asked.

"Someone poisoned a batch, but we don't know which one or when," Dario answered, and Enzo's face darkened as he understood what could've happened.

"It's okay, Angelo, I'm fine," she said, her voice so calm and such a contrast to how I was feeling.

"It's obvious that someone is trying to ruin me. I just don't know who or why. I'm so sorry that you were almost caught in the middle of this for a second time." I shook my head as the anger in my veins made me see red. "I'm going to find who the fuck did this, and when I do...." I didn't bother finishing the sentence.

Jasmine wrapped her arms around my waist and laid her head over my heart. I glared at the shattered glass. That was what my heart would've looked like if she'd been poisoned. All of my dreams had almost become my worst nightmare.

Not even the doors of hell could hold me from taking my revenge. Whoever did this would pay with more than a pound of flesh, of that I was certain.

Chapter Forty-Five

JASMINE

WITH EVERYTHING WE'D SHARED, sitting in the SUV together, I finally realized Angelo wasn't exaggerating about how he felt. He'd done crazy things to get my attention, from the first day we met. Everything from bullying, outlandish gestures to shock me, and anything else imaginable. It was his nature to be over the top.

Angelo didn't scare easily. I couldn't remember a single time I'd ever seen him scared over anything, but the terror in his eyes hadn't left since the distillery. His bouncing knee and the hard line to his jaw as he held my hand like I would disappear only added to my understanding.

Silence blanketed the car on the way to Athena's Palate. Not even Enzo, sitting in the passenger seat, looked back or said a word.

"Guys, I'm fine. Can we relax and try to enjoy the evening?"

The uniform look I received from all three of them was like I'd asked them to dance naked in the street.

"I won't be able to relax until whoever is attacking me is caught and punished," Angelo said.

"If they're after you at all," Dario commented. I glanced at the rearview mirror, but his eyes were covered with black sunglasses, so dark that I didn't even know how he saw the road.

"You think they are targeting Jasmine?" Angelo asked the question, but I also wanted to know the answer. "What possible reason would someone have to want to hurt her?"

"I'm not saying that is the case, just that it's a possibility we need to explore. We are only days out from Jasmine being attacked in the house," Dario said, and Angelo's hand tightened on mine.

I placed my other hand on his, and Angelo's eyes flicked to mine. If I didn't know Angelo, I would've said that the news wasn't bothering him, but his panic was obvious to me.

"Alright, I'm not leaving anything to chance. Enzo, when we get back, finding any leads or connections is your top priority."

He looked over his shoulder. "Already on it, and I'll put pressure on the lab testing the blood sample we collected from the one we winged."

Angleo looked at me. "Until we have some answers, I don't want you going anywhere alone. Not out to the garden or greenhouse, not even the bathroom." He knew I was gearing up to argue that he was going overboard because he brought my hand to his heart. "I'm asking you to please do this. Death might as well reach up and drag me to my grave if something happened to you because I wouldn't survive that."

I'd never seen him this emotional, and it was freaking me out more than him being an overbearing ass. Reaching out, I cupped his face and wiped away the tear running down his cheek.

"Okay, I won't go anywhere alone." He leaned in and kissed me, and there was so much emotion behind it that my eyes began to tear.

"Promise me," he said.

"I promise."

He shuddered and sighed, the tension easing in the car like my promise had let air in, and we could all breathe again.

"Thank you."

With a blink, he composed himself and sat up straight. I'd seen my papa do the same thing many times over the years, and it still amazed me how they were all taught to swallow emotions and take it, *'like a man.'* It bothered me, but if I said anything, I would bet he didn't even notice. It was so engrained into the fabric of who he was now. It wasn't fair—the masks worn *Of Mice And Men*.

"Oh wow, is that where we're going?"

"Sure is, best Mediterranean food I've ever tasted," Enzo said, and a smile graced his lips for the first time all day.

The restaurant glowed like a diamond in the dark. The white walls and large arching doorways with white sheers reminded me of my home back in Italy. I suddenly felt homesick. Just looking at this place made me think of Papa and Ciro. I missed my best friend and loved and missed my papa so much, but I had no idea what would happen if I reached out.

Dario pulled up to the valet stand and turned to look back at Angelo and me. "Stay in here until the men and I have done a sweep. We'll be back."

He jumped out, and Enzo followed. I watched them working like a unit as they walked into the restaurant.

"Is it always like this," I asked. "Being a Don, being the wife of a Don?"

Angelo turned away from the window and looked at me. "You didn't see any of this back home?"

I shrugged. "Very little. My Papa wanted to keep out of whatever he could. We rarely left the property unless it was with other Dons and their families. I assume all the inspections happened before we arrived. At home, as you know, there were guards everywhere, but I grew up seeing men in suits standing at doorways. I just didn't realize how unusual it was until I left. It has been nice not waking up to find a guard outside my room."

"Do you not want this life?"

I searched his face and gave him a little smile. "I want whatever life looks like with all of you, but I can't say the fear and worry is fun or that I'll enjoy it."

Angelo cupped my face and leaned in to kiss me. "That's fair," he said, breaking away. "I would keep you out of all of it if I could. I never want you to see or know what I've done."

I knew he meant killing and, most likely, torture. I also knew that no matter how clean one of the businesses looked, they all had another side that wasn't as legal. There were some things you just learned to accept growing up in this world, and I'd made my peace with who I was. Being Jasmine Falcone meant I couldn't just be the teen who walked down the street with friends, went to the mall, or watched movies and talked about boys. I was a target, someone to use against my family.

I sucked in a sharp breath, and Angelo's eyes went wide. "What's wrong?"

"What if it's not me? What if it's an attack on my family, and I'm just the easy mark?"

Dario opened the door, and I jumped. Worry had wormed its way into my mind.

"We will talk more about this when we get home," Angelo said and took my hand as he got out of the vehicle and forced me to exit the same side.

Dario and Enzo flanked us, and I could see the men who had been following us all day stationed around the building. When we stepped into the restaurant, my mouth watered, and my stomach growled. It smelled amazing, and I was ready to eat for ten.

"Welcome to Athena's Palate, my name is Rhea." The pretty brunette behind the maître d' stand said with a wide smile. She had her hair pinned, but a couple of curly strands hung around her face. "We have reserved the best table in the house and those surrounding it just as instructed."

"Very good," Angelo said.

"Please follow me."

We walked to the back corner of the restaurant, and I admired the bar area with the bright greenery and backlighting that made all the colorful bottles glitter. Angelo pulled out my chair for me to sit, as Dario and Enzo stood on either side of the table like sentinels. All eyes were on us, but I ignored the uncomfortable feeling and thanked Rhea.

"Rhea, is Gina working tonight," I asked.

"Yes, she is. Would you like me to let her know you're here?"

"Don't go to any trouble. I just wanted to say hi," I said and smiled. "No need to bother her."

"Very well, your server will be with you in just a moment," Rhea said and hustled off. I liked her professional and to-the-point attitude.

"You mentioned that this man you're meeting is a business partner?"

"No, I want to purchase a building and equipment from him to expand." Angelo looked at his watch. "I hope he's still coming."

"Oh, I think they're here," I said, nodding toward the couple walking across the room. I felt both baffled and frozen in my seat. They were incredibly stunning. So gorgeous that they looked like movie stars walking the red carpet, apparitions, or maybe something unearthly.

The woman wore a blue dress that matched her eyes, her long black hair flowing perfectly in time with her strides. The smile on her face felt warm and inviting, which was at odds with the man on her arm. The man I knew as Mr. Rhodes was no ordinary man. With one glance, I knew he was used to being in charge of everything. His aura was commanding, and amber eyes darker than my own were sharp and intelligent. There was no denying that he was unbelievably handsome. I wasn't a woman to typically stare at a man, but my eyes were drawn to him.

Angelo suddenly grabbed my hand, and I cleared my throat and sipped at my water as the couple stopped at our table. Angelo stood and held out his hand, and I stood beside him. I suddenly wished that I hadn't lost my gold dress in the crazy shootout yesterday. I looked down at the simple black number I wore and felt extremely underdressed.

"Mr. and Mrs. Rhodes, it's a pleasure to meet you in person. This is my fiancé Jasmine, and we'd like to thank you so much for coming."

"You can call me Riker. This is an informal dinner, and this is my wife and certainly the best parts of me, Minetta."

Minetta smiled at her husband, and my heart beat a little harder like I was watching a storybook romance play out before my eyes. She held out her hand to Angelo.

"You can call me Minny."

When she did the same to me, I was startled and stared at her for a moment. "So nice to meet you," I said, gripping Minny's hand and instantly feeling at ease. As intimidating as she seemed, a calmness washed over me with her touch.

I held my hand out for Riker to shake, but he turned it and lifted it to his lips. I'd always thought Angelo had the most intense and intimidating stare, but looking into Riker's eyes made the hair on the back of my neck stand on end. I swallowed hard as his lips met my skin. I was flattered but felt very uncomfortable with the extra attention and just wanted him to let go of my hand.

I could feel Angelo glaring out of the corner of my eye. It would do no one any good if he lost his cool. Riker lifted his head, a devilish look in his eyes as he smirked.

"I like both of you. That's good, we can continue. Please sit," he ordered. "So tell me, what is good to eat here?"

"That question would be for me." I hadn't noticed Gina walk up to the table, but she smiled at everyone, her bright white chef's coat neatly in place and her hair done in a tight bun on top of her head. "Nice to see you again," she said, smiling at me.

"You as well, Chef," I said.

"I will be personally cooking your meals this evening, and if I were you, I would try the chicken shawarma."

"Well, I'm sold, make that two," Riker said.

"The same for us," Angelo said.

"Excellent choice. This is Hector, and he will be your server for the evening." The man approached the table, and I blushed as he winked at me. I quickly grabbed Angelo's hand under the table before he exploded in a rage.

Minny turned to me as the men discussed wine orders.

"Yours is overprotective as well," she asked and rolled her eyes, making me smile.

"That is an understatement," I said and caught the subtle smirk from Dario.

Neither he nor Enzo had moved a muscle since we sat down, and I wished I could tell them to relax and sit with us, but this was the reality. Behind closed doors, we were so much more, but out here in the open, they were once more bodyguards, and it made me sad to see them treated that way.

"You look stunning. I'm sorry if I keep staring at you, but your dress is breathtaking."

"Thank you, that is kind of you to say." She reached out and laid her hand on top of mine on the table. Her voice was so soft I didn't know how I heard it over the music and loud male voices, but I did. "You look incredible. It's not the dress but the person who shines."

This wasn't how I envisioned dinner or the people we were meeting, but it felt right to be included in an important negotiation for a change. Minny was right. I needed to stop looking at myself through childish eyes. I was a grown woman, powerful and strong. I needed to own that and let it shine through.

"Thank you. I needed to hear that."

Chapter Forty-Six

ANGELO

THE STORIES and rumors didn't do this man justice. I'd heard everything from a business tycoon who took no prisoners to a demon from hell who would rip your soul out as he destroyed and dismantled your company. I thought they were exaggerating, but now I wasn't so sure.

I didn't know what to make of Riker, but I hated how he flirted with Jasmine. Or maybe it was Jasmine who couldn't take her eyes off him. It made my blood boil, and the angrier I got, the happier Riker seemed to get. Was he purposely trying to push my buttons? All I could think about was leaping across the table and strangling him while trying to keep a pleasant smile on my face.

"What do you think?" I finished and sat back, not wanting to give any trepidation away.

Riker swirled his drink, the wine circling the glass like a whirlpool, and I felt like I was being sucked down into the undercurrent as I waited for his answer.

"Let me understand this correctly. You want to purchase my building and all the equipment but don't have the downpayment we agreed upon, and you want to extend the payment plan?" His voice was calm and cool, but the way he spoke made me feel like I was sitting in front of my disapproving father all over again. All those old wounds and insecurities were trying to creep to the surface.

"As I explained, there was a snag with the investor, but rest assured, I will find another," I said, sipping my wine.

"By snag with your investor, you mean the Cogsworth. Is your next plan to steal what you need?" He smirked, and I choked on my drink. It felt like he could see into my mind and knew everything I'd ever done or would do.

"What would make you say that?" The weight of my family ring seemed to be burning right through my finger.

Riker's lip pulled up. "I may have done business a time or two with the Esposito family as recently as five years ago." He shifted the fancy Rolex on his wrist, and my heart pounded harder. "You are Mario's son, are you not? He mentioned a falling out between you, and I helped him with a little financial crisis. He still owes me money, but he pays on time, which bodes well for you. I'm just not sure I want to do business with another Esposito who is struggling to find payment. Could also be considered a conflict of interest."

I had no idea that my father even knew Riker, but I knew what timeline he referenced. Licking my lips, I tried to calm my racing heart, terrified he would blurt out the entire embarrassing ordeal.

Did he know all the details? Was he trying to drive a wedge between me and Jasmine by bringing up this painful part of our past? I glanced at Jasmine, very aware of her eyes on the side of my face, and my blood pressure began to rise.

"I assure you that any business you have with my father would never conflict with my purchase, and I will not default on the loan," I said.

"You say that, and yet you didn't have the downpayment ready for tonight." He leaned forward, pushing aside his dessert dish before resting his arms on the table. "You must see how that wouldn't make me feel secure in forging a partnership with you?"

My jaw twitched as my frustration and anger rose with this

entire situation. Jasmine laid her hand on my arm, and that simple touch calmed me.

"Mr. Rhodes, I can't—"

"Riker," he corrected, cutting her off, but he smiled at her, and I hated the red blush that crept across her cheeks. She was staring at him like he hung the moon. I didn't know what pissed me off more—that he seemed to know all about my personal and professional life while I knew very little, other than rumors, about him or that Jasmine's eyes were feasting on the most ruthless businessman in the world. It didn't help that he looked like he'd been chiseled to perfection by God's hand.

"Riker. I can't profess to be a business mogul like yourself, but I can certainly say that Angelo's word is ironclad. If he says he will get you the requested money with more time, then I assure you he will."

"You don't need to defend me. I'm perfectly capable of handling my business," I said, shooting her a glare, hating that she felt the need to say anything. I immediately regretted it as a flicker of hurt flashed across her face, but she recovered quickly, and it was gone. Jasmine nodded as she removed her hand, and I wanted to take back everything. Shit. I was fucking up on all fronts.

Riker leaned back in his chair, and his arrogance made me want to snarl at him. He pointedly looked at me and then Jasmine before smiling like the fucking Cheshire Cat.

"I'd love to hear what Jasmine has to say, even if you don't," he said, and I'd never been so easily stripped down in my entire life. Not even Giovanni had Riker's skill. I couldn't decide if I envied or hated him, but neither of the emotions made me like him. I was ready to grab Jasmine's hand and march out the door and say fuck it to the deal. He was right. I had other ways to get the money.

"No, it's fine. I've said all I was going to," Jasmine said.

"Not about Angelo. I'd like to hear more about you," he said and turned to stare at Jasmine even as his arm was wrapped around the back of his wife's chair. She didn't seem bothered by his behavior. She just shook her head or rolled her eyes, which made me wonder if this was a game he liked to play. Maybe they both did. Hell, maybe they were looking for someone else to be part of their relationship and Jasmine piqued Riker's interest. It was hard to tell, and my volatile yet desperate emotions weren't helping me to think straight.

"What would you like to know," Jasmine asked, folding her hands in her lap.

"Tell me this. Why are you with someone like Angelo? You were born with class, and it's obvious you could certainly do far better," Riker said, not only insulting me, but his voice sounded like he was already imagining licking her body.

I was out of my seat, with my hands balled into fists, before I even had time to contemplate the repercussions. Dario and Enzo turned in our direction, reaching inside of their jackets. Everyone close to our table stopped to stare at my sudden outburst. Riker slowly turned his eyes up to meet mine.

"If you don't want to do business with me, fine. I don't give fuck. I will find someone else who does, but you will not touch one hair on her head. Jasmine is mine," I growled, glaring at him, no longer caring about anything else. I looked down at Jasmine, her eyes wide as she stared up at me. "There is only one thing in this world that is worth more to me than any deal, and you are walking a very fine line." My eyes met Riker's once more. "I would choose your next words carefully."

"Ah...there he is," Riker said, and I had no idea what he meant. He polished off his wine glass and poured himself another before smiling at me. "Your truest desire is noble. You still need work, but your heart is pure and not most interested in what I can offer you. Sit, please. I'm happy to do business with you."

I blinked, my body relaxing as confusion mingled with anger. Lowering myself to my seat, I looked between Riker and Minetta and back again. "You've been playing me? All this time?"

Riker shrugged. "I wanted to see who you really were when pushed. I only do business with people I can destroy or like. There is no middle ground with me."

"And which category do I fall in," I asked, leaning my hands on the table.

"When I first arrived, I didn't know. But now, I do. I like you, Angelo. You are willing to fight for what your heart wants, and I admire that. I may have had to do the same thing once or twice." He glanced at Minetta, and I couldn't imagine how he talked her into marrying him.

"So you want to do the deal?"

"Well, I don't like that you don't have my money...." Minetta grabbed his hand, one elegant eyebrow arching as she looked at her husband. I held back the smirk as I watched him swallow hard. So the man was tameable, or as much as someone like him could be. Reaching out, I took Jasmine's hand, mad at myself for snapping at her like I had, and realized that some might say the same thing about me.

"Do you remember what we talked about on our way here," Minetta asked, her voice soft.

Riker pulled at his tie, loosening it around his neck. "I do."

"Then I suggest you do what we discussed, and we can get going or...."

Riker jumped up from his seat like he'd been electrocuted. The glasses rattled on the table before Minetta could finish her sentence.

"I'm sorry, but I need to get going. How about this? I'm feeling generous. We can do the deal for twenty percent less than the original price with no downpayment. My lawyer will be in touch to finalize everything."

"Nice to meet you, Jasmine and Angelo," Minetta said as Riker wrapped his arm around her waist.

"Nice to meet you as well," Jasmine said, standing and shaking their hands. I followed suit, very confused about what just happened.

As soon as I let go of Riker's hand, he nodded and practically dragged Minetta from the restaurant.

Dario slowly turned and looked at me. "That was the strangest meeting I've ever seen, and I don't say this lightly. That man unnerves me. No one unnerves me."

"Did that just happen," I asked and flopped onto my chair.

"I heard it," Dario said.

"Same," Enzo said.

I turned to Jasmine, but she wasn't smiling.

"Tonight, we are going to celebrate." I leaned closer to give her a kiss, but she leaned away.

"Think again. You disrespected me and put me down in front of a potential business partner." Jasmine tossed her napkin down on the table and stood.

"Jasmine...."

"No, I don't want to hear your apology right now. I'm angry, and I have a right to be. I'm going to the bathroom." Enzo followed her without a word, and I slumped back into my chair.

"Fuck."

Dario smirked. "You really need to work on the foot-in-mouth disease you have," he said, picking up Jasmine's fork and polishing off the last mouthfuls of dessert.

"You could learn to mind your own business."

"Impossible, it's part of my job description to call you out when you're a flaming dick. You had me agree to it years ago." I glared at him. "Although, I'm starting to come around on Enzo's thought process. It's nice that you're such a fucking ass. It makes the two of us look great in her eyes."

"I fucking hate you."

He chuckled. "I'll go get the car."

Dario had a point. Everything I did took me two steps forward and one step back. Fuck my life.

Chapter Forty-Seven

JASMINE

OKAY, sleeping in my room didn't feel like as much of a punishment for Angelo as it was for me. He was annoyed and upset, but Enzo was working late, and Dario went to see Kenji, so I slept alone. That was a stretch. Staring at the ceiling frustrated was more accurate. How quickly times change.

"Ugh, this is useless." Tossing the blankets off, I walked to my door and opened it a crack. Angelo didn't want me wandering the house alone, but I wanted a drink and would be quick. The guard at the end of the hall stared out the window, so I slipped out and tiptoed in the other direction. This reminded me of when Angelo and I would sneak around my home, and despite my anger with him, excitement soared through my body.

I managed to dodge another guard and was surprised I didn't knock over an expensive statue, break a glass, or walk into a wall. The kitchen was quiet, and of course my stomach dropped with disappointment that I didn't find Angelo waiting for me. I poured myself a tall glass of cold water and took the long way back to my room. Turning down the hallway that led to the back stairs, I froze when I heard a loud thud. I looked down at the vibration that I'd felt through my bare feet.

My first instinct was to press my back against the wall and keep an eye on both directions. The thud came again, but there was also a faint grunt. A normal person would turn around and run away, but not me. Nope, I had to know what made the noise and continued down the hall, listening.

Rock music poured from behind the next door, and I paused to listen.

"Ah!" *Thud.*

I jumped when I heard the yell, and my pulse spiked. It took a second, but I recognized Dario's voice, and my curiosity got the better of me. Like a thief in the night, I opened the door a crack and peeked inside. The glass almost slipped from my hand as I spotted the cause of the noise.

Dario stood in front of a wall of mirrors without a shirt, and I bit my lip as I stared at the massive, roaring gorilla. It took up his entire back and contrasted sharply with the calm gorilla tattooed on his chest, but they were both so much like him. He wore black track pants, and my mouth watered as he squatted, his hard ass pressing against the material. With a roar, he lifted the heavy weights, his back and arm muscles flexing as he pushed the bar above his head before dropping it to the floor in front of him with a bang.

"You can come in, you know," Dario said, looking over his shoulder at me.

Startled, I jerked, and my water sloshed in the glass and splashed the front of my top.

"Shit," I grumbled. "Great." My face heated as I wiped at the wet mark, my embarrassment alive and well. He caught me being a peeping Tom. Maybe for my next trick, I would take up stalking like Angelo.

Dario pulled the door open wider, his eyes taking in my wet shirt as he looked me up and down. "You're not supposed to leave your room without a guard," he said.

"Are you going to tell Angelo?"

He smiled and reached out to pull me into the room. The door closed behind me, and I swallowed hard. Dario stepped into my body, and I moved back until there was nowhere to go. Reaching around me, he flicked the lock.

"I'm sure you could bribe me to keep my mouth shut," he said, and I rubbed my thighs together.

"I thought you were the nice one," I teased, and he smiled, making my heart skip a beat.

"Oh, I am the nice one. Angelo would have you over his lap, spanking your ass by now for disobeying him." I smirked as he stepped in closer. "Unless you want me to spank you." Dario dropped his head to my neck, the rough five o'clock shadow brushing against my skin. "I would happily lay you over my lap."

"Are you trying to seduce me?"

"I'd say that's the other way around. You found me in the middle of the night with a wet tank top, no less." He nipped my ear, and I closed my eyes as my fingers tightened on the water glass like it was the only thing keeping me on my feet. "What am I to do with you now? Should I tell Angelo or punish you myself?"

It was as if someone set fire to my body. The little shorts and tank felt too constricting, and I was tempted to dump the glass of water over my head. It was as rare as an eclipse that Dario let himself be playful. He was always too worried about protecting, keeping up appearances, and hiding his ture feelings infront of the wrong person. It made moments like this special.

"I don't think Angelo needs to know about my little nighttime adventure to the fridge. I'm sure we can keep this between us," I said. I could feel Dario smiling against my neck, sending the twinges of need soaring throughout my body. "Should we take this back to my room?"

He pulled back and looked down at me before plucking my water from my fingers. Why was watching a man drink so sexy? With each swallow the clear liquid disappeared down his throat, and I bit my lip unable to look away. Who knew you could be jealous of water? He licked his lips before he sat the glass down on the ground.

"Oh, we aren't going to your room." Reaching out, he lowered the bright lights to a soft glow. "I plan on punishing you right here."

I squeaked as he grabbed me around the waist and lifted me up like weights. Staring down into his eyes as he walked across the room, I had no fear that he would ever drop me. Dario made you feel like he would kick the doors of hell down to save you, and I believed it. Saying he would die for me was not him spouting pretty words. It was beautiful and terrifying at the same time. My eyes flicked to the narrow bandage on his shoulder, but if the wound bothered him, it never showed.

"Are there no cameras in here?"

"Oh, there are cameras." He smirked. "I just don't care."

A thrill raced through my body as I pictured a furious Angelo watching and jerking off to me and Dario.

Setting me on the cushioned mats, he tilted my head and stared into my eyes without saying a word. It didn't matter. I felt the passion in his stare and the love he conveyed as his lips touched mine. Nothing felt rushed with Dario, and with every second that passed, the desperation to feel his touch on my body drove me near insane with need.

My fingers traced the lines of muscle down his chest and abs. He was so fit that each dip seemed carved from marble. My breath caught as my fingers came into contact with the front of his track pants and the massive package that forced the material to stand out. He groaned as I wrapped my hand around him, and he pushed harder into my grasp.

"You are wearing far too much clothing, especially when I get to watch you in the mirrors," Dario said against my lips, making me smile. The butterflies in my stomach took flight as I looked at around the room and realized we were surrounded by mirrors.

Lifting my arms, he pulled the tank top off and let it fall to the floor as he squatted in front of me.

"Uh," I gasped as he kissed my stomach. Dario's fingers hooked into the waistband of my shorts, and with each inch that he pulled them down, his mouth followed until I was a gasping mess in his hands.

"So sexy." His tongue flicked out and swirled around my clit as I moaned. "Let's get rid of these," he said, and I stepped out of the shorts.

Dario looked up at me as his hands ran down the back of my legs, and I couldn't say why, but I wanted to cry—the reality of having him back had finally hit. My life the last few years had been filled with so much emptiness that it kept trying to drown me until it felt like every day was a gasp for breath. This last month had been a whirlwind of emotions, and now it didn't seem real.

"You're so beautiful that my heart sings looking at you." My cheeks heated with the compliment. He slowly stood, forcing me to look up. "My soul aches whenever I have to close my eyes." Placing his hand over my heart, he searched my face. I wanted to say something romantic back, but poetic words had never been my thing. "When I knew we weren't coming home...." He shook his head, and the pain in his eyes choked me. "I'd always accepted my position until that moment, but I got down on my knees and prayed to be more than a soldier. I asked to go to sleep and to wake up the son of a Don, but it never happened and the bitterness sucked all happiness from my soul. To be worthy of you and ask for your hand was all I wanted."

I cupped his face, hating that he saw himself as a lesser man. Titles didn't make the man inside the skin. "You've always been worthy. Don't ever say that to me again."

His lip curled up. "Living here is like being in the Wild West. I get to pretend whatever I want, and maybe in my heart, you are right, but back home, I would be shot for touching you. Yet, I would still take the risk and happily accept whatever fate came for me, just for a single night alone like this and the chance to hear that you love me."

The tears I'd been fighting back trickled free. "I do love you. I love you with all of my heart."

He smiled. "Then, no matter what comes, I will die a happy man."

"Stop that." I placed my finger on his lips. "Don't you dare mention dying again. I mean it. I order you not to," I said, and he chuckled.

"Well, I can't disobey a direct order."

My breath hitched as he slid his hand up and wrapped it around my throat. He walked around, so I stared at myself in the mirror as he stood behind me. His hand was large and imposing, yet his strength was controlled. I'd always wondered what he would be like if he was more like Angelo, aggressive and domineering, but then I realized he was exactly who I needed him to be. Dario was every fantasy I could conjure in my dreams about love and respect. If I wanted him to be rough, he would, but he was just as happy to gently seduce me and drive me wild like he was now.

His hazel eyes pierced mine in the mirror's reflection as he snaked his other arm around and pulled me back into him. I shivered at the feel of his cock pressing into my ass. I couldn't take my eyes off his hand as it traveled all over my body before dipping between my legs.

The deep growl in my ear as his finger teased me made me wiggle in his hold.

"Look at how beautiful you are when you come," he said as his fingers pushed into me. He set my skin on fire, and I moaned with every little movement. "Yes, that's it. Spread your legs for me," he said, nipping at my ear. I stepped out wider for him and moaned as his finger sank deeper. "Yeah, that's it, fuck my fingers. Feel how badly I want you." He pressed his cock harder into my ass, and I wanted to feel him without the track pants on, but his hand was relentless, and I could feel the orgasm rising. "I can feel you climbing. Don't hold back." My eyes closed as I bounced on his fingers, his hand tightening around my throat with a growl. "No, open your eyes. See what I see. I'm addicted to your body, Amorina. I need you to come, do it. Come for me," he ordered. The rasp in his voice making me shiver..

My legs shook as the climax hit, and I would've screamed, but he tightened his hand just enough to quiet the wail as I came. I writhed in his arms as the pleasure flowed until I slumped over. My eyes focused on him as he sucked his fingers, and more heat spread throughout my body.

"So good. So fucking good," Dario said, pulling them from his mouth.

My knees shook as Dario stepped away and brought back a large yoga ball, setting it on the floor.

"Sit on this."

I had no idea what he was up to, but I lowered myself onto the rubber ball, squealed as I almost rolled off. Laughing I looked up at Dario and covered my mouth to quiet the giggles.

"You're adorable," he teased as he chuckled with me. Lifting my chin he dropped his lips to mine and the embarrassment faded away.

"Good, now slide forward and lay down," he said, but I was completely distracted as I watched him kick off his sneakers and bend over, pulling his track pants down. I licked my lips as I got an unobstructed view of his hard ass. He looked at me in the mirror, and our eyes locked. "I feel your eyes on me, and you're not in position."

"How could I not stare at that view?"

He stood up straight and turned toward me, and I shivered at the sight of him fully naked. There was nothing to hide his monster cock or the hard muscles all over his body. Even his legs and forearms flexed as he walked closer, and if anyone could be frozen in place by the sight of another, then I was now.

He stood in front of me, and I reached for his cock, but Dario grabbed my hands before I could stroke my prize. My lower lip pushed out, making him laugh.

"This is your punishment, remember? You don't get to play with the toys you want until I say you can." His glare wasn't genuine as humor danced in his eyes, but I slowly laid back like he wanted. I was once more arched backward, but this time, I saw myself upside down and watched Dario lower himself between my legs.

My galloping heart thundered like a million hooves inside my chest. The fast thumping echoed louder as he pressed my thighs wider.

"Lift your legs and hold them in a V," he said, and I swallowed. "Don't worry, I won't let you fall over."

Doing as he said, I lifted my legs and spread them wide. Dario's head dropped, so I could only see his eyes in the mirror as his mouth drew little cries out of me.

"Better be quiet. You don't want the guards to come running thinking that something is wrong," he said and dove back in again. I slapped a hand over my mouth to try and contain the sounds I wanted to scream at the top of my lungs. "Mmm, you taste so fucking good," he said between the deliciously tortuous licks.

The ball under me was shaking along with my body as another orgasm loomed. His hands were on my thighs and held me firm as I gripped his hair and pulled him into harder into me.

I wiggled my hips in time with his tongue, and he groaned. His deep voice sent vibrations through my body.

"Fuck, I could do this all day," he growled. I didn't think I could survive an entire day. My body already felt wrecked. "Wrap your legs around my neck."

"What if I hurt you?"

"There would be no sweeter way to go than suffocated by your pussy. Now, wrap your legs around my neck."

As soon as my legs were locked around his head, he pushed my thighs tighter together. I screamed as he sucked harder, his finger slipping inside and fucking me fast. Unable to help myself, I grabbed his hair tighter, the need so intense that it was on the verge of painful as my body ached for the release. He growled and groaned, his tongue lashing at every sensitive spot until I was screaming his name.

I came in a mad rush as I was pushed over that high peak and tumbled headlong down the other side. My back arched on the ball, and if it weren't for his strong hands holding me in place, I would've tumbled off.

Panting hard, I released his hair, and my legs fell away from around his neck. Dario raised his head and I blushed as he licked his lips.

"Tell me when and where, and I will drop to my knees every time. You taste so fucking good." He stood and pulled me up off the ball. "Please order me to do it in front of Angelo." He smirked, making me smile.

"He would like that too much," I said.

"Maybe, but so would I."

Wrapping my arms around his neck, I kissed him hard as my ankles locked around his waist. I felt him nudging at my pussy as he walked, and I squealed loud when my back pressed up against the mirror.

"Oh, shit, that's cold," I hissed.

"Don't worry. I plan on warming you back up, but I couldn't have you in here and not have that view." He nodded to the side and looked over to see a side view of us. "Give me your hands."

I grudgingly unlocked them from around his neck, and he lifted them above my head, holding them in one hand. I couldn't tear my eyes away from the image of us as he rubbed his cock against me. I moaned as he pushed into me, and as impossible as it seemed watching us, he slid in, stealing the last of my breath away.

"Oh fuck," Dario groaned, his shoulders flexing as he bottomed out. I closed my eyes as he captured my lips and stole the moans from my mouth as he started to move.

He picked up the pace, and the sound of my ass slapping into the glass grew louder with every thrust.

"Ah!" I screamed as I bounced on his cock that was rubbing against my G-spot and pushed me toward another climax.

"Fuck yes." Dario's voice was husky with a deep, gravelly sound as he pistoned faster. Each powerful thrust was right on the point of pain and exquisite pleasure. I screamed his name. "Yes, come for me again."

His finger tweaked my nipple, rolling it just the way I loved, and I was done. I froze with my scream trapped in the back of my throat as he pounded into me, and I came all over him.

"Yes, fuck yes," Dario groaned. Releasing my hands, he yanked me away from the mirrors and laid uson the floor. I had no idea how he didn't lose his rhythm, but my mind was too scattered to contemplate it. Wrapping my legs around his waist, I clung to his wide shoulders, and dug my nails in.

"You're like fucking heaven," he said against my lips before kissing me harder than ever before.

"Oh god!" I yelled at the top of my lungs, not caring if anyone had heard.

"I'm going to come," he growled, and his pace turned erratic. "Fuck! Oh, sweet fuck, Jasmine." He pushed in hard and yelled my name again as he came. With each slow thrust, I felt him coming inside of me, and the earlier climax sent smaller shock waves through my body.

Breathing hard, Dario stared at me, and it was like I was staring at home.

"I love you so much, I can't find the words," he said.

"I feel the same way," I said.

The door to the gym was kicked open, and I screamed.

Dario dropped his arm to act as a shield as he stared at the guards who filed inside.

"You have fucking terrible response time," Dario growled. "What if I was an actual attacker?"

I bit my lip and buried my head in the crook of his shoulder, too embarrassed to look at the men.

"Um...."

"No, ums, you should be disgusted. Tomorrow, we'll be going over rounds and times. Understood?"

"Yes." They chimed in unison.

"Good, now get the fuck out of here, close the door and don't come back."

"Yes Sir," they said, and the door closed again.

We looked at one another, and I couldn't help but laugh. Dario smirked and then joined me until tears were running down our faces.

"Come on, let's get you back to your room. I think a sexy shower is in order."

"I'm not sure I can even walk," I said, smiling as I teased him.

"I'll carry you, just like I would carry you every day and night if you needed me to."

As he kissed me softly, the world felt whole. The once shattered pieces of my fragile heart had mended, and tonight, the final shard was put back into place. It was clear that my world would never be whole without them. Nothing was as terrifying as allowing myself to be that vulnerable all over again, and yet my heart hadn't given me a choice. It was done. My heart was theirs, and they were mine.

Chapter Forty-Eight

ENZO

WALKING ACROSS THE LAWN, I nodded to the guards standing at attention outside the greenhouse before pushing the door open. It was amazing how fast the builders erected the structure once the concrete floor was poured and set. This place dwarfed the old greenhouse, and I had no idea what Jasmine would grow to fill up all the space.

I followed the sound of music down the long building and wondered where Jasmine was when she suddenly stood up from behind one of the long planter tables.

"Oh, geeze, you scared me," she said, her hand on her heart.

"Sorry about that. I thought you might like a coffee?" I held out the hot mug, and she smiled as if I had offered her a tray of gold.

She wore jean overalls with a white t-shirt, which was unbelievably adorable. She always looked great, but for whatever reason, seeing her with dirt on her face and her hair a mess turned me on like nothing else.

"Thank you," Jasmine said as she took the coffee from my hand.

Her lips made a perfect O as she blew on it, and my cock instantly woke up inside my jeans. I quickly looked away and sipped mine.

"What are you drinking? It smells fabulous."

"Hot apple cider with fresh cinnamon. Would you like some?"

"I've never had it before," she said.

My mouth fell open, and I held out my cup for her. She took the cup and closed her eyes, sniffing it like a whiskey she was inspecting. The thought conjured the image of her at the distillery, and my smile fell. As it turned out, that bottle was safe. The chemical analysis results had come in this morning, but it was still terrifying to think of what could've happened.

"Mmm, this is delicious."

"You can have mine if you want to swap. I'm easy," I said. "Well, not easy like that. I just mean that I'm easy about what to drink, and I'm going to stop talking now."

Jasmine's laugh made me smile. Her eyes lit up and reminded me of the first day we met. It was hard to believe it was only a few weeks ago when it felt like years had passed, all in a single day.

"It's okay. I love my coffee, but I will take you up on one of those sometime." She held out the cup, and my fingers brushed against hers as I took back my cider.

Clearing my throat and ignoring my dick which had a mind of its own, I turned to the long tables that were still mostly empty.

"Would you like some help setting up?"

"You don't mind?"

"Are you kidding? I'd much rather hang out with you than sit in on another of Angelo's meetings with Riker's lawyers." I made a snorting noise, and Jasmine smirked.

"I'm happy to have the help. It will feel like when we first met," she said and looked down. "I should apologize to you as well. I was upset that you were untruthful with me, but I gave you a false name and lied about why I was here."

Reaching out, I ran a loose curl through my fingers, loving the soft silky feel. "I'm pretty sure me filling your home with cameras and then sneaking in with Angelo negates any lie you told me. You could probably tell me a hundred more and it still not make up for what I did." I ran my hand through my hair as I thought about what to say. "I really am sorry. I...shit. Surveillance is part of what I do for Angelo, and I hardly knew you, not that it makes it right, but you know we live differently than most. He asked me to put cameras in every corner of your house, and I took him at his word."

"I know."

"And the sneaking in...I didn't want to, I...shit, I still did it. I own that, but it never felt right."

Jasmine waved her hand, stopping me. "Let's not rehash all of that. I don't approve of what you all did, not even in the slightest. The thing is, I can either be pissed off for the rest of my life and leave Angelo, you and Dario behind or...I can let it go and accept that Angelo is the way he is, and I'm never going to change the asshole he can be when he wants something. It's behind us, and I'd like to keep it there for my peace of mind." She held up a finger. "But don't tell him that. I prefer for him to believe I'm still angry. It's better that way."

I chuckled. "Fair enough."

Sitting my cup down, I picked up the bag of soil Jasmine had slit open and dumped it into the tabletop she was working on.

"I know we don't have a history like you do with Angelo and Dario, but I do really like you. I was never faking my feelings for you. I was going to leave Angelo, tell you the truth and ask you to run off with me. I know stupid plan, but I knew that if I didn't fight for you then Angelo would cut me out."

Jasmine squatted and cut open more bags, and I obliged by dumping them where she pointed.

"I like you a lot, too," she said, and I smiled. "You were really going to go toe-to-toe with Angelo?"

"I was. I've never felt like I had someone to fight for before. You are different, you were from the the first second you opened your door. I'm never believed in love at first sight, but...um...anyway the point is, I was never faking how I felt." I'd already fallen in love with her, but it felt too soon to tell her.

"That's good to know. I can't deny that I was hurt thinking you were only coming around to see me as part of your job." She didn't look up as she evenly patted the soil and I felt terrible for ever making her feel that way. "I don't remember you at the same school as the three of us." Jasmine wiped off her hands and took another sip of her coffee. I needed to stop staring at her lips before I threw the cup away and kissed her. "Enzo? You okay?"

"Huh?" My eyes snapped up to hers. "Yes, um...." My brain raced as I tried to remember what she asked. "I didn't go to the same school. I didn't meet Angelo until he came to Chicago. I was already there working and doing odd jobs for different people, but when Angelo came to me to figure out who was attacking his family from the inside, he hired me full-time." I shrugged. "We've been together ever since."

"What do you mean his family was attacked from the inside?"

"I'm not sure if I'm supposed to talk about the details," I said, and she crossed her arms and glared. I swallowed hard. "Okay, I'd rather deal with Angelo's wrath. It was the whole reason he went to Chicago in the first place. His father was fed information that his Chapo and all those working directly under him were dirty. They were supposedly stealing and looking to take over. Don Esposito ordered their deaths and sent Angelo to run everything and finish killing the traitors. When Angelo arrived, he discovered that all the documentation and videos were doctored and false, but not before he'd cut through dozens of men. The family business was stripped down and needed to be rebuilt, but everyone was now terrified to work for him. Whoever set up the Esposito's made them kill themselves like a snake eating its tail. A smart and deadly plan."

"That's why he suddenly said he had to stay and cut off all contact," Jasmine muttered. She rubbed at her chin. "My father would never have let me go to Chicago, especially if he thought there was unrest and I might be in danger."

"Correct. I remember Angelo mentioning that he was trying to negotiate a deal for the woman he loved, but her father wouldn't answer his calls. I remember the night, he and Dario cut off contact.

They both got shitfaced and passed out on the floor of the office. I found them like that the next day. He didn't tell me all the details. We weren't close yet, but it had to be you. No matter what you saw, the only person he ever talked about was you."

"Are you here to get me to forgive him for the fiasco at dinner?" Jasmine tilted her head.

"Hell no. Angelo deserves whatever you want to throw at him, no pun intended, but in all seriousness, talking down to you like that was...fucked up. I wouldn't let him off easily."

She smiled. "Good, I plan on making him grovel."

"Fuck can you film that for me, please," I asked, and Jasmine laughed. "Anyway, almost every coveted position needed to be filled while Angelo looked for the person responsible. We still didn't know when we left, but at least trusted people were in place."

I dumped two more bags, and the row was almost full. Jasmine swore as she gripped the side of the table and looked down.

"I didn't mean to upset you," I said.

"It's not that. I just wish Angelo had communicated with me, and I can't change anything now, but...."

"It's frustrating," I offered.

"Yes, exactly. In all his hopes to win me and protect me, he ended up pushing me away and hurting me." She shook her head. "So much lost time."

Nodding, I helped level out the soil, the two of us working in a comfortable silence even though I could still feel her anger bubbling under her calm expression.

"I'm going to say something really selfish," I said, and she raised her eyebrows with the silent question. "I know everyone is hurting and I want to make it clear I'd never want you to be hurt or anything else, but...." I licked my lips. "If Angelo hadn't needed to hire me and the two of us become friends than I never would've met you. I can't say I'm not happy we met or that you want me in your life. That makes me sound like the biggest dick." I shook my head.

"Maybe a little, but at least you're honest. That is rare in our world." She polished off the coffee and sat the cup aside, but was focused on the moisture on her lips.

"Have you ever been go-carting?" I blurted out.

Jasmine's hand stilled. "No."

"Would you like to go with me one evening? I know a fun spot not far from here. Just the two of us. Well, the two of us and some guards, but that's beside the point." I polished off my drink as I anxiously waited for a response. It was a stupid idea for a date with a princess. What was I thinking?

"Only if you don't let me win," she said, her lip curling up in challenge, and if there was any doubt left that I loved her, it was gone.

Grabbing her hand, I pulled her in close and tickled her side. She laughed and jumped away, but I still held her hand and tickled her again.

"Stop it...." She laughed hard as my fingers moved over her ribcage.

She had the best laugh, and I loved her smile. It could light up the darkest room. She wiggled out of my grip and took off running. Oh, hell yeah. We ended up in a mad dash around the room as she evaded me.

"I'm going to get you," I teased and jumped up on the table.

Jasmine took off again and I ran beside her on the table. Jumping down I wrapped my arm around her waist and she let out an adorable little squeal. Picking her up easily, she screamed as I spun her around and pressed her up against the wall.

"Please, no more," she begged as she wiggled in my hold.

Instead of tickling her, I dropped my lips to hers and groaned as she opened for me. Cupping her face, I attacked her mouth, tasting every inch. Jasmine pressed her body into mine, moaning as she ran her fingers through my hair, and I lost the little bit of control I had left.

"I want you, all of you. Right now," I said against her lips, my heart pounding and my cock aching with it pressed up against her. I plucked my cell out of my pocket and dropped it on the closest table. "No phone to interrupt us this time."

The desire in her eyes matched my own, but I held off even as everything in me screamed to finally take what I wanted and have her all to myself.

"Then what are you waiting for," she asked coyly.

"Sweetest words I've ever heard." I kissed her again, fumbling for the door to the storage room. I found the handle, turned it, and pulled her inside. Laughing, I groped the wall for the light, then remembered there was no electricity yet.

"Shit," I growled. "No lights."

Jasmine pulled away, and my heart sank until a light clicked on. I smirked as I stared at the flashlight in Jasmine's hand. She looked utterly devilish in the sexiest way possible, with the light shining on her face like she was telling a ghost story.

"You're fucking brilliant," I said, taking the light and sitting it on the metal shelving unit. Yanking off my shirt, I tossed it on the shelf to join the flashlight before pulling Jasmine back into my arms.

She leaned back before I could kiss her again. "We need one rule," she said.

"Okay?"

"I can only have one of you grabbing strange crap to shove into me. Angelo has that covered, so even if that broom looks enticing, or the flashlight seems like a bright idea, I will beat you with it if you try."

Smiling wide, I cupped her face. "There is only one thing that I want to shove in you, and it isn't a broom or a flashlight," I said and chuckled as her cheeks reddened. "I'm going to kiss you now."

Fuck she tasted good. There was an addictive sweetness, but under that were remnants of her coffee and a hint of sweetness. I wanted to devour her. I slipped my hands into the back pockets of her overalls and gripped her ass. I'd been dying to do that for a while now and pulled her hard into my body. Jasmine ran her hands down my back, but it wasn't enough.

A mad desperation took over, and I needed more. Stepping back, I traced her lip with my thumb and committed her swollen lips and the dreamy look on her face to memory. I lifted my arms up and behind me to grip the tall metal shelf.

"Touch me however you want. I want to feel your hands all over my body."

The shock on Jasmine's face only lasted a moment before she unclipped the straps on her overalls, letting the top half fall. She pulled off her white T-shirt, and I wanted a picture of her just like this. Her hair was wild, half in and half out of her hair clip. With the skimpy white lace and folded-down overalls, she could've been on the cover of a sexy gardener magazine. The sweet smile turned into a naughty grin as she reached behind her back, and her bra slid down her arms.

"Oh fuck me," I mumbled under my breath as I stared at her hard nipples. My mouth watered, but I loved this torture. The more my cock ached, the better the orgasm, and right now, as Jasmine ran her hand up my chest, I thought I might come. "Fuck yes, use your nails."

Shuddering, I closed my eyes as she traced my body. I knew there would be lines on my skin, and I welcomed every one of them. Arms, chest, abs, and even my legs, Jasmine's hands roamed, and my cock strained behind the fly of my jeans. I was panting hard by the time she tugged at the button. That simple release was almost enough to make me shout. I'd always been a commando guy, and when she pulled the zipper down, I sucked in a ragged breath as my cock was finally freed and stood out straight.

"You like this," Jasmine asked, her voice soft like she was purring. Her fingers skimmed all around my cock, but never touched it. "It seems like you do," she said.

"Yes, I fucking love it." I groaned as she drew one finger the entire length of my cock from base to tip. "Oh fuck, yes." She stopped long enough to swirl her finger around the tip and spread the precum over my head before trailing her finger back down. "Ah! God yes! Please keep touching me. Please don't stop," I begged, forcing my hands to grip the shelving tighter.

I sucked in a ragged breath as she gripped my hips and sucked my nipple into her mouth. The feel of her hot tongue went straight to my cock, making me shudder. I let my eyes close again and soaked up the feeling of her mouth traveling across my body and leaving wet lines down my abs.

"Does touching me make you wet?"

"Yes," she said and placed a chaste kiss on the tip of my cock.

"Are you wet right now?"

"Yes. Very," Jasmine said, and I groaned, my cock kicking out like it was begging for more.

"Does it turn you on when I tell you to suck my cock," I asked, muscles straining to remain in place. The dim light made Jasmine's eyes look like a predatory cat as she stared up at me from under her thick lashes. Fuck that was the hottest look I'd ever seen. All the wires in my brain scrambled as I stared into her eyes. Putting words together that made sense was increasingly difficult.

"Yes," she said and ran her tongue over the tip like I was an ice cream cone. Holy hell, it took every ounce of my control not to grab her and throw her over the pile of fertilizer bags and take her.

"Then do it. Suck my cock like a good girl." She cocked a mischievous brow at me. "How about a naughty girl then?"

"I like that much better," she cooed, teasing me as she bobbed her head.

The shelving creaked as I squeezed hard enough to make my muscles shake. A moan vibrated down my shaft as Jasmine sucked me deeper into her mouth. I groaned and arched my hips up to get deeper into her throat. Her mouth was deliciously hot and wet, making my balls churn, and I was close to coming way too soon.

There was only one thing that would be better than watching my cock disappear inside her mouth, and that was my cock sliding into her pussy. I'd been denied the real thing when we snuck in to her room and if truth be told I was just as happy, but now I had nothing holding me back.

"Fuck, fuck, fuck," I growled, unable to take anymore. Releasing the shelving unit, I wrapped her hair in my hand and pulled her off my cock. Grabbing her adorable pouting mouth, I kissed her until she was shaking.

Picking her up off the floor, I bent her over the large stack of bags. They were so tall that she was on her tiptoes, but it put her ass at the perfect height, and I couldn't wait to get inside of her. Yanking back hard enough on her hair that she was forced to look at me, I leaned forward and kissed her hard, then nipped at her lower lip. I didn't miss a single moan and captured them all. She looked exactly like how I imagined. Sexy as hell.

"You really are a naughty girl, Jasmine. You made my cock ache. Now all I can think about is fucking this sweet pussy," I whispered in her ear.

"Is that so," she sassed, wiggling her ass back and forth. The jean material softly brushed against my cock and sent what felt like electrical jolts down my spine. "Should I say sorry or fuck me hard?"

"Fuck me, I think I'm in love." I couldn't get the overalls pulled down over her hips fast enough before shoving my cock into her in one hard push. "Ah!" We yelled together as her tight pussy enveloped me. Teeth clenched, I held still, soaking in the feel of her. My hand and the fantasies dancing around my mind at night couldn't do justice to the real thing. Reaching around her body, I rubbed at her clit, and she moaned and bumped her ass back at me, but I didn't budge.

Her moans and wiggling ass pressed up against me were fucking heaven, and teased my cock to new heights as she tested my restraint. There was a moment where I could feel her getting ready to come. I stopped rubbing her clit and grabbed her hips before letting loose.

Jasmine screamed and swore like a sailor, and every fuck that fell from her mouth was music to my ears. She could yell at me all night as she rode my cock.

I smacked her ass, the sound more jolting than any pain. Jasmine jumped and slammed back into me, screaming. The sound our bodies made echoed inside the mostly empty room.

"That's for being a naughty girl. You better come on me unless you want me to shove my cock back down your throat."

Reaching forward, I grabbed her by the arms, savoring her yell as she came, and her pussy clenched me tight. Shuddering, I thrust into her hard and groaned as I came while she quivered around me. I slumped forward and wrapped my arms around her. She turned my world on its axis with a single touch and I knew that I was forever lost.

"You okay," I asked, kissing the side of her neck.

Jasmine opened her mouth to reply, then screamed as the door was thrown wide. "Oh my god, not again," she said, and I grabbed her off the stack to hide her body from the guard's view. I had no idea what she meant, but Angelo's annoyed face as he stepped in front of the men worried me.

"Really?" Angelo drawled. He shook his head. "Enzo, I've been trying to reach you." He held up my phone that I'd left out in the greenhouse. "I now know why you're not bothering to answer." Even though he couldn't see Jasmine, it felt like he could look right through my body as he glared. "And Jasmine, could you maybe let the guards know when you plan to scream the world down? This is becoming a habit."

I felt her tense as I held her tight.

"It was my fault. I dragged Jasmine in here," I said, looking over my shoulder at Angelo. I kept my arms firmly wrapped around Jasmine, feeling protective over her from his angry gaze.

"Of that, I have no doubt, but I also know that Jasmine wouldn't go with you unless she wanted to, and this is the second time in two days that the guards have seen her naked and being fucked." Jasmine swore softly and pinched the bridge of her nose. "Unless, you'd like to explore a more exhibitionist type relationship. I'd be happy to take you to town and fuck you in front of everyone. Or is your hope to add a few of them into the relationship, Jasmine? I mean, once you hit three cocks, what's a few more?"

Angelo was looking for a fight. I could feel it rolling off him. "Really man? You're gonna be a dick like that," I said, holding his hard glare.

Jasmine swung her arm around my body and pointed. "Sure, I'll take him," Jasmine said, and the guy her finger landed on looked like he might pass out as Angelo looked at him. The guard put his hands in the air and backed out of the room.

"Well, that's one down, would you like to try for another?" Angelo asked, sarcastically.

"You really want to do this Angelo?" Jasmine asked. "Because I will, but you won't like what I have to say."

I could almost hear his teeth grinding from the doorway. "Enzo, when you're finished, I need to see you. It's important."

He dropped my phone onto the shelf and shook his head before turning and walking out. The door slammed loudly behind him.

"Is it wrong that I'm thrilled I pissed him off," Jasmine asked, and I laughed.

"Nope, not at all. Angelo deserves it, probably deserves more than that." Releasing her, I bent over and eased her overalls back up over her hips, making sure to leave little kisses up her body until I reached her addictive lips.

"I better go before he has a nuclear meltdown, but this was the best coffee break I've ever had." She smiled.

"Same."

"We should make this a daily habit," I teased, but would totally go for it if she agreed.

Jasmine wrapped her arms around my neck and I could see my future in her eyes. If we went home I could not imagine holding her when I wanted to. It scared me how things would change and I knew they would have to. I was secretly hoping that Angelo never found a way for us to go back if it meant I could live free like this with her forever.

"How about we take it one day at a time," Jasmine asked, but a playful look shimmered in her eyes.

"Fine, I guess that will do," I said dramatically, making her laugh.

I dropped my lips to hers and savored this moment. It may not have been the most romantic, but it was still our true first time together and I wanted to remember everything. Sighing I stepped back and grudgingly pulled on my T-shirt, zipped up my jeans and grabbed my phone that showed twenty missed calls. Before I could walk away, she grabbed my arm.

"He won't hurt you, will he? If so, I'll kick his ass." I loved the fierce look in her eye, and I didn't doubt she would.

"Nothing I can't handle. I mean, Angelo's already shot at me twice over you."

"He what?" Jasmine's mouth fell open as I laughed.

"I told you I would fight for you. Besides, if he wanted to kill me, I'd already be dead. He was just reminding me who was the bigger dick in the room. Metaphorically speaking, of course," I said.

"Yes, of course," she giggled. "Still, I'll talk to him."

"No need. Truly, we're in a much better place now. When you said you wanted him and would stay, it eased almost all the tension between us. I genuinely think he thought you would choose me over him." I smiled. "But, he doesn't understand that I would never make you choose as long as he didn't try to cut me out. I want you no matter what."

Before she could say anything and tempt me to stay longer, I kissed her softly and slipped out the door. The guards smirked as I jogged past them and into the house.

"I'm going to fucking kill that fucking piece of shit!" Angelo yelled, and something smashed in the room. Or maybe he was going to kill me, and I should've brought Jasmine along. "Fuck!" *Crash.*

"Okay, maybe this is not a good time," I said and turned around as something else flew across the room. I was getting the fuck out of there to let Angelo calm down when he called my name.

"Enzo, get the hell in here. I see you lurking."

"I'm dead," I mumbled as I turned around.

"Close the door," Angelo ordered, and I stepped into the half-trashed office, but Dario looked just as mad, which confused me. I didn't think either of them would be this angry over Jasmine and me having alone time.

"Look, man, I'm sorry about the greenhouse. I didn't think you'd be this pissed off," I said, and Angelo turned around to look at me with a bottle of whiskey in one hand and a glass in the other. There was a fifty-fifty chance he was going to whip the glass at my head.

"I don't give a fuck about that," he said.

"He lies. He does. Just something else has him more pissed off than Jasmine cock blocking him," Dario piped in and earned a glare.

"Fuck!" Angelo bellowed, and I looked between him and Dario as Angelo slammed the glass down and chugged the whiskey straight from the bottle. There was very little that bothered me, but whenever my father was stressed, he drank like this. It bothered me when he did it, and it bothered me now. The tension in the room was palpable, making me antsy.

"What the hell is going on?"

"You tell him," Angelo said, stomping over to the window and staring outside.

I looked at Dario for the answer and felt like yelling, spit it out already. "The blood is back. It was Lucas."

Chapter Forty-Nine

JASMINE

I DIDN'T KNOW what the hell was going on, but the guys had been cagey and not around at all. It didn't matter what time of day or night I went looking for them. They were locked in Angelo's office in a meeting, not in their rooms or not home. If this was some new way Angelo had conjured up to get back at me for being mad at him, it worked because I was irritable and couldn't concentrate. I finished patting the dirt into place for the newest row of seeds I'd planted and sighed as I stared out the window to the gardens that in a couple months would be covered in snow.

Pulling off my gloves, I stepped outside and walked over. I didn't bother to tell the guards not to follow me. They wouldn't listen, and I was past the point of caring. Two stood outside my bedroom door at all times, two more at each end of the hall, and so many outside that I could've thrown a stone from my bedroom and hit any of them. The sun was warm, and I soaked it in as I walked the short path to the lone bench.

The roses reminded me of my mama, and I sat beside the bright red bush and watched as a honey bee landed on one of the large flowers. I was captivated by the little insect as it worked, my mind drawing parallels to my own life. So many little pleasures surrounded us as long as we were willing to look and appreciate them. It wasn't until my mama was in the final days of her disease that I understood what separated me from my schoolmates. The other girls made fun of me because I was different. It became so clear that they'd never been forced to appreciate the next day and simple things like walking around a garden with a loved one or laughing one more time. I'd watched my papa grieve like he was the one sick with each passing day, and it tore me apart that it didn't matter how much money we had. No one could help her.

"May I sit?" I was startled by Angelo's voice and looked up to see him standing a few feet away. I nodded. "You can wait by the greenhouse. We're fine," Angelo said to my two shadows before sitting beside me.

He laid his hand down between us, his palm open, but didn't say anything. I knew this was his way of apologizing. Angelo wasn't great with words. He was a man of action. Sighing, I placed my hand in his, and he scooted closer.

"It's stunning out here, isn't it?"

"Yeah, it is. I didn't take you for being much of a garden guy," I said. His face was bathed in sunlight, and the intense worry lines he usually carried around were smooth.

"I built it for you," he said. He smiled as he looked at the skeptical look on my face. "Okay, not for you exactly. I built it for me, but because it reminded me of you. I'd never tell Dario or Enzo that," he said, and my mouth tilted up in a lopsided grin.

"Does this mean you're not upset about Enzo and me the other day? I feel like you've been avoiding me," I said, and all humor was wiped from his face.

"I will never be okay with you and someone else when I'm not involved, but...." He rubbed the back of his neck. "I'm learning to grow as a person." I giggled at that, and he bumped my shoulder like when we were kids. "No, I'm not angry, and I wasn't avoiding you. I've had some business to work out."

We heard a honking noise and saw six white swans flying overhead. "Wow, they're beautiful. I've never seen them this close."

"They love the pond."

"I'll have to go see them later," I said, excited to see the majestic birds up close.

Angelo cleared his throat. "So, I've wanted to apologize for treating you like I did at dinner with Riker and Minetta. I shouldn't have disrespected you, but in front of them, it was worse."

"Why did you?"

Angelo looked at me, and his eyes were so blue today that they sparkled like the ocean. I could almost see the waves from back home in his eyes. It was beautiful here, but I wanted to take him home and explain everything to Papa. It was risky. Papa could hold a grudge, but I didn't want to marry Angelo without him there to give me away. I didn't want my wedding in hiding and in a town I hardly knew. Angleo put my hand in his lap, and the tension seemed to seep out of him as he held on like a life preserver.

"Tell me, Angelo, what's wrong? I know something is wrong."

"I can give you a dozen reasons, Tiger. I can tell you that it was an old habit or that I grew up this way, and it's all I know. I can tell you that I've always had to prove myself, and to have anyone, not just you, defend me like that would have earned me a slap from my father, as he called me weak. I can tell you that something about Riker and how he looked at you terrified me, and when you spoke, I felt emasculated in front of him."

Angelo turned on the bench and laid his hand on my thigh. "I could even tell you that I've been under a great deal of stress, and I'm not handling it or my fear for your safety very well. All of that would be true, but at the end of the day...they remain nothing but excuses." He licked his lips and held my hand a little tighter. "I've never been a good person, Tiger. I've never been considerate or kind like you. I've never put other's feelings first or cared about the consequences of my actions, but you make me want to be better. No, you make me want to be great. I just fear you'll be fed up and gone by the time I get there."

I cupped his cheek, and he leaned into my touch.

"I'm going to mess up again. It's not a matter of if. It's a matter of when, and that scares me."

"Angelo, you once more underestimate me. I won't stand for you treating me like you did, and yes, you will need to grovel for me to forgive you." Angelo smirked. "But how I feel has never wavered even when it should've. If I could turn it off, I would've done it long before now. I don't expect you to be a perfect man or husband, but I deserve your respect."

"You're right, you do." He groaned and rolled out his shoulders.

"Angelo, you aren't your grandfather or your father." His eyes locked on mine. "You are your own man. You choose how you treat people, how you treat me."

"My father never hit my mom," he said far too quickly. I didn't know if his father had or hadn't, but the worry was back in his eyes. "Not that I ever saw, anyway."

"I never said he did, but I wasn't talking about how he treated your mom. I was referring to how he treated you. I don't remember a single party or meeting I was allowed to attend where he didn't make fun of you or talk down to you. He was always poking at your intelligence or how you would never be a real man and end up embarrassing him."

Angelo suddenly stood, and paced across the small cobblestone garden. His shoes thumped loudly as he attacked each step like he was mad at the ground. Dark shadows crossed his eyes. They didn't last long, but I knew I'd hit a nerve.

"Don't pity me. Don't do that," he finally barked out.

"Is that what you think I'm doing?"

"Isn't it?"

The anger in his eyes was evident, but I saw what was hidden under the dark glare. In some ways, he was still a little boy looking for his father's approval. But he never needed it. That was what he didn't understand.

I shook my head and stood. Walking toward him, he stepped back, reminding me of a caged animal. Grabbing his fists, I waited until he took a breath and opened his hands before linking my fingers with his and holding them to my heart.

"When you look at me, what do you see," I asked. The defensive look softened, and his hands held mine tighter.

"I see the closest thing this earth has to an angel. You are the best parts of this world and strong enough to deal with the crap it tosses at all of us. Your unwavering spirit is what always ignited my desire for you. I hated that when I bullied you, you wouldn't stay down. You confused me so much, but now...now, I would protect that light at all costs. You're someone I never deserved, but I wanted all the same, and I'm enough of an asshole to keep you."

I swallowed the happy tears and emotions that threatened to derail my thoughts.

"But you don't pity me because my mama passed away or see me as less of a woman because I miscarried our child."

His face paled. "What? No, never. I would never."

"Then why do you think I pity you for the things that made you stronger? I see a good man, despite the callous way your father treated you, someone who deserves all the accolades and is worthy of love. All I'm asking is for you to see yourself through the same lens you see me and treat our relationship with mutual trust, honesty, and respect. Thinking you're a bad person and unworthy of me isn't healthy for either of us."

He stepped away, as all the walls and doors he used to hide the tender man that lived inside of him slammed closed before my eyes. I couldn't understand why he was so vehemently against seeing himself in a different light, but it was obvious that he did.

"I can't talk about this right now. Will you meet me for dinner? Just the two of us in my office? Say seven?"

I let it go for now and nodded. Angelo kissed my hands before dropping them and walking away. It felt like he was still hiding even when he should be screaming his accomplishments from the top of a mountain. I looked around at the large country property and didn't understand why Angelo was even here. Why wasn't he back home ensuring he had his seat at the table? What the hell had his father done to make him run this far from home? This far away from me?

I glanced over as the two guards, who had become my babysitters, stepped up to the mouth of the garden and took up their posts once more. My guards were much like the walls in Angelo's mind. They may protect us, but they were no less debilitating to our freedom.

Leaving the sadness and heavy talk behind, I brushed my fingers along the soft red petals of the roses and walked to the greenhouse. I'd planted a seed in Angelo's mind, but just like everything else, I couldn't force it to grow.

Chapter Fifty

ANGELO

I CAN DO THIS.

I can do this.

I repeated the chant as I waited for Jasmine to arrive for dinner, but it wasn't helping. Grabbing the window frame, I stared out at the darkening sky, and terror gripped my throat. Coming clean about everything I'd done since leaving her was a weight hanging around my neck that threatened to drag me down. The killing, torture, and partying in excess were only the tip of the iceberg of shit I could never take back.

When Don Falcone said no to me for the final time, I shut down and stopped caring about anything other than a job well done and numbing the pain. Jasmine deserved to know everything, yet the thought of her leaving...no, that couldn't happen.

I pinched the bridge of my nose, trying to ward off the headache that had been threatening since my conversation with Jasmine. She was right, but I didn't know how to fix everything. She believed in me. The love and trust in her eyes was like pouring salt on the stab wound in my heart. But, if the two of us were going to have a future, I needed to be honest and lay out the hand I was dealt and the cards I'd drawn right or wrong.

That was all before I made amends to her father, and I had no idea how to do that without him shooting me. I would shoot me if it were my daughter. How could I expect or hope for forgiveness?

Don Falcone, I'm sorry that I snuck into your daughter's room, took her virginity, got her pregnant, left her, stopped speaking to her, and wasn't there for her when she needed me the most. I'm sorry I humiliated your family and stole your family heirloom worth millions. While we're at it, let's tack on everything since Jasmine came here, like almost getting the most precious person in your life killed.

There was no fixing it. At every turn, I shot myself in the foot. My stomach churned as the headache got a little worse. The harder I tried to hang on to her, the further she slipped away. I wanted to whisk her off to some far corner of the world with no one and nothing but us until we died in each other's arms.

To make matters worse, I'd made a deal with the devil to save my own skin, and that deal was coming home to roost. Fucking Lucas. I should've known he would try something like this, and I would bet every last cent I had that the second attacker was Jacapo.

After finding out what Kristof learned about how Jacapo had leaked the information about a traitor to my father, I knew it was him. How the two of them ended up in bed together didn't matter. What did matter was that Jasmine was now their target. Jacapo was after the head seat at the table, and Jasmine was in his way unless she married him, and she would never agree to that. My best guess was that he knew she was going to marry me. The fucker probably watched me fuck her and set his trap. He knew I was young with ambition, and my father and his approval were weaknesses. He set out to destroy us and almost succeeded until Jasmine happened to come here. Had he followed her? Did he have some tracer on her? I didn't know, but she would never be safe until she was married and her father signed the papers.

She hated the man already. If she learned about this, I could see her storming back to Italy to shoot him herself. The addition of Lucas was all on me. *Fuck my life.*

A thought came to me, and I pulled out my phone, dialing Giovanni's number—not the stupid burner cell, but his business line. I wasn't surprised when it went to voicemail. The prick was avoiding me.

When the message beeped for the voicemail, I growled into the phone. "I understand your coded message. If you don't get control of the cuckoo and put it back in its cage, then I swear I will make sure every Don knows about what he did and how you covered it up. I still have a copy of everything, including the video footage, locked away for safekeeping. And, just so you know he took another run at Jasmine and I will put a bullet between his eyes if he tries again. I will destroy anyone in my way to protect what's mine and happily die dragging you to hell with me. My soul already belongs there, but I'm happy to have company. Get. Him. Under. Control. Now. Don't test me." My voice was steely and threatening as I hit the end button and slammed my cell on the desk.

I didn't care if he was the Don of Dons. No one went after Jasmine without feeling my wrath. The earlier rage threatened to spill over once again, and I sucked in a deep breath to try and get it under control.

"Angelo?" I jerked, my heart jumping as Jasmine spoke.

I smiled at the sight of her in the doorway. She was a vision in the ice-blue lace dress. My heart pounded hard, and the blood thrumming through my body pushed the anger aside.

"You look beautiful, Tiger."

Stepping around the desk, I walked across the room and pulled her into my arms as I kissed her hard. My hand snaked up into her thick, wavy hair, and I was tempted to skip dinner and jump right to dessert. I'd never thought of myself as a coward and aimed for the top of everything I did, but when it came to losing Jasmine, I was weak. I just couldn't tell her as much as I knew I should. Even if she forgave me, which I couldn't see, her father never would. Marrying her would force his hand, and I prayed he cared more for her happiness than wanting my head on a spike.

"Are you okay," she panted as I broke the kiss and held her tight.

"I am now. Come in, I'll let the chef I hired know we're ready."

"Wow, this is beautiful Angelo. You did all this for me?" She reached out and ran her hand down the vines and twinkling lights I'd hung. They reminded me of the wineries back home. The table was set for two with silverware and flowers while wine sat on ice, chilling.

Tugging at her hand, she laughed as she twirled and was once more in my arms. "There is nothing in this world that I wouldn't do for you. Nothing."

"Are you sure everything is okay? Not that I don't mind this romantic side, but you seem upset."

I wanted to spill my guts as I stared into those honey eyes that had stolen my heart so long ago. Instead, I rested my forehead against hers and closed my eyes.

"I'm just so happy. Happy scares me."

"I'm happy, too."

"I better let the kitchen know we're ready, or I'm going to tear this dress off you instead."

I felt her smiling even with my eyes closed. Her body radiated happiness, and I soaked it up as I would the sun's rays. "Well, you went to all this trouble. It would be a shame for it to go to waste."

I beat back my uncontrollable fear and pulled out her chair. "And I bet you haven't eaten any lunch?"

"Guilty as charged, but the new greenhouse is really coming along. I'm so excited." She beamed as she spoke, and my mood started to shift. We were safe for now. I needed to just enjoy this time with her.

I sent the text message to the kitchen, and a moment later, a tray was wheeled in through the open door. "Chef Louis has prepared all of your favorites."

One by one, the silver trays were placed on the table, and Jasmine's mouth fell open. "Oh my gosh, this looks divine. Thank you."

"My pleasure Mademoiselle. If you should need anything further, I will be in the kitchen preparing the dessert."

As soon as the door was closed, I leaned in and kissed the side of Jasmine's neck. I loved that I made her shiver.

"Fuck, I want to lick this food off your body."

Jasmine laughed and pulled away, her hand going to my chest. "As much as I want you to lick something off my body, I don't think that squid ink carbonara is the dish for it."

"Fine, but if he brings whipped cream in here, all bets are off," I teased, nipping at her ear.

Halfway through our meal, Jasmine spoke, and I froze.

"Just spill it," Jasmine said.

"Spill what?"

She turned toward me, her intense stare stripping me bare. Jasmine dabbed at her mouth with a napkin as she gave me her 'Don't mess with me look.' I knew this look well. She'd given me that same look since she was six years old.

"Why are you so nervous?" She looked around the office. "It's just you and me in here. We have music playing and a wonderful meal, and your knee hasn't stopped bouncing the entire time."

"It's nothing."

"Angelo Riccardo Esposito, don't you dare lie to me. I want to know what is going on right this minute." I licked my lips and stood as my turbulent emotions warred over the right thing to do. I gripped the bookcase and stared at the tiger box and wished I could just tie her up and fuck her again.

"I want to get married," I blurted out, cringing at my weakness. How could I shoot a man in the head without blinking but was terrified to lay all my atrocities at the feet of the one person I loved?

"I know. I want to marry you, too." The confusion was evident in her voice. Turning around, I opened my mouth and closed it like an idiot. "Oh, dear god," she said and covered her mouth.

"What?"

"Don't you dare." She stood suddenly, and now I was confused.

“Don’t you dare say it.” Panic was written all over her face, and she backed away when I took a step in her direction.

“What do you think I’m going to say?” I stepped forward again as her eyes filled with tears, and this time, I grabbed her shoulders, not letting her back away. For the life of me, I couldn’t figure out what she thought I was going to say to cause this kind of reaction.

“Don’t you dare tell me you’re already married or have a family with someone else,” she said, and relief washed over me, making me smile. “Don’t Angelo, don’t make fun of me. Just tell me straight.”

Lowering myself to one knee before her, I grabbed her hand and kissed her ring finger. My ring would be on it very soon.

“No, Tiger. I am not married to someone else, and you’re the only person I’ve ever had unprotected sex with. I have no children.” The tears still flowed, but the fear that had been there a moment ago vanished from one blink to the next. “I have never loved another.”

“Then what is wrong? You’re freaking me out.”

Rolling out my shoulders, I looked into her eyes and decided that losing her was worse than burying my crap deep inside.

“I want to marry you right away. As soon as we can get the paperwork, I want us to be official.” Pushing myself to my feet, I cupped her cheeks and wiped the wet tears away.

“You don’t want a proper wedding with our friends and family?”

“The only friends and family I have are in this house. I don’t want to wait another second. We have had so many obstacles already, and I’m sick of everything trying to tear us apart.”

She nibbled her lip. “I wanted Papa to give me away.”

“And he can at a proper wedding we have later, but right now, I just want to call you mine. For real, this time. I also don’t want your father to have any choice but to accept us. If he knows about the pregnancy and the miscarriage, I’ll be lucky if he doesn’t shoot me on sight, let alone permit me to marry you.”

She sighed, and I hated playing this card. It made me feel dirty, but losing her wasn’t even in the deck to be dealt as a possibility.

“I know you’re right about that. I just always imagined a garden wedding and my papa at my side. It's hard to picture having a shotgun wedding."

"I don't want anything else to come between us. Being together and facing whatever comes is what is most important to me. Together, we can conquer anything, but I need you to say yes, that you'll do this."

"This feels desperate, Angelo. Are you rushing for another reason?" She narrowed her eyes and searched my face.

"I do have another reason. We have had major scares recently, and that has put things into perspective, but I also want to start trying to have a family again. I know it feels fast when we've just reconnected, but we've already lost so much time. Please say yes. Please, and I promise we will have another wedding, the one of your dreams, with your father there."

I was not in the mood to play fair and dropped my lips to hers and kissed her until she moaned and relaxed in my arms.

"Say yes," I mumbled against her lips.

Jasmine opened her mouth just as the door opened, and Dario stood in the doorway.

"Kind of busy here."

"We have a problem," he said, and my muscles flexed as I braced for whatever he said next.

"And?"

Dario looked at me and then Jasmine.

"It's best if we speak out here."

I groaned and kissed Jasmine's cheek. "I'm so sorry. I'll be right back."

Stepping out into the hall, I closed the office door, and Dario walked us further away.

"This had better be good."

"Three cars just arrived," he said, and I immediately grabbed my gun. "Ciro is here, and he's not alone."

"I'm going to fucking kill him," I growled and marched for the door.

Chapter Fifty-One

JASMINE

UGH, I despised being cut out of conversations. I really should've been born a boy. Walking over to the wall of monitors in the corner, I turned them on, surprised to see the main house and not my little rental. Several screens showed people moving around, but I spotted Dario and Angelo right away.

My ability to read lips was poor, but whatever Dario said made Angelo pull his gun and storm off. Fear raced down my spine. What danger were we in now? I followed him through the hallways as he headed for the front door, and I gasped when I saw who was standing outside.

"No, no, no."

Dashing to the door, I whipped it open and shocked the guard as I sprinted past him. Pulling up the front of my dress, I ran as fast as I could. Angelo would kill Ciro. There was no doubt in my mind. I had no idea how he found me, but I wouldn't let Angelo kill him.

"Stop! You can't go down there," the guard chasing me said, his fingers brushing my arm, but I jerked away and ran faster.

"Angelo, don't," I yelled, hoping he would hear me as I made the final turn.

"Stop. I said stop." The guard reached for me again and grabbed my arm, but I turned and jerked to a stop. Momentum was not on his side, and he ran right into my fist. I regretted the decision when the bones in my hand crunched. "Fuck."

I took off as the guard stumbled back from the blow. When I reached the foyer, I screamed for Angelo. His gun was up and touching Ciro's forehead. While Dario and Enzo had their weapons raised along with every guard, and Ciro looked terrified.

"Stop, all of you, stop this." I ran forward, not caring that I was dashing between the loaded weapons, and stepped beside Ciro. Angelo's face was a mask of darkness. He was a completely different person from the man begging me to marry him. I didn't dare touch him. Any little flinch might cause him to pull the trigger. "Angelo, stop this, please."

His eyes flicked to mine, but his arm remained steady. Ciro hadn't blinked or said a word like he knew he was on the lip of a dangerous ledge. I was used to the men back home pulling their guns, but it was rare that anyone truly meant harm. The tension in the air tonight was different. I stared into Angelo's eyes, pleading with him.

"I can't marry you if you do this," I said, and his jaw twitched.

"I'm not letting him take you from me." Those few words held so much emotion. No one else would pick up on the panic, but I did.

"He won't, Angelo. Lower the gun."

"You don't know that," he argued.

"I do. Ciro doesn't want me, not like you think."

"Don't try and save him. He sealed his fate the moment he got engaged to you."

"Ciro is gay," I blurted out. "We are best friends, not lovers. We've never kissed or had sex or anything else you have running around in your mind. Please, put the gun down."

Angelo's head slowly turned in my direction, and he blinked. "What?"

"She said that I would prefer to bend you over rather than her,"

Ciro said, impressively sounding bored even as I shot him a glare to shut up.

"I'm not lying. Didn't you wonder why Ciro and I would go everywhere together and never dated? Think, Angelo. All the times Ciro was my date for events, and never once did you see us kiss, flirt, or even hold hands."

"Then why are you engaged to him?"

"Can you lower the gun before we continue this conversation? As it is, I'll have to clean my boxers," Ciro said, and I'd never wanted to smack him more.

Angelo slowly lowered the gun and looked around at the rest of the men as they did the same.

"All of you as well, guns down and go wait by the cars," Ciro ordered as he stepped into the house. "I need to speak to Jasmine, but I'm not here to force her into marriage."

"Fine, but if you think you're talking to her alone, think again. Follow me."

Angelo growled and linked his arm through mine. I shook my head at Ciro as he rolled his eyes. I loved Ciro, but he was dramatic and preferred to keep fueling the flames.

"What the hell happened to you," Angelo asked the guard I'd punched in the face.

He glared at me. "Your bitch punched me when I grabbed her arm to stop her from running into the foyer," he said.

I didn't even have time to process the words before Angelo shot him in the leg. I cringed as blood poured from the wound, and the guy dropped to the floor, yelling in pain.

"If you disrespect her again, the next one will be between your eyes." Angelo glared over his shoulder at the guards, who seemed frozen. "Get him help, clean up this floor, and consider this your only warning. I will bury you if you ever touch or disrespect Jasmine. Is that fucking clear?"

"Was that necessary?" I whispered as we walked away.

"Very," he said.

We stepped into the office with Dairo, Enzo, and Ciro in our wake. The small table with the delectable meal remained, but the sparkly little lights and romantic candle flickering didn't match the current mood. Dario closed the door behind us, the sound far more ominous than it should be.

Angelo marched us to the couch and sat with me on his lap.

I narrowed my eyes at him, but the look of murder on his face never wavered. "Is this really necessary?"

His eyes darted to mine briefly before focusing on Ciro once more. "Very."

Unbelievable.

"You're really going to make me talk to her like this," Ciro asked, dropping down into the chair I'd sat in for dinner.

"Either like this or with a hole in your head, your choice," Angelo said as if this was a business meeting.

"Angelo, please," I said, hoping he would relax, but my plea fell on deaf ears, his face remaining hard as stone.

Ciro sighed and then focused on me. "I came to apologize for how I acted and what I asked of you. It wasn't right or fair. I also came to see if you would come home."

"No," Angelo bit out, his hand tightening around my waist.

Ignoring Angelo's outburst, I said, "I thought you weren't here to talk me into marrying you?"

"I'm not. After you left, I realized how much of an ass I'd been to expect you to take on my burden for the rest of your life. I finally told my father that Marcus and I are a couple and that I wanted to marry him."

I squealed and leaped off Angelo's lap, enveloping Ciro in a hug before Angelo could stop me. "Oh my god, are you serious?"

Ciro laughed and nodded. "Yes, I finally did it."

"And, tell me everything, how did he take it?"

"Shockingly and annoyingly well. Years of worry and all I got was him asking if I would still give him a grandchild. I said that Marcus and I had looked into options. He said fine and walked out of the room. He has been completely normal ever since." Ciro shrugged. "Maybe he already knew or he really doesn't care, but I seriously need a therapist just to unpack the whole thing," he said.

"That was it?"

"That's it. Ask me how stupid I feel for keeping it hidden for so long?" I gripped Ciro again but let go when I heard the strangled growl behind me, and I went and sat on Angelo's lap before he had a coronary.

"So this is why you came? How did you even find me?"

"I came because I can't get married without my best man or, in this case, best woman. I want you to stand up for me at my wedding. I need the one person in my life that I love with all my heart, other than Marcus, of course. You've been my best friend for as long as I can remember, and it just wouldn't feel right. Marcus feels the same way."

I covered my mouth, tears of joy streaming down my cheeks. "Yes, yes, of course, I will. Oh my gosh, there is so much to do. Have you picked colors yet? How about flowers? Oh no, when is the wedding? I need my notebook."

I went to stand, but Angelo pulled me back down onto his lap, and I glared at him.

"Angelo?"

"Answer the second question. How did you know that Jasmine was here?" I could tell Angelo still wasn't convinced that Ciro wasn't a threat, but I knew Ciro and trusted him. Although, I was curious as well, so I waited for Ciro to answer.

"Um...well." Ciro cleared his throat. "Jacopo showed me a news report online that named you as a person of interest. It wasn't too difficult to track you down after that. I mean, you used your mother's maiden name."

"Of course he did, fucking Jacopo," Angelo growled and stood, setting me on my feet.

"Wait, forget Jacopo. What do you mean I was a person of interest? In what? And where?" I was horrified that my face was shown on the news.

"It was for multiple murders," Ciro said, and I spun around to face Angelo.

"Did you have something to do with this?"

"Oh shit," Enzo mumbled low from where he stood in the corner, but I heard him as clear as day.

"What the hell did you do, Angelo?"

He crossed his arms as he leaned against his desk. "You were drawing the attention of some men who were bad news. I took care of the person of interest issue and made the men disappear."

My mouth fell open. "When? What?" My brain jumbled the words, and I rubbed my eyes to wrangle the confusion. "When was this?"

"Does it matter?" Angelo shrugged his shoulders. "They're already dead."

"Oh my god. How many people?"

"Just since you came here or in total?" I couldn't tell if he was joking. That had to be a joke. Right? "I told you I would do anything to keep you, and I meant it."

This was one of those fucked up times where I found myself wondering if I had a problem. I wanted to say he was being sweet, but then I remembered that he killed people, and my emotions got crossed like two wires shorting out.

"We will discuss this later," I said and turned back to Ciro. "So, when is the wedding?"

"Next spring, but I was kind of hoping you'd come home." He looked around the room at the three men. "At least for a little while. Your father hasn't been in a good state since you left."

"Is he okay? Is something wrong with his health?" Panic hit, and my heart ran alongside my mind, quickly spiraling to the worst possible scenarios.

"Nothing like that. Sergio just hates that he drove you away. He hasn't been himself, and he hardly eats. Marcus is worried about him, and Jacopo has made snarky comments about your father being no longer fit to lead the family." Ciro leaned back in the chair and grabbed a piece of fresh bread off the table. "God, I hate that guy. Do you mind if I eat this? I'm starving," Ciro said, holding up the bread.

"No, go ahead. We were finished."

"I guess we were," Angelo said softly.

"I could come home long enough for him to see I'm alright. I do miss him," I said, and Angelo's fist hit the desk, making me jump.

"No, not until we get married," he said, but it was an order that made my hackles rise.

"Excuse me?"

"You heard me. We get married first, then we can see your father," Angelo said.

"I never agreed to elope."

"You were about to until he showed up." Angelo pointed at Ciro.

"What is going on with you? Do you trust me so little that you think I wouldn't return?" Anger was beginning to bubble up inside of me.

"It's not you, I don't trust," Angelo said.

"Ha, that's funny," Ciro snorted, dipping his bread in the flavored oil. "What the heck are you doing here with these three anyway? After everything, I would've thought they would be the last people you'd want to see."

"I don't think we need to rehash all of that again," Angelo said as he glared daggers at Ciro.

"Angelo is right. We discussed what happened, and I've chosen to move on."

There was a subtle shift in the room, and Angelo wasn't the only one nervous now. I looked around, unsure if I imagined it. I'd only ever had this feeling twice in my life. The first time was when Mama passed away, and the other time was the last time I spoke to Angelo on the phone before he cut off communication.

Ciro leaned back in the chair and looked between my men and

then at me. "So, you're really okay marrying the man that...." Ciro stopped as Angelo lifted his gun and pointed it at him.

"Angelo, what the hell are you doing?"

"Don't say it. Don't do it," Angelo said, his eyes wild.

I didn't like whatever was happening, and I deserved to know why he was so afraid of me finding out. Not caring, I stepped into his line of fire and felt Dario and Enzo move away from the wall where they'd been watching.

"Put the gun down," Dario said.

"Get out of my way, Tiger." Angelo's hand shook, and the fear was evident in his eyes.

"No, I won't move. I have a right to know what is going on," I said.

"Put it down, Angelo, if it goes off...." Dario didn't finish the sentence, but the threat was under the surface. I took a deep breath as Angelo lowered the weapon.

I kept my eyes on Angelo as I spoke. "Ciro, finish what you were going to say."

"I'm not sure this is the best time," he said.

"Everyone needs to stop hiding shit from me. Tell me, Ciro," I ordered, my hands balling into fists.

"Um...well, I was going to ask you if you were really fine marrying the man who stole your mother's Fabergé egg and effectively stole your inheritance. I just never thought you would be okay with that."

"What?" I whipped around and looked at Ciro. All the blood rushed to my head while my stomach dropped to the ground. "You can't be serious. What are you trying to pull," I asked, but deep down, I knew it was true.

Dario and Enzo would no longer meet my eyes, and Ciro's words were confirmed when I turned to face Angelo, who was leaning on his desk with his head down.

"You? You stole my mama's egg?" I was too angry to cry. I turned in a circle. "The three of you?" No one moved or said a word. "Answer me!" Hands balled, I yelled at Angelo.

"I thought you knew. I prayed you did and had chosen to forgive me. I only started to suspect you didn't know the other day." Angelo pushed away from his desk, his eyes desperate. "Please, let me explain."

As soon as he was close enough, I let my hand fly and smacked him hard. The room was so quiet you could've heard a pin drop.

"Don't. There is nothing you can say to make this okay." My body shook with anger at the betrayal. "Is that how you built your fancy distillery and purchased all the properties you own? What happened? You couldn't get your hands on my papa's money the easy way by marrying me, so you resorted to stealing it," I said and backed away from him. "Oh, my God, that is what Riker meant by steal what you needed. How is it that everyone knew, but me? What a fool I must have looked sitting there with you."

"Jasmine, please...."

"No. You yanked me back into your life after you ripped my heart out of my chest. I believed in you. I believed in us, and all I was to you was a golden egg. Your ticket to the top where you always wanted to be." I smacked my forehead as things began to snap into place. "This is why you wanted to elope. You wanted to make sure I was tied to you first. Unbelievable."

"It wasn't like that. I stole it for us," Angelo said, and I marched forward and shoved him hard in the chest.

"Don't! Don't you dare turn this around. I cried when it was stolen. The only thing of hers that had been in the family for generations, and it was ripped away from me by the same person who stole and destroyed my love. Just don't." I wheeled around and looked at Dario and Enzo, who wore similar expressions of sadness, but I couldn't separate them on this one. "I can almost understand why Angelo would go to such lengths and then not tell me, but you two as well?"

"I have no excuse for my behavior. We never should've stolen the egg, and I suspected you didn't know and didn't say anything. I chose to keep quiet," Dario said. "Losing you seemed like a worse fate than to hold my tongue."

"I felt the same way. I'm sorry, Jasmine. I didn't know you then, but I do now, and I...I felt like an asshole and didn't want to lose you either," Enzo said.

I laughed, but there was no joy in my heart. They had stolen it all. Looking between them, I shrugged. "But you lost me anyway."

"Jasmine, don't go. Let me tell you the whole story. I'll tell you everything, anything you want to know," Angelo said, grabbing my arm.

"Let go of me." I jerked in his hold, but he wouldn't let go.

"Jasmine, it's not what it looks like," Angelo said, his fingers firm on my arm.

"It doesn't matter why you did it. Not anymore. You played me. You've had weeks to tell me the truth and ensure I heard it from you. But, you kept quiet and tried to manipulate me into a fast wedding." I shook my head. "If Ciro hadn't shown up tonight, I still wouldn't have known. Right?" He didn't argue with that. "Let go of me, Angelo, or so help me God, I will call Papa and tell him where you are. Right now, and only because I foolishly still love you, I will pretend I never saw you. That's my parting gift to all of you. You get to continue living your life, making money, fucking anyone you want, and striving for the top, free from my papa's wrath. If I were you, I'd take the deal."

"Let her go, Angelo," Dario said as Angelo's hands shook. Dario walked over and touched Angelo. "Let her go, she wants to leave."

I hated the terror and sadness in his eyes, and I hated myself more for caring that it was there at all. One finger at a time, his hands loosened, and I stepped away.

"Goodbye," I said, looking at all three of them. "I love you. I love all of you, but you don't deserve it." Ciro slowly stood and walked to me. "Let's go home," I said, walking out of the office door and leaving them behind.

The scabs that had formed over the scars on my heart had just been ripped open, and they were bleeding raw in my chest. I knew I would never heal from this. I might never love another again, but I couldn't stay, not now. There were too many lies, too many secrets, and too much pain.

"I'm sorry, I thought you knew," Ciro said as I slipped into the back seat of his car.

"It doesn't matter. I should've known. He should've told me."

"Would you have forgiven him?"

"I don't know, but it would've been my choice. Instead he kept me in the dark."

I looked out the window at the large home and the three men standing outside. I held their stares until we pulled out of the driveway. As soon as we were alone, Ciro pulled me into his arms, and I cried as the other half of my heart withered like a rose.

Chapter Fifty-Two

ANGELO

THE TOXIC STORM of rage and despair rode me as I tore my office apart. Nothing was safe. When I ran out of bullets, I grabbed my knife.

"Ah!" I yelled as I pulled the last of the foam from the leather couch. I stood back, breathing hard, and looked at the chaos in what had once been a neat and orderly room. The books were torn, my monitors were smashed, and pictures were ripped from their frames. Dropping to my knees, I stared at the gold tiger statue just out of reach, and the agony gripped me as surely as a hand around my throat. Crawling to the golden figure, I picked it up and sat down against the wall.

Each breath ached as I tried to get air like my lungs had forgotten how to work with the thought of never seeing her again, never kissing her sweet lips good morning or holding her as she fell asleep at night. I lost her. I lost her all over again, and there was no one to blame but myself. Every decision I'd ever made mocked me.

I slumped against the wall and couldn't tear my eyes away from the tiger. No matter how closed the door felt to Jasmine in the past, I'd always kept hoping that I would make it home and win her back.

This felt final like I'd written the last chapter in our book before I even recognized it.

No, I wouldn't accept that. Jumping up, I walked to the bookshelf and pulled on the book that released the hidden panel. Twirling the knob on the fancy metal door, I unlocked the first of three separate locks for the walk-in vault. Placing my palm on the last one, the door hissed as the seal separated. Yanking it open, the lights flicked on, and I grabbed the black go bag and quickly unlocked the second smaller vault that held everything I'd stolen from Don Falcone. I hadn't spent a dime or sold anything I'd taken. It was never to better myself financially. Jasmine had that wrong. I would do what I should've done long ago and give this back to Don Falcone, and I prayed that Jasmine would hear me out. No, I would find a way to make her hear me out. That was the end of it.

As soon as everything was zipped up tight, I walked out into the office and locked the vault back up. Pulling my phone out of my pocket, I hit Riker's number.

"Come on, answer, answer," I mumbled as I marched around the room, gathering anything else I might need, including my guns.

"Riker, here."

I ran my hand through my hair and sucked in a deep breath. "Riker, it's Angelo."

"Are you calling to say you've changed your mind about the deal," Riker asked.

"No, why would I do that?"

"No reason. What can I help you with? You don't strike me as the social call type," he said.

"I need your help, and I'll pay whatever price you ask of me. I don't care what it is. I'll be forever in your debt."

"You screwed up and lost her, didn't you," Riker said. There was something annoyingly father-like about his tone.

"I don't want to talk about what happened, but I need to borrow your jet," I said, sitting on the edge of my desk, the only thing that wasn't destroyed.

"Let me get this straight. You want to borrow my multi-million-dollar jet, but you don't want to tell me why? I don't think so. For all I know, I could be helping a fugitive. Oh wait, you already are." He chuckled, and I ground my teeth together.

"Are you always like this," I asked, and he laughed harder.

"Minny would ask the same question, but now she just rolls her eyes," he said.

"Come on, what do you have to lose? What did you do?" Riker persisted.

"There is too much. I don't even know where to begin. I fucked up. Can I have the jet now?" Talking to him was worse than talking to my father. I had a similar conversation when I had gotten a speeding ticket in his Bentley.

"Let me guess this about her mother's heirloom you stole?" How the hell did Riker know it was her mother's? "She didn't know it was you, and when she found out from someone else, she left? Am I close?"

"What the fuck? Are you spying on me?"

"Please, like I have time for that. I told you, I like to know who I'm dealing with. Let's just say I had a feeling she didn't know. You seemed pretty uptight when I danced around what you did. Tell me, Angelo, did you sell it?"

I ground my teeth together, annoyed that he read me so easily. "No, but it doesn't matter. She didn't want to hear about it, why, or anything else I had to say. That's why I need the jet. I have to make this right and see if she will give me one more chance," I said.

Riker laughed, and annoyance flared in my chest. Who the hell was he to laugh at me?

"I'm impressed. I didn't know if you were serious when you said you'd happily go to hell for her. Good on you." I stared around my office and then at my phone. Did he have me bugged?

"How did you know I said that? I don't remember saying that at dinner?"

"You must have. What the two of you have is true love. Love like that is rare, and you never stop fighting for it. Take it from someone who knows what it feels like to lose your soulmate. When I thought Minny was forever lost to me...I didn't care about anything anymore."

"Which is why I need the jet. I need to try. She is my everything. I would give everything up for her. Not only that, but I think she's in danger. Two men attacked her here, and if my hunch is right, they will try again, and she has no idea they're a threat. Riker, I wouldn't come to you unless I was desperate."

"Fine, you convinced me. My jet is still in town. You can use it. I'll text you the address of my private airstrip," he said, and a glimmer of hope sparked in my chest. If I could convince Riker to help, there was hope for me yet.

"Do you have a private hanger everywhere?"

"Pretty much, I don't like people."

That explained a lot. "Thank you," I said.

"Don't thank me, just go, and when you get back, we'll talk about the business. I have a few ideas. That is if Don Falcone doesn't shoot you in the head, of course." And just like that, he dashed the hope. He laughed as the phone clicked in my ear.

"Ass," I mumbled as the door to the office opened, and Dario and Enzo walked in with large black duffel bags in hand.

Dairo threw one at my feet. "We're going after her. You're already packed."

"How did you know I was talking Riker?"

"Riker? How would I know you were talking Riker?"

I shook my head. "Never mind. We're borrowing his jet." Grabbing my duffel, I marched out into the hall. No more lies or games—it was time to push all my chips to the center of the table.

Chapter Fifty-Three

JASMINE

I SAT in the car and stared up at the mansion I had lived in my entire life, and it felt different. It was still home, but something was missing. I felt the same way after Mama passed. Rooms felt colder, and leaving and coming home, knowing she was no longer there to greet me, was a twist of the knife in my heart. I hadn't spent a single day with Angelo, Dario, and Enzo in this place, yet my heart hurt the same.

"Do you want me to go in with you?"

I turned my head to look at Ciro. His expression had been worried the entire trip home. He'd insisted that we stop at a couple of our old haunts and pick up my favorite things. I knew he felt terrible for outing Angelo and the guys. As much of an ass as Ciro could be, he would never want to hurt me, but I was happy he said something. If I'd found out after I married Angelo, I would never be able to forgive any of them, and what kind of a future would we have had?

"No, I'll be fine, Ciro. Let me know when you want to start wedding planning. I'm really excited for you."

He grabbed my hand before I could reach for the door. "Are you sure you don't want to go back and talk to Angelo? I...shit, he looked devastated. I never...."

Leaning across the seat, I hugged my best friend. "Don't blame yourself, you did nothing wrong. Fate pushed us back together, but he wasn't upfront with me, and we have nothing if we don't have trust, honesty, and respect." Pulling back, I smiled at him. "It's good to see your face. I've missed you."

"I missed you, too, and don't you ever take off like that again. You gave me a fucking ulcer with worry, and I hated myself for being such an ass. I swear you did it because you knew not being able to reach you would be the worst possible torture."

"Oh, that was definitely it."

"Be-otch," he said, rolling his eyes at me before bringing my hand to his lips for a kiss. "Never change. I love you, Jazzy."

"I love you, too." The front door opened, and Papa stood in the doorway, the light illuminating him, and the corner of my mouth tugged up. "I guess it's time to face the music."

Stepping out into the night, I took a deep breath of the salty air and could just make out the sound of the sea. I'd missed that. I didn't even reach the bottom step before Papa jogged down the steps and gripped me in a hug.

"My daughter, look at you. It feels like forever. I've missed you. I'm so sorry," Papa rambled as he hugged me tighter. The scent of his cologne mixed with the light hint of his favorite cigar filled my senses.

"I missed you too, Papa."

"Come inside. We need to speak." He wrapped his arm around my shoulders as we walked into the house. The guards standing around nodded as we walked past, and I sighed with relief not to see the four women who used to follow me around. They were nice enough, but I didn't want that.

We stepped into Papa's office, and as soon as the door was closed, he pulled me back into a hug. I could only comprehend at this moment how much my leaving had hurt him, and my gut churned with guilt.

"Would you like a glass of wine," he asked, pulling away and heading to his desk.

"Yes, please."

I sat on the couch where, not long ago, I'd received the news that made me decide to leave. Why did it feel like a whole other life?

"Here you go."

I took the offered glass as my Papa sat down beside me. "I'm so sorry. I...I promised your mother I wouldn't force you into an arranged marriage, and I sadly almost did it twice."

"Twice? Who was the other?" I already knew it was Lucas, or at least that was what Angelo said, but Papa had never mentioned it until now.

He looked embarrassed as he stared into his glass of wine. "Lucas." He shook his head. "I don't know what I was thinking. He seemed changed, and Giovanni made a compelling case, but he is as evil today as he was as a boy."

So that was one truth from Angelo. It would've been another wound to my soul if I'd given over my virginity to someone who had lied and then thrown us away. The later betrayal was bad enough, but to be duped at the start....

"You know I love Ciro, but just not to marry him, right?"

"I do. Ciro came to me and told me why you left." He shook his head. "I had no idea. I should've guessed. Ciro spent more time here than at home, but I never put it together. I was more worried he would do something inappropriate with my teenage daughter." He rubbed his eyes. "Your mother would be furious with me. When I close my eyes at night, I hear her telling me off."

I smiled. "Papa, can I ask you why you never dated or remarried? You are still a young man and a catch for any woman. Why do you choose to live alone?"

He looked around the room, and the corner of his mouth pulled up. "Because your mother was the love of my life. It always felt like our souls were connected, and I had no interest in anyone else after she passed away. I still feel her with me sometimes."

"But, aren't you lonely?"

"Define lonely? This room could be full of people, and I would still be lonely without your mother. It's not just any people that make you feel whole. It's the right people."

I sipped my wine and knew what he meant. Angelo, Dario, and even Enzo made me feel connected in a way I'd never felt with anyone else.

"Papa, did Angelo come here asking for my hand in marriage when he returned from Chicago?"

His cheeks flamed red, anger in his eyes. "Yes, he did, and I sent him packing. After what he did, what he took, and how he left you...I was never letting him near you again."

I looked down at my hands. "I wish you had," I said softly.

"What?"

My eyes stung with tears. "Why didn't you tell me Angelo stole Mama's Faberge egg?"

He stood and leaned an arm on the mantle, his finger tapping on the edge of his wine glass. "Is that who you went to see?" His tone changed, and his eyes grew hard.

"I didn't plan it, but yes, that is who I was with."

He rubbed his forehead. "Why Bambolina? He is bad news."

Even though he was right, my back stiffened. "Papa, please just answer the question?"

"I didn't tell you because I knew you were still holding a candle for him. I could see it in your eyes and felt your heart aching. I couldn't tell you what he and his friends did. It would've crushed you." He shook his head. "I can't believe he ever thought he was worthy enough to marry you."

"Stop it, Papa. This is exactly why I left. This attitude of you thinking you know what I need or who I should be with." Standing, I stepped around the low coffee table so my papa couldn't look away. "I loved him, and whether right or wrong, he had reasons for cutting off communication, and he didn't know I was pregnant." He made an annoyed sound and chugged his glass of wine.

"You never should've been pregnant, it was manipulative. He tried to force my hand when he knew he wasn't worthy of you. Doesn't that bother you?"

"Papa, I knew about Lucas," I said, and his mouth fell open. "I knew you already tried to sell me off like a broodmare to the highest bidder. I chose to be with Angelo. He didn't force me to sleep with him. I fell in love with him, and yes, I still love him."

"I don't want to hear this." He tried to back up, but I wasn't letting him off that easy, and I walked around the couch to step into his path.

"We need to talk about this," I said, holding his glare.

"You want to be with someone who stole your virginity, your heart, and your inheritance? Then go, but do not ask me to approve a marriage to that man. I will not. I cannot."

Tears trickled free. "I'm not marrying him, but it could've been so different if everyone in my life had been honest and stopped sheltering me. You and Angelo keep making the same mistake. You underestimate what I can handle, and in the end, you both hurt me." I shook my head. "You tried to marry me off twice, Papa, and kept your own secrets. So do not cast stones inside a glass house."

"I am sorry for that, but Angelo...."

"What? Angelo what? Let's take the robbery and even the sex before he got your approval to marry me out of it. Would you have approved of him?"

"I need more wine." He walked over to the desk and poured a full glass.

"Answer me, Papa. I am so sick of lies and secrets. Everywhere I turn, there is another one," I said, clenching my hands into fists.

Papa wheeled around and looked at me. "No, I wouldn't have approved a marriage."

It felt like he slapped me across the face with his words. Angelo was right. "Why?"

"Because his family is tainted with rumors and baggage that would've cast shadows over you for the rest of your life. And, because I know he was the one who made you cry when you were little, mia Bambolina. So, no. I protected you because you are my daughter, and it's my job as your father. I love you and only want what is best for you."

"But you didn't trust me to make that decision for myself," I said softly, my heart hurting.

"He said he called you from Chicago. Is that true?"

As soon as he looked away, I knew, and I covered my mouth as more tears fell.

"You realize he probably stole the egg to get back at you because of me?"

"Is that what he said," he asked, his jaw twitching with anger.

"No, I don't know why. As soon as I found out Angelo took it, I left. I was too hurt and angry to hear why because it didn't matter. But it's something he would do. He spent his entire life trying to escape the shadow you condemned him to. Papa, I should've had the choice. Even if I said no, it should've come from me, and if I said yes, then you should've loved and supported me."

"Why must you always be so...difficult? Even as a little girl, you were always getting into trouble and telling everyone off like a man." As soon as the words were out of his mouth, he cringed. "I'm sorry, I didn't mean it like that."

"Yes, you did." I stepped back. I would never be an equal no matter what I did or said. I walked away and picked up my wine glass, polishing it off. "You know what's funny? Angelo, for all his 'unworthiness,' is the man who loved me for my fierceness, intelligence, and difficult behavior." I pointed at him. "Let me make this clear, Papa. I may not be the son you wanted, but my heart is stronger than a dozen men, and Mama raised me to be myself, whether you agree with that or not. I will not be a piece on your chess board placed before who you think is my best suitor. I do not need a man to be powerful. I will make my own way."

I turned around, stomping toward the door.

"Jasmine, wait."

I stopped as Jacopo opened the door and stepped into the room with two guards behind him. He resembled a sniveling weasel, as his shifty eyes looked between Papa and me.

"So the runaway daughter returns," he drawled, his mouth pulling up into a grin that sent shivers skipping along my skin.

"Jacopo, this is a private, family conversation," Papa said.

"Oh good, then I'm right on time," he said—his arrogant tone, like nails on a chalkboard.

I sucked in a shocked breath as he pulled his gun and walked around the room like he owned it.

"What are you doing? Get out." Papa ordered, moving to stand near me.

"Why would I do that? When I need both of you. You really made this easy by being in the same room?"

"Guards," Papa called out. "Get him out of here." He pointed to Jacopo, but they didn't move, and a cold trickle of fear traveled down my spine. I never trusted him, but the look on his face was pure evil. I always knew he was, but he covered it with a placid mask. The fact that he was letting us see the darkness under the false façade was not good. "Why are you just standing there? Throw him off the property."

"Oh, I don't think they will be doing that." He smiled, and I wanted to hit him. "You see, they feel the same way that I do. You have let your daughter make you weak. But, I have a solution where we all live happily ever after."

Papa looked at the guards and then Jacopo, his eyes furious. "What the hell do you want?"

"It shouldn't be that hard to figure out. I want to be the head of the family. So this is what's going to happen. I will marry Jasmine tonight. I brought all the paperwork with me, and then you will retire and hand the family over to me. You get to live out your days anywhere you want but here."

Bile rose in my throat as he pulled out paperwork from inside his jacket.

"You can't be serious?" Papa glared at Jacopo. "I practically raised you like a son, and this is how you repay me? Have you lost your mind?"

"Ha! You mean I suffered all these years waiting for you to die and give me what is rightfully mine. Instead, you try to marry Jasmine off to Ciro. Like that fucking guy could ever rule the family as well as me. He doesn't deserve it," Jacopo yelled, his voice wavering on the edge of manic. "But I do, and I deserve her. I will turn her into a respectful woman who knows her place."

I took a step in his direction, ready to rip his balls off, but Papa grabbed my arm. "I'll never marry you," I growled.

He lifted his gun and pointed it at my papa. "Oh, I think you will, or I'll shoot your father right now in front of you. Then I'll frame your lover Angelo and still marry you."

Papa pulled me back and stepped in front of me. "You will do no such thing. I would never let a monster like you marry my daughter."

"Well, in that case, I have no need for you."

I screamed as a gun fired, and Papa slammed backward into me. "No," I yelled, grabbing him as he fell. But, as we tumbled, confusion took over. The two guards were dead on the floor, and Jacopo was down, rolling around on the ground in pain. Dario and Enzo stood over him, but when I saw Angelo on the ground in front of my papa, terror lanced my heart.

"Angelo, oh my god." I quickly crawled to him as Dario ran over.

"Hey, Tiger," he said as blood pooled on the floor beneath him.

Dario pressed on the wound in his abdomen. "Call an ambulance."

"I already have them on the phone," Papa said as I picked up Angelo's hand.

"What are you doing here? What are you doing getting shot, you fool," I growled at him.

He smiled wide. "That's my Tiger, always so fierce." He clutched my hand tight. "Fuck, that hurts. Do you have to press so hard?"

"Do you want to live or bleed out," Dario asked.

"That's a stupid question," Angelo said, wincing and holding my hand tighter.

"Then shut up," Dario ordered.

"The ambulance is on its way." Papa knelt by Angelo and looked at him. "You saved my life."

"I owe you more than that." Angelo pointed to a black bag near the open window, and I suddenly knew how he had gotten inside. "Everything I took is in there. I'm sorry." Angelo turned his eyes to mine, but I could hardly see through my tears. "I'm so sorry, Tiger. I only took it to look like a hero when I found it. I just...I couldn't think of another way to make myself worthy. I thought being a hero would do it."

"You know that's stupid, right?" I ran my hand through his hair. "You never needed to prove yourself to me." I watched as my papa set the bag on the desk and pulled out folders and velvet bags before pulling out the egg's black protective case. "I thought you sold it."

"It was tempting, but I couldn't do it. I only ever wanted the egg to win you, but that plan got ruined because of that piece of shit," Angelo said, pointing at Jacopo. "I'm feeling a little lightheaded. That can't be good.

"Where is that ambulance?" I yelled as I heard boots running down the hall. "I love you, don't you dare die, you ass. I need to yell at you some more."

Angelo weakly smiled before I was forced to let go of his hand and move out of the way. Everything moved in fast motion. Guards piled into the room and helped Enzo drag Jacopo away while Dario held me back to let the paramedics load Angelo up on a gurney. Dario spoke as we walked out to follow the ambulance, but I didn't know who he was talking to or what he was saying. All I could picture was Angelo on the floor, bleeding. If he died...closing my eyes as we got into the vehicle, I ran through every touch, look, and conversation we'd shared. No, he had to be okay. He had to be.

Chapter Fifty-Four

ANGELO

CONFUSION AND WHITE-HOT PAIN. What the hell happened? My mind raced as it grabbed at the memories on the periphery of my brain fog.

Blinking, I slowly opened my eyes and stared at a darkened ceiling I didn't recognize. I would never stay somewhere with cheap drop-down ceilings, so this wasn't a hotel. Rolling my head to the side, I took in the monitors, and it all came racing back. The mad dash to get to Jasmine, the dead guards, sneaking up the wall like I was fucking twenty again, and the impossible timing as I raced across the room to jump in front of Jasmine and her father. If I'd been even a minute later, Don Falcone would be dead.

"No, you're not dead. But you may wish you to be by the time we are through," I swallowed and winced at the razor blade feeling traveling down my throat.

Don Falcone walked into my view as he came to stand beside my bed. I thought I would be terrified to face him, but a sense of calm had taken over my soul on the flight here. There was peace in accepting whatever fate awaited me. All I wanted was one last chance to make things right, and I did that...mostly. I would take another conversation with Jasmine before they carted me off to my death, but aside from that, I stopped Jacopo, saved Don Falcone, and returned everything that I'd stolen. The only thing I couldn't and wouldn't give back was Jasmine's heart. I would remember the love in her eyes no matter how many hours or years I had left.

"Excuse my language, but..." I licked my dry lips. "I don't give a flying fuck what you do to me now. I made my bed, and I know what comes next."

His lip curled up. "Are you so quick to accept death over being with my daughter?"

"That is not even a choice. I would choose Jasmine a million times over and fight with my last breath to have her, but I also know I have made too many mistakes." I refused to look away from his eyes.

"Tell me why you stole the egg?"

Sucking in a breath, I braced against the pain and pushed myself up higher on the bed. It felt like a fucking marathon just to gain a couple of inches.

"I never meant to leave Jasmine. I tried negotiating with you to have her come to Chicago when I realized the few months had no end date. When you said no, I cut things off. I couldn't lead her on for years when I didn't know when I would return. It had stupidly been my dream to prove my worth and take over as head of my family." I snorted and looked away. "My father was never going to consider me worthy. I was a lost cause, and looking back, I should've just left and come for her instead."

"Then you came home, and I refused your offer again. Was taking the egg revenge?"

I chuckled and grabbed my side as the pain stabbed me. "You would think it's that simple, but no. I still wanted Jasmine. So, I devised a scheme to steal the egg and make it look like a robbery. The plan was to wait a few weeks, knowing you would offer whatever it took to get it back. I wanted her. I was always going to return it. So fucking stupid. The alarm going off was what I hadn't been banking on. I had a guard on the inside who knew how much I loved Jasmine and offered to help for a price. Enzo dismantled the alarm, but Jacopo got wind of what I was planning. Long story short, Jacopo had his own plan, and I was fucking with it, so he set off the alarm." Sighing, I looked up at Don Falcone and couldn't tell what he was thinking. His face was set in a frown that didn't give me much hope. "Jacopo was also the one who had me shipped off to Chicago in the first place. I just found that out and how he manipulated my father." I shook my head. "If I live, I'm killing him with my bare hands. All I can say for my actions is that I was desperate."

The heavy silver rings he wore glinted as he rubbed his chin, and I expected his fist to mess up my face very soon.

"You love my daughter that much?"

"She's the only person I have ever loved. I would do anything for her, and I do mean anything."

"Why start this deadly game, to begin with? You never spoke to me about arranging a marriage. I probably wouldn't have granted it after you terrorized her for years, but why didn't you try?"

I swallowed again. "I should've known you knew about that, too." I rubbed my face. "Honestly, I didn't think I was worthy. I've never thought I was worthy of anything, but she made me feel like I could conquer the world." Grabbing the plastic cup, I took a sip of the gross, warm water, but it helped my aching throat. "I also knew that if I asked you, she would say no even if you considered it because I'd been an ass most of her life. I was too arrogant to accept that as an option." I shook my head. "So, I needed her to say yes, first. I wanted to win her heart, and if that twisted your arm in the process...."

"All the better?"

"Something like that. I am sorry I wasn't here for Jasmine during the miscarriage. I didn't know, I...it doesn't matter now. But that's the whole story."

The sun was coming up, and I couldn't help wondering how many more sunrises I would see, if any. I stared at the deep orange rays and remembered lying in bed and watching Jasmine sleep as the sun rose, making her face glow like an angel sent just for me.

"My daughter tells me you've created quite an impressive business for yourself in Beastville. Is that true?"

"It is. I own multiple properties and have a distillery making whiskey. All of it on the up and up...okay, I have an underground casino, but does that really count as illegal?"

Don Falcone chuckled. "I've never considered it to be. I will assume the whiskey business is to get back at your father?" His lip curled up.

"I wouldn't do such a thing," I joked. "But if it is doing better than his, then..."

"All the better?" Don Falcone laughed, and I could see why all the families respected him. Even Giovanni had only spoken about him with reverence. Jasmine was a lot like her father, and I saw the same spirit in them both. "Well, son, if you're this determined to marry my daughter, then I guess it is time I stepped out of the way. Only if she agrees to take you back, of course."

My mouth fell open, and my heart pounded hard. I couldn't have heard that correctly. "Are you serious? You're not going to kill me or have me locked up and throw away the key?"

"I can't deny that I have dreamed of doing that, but I only ever wanted my daughter to be happy, and I think you've proven yourself worthy of her hand. I've always considered myself a fair man, and anyone willing to go to the lengths you have deserves a chance."

It took all my strength, but I swung my legs out of bed one leg at a time and slowly rose to my feet to look him in the eyes. I ignored my screaming side as I held out my hand.

"Don Falcone, I don't know what to say. Thank you."

"If we're going to be family, call me Sergio." Ignoring my hand, he gripped my shoulder and leaned closer. "But if you break her heart again, I will rip yours from your chest." He smiled wide, and I'd never felt so free. My heart sang, but the battle wasn't over. I still needed Jasmine to agree, but this was a win.

"I will never hurt her again, I swear to you."

He walked to the door and opened it. "I'm not the one you need to swear to."

Jasmine stepped into the doorway, and her face lit up as our eyes met. Then they turned embarrassed. I couldn't hear what he said to her, but she laughed, and tears filled her eyes as she smiled wide.

Don Falcone looked at me and nodded. "Thank you for saving my life."

The door closed behind him, and I didn't know what to say. There were so many jumbled thoughts running around my mind.

"God, I'm so sorry. I should've done so much differently," I said.

Jasmine saved me from whatever stupid thing I was going to say next as she rushed across the room and hugged me. I didn't even care that it hurt. It felt so good to hold her.

"What the hell were you thinking? You stupid ass." She mumbled into my chest.

"I was never letting you go. I told you that. And no death scares me as much as losing you. You were right. My father's acceptance haunted me and blocked me from what I really wanted. I needed to stop pretending to be something I'm not," I said, kissing the top of her head. As soon as she let go, I wiped her face.

"Can you let Dario and Enzo in?"

Opening the door, she waved in the two men and closed it again before coming to stand in front of me.

"Guys can you come over to this side."

They gave me a suspicious look but did as I asked. Grabbing the side of the bed, I groaned as I lowered down to my knee, and Dario gripped my arm to keep me steady.

"Angelo, you're going to tear your stitches," she said, worry etched into her features.

Panting, I looked up at her. "I'll get up once I've said this. Once upon a time, I thought your unpretentious nature was a sign of weakness, and I wasn't very nice to you. But at every turn in our lives, you've proven me wrong. I've spent my life wishing to be powerful and have all the riches in the world because I thought that would prove my worth and I'd gain honor and respect."

I took a deep breath, taking in her honey eyes and the fresh tears traveling down her cheeks.

"I failed to realize that my wish had already come true, but I was too blind to see it. It was always you who made me the richest man in the world—every second I spent with you helped me realize my self-worth. You gave me the confidence to reach for the stars and dream of a future. I would give up every last cent and walk away from everything just to be by your side forever."

Her hands shook as she covered her mouth, but her eyes were filled with love.

"Jasmine Falcone, my Tiger, you've taught me so many things, but the most valuable lesson I've learned is that humility is not weakness. You humble me. I love you, I've always loved you, and I would be honored if you took my name but married us. This is me placing the decision at your feet. There are no more lies or secrets and I promise nothing will ever come between us. With you, I am rich, without you, I'm half alive. I'm just Angelo." I nodded to the other two men and caught Dario's smile.

She opened her mouth, and I held up my finger. "Dario, do you have the box I gave you?"

"Right here," he said, handing over a small velvet box.

With a snap, I opened the lid for Jasmine. She gasped as she stared at the amber diamond, the same color as her eyes. "Now you can let your heart decide," I smirked.

"Always an ass. Yes, I will marry you." She looked at Dario and Enzo. "All of you," she said, bending over and kissing my lips.

"I promise you, Jasmine, we will build a whole new world together."

Chapter Fifty-Five

ANGELO

"DID you get everything I asked for?"

Our boots echoed on the stone floor as we traveled deeper into the cavern that Giovanni called *The Belly of the Beast*. The men he sentenced to the cave never came out, at least not in one piece.

"I did," he said, his somber voice echoing off the stone.

Every few steps, a guard was stationed, and I knew that even if one of Giovanni's prisoners made it out of their cell, they would never make it up the steep climb before being shot. Dario and Enzo kept pace a step behind. They had reservations about us coming here, but with Don Falcone notified of my whereabouts, not even Giovanni would try something that stupid. I hoped.

I'd only been down here once a few years ago to watch a man—who had stolen from my father—executed. How times had changed? It had been a month since I was shot, and I'd only seen my father once in that time, but I suspected I would never see him again.

"My son, you look so grown up." I stared at my father as he waltzed into my hospital room as if he owned it and wondered what the hell he wanted. He was the last person I thought would stop by. "Jasmine,

you look ravishing as always." He walked over to where she was seated and held out his hand.

Nothing in this world could've surprised me more than when she closed the book she'd been reading, looked at his hand, and then up to his smug face, but never moved to accept the gesture.

"Why are you here," Jasmine asked.

Not too long ago, I would've been offended as she went on the attack for me, but now...now, I was happy to sit back and watch the show. She was going to eat my father up and spit him out.

My father's face twisted in confusion. "I'm here to see my son, of course."

"You mean the son you didn't want anything to do with until now, when word has spread of our engagement?"

"Where is this aggression coming from? I merely wanted to see my son."

"No, we don't need your phony devotion." Jasmine looked at me. "I'll come back when your father is gone." Jasmine stood and walked past my father like he didn't exist, and I couldn't help but smile. That was my Tiger. I fucking loved the look she gave me as she walked out the door, and if I weren't bedridden, I would've had her over my lap. Fuck, it was hot.

"What have you said about me?"

The sweet man who had greeted Jasmine was gone, and all that was left was the monster I'd known all these years. I still didn't know if he abused my mom or if the story of my grandfather was true. I suspected that it may have been my father who hurt her and my grandfather had stopped it, but I didn't think I would ever know the truth.

What struck me as funny was that his dark and menacing glare didn't affect me as it once had. I felt no need to prove my worth and didn't think I was a failure. I also wasn't worried about any mental or emotional manipulation, which had been his favorite tool. I could see the narcissist that lived under his skin, and I no longer cared. I felt free.

"I have only ever spoken the truth. Why are you here? You made it clear that I'd screwed up for the last time, and you no longer wanted anything to do with me."

The dark stare turned glacier, and I almost laughed. It was always the same, and why the pattern had eluded me for so long could only be attributed to the fact that he was my father, and I wanted to believe he was a great man.

"I didn't want anything to do with you for good reason. You'd stolen a precious artifact from another Don. I couldn't be caught up in your drama. The whole family and our holdings would've been called into question. As it was, the humiliation you caused was almost irreparable and I've been paying on that debt ever since." He straightened his suit jacket and dusted off the arms. I would never see him as my father again. "I should've known you would find a way to twist your banishment on me. You never could handle true responsibility."

"The banishment was warranted. You cutting me out of your life, your will, and telling everyone I was dead to you was all so you could play the victim. You never even let me explain what happened, and yet you were happy to send me to Chicago to clean up the mess you created by not looking into the allegations closer. I killed dozens of our men, all of them innocent, because you couldn't be bothered to do your job. So which of us can't handle responsibility or consequences?"

"How dare you speak to me like that. I came here to let you know that you have officially been named my succor, and this is how you treat me. Not an ounce of gratitude?"

These were the words I'd always longed to hear. My father had held who would take over above my head like a carrot. I jumped to his tune like a marionette on a string, but the excitement that not long ago would've filled me didn't spark. I was no longer going to be anyone's puppet.

"I don't want it. Name one of my cousins or whoever you've manipulated into thinking that stepping into your shoes is a prize, but as of today, the only thing we will have in common is our last name. I've made arrangements to take over the payments owed to Riker Rhodes and as soon as I'm finished paying it off I will pay you back every dime you spent to date. I don't want anything from you, not ever again. Now, get out of my hospital room. I need to rest."

• • •

"As promised," Giovanni said as we stopped in front of a cell I hadn't seen before. Had I been transported into *The Silence of the Lambs*? The cell was lit with lamps, and a glass wall allowed you to see the plush bed, desk, and chairs. Lucas lounged on the couch reading a book like he was at a fucking resort, and I looked at Giovanni like he'd lost his mind.

"I said take care of him. I didn't mean to treat him like a pet. What the hell is this?" I held my hand toward Lucas, who looked up and spotted me. He sneered as he slammed the book down and marched toward the glass.

"He can't hurt anyone in there. I know I can't let him roam free—that didn't work—but I can't kill him. He is still my son."

"Your son is—"

"I know what he is. I don't need you to remind me." Tension grew around us, the guards shifting as they waited to see what I would do next.

I shook my head. "He better not get out of there, not ever. Or I will hunt him down and do what you can't."

Giovanni stared into my eyes and finally gave a single nod. "Understood."

"Let me the fuck out of here," Lucas yelled, his fist hitting the thick glass. He stomped across the room, grabbed the desk chair, and came back to slam it against the wall like a child having a tantrum. "This is all your fault, Esposito, and when I get out of here, I'm coming for you and your little bitch Jasmine, too."

"Your poetry is getting better, Lucas. Keep it up. You have nothing but time to perfect the skill," I called back and smiled. The Hulk-like meltdown was well worth it as he tore his shirt off and screamed at me. I shot a glance at Giovanni. "Yes, I can see now why you want to keep him around. This is quite amusing."

"Make fun all you want, but one day you will have a child, and when you do, you will see that you would do anything for them."

He might be right about that, but I would have to see when I got there. We followed along the hallway until we came to a far less lush and cushy cell. A man hung in chains, stripped of his clothes, while the dank scent of mold and shit wafted out of the small space.

"Hello, Jacopo," I said, and his head lifted to look at me. "You don't look pleased to see me," I drawled. "Were you hoping your bullet killed me? You've certainly done your best to try and ruin me multiple times."

"You were in the way."

I shrugged out of my jacket, rolled up my sleeves, and nodded to the guard manning the door.

"I want to thank you," I said, and his eyes narrowed. "If you hadn't gone to such great lengths to get me out of the way, I wouldn't have understood what I had. I am the man I am today because of what you did."

"Well, that's lovely. How about you let me go as my reward then?" Even the beard he was now sporting couldn't hide the evil of his smile. "I promise to be a good boy."

"No, I don't think so. The day you laid a hand on Jasmine was the day you signed your death certificate." Getting up close, I made sure he saw hell in my eyes. "Not to worry though, I have decided on a fitting death for you."

"Do your worst. Nothing you do will scare me."

I smiled as my fist landed a blow to his side. He grunted and winced away from the impact. "We'll see about that."

"That's it? That was your big threat?" Jacopo laughed as he was unhooked from the chains. I didn't want to go too far, but I made sure that every punch was a statement for the deaths he'd caused and the life he tried to take away from me.

The guards dragged him across the stone floor, blood dripping from his mouth and eyes swollen shut. The wild laugh that came out of him sounded insane as the massive door, far thicker than all the others, locked into place.

Jacopo sat in the middle of the floor like he was pretending to do yoga and continued to throw insults in my direction.

"I must admit this was an unusual request, but I'm looking forward to it," Giovanni said.

My gaze briefly met Dario and Enzo, and they looked as calm as I felt with my decision. Giovanni raised his hand to the guard, and with a grinding sound, the wall shifted to the side.

Jacopo stopped his ridiculous rambling and looked over his shoulder to the dark void. The hair stood on the back of my neck, anticipation filling me as a soft, throaty growl came from the darkness. Jacopo spun around and got to his feet just as one orange and black paw stepped into the light.

"What are you doing? Let me out of here?" The panic in his voice made the dark parts of my heart smile.

The massive Bengal tiger slowly stepped into the cell, its golden eyes piercing and fangs easy to see as it pulled its lip up and growled again. One paw was the size of my face, and we all took a big step away from the bars.

"You can't do this. Let me out of here," Jacopo said, slowly moving around the cell to keep distance between him and the predator. Its nose lifted in the air, and I wondered if it could smell his fear as easily as the blood running down his body.

"My Tiger will have justice," I said.

Jacopo ran for the open door where the tiger had emerged. He didn't make two strides before the cat leaped and tackled him to the ground. The screaming was loud and echoed off the walls as fangs sank into the meaty flesh of his leg. Like something from a horror movie, the tiger dragged Jacopo across the floor. He thrashed wildly and kicked as it slowly hauled him into the dark.

"Please," he cried out, his eyes meeting mine as his fingers clung to the lip of a stone in the floor.

With a horrific scream, he was pulled beyond the light, and I shuddered at the sound of bone crunching.

Giovanni once more waved to the guard, and he hit a switch to close the door and cut off the sound of Jacopo being torn apart. We all stared silently at the empty cage and the bloodstain on the floor.

Turning to Giovanni, I gripped his shoulder. "He knocked on the Devil's door one too many times. It was inevitable that he would be let in sooner or later."

"You have what it takes to be a Don, Angelo. You might even have what is needed to be the Don of Dons."

Nodding, I let go of his shoulder, and with Dario and Enzo at my side, we marched toward the beginning of our new life.

Epilogue

JASMINE

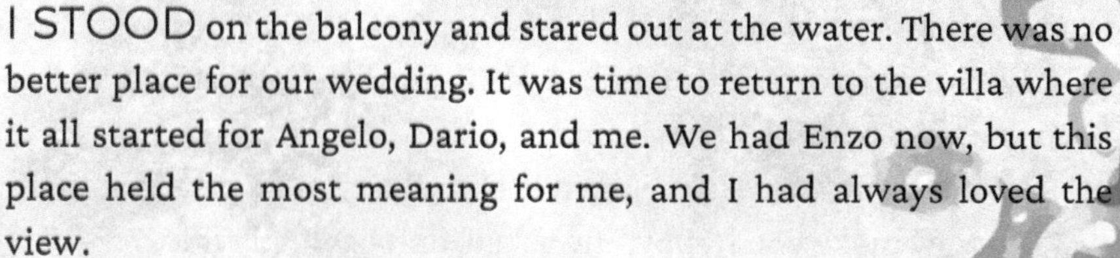

I STOOD on the balcony and stared out at the water. There was no better place for our wedding. It was time to return to the villa where it all started for Angelo, Dario, and me. We had Enzo now, but this place held the most meaning for me, and I had always loved the view.

"Is everything okay?" I turned and smiled at the sound of my papa's voice.

"Couldn't be better, just needed to cool off."

I smiled wide as he handed me a tall glass of water, and I was tempted to pour it over my head. One thing not advertised when purchasing a wedding dress was how hot they were.

"When do you leave to go back to Beastville?"

"After the honeymoon, but I want you to visit as soon as we are back. I want you to try Athena's Palate, and I'm so excited to show you what I'm working on."

Papa leaned on the balcony beside me. "It will be strange not having you here every day. I'm going to miss you like crazy."

"We'll be back. I've already told Angelo I want to come home every other month, and he seems to like the idea. This will always be my home." I touched his hand and felt compelled to tell him the truth about my relationship. "Papa, I have a confession to make," I said, sipping the water.

"Oh? You didn't really like the cake?"

My lip curled up at the joke. For whatever reason, the cake had turned into an adventure all of its own and caused arguments that turned so heated you would've thought we were talking about a pressing topic in the world.

"No. I married Angelo, and we love one another, but...um...." How did you tell your father that you were sleeping with three men? I had no idea.

He reached out and placed his hand on mine as I continued to stumble over the right words. "It's okay. I know about Dario and Enzo. I also know that I will have to keep it quiet." He nodded toward the ballroom. "Angelo told me, but I picked up on the vibes. I'm not so old or blind, you know?"

My cheeks warmed further, and dumping the water over my head sounded better by the second.

"And you don't care? I'm sure it is not what you pictured for me?"

"Do they make you happy," he asked, and I smiled wide.

"Very. Each is like a puzzle piece, and together, we fit perfectly," I said.

"Then I'm happy for you, and I know your mother would be happy too. All she ever wanted was for you to have the kind of love she and I shared. She would say, 'Sergio, make sure our daughter finds her soulmate. Money, power, and pretty places don't mean anything without the one you love by your side.' "

Taking him by surprise, I wrapped him up in a hug. "I miss her so much," I mumbled, fighting back the tears for the hundredth time today.

"I miss her too, mia Bambolina. You're not little anymore. You're all grown up." He pulled back and wiped off the tear on his cheek. "I wish she was here to see this, to see you on your special day. She would've loved everything you've chosen."

Angelo stepped outside just then. "Oh, sorry, I didn't mean to interrupt," he said, and I dabbed at my eyes.

"I was just about to come back inside." Kissing my papa's cheek, I whispered. "She's always here. You told me that yourself. She knows, she sees, and I feel her love through you."

My papa cleared his throat. "Go on, get out of here, and stop spending all your time with your old man."

"Ti amo Papa." He smiled, then turned away, and I knew he needed a few minutes to collect himself.

"Is he okay," Angelo asked once we were out of earshot.

"Yeah, we talked about my mama and how we wish she could be here. It's a bittersweet day," I said, and he gave my hand a gentle squeeze. He led me to the dance floor just as a slow song came on, and I twirled out and then into his body.

"I think we should start trying for kids right away. That way, he'll have grandchildren to entertain him," Angelo said, and I laughed.

"Is that so? Are you planning on using my papa as a bargaining chip for all your negotiations from now on?"

"Only with you," he smiled, giving me a wicked lopsided grin. He spun me around, and I caught sight of Dario and Enzo talking to Ciro and Marcus. I winked at them as we danced by.

"Fine, I'll go off my pill," I sighed dramatically.

Angelo's cheeks turned red, his eyes shining with mischievousness. "So, remember when I said no more lies?"

"Yes."

"I may have forgotten to mention that I swapped out your pills with placebos." He cringed like I was going to punch him. "It may not have been my best strategy," he said sheepishly.

I laughed hard, not able to be angry even though I probably should be. This was Angelo, and I'd just signed myself up for a lifetime of 'What the hell were you thinking' moments, but I wouldn't have it any other way.

"Well, that explains it," I said.

"What?"

"Why I'm two months late," I said. Angelo stopped moving, and his mouth fell open. I poked him in the chest. "No disappearing this time," I ordered playfully, knowing that wouldn't happen. I had wondered if it was possible I was pregnant but hadn't wanted to get my hopes up.

"I want to scream this from the rooftops. Are you kidding? I'm never going anywhere ever again." He pulled me into a hug.

"Maybe we should wait to—"

"Hey, everyone! I'm going to be a father!" Angelo yelled.

"Tell everyone," I finished as the first person congratulated us.

I sighed as we were quickly surrounded, but I smiled at Dario when he stepped in close, wrapped his arm around my waist and whispered that he loved me. Enzo's hand slipped into mine as he hugged me and whispered the same. I felt the two of them brimming with as much excitement as Angelo was showing, and I already knew that it didn't matter what time we made it back to the room. The party would continue for hours.

Not everyone was lucky enough to have a happily ever after, so I would hang onto mine and my men with both hands and never let go.

I am Jasmine Falcone-Esposito and I am the tiger.

Crossover Books

Greed by Brooklyn Cross (Riker Rhodes and Minneta)

Virtues Fairytale Novels

Patience by Mia Z Staysails (Gina)
Temperance by EJ Everette
Diligence by Jay Leigh Brown
Chastity by Kira Roman
Charity by Alexandra K Martin
Kindness by Sunday Mathers

Thank You

Thank you to all those that decided to pick up this book and read it. It is only with readers continued support that Indie Authors, such as myself, are able to keep writing which is why your reviews mean so much to us. If you enjoyed this book, please consider leaving me a review.

ABOUT THE AUTHOR

Writing is not just a passion for me. It is a lifeline to my sanity.

I have always loved writing but suffer from severe dyslexia and short-term memory retention issues. I struggled in school while I worked every night on re-training my brain.

I was frequently treated like I would never succeed, and I found myself putting my love for writing on a shelf.

Even at the age of six, I found it easier to communicate with animals than people, which was a big reason why I was drawn to dressage horseback riding. I remained focused on my passion for riding until I had to step away from the competition world for personal reasons.

Today, my desire for writing and storytelling has been rekindled. I have published multiple books and will never let anyone or anything hold me back again.
I am a proud romance author who offers my readers morally grey heroes, a ton of spice, epic journeys, and redemption stories.

-Follow Your Dreams- *Brooklyn Cross*

www.ingramcontent.com/pod-product-compliance
Lightning Source LLC
Chambersburg PA
CBHW030349310726
48979CB00001B/232

* 9 7 8 1 9 9 8 0 1 5 3 0 6 *